. . . and yet his body suddenly seemed less threatening and more powerful. She moved away the barest of inches, gasping.

"You have always shied away from touching me," he said, with an added gruffness that told her how her flinching had hurt him.

"You have avoided touching me as well," she whispered. She knew the fluttering in her voice betrayed all the pent-up longing she'd tried so hard to hide. She didn't care.

"Jillian," her name was a husky groan. And then he pulled her hard against his warm chest, and she felt the thundering of his heart beneath her ear. Slowly, he tipped her head back, and she felt his lips against her neck, her lips. . . .

She was his.

Captor of My Heart

Donna Valentino

A SIGNET BOOK

SIGNET
Published by New American Library, a division of
Penguin Putnam Inc., 375 Hudson Street,
New York, New York 10014, U.S.A.
Penguin Books Ltd, 27 Wrights Lane,
London W8 5TZ, England
Penguin Books Australia Ltd, Ringwood,
Victoria, Australia
Penguin Books Canada Ltd, 10 Alcorn Avenue,
Toronto, Ontario, Canada M4V 3B2
Penguin Books (N.Z.) Ltd, 182–190 Wairau Road,
Auckland 10, New Zealand

Penguin Books Ltd, Registered Offices:
Harmondsworth, Middlesex, England

First published by Signet, an imprint of New American Library, a division of
Penguin Putnam Inc.

First Printing, July 1999
10 9 8 7 6 5 4 3 2 1

I

October 1651

Jillian Bowen dreaded confronting Death on moon-drenched nights.

She agonized every time she pitted her meager skills against Death's awesome strength, but failure weighed particularly heavy when moonlight leached all color from the landscape and shadows swallowed all sound. The sky, the trees, the grooved ruts in the lane, everything, lay bathed in shades of gray and black, silent and lifeless as the inside of a grave.

She shivered, though her cloak provided more warmth than required on this October night. Her hands trembled, and her fingers cramped from her tight grip on the reins. She could not loosen her hold. Her agitation had nothing to do with fearing that patient, plodding Queenie would take the bit between her teeth and bolt. Nor did she feel overly exposed to the elements; she and her father were well protected, roofed and walled within the wagon's boxy confines. There was no logical reason for clutching the reins with so much fierce determination, no reason to believe that something stalked her in the night, waiting for the right time to pounce.

Those sorts of fears usually crouched in a low, simmering fury, always present, but under control until she'd been away from home for a few hours.

Jillian had accompanied her father on similar midnight journeys a hundred times, a thousand times, and had learned to keep her silent anxiety at bay. Why had her control failed her this night? Her nerves jangled. She could not shake the sensation that unseen danger lurked under cover of moonshadows, watching her, waiting for the chance to destroy her world.

Ridiculous. The very notion brought a light sheen of perspiration to her forehead. She'd woven a web of lies and deception to protect all she loved and valued and it had served her well for years now. Tonight, silvery moonlight seemed to cast all her efforts in a pathetic light, taunting her with all the demons she thought she'd learned to subdue: She could lose everything; she was helpless against forces beyond her control.

Her father sat half-slumped at the far corner of the bench seat, snoring, blessedly oblivious to her apprehension. She craved the sounds of life, but rousing Wilton Bowen from his nap would only cause heartache rather than relief.

Queenie's hooves crushed through the fallen leaves that layered the road, sweetening the cool, crisp air with the scent of autumn. A nightingale's call rang out once in counterpoint to the wagon's squeaking wheels. Other than that brief trilling song, those heavy, muffled thuds, nothing stirred. There was no point in hoping she might come across a fellow traveler. Lord Cromwell's iron-fisted restrictions meant honest Englishmen spent the nights indoors now, with doors barred and windows shuttered against those who might spy on them from without.

The lane curved. Moonlight revealed the silhouette of a mounted man sheltered beneath the shadow of a spreading elm. Queenie tossed her head, snorting a warning. Jillian's heartbeat quickened, with fear and with an equal measure of relief. Her instincts had not been wrong after all—someone *had* been watching her, waiting for her.

It was only Constable Fraley. She recognized the gaunt rider, aware of the irony. She was safe with Fraley, and Fraley had no reason to be out stalking her. As Constable of the Watch, Fraley worried more about the rogues and vagabonds who sought easy prey in Arundel Forest's quiet depths. And yet, much as she yearned for companionship, she would have preferred riding on alone, wrestling her silent fears, over the company of the Lord Protector's henchman.

"For God, for king, and for country." The constable's gravelly voice rang out harsh and loud against the quiet.

"For God and country, but not for king." Jillian parroted the approved response.

"Mister Bowen. Mistress Bowen."

"Fraley," she acknowledged. "You have ventured far off the main road tonight."

Jillian's father stirred and mumbled something incomprehensible before lapsing once more into silence.

" 'Tis a pleasant eve for rambling about." Fraley guided his horse in a slow arc around their wagon. Jillian knew his sharp eyes searched beneath the vehicle.

"Would you like us to climb out?"

"No need, mistress."

According to the rules of his Watch, Fraley should thoroughly examine the wagon for stowaways. Jillian supposed he'd grown tired of poking his sword into the empty space beneath the seat. He'd gotten bored, too, with opening the wooden box bolted to the back of the wagon only to find medicinals, blankets, and rope. He'd searched their wagon countless times without finding anything amiss, and so made only a cursory examination now.

Fraley would still expect her to explain why she and

her father were out riding that night. She did not wait for him to ask. "Jamie Metcalf's dying."

He grunted with perfunctory sympathy. "Your father will set him right."

"Not this time."

Fraley did not argue the point, but she saw his dismissal of her opinion in the way his mouth curled into a faint sneer and in the quick shift of his eyes toward her father, as if he expected Doctor Bowen to leap up and declare her wrong. She could not take offense, because his attitude suited her. She wanted everyone to think that she merely assisted their beloved Doctor Wilton Bowen. But for three years now, *she* had been the one to analyze a patient's condition and prescribe the proper course of treatment.

They would never forgive her, once they found her out. Nobody would accept treatment from a woman.

Fraley's interest had strayed. He narrowed his gaze toward the trees and then turned his head, probing the gloom, seeking, searching. " 'Tis rumored Charles Stuart might sneak through these parts trying to get back to France. You didn't catch sight of any tall, dark-haired louts skulking about, did you?"

"Not tonight."

"You be sure to scream out good and loud if you do. The sound will travel far on a night like this."

"I will." Jillian hoped her insincerity didn't show. She never reported the terrified, wraithlike souls she sometimes spotted darting through the woods, doing their best to elude Cromwell's dreaded patrols.

She silently wished the fugitive king well. She had met him once or twice, years earlier, when her father had been resplendent in his robes, a Royal Physician attending King Charles I. The younger Charles Stuart had been an agreeable lad, five years younger than she. She was happy he'd avoided his father's fate, but she did hope he would regain the sanctuary of France and spend the rest of his days there. Jillian did not chafe, as so many did, under the harsh rules imposed by Oliver Cromwell—they provided an order, a uniformity, that she found comforting.

Even so, she would never betray the exiled king. She and Charles Stuart were kindred spirits, though she would never tell him so, even if she chanced to see him again. He would certainly find it amusing to think that a woman who yearned to be acknowledged as a physician thought she had something in common with a man who yearned to be acknowledged as king.

But at least Cromwell's forces were enemies Charles could see. At least a person knew that traveling without permission could incur Cromwell's wrath and punishment. Taking calculated risks wasn't like falling victim to Death and being struck down without warning or provocation. Or like the irrational fears that left her uneasy if she stayed away from home for too long, or if people crowded too close. Or like the disease muddling her father's mind, gleefully eradicating his knowledge and memories, leaving him little more than an empty husk of flesh.

"I'll be riding this part of the country all night," Fraley said.

"Then we shall see you later, once it's finished with Jamie Metcalf."

"I won't disturb you then, mistress. I know such things weigh hard on your father."

"Thank you."

Fraley touched his forehead and then reined his horse away.

Jillian clucked softly to Queenie, urging her to pick up their pace. The wagon jolted a little, and Jillian's father blinked awake.

"Jillian?" His voice quavered. He swung his head, and she knew it surprised him to find himself surrounded by the night sky, the trees, the empty road, instead of his bed. Jillian took heart. Uncertainty came upon him only during his most lucid moments, when he emerged from the fog numbing his wits and realized that he held but a tenuous grip on his sanity.

"Papa." Hope surged through her. If he could cling to his sensibility for a little while, he might remember a treatment that could save Jamie Metcalf. She was all too chillingly aware that she'd learned only a small portion of the skills trapped in the lost depths of her father's failing mind. "You remember Jamie Metcalf—you set his wife Mary's leg when she got kicked by a cow and the barber-surgeon was so drunk he made a bungle of it. 'Tis her husband who ails. I have tried every remedy to ease breathing that you taught me, and nothing has worked."

Wilton Bowen blinked sleepily at her.

"Try to remember," she urged. "Jamie cannot sleep. When he tries, he feels as though a rock crushes his chest, and he must struggle upright, gasping for breath. He can no longer breathe without conscious effort. He is dying, Papa."

Wilton Bowen frowned. She wanted to burst into tears at the obvious effort he was making to think, to remember. And then his face cleared, turning as smooth and unaffected as a child's, and she knew she had lost him again.

"He cannot breathe," she whispered.

Her father patted her arm. "Nonsense," he blustered with the confident jocularity that always reassured the sick and dying. "You are a fine, healthy young woman."

"Not me, Papa. Jamie Metcalf. Try to concentrate."

"Try to concentrate." He echoed her words exactly, the way they'd worked out so that he could bend low over the sick and infirm while she fed him clues about what to say, guided him to prescribe the appropriate remedies. He fumbled with Jillian's hand, trying to disengage it from the reins. She allowed him, despair turning her muscles limp as he pressed her hand against his chest while he drew a great lungful of air.

"This is how it feels when you breathe properly. In. Out. Breathe as I do."

"It is Jamie Metcalf, and not I, who has trouble breathing."

"Small wonder you cannot breathe, young lady," her father chided sternly. "You have a nervous temperament and an argumentative nature. I shall have my daughter mix a draught to calm your nerves."

"I am your daughter, Papa," Jillian whispered while anguish racked her soul.

Her father was oblivious to her distress. "Do as I say. In. Out. In. Out." He gave her hand a reassuring pat and then settled once more into his corner. "Watch me now." He drew several enormous, ostentatious breaths for her benefit, and then bewilderment settled over him, and she knew he had forgotten why he was breathing so hard. Within moments, he fell back into sleep.

It was no use. Death would claim Jamie Metcalf on this sweet-scented, moon-washed night.

And so might her dreams die, too. For weeks now, she'd ignored the signs that her father's condition had worsened. She'd denied the evidence of her own eyes and ears. He no longer seemed capable of making the mental leap required to discuss the condition of a person who did not actually sit right in front of him.

The day would soon come when his hard-earned skill failed altogether, when they could no longer fool people into believing that Wilton Bowen could restore their health. Everything would end. Once everyone realized that her father was no longer competent to act as physician to them all, they would once again seek out the quacks, the charlatans, the superstitious old wives. Jillian would retreat with her father behind the walls of the secluded country house and nurse him through his final days and . . . and . . . and . . .

And nothing more.

Death of another sort. The end. She wished sud-

denly that her formless, faceless enemies would take
shape, so she could pummel them in her frustration.

The unfairness of it all coursed through her, pulsing
and pounding while her mind screamed in denial.
Jamie Metcalf was too young to die. Her father was
too precious and dear to lose in such a heart-
wrenching way. And she had spent too many years
hiding away before managing to deal with her fears.
She was growing braver each day, gaining confidence
as she stealthily acquired a physician's knowledge. She
could not bear to have it all snatched away so
ignominiously.

Death was a monster, she thought, whether it
sucked the life and intelligence from a man, or modest
dreams from a woman.

A monster.

She closed her eyes, wondering if her own sense
might not be deserting her. Perhaps she ought to stop
trying to hold on in the face of so much futility—
abandon the patient horse clopping along the moon-
washed road, forget all about carrying her father's in-
sensate hulk to a dying man she could not save. She
could just retreat behind the walls of her home and
stay there safe and untroubled. But Queenie's hoofbeats thudded on. Her father's indrawn grunts and
whistling exhalations continued their steady rhythm.
Sitting there wishing Death might come and spirit her
away would not solve anything. Reluctantly, she
opened her eyes.

She slammed them shut at once, to dispel the dis-
quieting vision that had taken shape before her.

But when she dared peek once more through the
cover of her lashes, she found Death waiting for her,
just as she had so recently and rashly wished.

Death stood in the middle of the lane, an apparition
in human form, but so huge and dark and formidable
that it seemed they would be swallowed within its vel-
vety blackness. Death wore a cloak that flapped in the

night wind and a Druid-like hood that concealed his face, but there was no mistaking his menacing intent.

He had come for her. She knew it with a gut-deep certainty.

Her heartbeat faltered, and then she rallied. "Get up, Queenie," she cried. She meant to run straight through that nightmare standing on the road. She had been bested by doubts and fears the whole night long. This manifestation of Death was merely an hallucination. . . .

The horse shied.

Steady old Queenie would not shy away from an apparition.

Before Jillian could react, before she could convince herself that perhaps the mare had sensed her fear, the monster's hand snaked out and grabbed Queenie's bridle near the bit, bringing their wagon to a skittering halt. Jillian clutched for balance, flinging one arm over her father to keep him from tumbling headfirst into the high, curving front wall.

And then Death vaulted himself over the half-door and onto the bench beside her.

He landed in place with the scrape of boot leather against wood, the hiss of wool sliding over the seat. He carried with him the scent of pine, as if he'd been hiding for so long in the road-hugging woods that his cloak had absorbed the odor of the trees. Warmth radiated from him; heat of a kind that drew her toward him the way a crackling fire did after a long night crossing the countryside. And though the moon silvered everything it touched, Jillian caught the faintest shimmer of midnight blue in his eyes, and the barest glimmer of burnished gold threading through the dark hair that escaped his hood.

He leaned over her. The movement plucked his hood away. The wind whipped at his hair and sent strands stinging against her face. The moonlight darkened hollows below his cheekbones and eyes, enhancing the strong masculinity of a face that bore the fine, clean lines of noble breeding. He so pulsated with virility and vitality that she knew he was a living, breathing man.

A warm, living man frightened her far more than Death.

She could not see beyond him, but she knew Fraley had moved on. She was alone.

She leaned back until she shielded her sleeping father. "Who . . ." she stammered. "What . . ."

He placed a finger against her lips. "Shhh."

She froze, while his finger pulsed against her and his whispered command washed over her like a caress.

Rabbits, she thought wildly, sometimes froze in terror when trapped by a hunter. She was no timid little rabbit, meekly accepting its fate. She screamed—or tried to. Drawing the required breath meant inhaling her captor's scent, and her scream came out sounding more like a yearning whimper.

"Shhh," he hushed her again. "Your father sleeps. You don't want to wake him."

She felt completely surrounded by him, by his warmth, by the elegant timbre of a voice that set the very air vibrating around her. She swallowed, and nodded her intention to obey his command. He did not move his finger away and so her lips stroked against him, up and down.

He smiled, satisfied with her acquiescence. A merry twinkle lit his eyes as the knave curled his finger and rubbed his knuckle lightly over her lower lip. No man had ever touched her so. Sensation rocked through her with the force of an explosion and roused an unexpected pleasant ache low in her vitals, as if that place and her lips were somehow intimately connected.

The tingling that rushed through her restored her senses. Good God, she lay soft and yielding as a besotted schoolgirl while a giant of a man made sport with her in the moonlight!

Fury—and embarrassment—lent her strength. She slapped his hand away. "Who are you?" she demanded. And then she remembered Fraley's warning about tall, dark-haired strangers who might be lurking about. One particular tall, dark-haired stranger. She quickly ran the stranger's features against her memories of a teenaged prince. "You're not King Charles."

His demeanor shifted from merry and teasing into hard implacability. "You cannot be sure, Jillian Bowen."

Nothing had ever frightened her so much as the sound of her name coming from this stranger's lips. "How . . . how do you know my name?"

"I know everything about you."

"But why?"

"Because." He gathered the reins from her nerveless fingers and slapped them lightly against Queenie's rump. The mare obediently pulled against the traces. "I had to make sure you were the right one."

"Right for what?"

He stared straight ahead. "No more questions."

"I'll scream," she said. The warning restored a bit of her confidence. "Fraley will hear and come rescue me."

He whipped around, and his piercing glare pinned her in her place. His hand flashed out and caught her by the chin, not so tight that it hurt, but not so gentle that she dared hope for mercy. He tipped her face up to his, and she read nothing but determination written there.

"No one can help you now, Jillian. For the next three weeks of your life, you belong to me."

2

Jillian Bowen smelled of soap and crisp autumn air. The sounds of surprise she made were feminine and soft and fell gently on his ear. Her breath, light and quick, misted around them.

His fingers rested at the ledge of her chin. He'd thought that hard work and even harder riding had roughened his hands beyond feeling, but touching her proved that wrong. Through his calluses he could feel her skin, warm and soft and yielding, and the staccato beat of her pulse racing beneath. She was slim and taut in the manner of a bowstring, vibrating with strength, waiting to be unleashed.

It surprised him to find her so alive.

He tipped up her face a little more, so he could search her features. He had to make sure he'd captured the right woman, the puppetlike creature he'd been watching for so many days. The curve of her cheek seemed right, the shape of her nose, too. He hadn't realized she possessed a quiet beauty, one granted by elegant bone structure and fine skin, probably because she tended to go about her errands head down and submissive as a scullery maid.

She always wore gray or a gown of brownish, rusted red wool that made even fading roses and wilting marigolds seem vivid in comparison, and tucked her hair into a nondescript white cap, whether walking in the village or working alone among the dry and dying flowers of her garden. Her movements were always calm, measured. She'd seemed completely ruled by her father's whims, and he'd had every reason to believe she would meekly accept his arrival and quietly go about playing out the role he created for her.

Her eyes blazed, telling him how wrong he'd been to think that.

A puzzle. She spent her days with her attention focused on her feet, her body hidden beneath dull-colored garments, her hair hidden, fawning at her father's side. Jillian Bowen at night was a subtly different creature, almost as if she found a unique freedom while being confined within the roof and walls of this small wagon. Her gown was unbuttoned at the neck. Her hair, in a loose coil, was bared to the moonlight. He fought the urge to pull free the thick strands. He imagined it tumbling down over her shoulders, past her hips, in a shimmering, flower-scented cascade.

She jerked free of his grasp, leaving his upraised hand holding nothing. He brought his fingers together, the rough brush of one callus rubbing against the other, and it seemed impossible that he'd touched her without marring her skin.

She leaned back against her father. He'd noticed that about her, too, the way she'd seemed to cling, and it had given him the impression she was weak and frightened of moving about on her own. Now he realized that she didn't cling so much as defend, the way a wary she-wolf might crouch over her helpless cub.

"Get down from my wagon," she said, a brave demand, even if it quavered a bit there at the end.

He sent her the sort of glower that always subdued even the most contentious of his men. She frowned right back at him, inching up her chin a notch. He felt his glower dissolve into amazement before he regained control. This wasn't the way the capture was supposed to work. She was supposed to be overcome with fear, paralyzed by dread, all but gibbering in her eagerness to do his bidding.

"I'll be giving you orders for the next few weeks," he muttered.

"Will you?" She seemed genuinely surprised rather than afraid.

"You must heed my demands."

"Why?"

"Because I am a desperate, dangerous highwayman."

There was the barest pause, and then she burst into laughter. She clapped her hand over her mouth to stifle the sound. She darted a glance over her shoulder and he knew she'd tried to muffle the sound merely to avoid waking her father. Or it could have been to conceal the slightly hysterical edge to her laughter. She could not possibly be as unaffected by the threat he posed as she pretended to be.

Perhaps she could. She leaned toward him and lowered her voice to a confidential whisper. "You look and sound like a nobleman playing masquerade."

"Ridiculous," he said, and then winced at the governess-instilled crispness of his utterance. "Nonsense." Good lord, but he could hear the Oxford-influenced accent in those two syllables as well. He ought to have growled something incomprehensible and menacing, maybe even curled his lip and bared his teeth for effect. But then, desperate and dangerous highwaymen probably didn't have much in the way of teeth, and considering he had a white and healthy mouthful, teeth-baring might have proven counterproductive.

The wagon, which had been rolling more and more slowly, shuddered to a stop. The mare shook her head and whinnied her displeasure at the lack of a guiding hand on the reins. Cameron scowled at the recalcitrant horse, but his disgust was directed at himself.

Instead of commandeering the wagon and domineering the woman, she'd goaded him into sitting there thinking about his teeth.

Jillian had somehow managed to turn the tables on him, and judging by the way she straightened and picked nonchalantly at a stray bit of leaf that had settled on her skirt, she was well aware of her success.

But he, too, was well aware of many things, including the way he towered over her, the certainty of his strength outmatching hers, the weight of the knife strapped to his belt.

A woman had once complained that he had such a cold, disinterested way of saying her name that it had sliced through her like a demon's voice calling her in the dark.

"Jillian."

A slight tremor shook her and he knew she wasn't as confident as she appeared. Perhaps he did have a demon's voice. He took little satisfaction from unsettling her, however.

"You would do well to respect the threat I pose."

"Believe me, sir, I am mightily regretting that I carry no knife in my pocket. If I did, 'twould be plunged into my heart right now." She paused, and drew a shaking breath. "And you would have to slake your lusts upon a corpse."

She pressed her knees together and lifted one slim hand to the undone buttons at her neck, the subtle gestures of a woman eager to deflect a man's lecherous intent.

Never once did she look toward her father for protection.

"You think I mean to . . ." Horror caused the words to clog in his throat. "I wouldn't . . . I mean, I have never forced a lady . . ."

"Oh?" She did not appear to be reassured. She laughed again, but this time it was forced and brittle. "How silly and presumptuous to think that a dashing fellow like yourself would have lecherous intents toward a plain woman like me. But then, this is the first time I've had a stranger leap into my wagon and declare that the next three weeks of my life belong to him. Pray enlighten me as to why you're so set upon claiming my existence."

This wasn't going well at all. She was supposed to be cowering, whimpering, telling him he could do anything, demand anything of her, if only he wouldn't hurt her. And then, when he told her he meant her no harm, her gratitude would lead her to do as he asked without question.

He'd known full-grown men to subside into weeping wrecks with less cause. She'd seemed a weak, ineffectual spinster of a woman, content to cling to her father's arm and go about with him, doing his bidding. He'd never suspected her slender build held the spirit of a tigress ready to sacrifice her own life rather than submit to the demands of another. Or that he'd want to touch the sweet curve of her cheek and tell her she was not a plain woman, not up close, and that any number of dashing fellows would find themselves helplessly transfixed by her allure.

"The less you know about me and my intentions, the more likely you are to survive this," he said, deliberately brutal. "Yes, Jillian, I am embroiling you in something that could get you killed. And if it came down to saving you, or furthering my cause, know this—everyone is expendable. Every one of us. I would watch you die without flinching."

She stared at him in wide-eyed silence for a long moment, barely even breathing. A soft fluttering commenced at the base of her neck, the only evidence to indicate she understood the full impact of what he'd said.

Now, she would cry.

She parted her lips, and he tensed, ready to clap a silencing hand over her mouth if she tried to scream.

"You'd best give me something to call you, for I

doubt you would like it if I addressed you by the names circling through my mind just now."

He fought down another surge of admiration as he relaxed. She taunted him, defied him, despite the terror that had her trembling like an autumn leaf caught in a stiff breeze.

"I am called Cameron," he said impulsively, and then bit back a silent curse. He'd given her his middle name, the one he gave to friends. He'd planned to use his innocuous Christian name, John, which was common enough to make her think it was false.

"Cameron. Cameron what?"

He did not answer her.

"Smith, then. Cameron Smith sounds a right proper name for a rogue."

"Smith will do."

"All right, then, now that we're past the formalities, tell me why you've descended upon us."

"You live in seclusion, yet close enough to Brighthelmstone to make it easy to drive back and forth in an evening."

"The pleasures afforded by Brighthelmstone are few." Her brow creased with thought. "Little more than the sea. I wonder why you would be so interested in a sleepy little village that lies along the sea?"

She was a quick-witted miss! "You can travel to Bramber, or Beeding as well, without raising suspicion."

"Those villages offer even less in the way of diversion. I'd suggest you'd find it more amusing to accost some poor female who lives closer to London."

"I have turned my back on London, just as you have, Jillian."

"You know nothing about my feelings for London."

"Oh, but I do. I know you lived there with your father until three years ago. I know your circle included the wealthy and titled, that your father was

among the Royal Physicians tending to the old king.
You must find this quiet life exceedingly dull."

He could tell that the extent of his knowledge
stunned her. And yet she continued to stand up to
him.

"It suits me," she whispered.

"And me. I require the freedom of movement you
enjoy during the night, and I require a safe haven
during the day."

"It is *my* haven." She vibrated with ferocity. "*Our*
haven."

"Not for the next few weeks. Even as we sit here
chatting, my man has moved my belongings into your
home and taken a place for himself in your stables.
He will attend to me, and keep watch if you try to do
anything foolish, like run away or attempt to summon help."

"He sounds a regular paragon," Jillian said bitterly.
"What will *you* be doing while your thug stands guard
over me?"

"I will sleep in your home. I will eat your food and
drink your wine." She stiffened a little with each right
he claimed. "I will tell you when to light candles and
when you must move about in the dark."

Detailing how he meant to control her every movement eventually penetrated her fragile bravado. Wet-
ness glimmered in her eyes. "Why are you doing
this?"

"You will learn as much as I choose to tell you,
when I choose to tell you. For now, it is best if you
don't know."

"Cameron Smith, I am growing heartily tired of you
telling me what is best for me."

"Then cease asking questions, and do as I bid."

"No. You cannot simply expect—"

He pulled back on the reins, bringing the horse to
a stop. He whirled about on the seat, bending over
her. She met him with a defiant pose, her chin tilted

high, her eyes sparkling with challenge. Admirable, where he required amenability.

"I *expect* your complete and utter submission to my will." He'd practiced those words, thinking himself quite fierce and frightening; saying them to her, he felt like the worst sort of scoundrel.

Her fingers clutched the edges of her neckline together again. Damn, they were back to that.

"I won't touch you," he said, all too conscious of a craving to once more feel the silk of her skin beneath his rough touch.

"There is no threat that will make me do your bidding."

"Oh?"

She squared her shoulders. "Do your worst. I've spent most of my life afraid of one thing or another. You are simply . . . another. I am prepared to die."

Her bravery roused a bittersweet tenderness. He'd gotten one thing right about her—she was an innocent, who had no clue as to the depths a scoundrel could plumb. He would have the dubious pleasure of shattering that innocence and taming her to his needs with one vicious threat.

"Defy me, Jillian, and I will wreak my vengeance upon your father."

"No!" She pressed one hand against her lips while her other hand splayed protectively toward her father. "You can't hurt him. He's . . . he's gentle and kind and . . ."

"And going insane," Cameron said. He lifted the reins and took control. He lightly slapped the horse back into motion. "Do as I say, or I'll tell all the world your father's lost his mind."

Fury surged through Jillian, so raw and violent that she knew if she did have a knife she'd plunge it straight into the highwayman's heart instead of her own.

Physical threats, to herself or to her father, could be fought against, and if she acquired a few bumps and bruises in the process, no matter—the human body usually managed to heal itself. The damage threatened by this arrogant, smiling rogue would be far more devastating.

She'd been so careful when making plans to leave London that nobody suspected the extent of her father's decline. She'd hired a man of utmost discretion to scour the countryside, looking for a snug, lovely home far enough from prying eyes that her father's every movement would not be remarked, and yet close enough to people in need that he could continue to practice the medicine he so loved, as long as he was able. She'd never expected that she would come to love it, too.

"How do you know so much about us?"

"I told you. I've been watching you."

"But I've been so careful. . . ."

He slanted a glance at her. "You and your father have become familiar figures in this area. The people here are not as learned or sophisticated as Londoners. These villagers see you behaving much as usual, and accept that nothing's changed—the way a mother often fails to notice how rapidly her child has grown."

"But you spied upon us, harboring no such delusions."

"Aye."

Jillian's mind whirled. It seemed impossible that she sat here discussing her innermost secret with an utter stranger who admitted to spying upon her. She should have noticed. She had promised her father, with her hand pressed over her heart, that she could keep watch over him and hide him away before he became a mindless wreck, like his father had before him.

But she had not lived up to that part of her sworn bargain. She had never expected that removing herself from the terrors of London would allow her the freedom to serve as her father's assistant. She had never dared to indulge her wild dream of becoming a doctor like her father until living here, feeling safe, had allowed her to risk venturing out at her father's side. Even if she'd had the courage to try this in London, society would not have permitted it. Here, she'd come to realize that the mere accident of being born a woman did not mean she lacked the intelligence to do what she wanted.

She had reveled in her work, and as the days had passed and her father worsened, she'd consoled herself by saying that she was still successfully hiding his deterioration. But this stranger had noticed. She had broken her vow, all because the thought of retreating behind her home's stone walls and spending the rest of her days as nothing more than an anonymous nurse sent despair coursing through her.

When had safety, and the assurance of knowing that one day would be exactly like the one before, lost its allure? She'd always known that taking risks led to disaster. She'd spent her whole life avoiding the slightest hint of risk.

These past few years spent sequestered within their country home, using the endless quiet hours to explore the countryside and nearby villages until everything was as familiar to her as her own kitchen, must have softened her wariness, must have lulled her into forgetting the taint in her blood. She'd felt safe here, certain that no outside force could shatter her happiness the way her world had been destroyed when her free-spirited mother had gotten herself killed. How could she have forgotten that she was her mother's child, and prone to destructive dreams?

"I never noticed you," she whispered, wondering if she'd deliberately ignored the warning signs, the way she pretended not to notice her father's decline.

The corner of Cameron's mouth tilted with satisfaction.

"These days, Jillian, we all travel about feeling that unfriendly eyes are watching us. 'Tis difficult to separate real threats from vague sensations. Who would think," he added, almost to himself, "that free men in England would find themselves in such straits?"

A profound hunger bled from him, so overwhelming that at first she was too affected to respond. Only someone like herself, who had witnessed the dissolution of all she'd loved and hoped for, could possibly know such loss.

And then she felt a wild, improbable surge of hope. It was dangerous to yearn out loud for the many freedoms that had been lost with the assassination of one king and the exile of another. Cromwell's patrols did indeed watch every movement, listen for the slightest whisper of treason or discontent. Comments such as Cameron Smith's earned the Lord Protector's wrath. Jail, hanging, torture—no punishment was too severe. And severest of all were the punishments exacted on those who harbored or abetted those still loyal to the exiled Charles Stuart.

Perhaps this entire escapade had been an elaborate hoax arranged by Constable Fraley to try to trick her into revealing her own political inclinations.

"You, sir, speak Royalist treason." There—she'd spoken the correct sentiment, even though the secret part of her that loved and honored the king rebelled. She held her breath, praying he would chuckle and admit she'd caught him out.

"I had hoped you might share Royalist sympathies," he said, dashing her slender hopes.

"We are neutral."

"Not anymore."

"Jillian?" Her father came awake. Blinking with alarm and confusion, he gripped her shoulder. "Who is this man?"

"Cameron. Cameron Smith," the rogue announced loudly and so cheerfully that no one would expect he'd just admitted he'd drawn them into a cause that could end with their deaths. "Your new apprentice, Mister Bowen."

"My new apprentice?" Her father clutched at Jillian. "Jillian?"

She could refute Cameron. Perhaps she could rouse her father into anger and between the two of them they might force the rogue out of their wagon. They would be well out of his secret Royalist plot, but then he'd be free to carry out his threat. By morning, all the people in all those places he named—Bramber, Breeding, Brighthelmstone—would know the terrible truth about her father.

"Papa." She patted her father's hand and hoped he would not notice the tremor in her voice. "It's about time he showed up."

"It's about time he showed up." Her father frowned at Cameron. "Very well, then. I do hope you are well-trained. The last apprentice I consented to sponsor had no right to call himself doctor. We have a very tragic case on our hands tonight, very tragic indeed. There's little time to chart a course of treatment."

The hope surging through Jillian almost banished her anger and dread. "Oh, Father yes—we must discuss Jamie Metcalf."

But to her horror, her father leaned forward so he could look around her, straight at Cameron Smith.

"Your credentials, young man?"

"Same as yours," said the liar.

"Why, the same as I!" Wilton Bowen brightened. "A Doctor of Surgery graduated from the University of Padua, no doubt." Cameron nodded his head. "And have you spent time at the Royal College of Physicians, as I have done?"

"Certainly." Cameron lied so easily as he leaned back against the cushioned seat that Jillian wondered if he ever spoke the truth. "Oxford, as well."

"Do you hear that, Jillian? He's followed the exact

course of study you claim you would have liked to
do." Jillian's father leaned even more precariously forward and added to Cameron Smith in a confidential
whisper, "She could not attend university or college.
She's a female, you know."

Cameron sent a slow, lazy sweep of a gaze over her.
"So I have remarked."

Jillian didn't know what infuriated her more: to
have the rogue stare at her person as though she were
no better than a common strumpet, and right in front
of her father; or to have him claim with such indifference that he possessed the knowledge she ached to
acquire.

How cruel, that her gender denied her the right to
pursue what she craved, while this . . . this *bounder*
could waltz through the university doors and claim it
as his right. But he had not troubled to do so, and
still claimed he'd done so, and there was no one to
challenge him over it.

"Oh, this will never do," her father fussed after
craning his neck to send a few more questions the
rogue's way. "Jillian, switch places with him. You
drive while young Smith and I discuss the Metcalf
case."

"Oh, yes, we must discuss the Metcalf—" Jillian
began before the reality of what he'd said sank in
on her.

Young Doctor Smith! Her father expected her to
act as coachman while he and the interloper chattered
on as if she wasn't even there.

"Papa," she whispered. Betrayal lanced through
her, freezing her into immobility. With that casual
phrase, her father had told her how little he valued
the skill she'd tried so hard to learn at his side. With
that casual phrase, he'd cast her aside in favor of this
so-called apprentice.

Cameron pressed the reins into her hands. With
quick and frightening strength, he caught her around

the waist and lifted her over his lap to his other side. He lounged back onto the seat, at ease between herself and her father.

Her father leaned forward and talked in low tones while Cameron nodded and frowned, the very image of an esteemed colleague instead of a complete imposter. Those indecipherable murmurs, the clip-clop of Queenie's hooves, the chill sigh of the wind, were all she could hear.

The reins she gripped still held the warmth of Cameron's hands. Her waist still tingled from the strength he'd used to shift her out of her place. Her bottom . . . she blushed at realizing she sat in the very spot he'd so recently occupied, on warm cushioned leather that still bore the shape of him.

Her own slight weight had never made a lasting impression in the seat.

Her father had never called her *young Doctor Bowen*.

Cameron's broad shoulder bumped up against hers and she had to brace her feet against the floorboards and push back to avoid yielding even more seat space to him. If she didn't fight for every inch, she'd soon find herself squeezed out onto the road. With that hulking lout blocking her father's view, and demanding all her father's attention, Papa might not even notice that she wasn't there anymore.

She clenched her teeth and shoved against Cameron's weight, until she realized that the rogue was thoroughly enjoying the sensation of her pressing so hard against him.

She relaxed, and promptly found herself squashed into the corner.

Jillian had never felt so lonely in all her life.

3

"You are too heavy," she said. "I am getting smashed over here."

"No woman has ever complained . . . about my size." The quip had come easily to Cameron; he wondered if she would understand its double meaning.

She kicked him in the ankle. "Move over."

He swallowed his grunt of pain. "Sharp-toed boots to go along with your sharp tongue, I see." She sent him a triumphant smirk. "Very well," he said. "If it's more room you want, I'll just move my arm out of the way."

He withdrew his arm from its very enjoyable position crushed up against Jillian's arm and the tender swell of breast that protruded beyond. He stretched his arm across the back of the wagon bench. The tips of his fingers dangled down over the edge, brushing her far shoulder.

He counted. It took her three heartbeats, no longer, to realize she sat more intimately pressed and enveloped by him than before. She stiffened herself into a fair imitation of the prow of a ship, leaning forward into the wind, deliberately choosing discomfort over relaxing against him.

She would come around.

His certainty grew with each turn of the wagon wheels. When they'd gone a quarter mile without her bursting into hysteria, he knew she'd unconsciously begun accepting the situation. A half mile, and old Doctor Bowen cocked his head at him curiously, and then launched into a surprisingly interesting discourse on the nature of the human liver. A mile, and Jillian's trembling stilled, her breathing settled. She ceased darting furious little glances his way. By almost infinitesimal degrees, she relaxed until she sat normally upon the seat. Her sleeve brushed his shirt, raising delicious little tickles on the tender skin along his side.

He shifted, breaking the contact for the sake of keeping his thoughts focused where they belonged, not where they longed to be.

Another mile, and a worried pucker replaced her stricken expression. He congratulated himself for choosing the perfect time to carry out this part of his plan. With her concern over the dying tenant farmer consuming her, Jillian had set aside her own woes. Doctor Bowen lectured him as if he'd missed having an apprentice learning at his knee.

The Bowens had accepted the inevitable. For now. And Cameron doubted very much that they realized they'd already conceded any hope of escaping him. Later, when their business with the dying farmer was finished and they were safe within the walls of their home, the Bowens would belatedly realize what he'd done. They'd probably lash out against the restrictions he'd forced upon them. But later would be too late. Any fury, any outrage they managed to summon would be a pale, weak shadow, now that it had been tempered by acceptance.

His father had been right. People behaved much like sheep. Point them in a direction they wished to take, and they'd go along no matter how uncomfortable or how difficult you made the journey. Cameron studied Jillian covertly for a long moment and found himself wishing that his father had been wrong, just this once.

"Why are you doing this to us?" Jillian asked.

"Because I can."

He had no intention of telling her his intentions, and most people would have been cowed enough by his blunt statement to subside into wordless acceptance.

"You owe us the decency of an explanation."

"I am a man without debt or obligation." At least he was now. Two years ago had been another matter. But that was ancient history, best left buried.

"Tell me your purpose in doing this. Perhaps . . . perhaps I might share your convictions and help you instead of hinder."

She startled him. So much so that he let himself respond incautiously. "You will come to trust me, Jillian, whether you want to or not."

"No."

"Yes. 'Tis a strange phenomenon, but it has been proven again and again that captives develop trust for their captors. You will find yourself caring about me, and embracing my cause as your own."

"I have never heard such ridiculous rantings. What devil spawn gave you such an idea?"

"Why, none other than a knight of the realm, a man so thoroughly steeped in loyalty to his profession that he cared for nothing else."

"Knights are chivalrous and would never treat a lady the way you are badgering me."

"This particular knight would've had your mind changed about that in an instant."

"You lie. About knights, and about knowing one. There are no knights anymore."

"Ah, that is so." Indeed, Cameron knew this to be true with piercing certainty. His failure to attain knighthood had forever embittered his father, no matter that times had changed and men did not have the same opportunities that Sir John Delacorte had enjoyed. "But the fellow who taught me these things was quite old. Good Queen Bess herself dubbed him."

"Well, I wish he were still about and would come to my rescue," Jillian muttered.

He swallowed the laughter that bubbled within. She was an amusing, if incautious, little thing. "Old Sir John came to no one's rescue, unless there was something for him to gain."

"So what did he gain from teaching you all his mercenary tricks?" she asked.

The conversation had drifted too close to Cameron's personal life. Jillian Bowen possessed more intelligence, more bravado than he'd expected. A moment ago he'd thought her incautious—instead it was he who'd relaxed his guard, and all because . . . because . . .

She had made him laugh.

It had been a good long time since he'd laughed. If this is what laughter did, causing him to lower his guard, dulling his determined edge, he'd be better off snarling like a wolf all day.

He gathered the remnants of his control and mentally honed his edge. "You will be forced to bend to my will, Jillian, so you might as well give in to me now."

"Never."

"Your father will look to me for guidance. You will turn to me for strength. You will trust me, Jillian."

She sniffed. "You obviously have never known the true thing if you cannot tell the difference between shadows and substance. My father and I will do what we must to survive. If you choose to believe that is real trust, then I feel sorry for you."

Her observation staggered him. She, who ought to be sitting there with teeth chattering in abject terror, felt sorry for *him*?

He could cure her of that misplaced pity easily enough.

He just wished that her comment had not roused a yearning within him to know what it would feel like to truly earn this woman's trust and respect.

She'd gone back to sitting brutally straight, her knees pressed so tightly together that the bones must scrape each time a wagon wheel dipped into a rut. She had tucked the folds of her gown beneath her legs as if she didn't want even the cloth of her skirt to brush against him. He wondered if she realized how she'd drawn the fabric so taut that it molded the sweet curve of her hips, the elegant length of her thighs.

"Stop looking at me," she whispered.

"Jillian." He used his demon-voice again, and knew it stirred her fears when she blinked a little too rapidly. "You must accept that I can do anything I want. Anything. I can look my fill, whether I'm looking at you, or at these fields we're passing through."

"As if a rogue like you would have any interest in fields."

"Ah, but there you are wrong—there's little I enjoy more than the sight of well-managed fields."

He'd always had a passion for riding out at night after the harvest had been taken in. He'd go when the sky was dark, for there was a special beauty in the silvery glow bathing fields picked neat and clean, when the corn had been gathered into bulging stooks and the hay stacked high to await winter feeding. He'd not been able to indulge that passion since losing Benington.

"These," he commented, after a brief, sweeping assessment, "these are not well-managed fields."

"They were thriving, until just recently. They were farmed by Jamie Metcalf, the man we ride to see."

No stooks rose high and fat to mark a fruitful harvest. The moonlight revealed the withered tips of mangolds still poking from the ground. Grain stalks whipped nearly empty seed heads against each other in the breeze. The valuable root crops had been abandoned to rot in the ground, the precious life-sustaining seed to fall to the earth. Jamie Metcalf's animals would starve this winter. Jamie Metcalf's family would no doubt fare the same.

"His family, his neighbors, should have seen to his harvest," Cameron murmured, appalled at the waste of a season's hard work.

"For what purpose? So that Cromwell's army could confiscate it later?" Jillian snapped back. "At least this way, the seed will fall to the ground and might sprout come spring, and if winter doesn't turn too harsh, Jamie's wife might salvage some of the roots."

"If her overlord is a good husbandman, she won't be here long enough to benefit," Cameron pointed out. "Were these my lands, I would already be casting about in my mind for the name of a likely man to take over these fields."

"I pray for the sake of Mary Metcalf and her babes that Lord Harrington is a kinder man than you."

"Most men are kinder than I, Jillian."

"You need not remind me."

But though she flung verbal barbs his way, he could tell her attention was more fixed upon the upcoming cottage than her own predicament. Just as he'd planned. Doctor Bowen, as well, had straightened and peered toward the squat, ugly dwelling with concern creasing his features. Despite having their lives uprooted, these two seemed to have forgotten their own woes in their worry over the dying tenant farmer. Also just as he'd planned.

He hadn't planned, though, on finding himself affected by some unknown tenant farmer's battle with death. Jillian's accusations stung, all the more because he had to admit they were true. A scant hour ago, hearing that a tenant farmer had allowed his ill health to interfere with his harvest would have roused Cameron's annoyance, but not necessarily his sympathy. He might not have spared the bereft family a single

thought, not given a fig for their future as he ordered
his bailiff to evict them from their home, replacing
them with a new family.

It must be the damned neglected fields, the abandoned crops drooping in the moonlight, that had
tugged at his heart, reminding him of all he'd lost. If
he still owned Benington Manor, the rich fields would
be prepared for winter already, with the grain safely
stored and the furrows turned, awaiting the sowing of
protective cover crops.

Benington's new owners—who knew what the new
owners had done? The land might have gone to weeds
by now. Cromwell had not cared about keeping the
land in good heart. He'd merely confiscated the lands
of those who had supported the king and parcelled it
out to those loyal to Cromwell's Commonwealth
cause. Cameron had never had the stomach to ride
back for a look at what had been so cruelly stripped
away from him.

As they neared the small cottage, he could see that
one window had been left unshuttered, with the stub
of a candle guttering low on the sill.

A woman's heartsick wailing, punctuated by the
frightened sobs of young children, bled from the cottage, drowning the squeaking of their wagon wheels.

"We're too late," Jillian said. She stopped the
wagon, and closed her eyes in the manner of one sending a short prayer toward heaven. When she blinked
them open, she looked tired and more defeated than
any woman should look. This, too, was according to
plan, so why did something inside Cameron rebel,
making him want to touch her with a tender caress
and restore some of the fire and spirit he found so
oddly appealing?

Jillian and her father climbed from the carriage with
the purposefulness of those who have moved in similar
accord times beyond counting. They'd reached the

door when the old man looked over his shoulder and realized Cameron was not behind him.

"Young doctor?"

Cameron hesitated, and then reluctantly slid from his perch to join them as they entered the cottage.

A meager fire blazed on the hearth, illuminating the waxy countenance of a man who had not gone easily from this world. His woman knelt by the bed, swaying. The suppleness of her body marked her as far too young for the years alone to have carved the lines etching her face.

The high-pitched keening they'd heard outside still sounded through her clenched teeth. Her children clung to her. The head of the oldest came even with his mother's chin. The next two—twins by the identically stunned look of them—stood no taller than her shoulder. The youngest, a babe still in clouts, sat wailing on the ragged hem of its mother's skirt. Judging by the bulge stretching the woman's apron, another child would soon join the brood.

"Mary?" Jillian's voice cracked. Her devastation over the farmer's death momentarily overcame her dismay at Cameron's own untimely arrival on the scene.

The grieving woman slowly turned her head. "What shall we do?" Her voice sounded flat and dull. "Whatever shall we do?"

Her anguish seemed to stem from fear for her future more so than grief at the loss of the man who had been her husband. The attitude echoed what Cameron had grown up believing—women, no matter their station, cared little for the men who shared their beds. They cared only for the money, the food in their bellies, the shouldering of responsibility.

And then he saw Mary's fingers stroke her husband's wrist. "Oh, mistress, I don't know how to help him. Jamie's so cold. So cold." Her whimper ended in a quiet sob. She tugged Jamie's shirtsleeve down and buttoned it, and then hurried to fasten the threadbare shirt up to his chin as if she sought to shield him from the unremitting cold that would forever enclose him, and Cameron felt ashamed of his earlier thoughts.

Jillian knelt alongside the grieving woman and with a subtle movement inserted her body as a shield so Jamie's family could not see what she did. Her fingers touched his neck near his ear and then brushed down over his chest. She thumbed at one half-closed eyelid, and when Cameron saw the opaque stare, he was glad that Jillian's thoughtfulness meant Mary and her children could not see this certain evidence of death.

"I will send Aggie to you," Jillian said when her butterfly-touch inspection was done. "She will take care of him now."

"What shall become of us, mistress?" Mary's hand groped like a kitten's claw for the security of Jillian's skirt.

"My father will speak to Lord Harrington for you." Jillian gently disengaged Mary's hand and placed it on the smallest child's tangled curls. "Is that not right, Father? He might allow Mary to bide here for a while if you will speak to Lord Harrington on Mary's behalf."

"I will speak to Lord Harrington on Mary's behalf," Doctor Bowen said. "Certainly, certainly."

"Oh, thank you, sir." Tears welled in Mary's eyes and spilled, leaving a new set of glistening tracks against her reddened, puffy skin.

"Do you have wine?" Doctor Bowen asked. "A cup, well mulled, is a great restorative." Mary shook her head, and Cameron thought of those unharvested fields and knew Mary Metcalf would be drinking nothing more than hot water, steeped with foraged herbs, through the coming endless winter nights.

"Come away from Jamie, now," Jillian said.

"Yes, Jillian, take Mary away now and make her

something fortifying to drink from our stores while young Doctor Smith and I attend to a few things."

"But, Papa, I always help you—" Jillian began.

"Young Doctor Smith here shall assist. He is my new apprentice, you know." Doctor Bowen looked very pleased with himself at making this announcement.

Jillian paled and looked about to protest when Mary collapsed into a sobbing huddle against her shoulder. She shot a stormy glare Cameron's way as she led Mary the few steps to the fire.

"Come." Dr. Bowen kept his voice low as he motioned Cameron to his side. "Have a look at the body. I will point out a few things you must keep in your mind for the next time you see a case like this. But take care that you don't fill your head to bursting." Doctor Bowen paused, while his face wrinkled with puzzlement. "There is a limit, it seems, to what the mind can absorb before it begins shedding some of the things that were hardest won."

Cameron's throat tightened with sympathy. He wanted, crazily, to comfort the bewildered old physician, and that made it easier somehow to approach a dead body he had no desire to see. In fact, he didn't want to be in this cottage at all, didn't want to witness the depth of grief a family displayed for a man who would soon be slid into a solitary grave.

Nor did he want to be aware of the depths of compassion possessed by Jillian and her father. He'd assumed it would be so simple, so easy, to force himself into these peoples' lives, to go along with them on their late-night errands of mercy. He'd never imagined the wrenching sight of Jillian's practiced hand judging whether life still lingered inside a man. He had the awful sensation that he was interfering with something holy, and that for all the sins he'd accumulated on this earth, this one would be the one responsible for consigning him to eternal hellfire.

Dr. Bowen sensed Cameron's hesitation and misread it. He gave Cameron a bracing slap across the shoulder. "You must not take this man's death too much to heart, young Cameron. There is no remedy that would have saved him, unless they've come up with new treatments since my days at the University."

"None that I am aware of, sir," Cameron said.

Dr. Bowen ruffled Cameron's hair in the jocular manner of a fond father bucking up a favorite son, a gesture Cameron had often seen but never received. He'd been little more than six years old when he'd convinced himself that hair ruffling was a silly thing to do, providing nothing more than the inconvenience of combing one's hair back into place afterward. Silly. Until now, when a near-senile old gentleman sought to reassure a full-grown man who had insinuated himself into his life by lies and subterfuge.

"I can see you have the makings of a fine physician. Don't overfret about this. You and I will do much good in the nights to come." Doctor Bowen's eyes were warm with concern and confidence.

Cameron coughed into his hand to loosen the further tightening of his throat. It was the sorrow pervading the room, he told himself, that caused him to feel so unusually emotional. But he was assailed by guilt even as a part of him rejoiced to hear someone express confidence in him, even if it was something as ridiculous as a befuddled old man who thought John Cameron Delacorte might make a good doctor. Ridiculous.

Cameron stared down at the dead man while Doctor Bowen brushed sweat-matted hair off the cooling forehead. "So sorry I could not help you, young Jamie," the physician murmured. "So very sorry."

Cameron forced himself to cough again, and hoped that his pretended hacking would provide an excuse for the dampness he felt springing to his eyes. He didn't understand. It could not be grief, because he had not known the dead man. But something inside him ached.

Damned inconvenient, that after twenty-eight years of lying dormant, the maudlin streak his father had always accused him of having would choose to show itself just now, when he had to be his most callous.

He tightened his jaw, willing his momentary weakness into abeyance. He swung his gaze around the daub-walled, low-ceilinged room, fastidiously clean despite having six human beings crowded into its space. The worn and primitive nature of the furnishings told him Jamie Metcalf had spared none of his earnings on comfort—it had all gone, no doubt, into land, into dreams for a future that was now denied to him. So poor and yet so proud, so hopeful . . . Cameron scowled at finding that maudlin tendency rearing its unwelcome head yet again.

One of the twins caught sight of his fierce glower and shrieked in alarm, hurling itself into Jillian's arms. She caught the child to her breast and turned an accusing glare upon him, and he wanted to turn away at once from the sight of her holding a crying young child against her shoulder, but doing so might expose his distressing new weakness. He carefully fixed his face into an expression mingling boredom and impatience.

"Nothing more we can do here, then," he clipped out. "Let us be on our way."

"I am . . . I am sorry." Mary Metcalf stumbled to her feet, clumsy and near-blind in her grief. "You have come all this way, and I have nothing to repay your kindness." She held out her hands in an age-old expression of gratitude. "Doctor Bowen . . . Doctor Smith . . . Thank you so much for all you've done."

"Poor Mary." Doctor Bowen awkwardly patted the bereaved woman.

"We will speak to Lord Harrington on Mary's behalf," Cameron reminded him.

"We will speak to Lord Harrington on Mary's behalf." The doctor nodded, accepting coaching from Cameron as easily as he'd done from his daughter.

A strangled-sounding moan came from near the hearth. Cameron slanted a look at Jillian over his shoulder. She'd gone nearly as white as the dead man, and she swayed as if the tiny child she held taxed her strength. She understood full well what he'd just accomplished with her father, with the widow who should rightly be thanking Jillian rather than Cameron.

A gentleman would reassure her.

Cameron deliberately fixed her with a triumphant sneer, and turned away from her, dismissively. He clapped a hand on Doctor Bowen's shoulder. "Time for us to go, sir."

4

This cannot be happening, Jillian told herself as she pretended to guide Queenie along the moon-drenched lane. *Cameron Smith does not exist. He is an awful, terrible dream, brought on by my worry over Jamie, by Cromwell's incessant watching. . . . I will waken soon, and everything will be exactly as it was. . . .*

"You will cut your hands if you continue to grip those reins so tightly." Cameron's voice, unfamiliar and yet all too familiar, chased away her fantasy that the past night's events had been a nightmare.

"Two hours as a doctor, and already you are dispensing advice," she snapped before she could control her outburst. She was glad of the dark, knowing it would hide her blush. She'd given herself away by letting him know how his easy assumption of her role had irritated her.

His hand hovered over hers. One long, strong finger ran across the tender indentations between her fisted knuckles. "Loosen your grip, Jillian."

"Don't you touch me!" She jerked her hands away, inadvertently tugging Queenie's bit, which caused the mare to whinny in surprise. "And don't you tell me how to drive my mare."

Cameron lifted his hand in a gesture of surrender and obligingly slid an inch away. But she felt no more in control.

"Your eyes search the woods and the clearings as if you hope to find someone lurking there," he said, quiet enough that she could not chide him for risking waking her father.

"Fraley—Cromwell's man in these parts—often approaches us during these late-night rides."

"And you hope he will be your savior, hmmm, and rid you of my presence?"

"He would. I will tell him everything the minute he hails this wagon." Her anger, mingled with frustration and jealousy, overrode her good sense. "I would rather the whole world know the truth about my father's condition than see you playacting the role of learned physician."

"Ah, Jillian, do you think me such a poor planner? I listened from the woods when you talked earlier with the man. Perhaps you don't remember—he told you he would not approach you again this night. 'Tis why this night, of all nights, finds me riding alongside you."

"I hate you."

"I don't blame you."

She gave a small moan of impotent fury, and woke her father in the bargain.

"Goodness!" Doctor Bowen blinked awake. "I bored myself to sleep in midlecture."

"Nonsense, Doctor Bowen," Cameron said smoothly. "You were merely taxed by the rigors of recalling William Harvey's revolutionary studies of the human circulatory system."

"Ah, yes, a most complex and difficult subject, isn't that right, Jillian? She's been after me for months to repeat all I know of the subject."

Curse Cameron Smith! She *had* been trying for months—close on to a year now—to pry this particular knowledge from her father's faltering mind. A mere two hours in Cameron Smith's company and her father began spouting medical lore as if he couldn't spit out the words fast enough.

She, who had spent most of her life taking pride in her self-control and calm demeanor, wanted to throttle her father into silence. However, she also wanted to absorb every word he said. She was jealous of every tidbit of knowledge he sent Cameron Smith's way, and so hungry to learn that she would listen secondhand if she must.

She wished she could take the ends of the reins and whip them across Cameron Smith's grinning face as he sat there, knowing full well the predicament she found herself in.

"Before I begin again, it might be best if you stop the wagon alongside that thicket, Jillian. A brief stop and I'll be more comfortable."

"Certainly, Papa."

Queenie resisted stopping, but stood there snorting and stamping impatiently while Doctor Bowen clambered down from the seat and carried himself to the far side of a tangle of brush.

"You ought to follow him," Jillian said to the rogue, who had lounged back into the space vacated by her father. If she could get him out of the wagon . . .

"Bladder tough as a wine cask." Cameron slapped low on his belly, ignoring her outraged gasp.

"Necessary, no doubt, for scoundrels engaged in your line of work."

"It does lend one a certain advantage."

He was enjoying this, the rogue! "My father might run off."

"Hmmm." He scowled, but she could tell he was fighting a smile. "But if I venture too far into the woods after him, I could get lost."

"Only if God is smiling down on me."

He didn't bother to stifle his laughter any longer, and it infuriated her that she'd given in to her frustration and caused him amusement.

"There is no need to openly mock my father's inability to make an escape attempt."

He sobered. "I am not mocking your father, Jillian. In fact, I may give him more credit than you do, because I can see he manages to think very well from time to time. I *would* go after him to make sure he doesn't try running away, but then there would be nothing to stop you from whipping the mare and galloping off to find help."

She tensed involuntarily, betraying that she'd been hoping that very thing. It took her a moment to realize, with stunned surprise, that she'd truly been thinking of running toward Bramber, seeking help, rather than bolting for the familiar shelter of her home.

"Of course," he mused, "if you ran off, that would leave me alone in the woods with no one but your father to absorb my rage."

"I would never leave my father at your mercy."

"I know that, Jillian. In fact, I am counting on it."

"I hate you," she whispered.

"It seems you possess a limited repertoire of insults. Perhaps you ought to save them for another time, especially as it seems clear that—on this night, at least— I deserve your undying gratitude."

"Grateful to *you*?" She could barely stutter a response. "Why on earth should I feel grateful to you?"

"For working something of a miracle. Your father's mind seems to be temporarily unlocked."

"It won't last. He often has lucid spells."

"Perhaps. But so long as this one lasts, your threat to hand me over to Constable Fraley strikes me as quite empty. My disappearance might send your father into even greater depths of dementia."

Tears sprung to her eyes, which she hated more than she hated him. "You have stolen my life away from me, and now you are robbing me of this precious time with my father. I will never forgive you for this, never."

He clasped a hand over his heart and pretended to

sniff away false tears. "Ah, your sharp tongue cuts me to the core. I wonder if I shall survive."

There was no time to hit him with a rejoinder. She was not quick-witted enough, it seemed, to hurl barbs capable of wounding him. Her father returned to the wagon, and Cameron Smith lent him a hand to pull him up. He leaned forward and reached around her father to close the half-door, giving it a little tug to make sure it wouldn't spring open. His thoughtfulness, his easy sharing of his strength, roused a strange ache inside Jillian. She'd never felt this way; she certainly hoped it didn't mean she was about to cry. Her cheeks were not wet when she dashed them with an angry swipe of her hand.

"Did I tell you that William Harvey and I were schoolmates," Doctor Bowen began as Jillian slapped the reins against Queenie's rump. The wagon lurched, and the wheels squealed in protest over the ruts. The sound echoed the thin wailing in Jillian's soul.

Her hands shook. Now that she'd convinced herself she had no option, she had to get home, as quickly as possible. Things would be better once she returned to the stone womb that sheltered her from harm. With a quick look around, she pinpointed their location and weighed the possible routes against one another. She pulled on the reins, tugging Queenie off the lane and into a field.

"What are you doing?" Cameron questioned sharply, at once.

"Cutting through this field will shave at least thirty minutes from our trip." The wagon lurched, sending the lout crashing right into her. She pushed at him with one hand until he edged away. "If you've been following me for a while, you know I don't often stick to the roads."

"Aye. Your familiarity with the countryside is part of the . . . charm . . . that drew me to you. A rather unusual skill in a woman."

She grew numb. "A necessary skill."

"Mmm. These roads must be near-impassable during the wet seasons."

"The shortcuts save time."

"Important when rushing to a sickbed."

"That, too," she conceded, before realizing how much it revealed about her weakness to admit this. And he caught her misstep, curse the rogue!

He shot her a questioning look. "There are other reasons?"

She shook her head. She would die before admitting the truth—that she'd been terrified of leaving her house when they'd first moved here, the way she'd been too frightened to venture outdoors in London.

She'd taken herself in hand, though, buying this wagon with its high-rising walls that enclosed her so completely on three sides. The front wall curved high, almost to her chin. So there was just that small gap along the sides, where the half-doors swung open to allow her to climb in and out, and the necessary opening from which to watch the road in front.

She'd ordered that specially made wagon two years before leaving London, knowing she'd never dare making the trip in a more conventional and open conveyance. She'd felt safe enough in it that once she'd settled into their new home, she'd forced herself outside again and again, going a little farther each time, until she'd taught herself a hundred and more different ways to get back home. If a bridge washed out, if a tree fell and blocked a road, it didn't matter. She would not be trapped away from her home.

And now this rogue informed her that the very knowledge that allowed her more freedom than she'd ever enjoyed in her life was the same knowledge that had drawn him to her.

She should have never left the house. She'd learned, when only a very young child, that venturing outside to do forbidden things led to death and devastation.

Her mama had been forever stealing away to indulge her passion for plays and operas, a passion inborn in Jillian as well. They would steal out on those nights her father was called to tend the king. It had been on one of those secret, late-night trips home from the theater when footpads had overtaken them.

Run, Jilly, run home! She could still hear her mother's frantic cry. It had been a very long time since she'd thought back to that horrible night, and she cursed Cameron Smith for making her remember.

Nothing bad had ever happened to her when she stayed safe and quiet in her room. She trembled now with the need to close herself within those walls, and she almost sobbed her relief when the low smudge on the horizon told her they approached the stone wall encircling her home. She lifted the reins and gave Queenie a light slap. The startled mare plunged into a rough canter that sent the wagon bouncing with tooth-jarring effect over the stubbled field. Her father cried out in alarm.

"Stop." Cameron issued the curt order.

She ignored him.

"Stop!" He shouted the command this time, and though she continued to ignore him, the unexpected male bellow frightened Queenie into a full gallop. Cursing, Cameron swept the reins from Jillian's hands and almost stood with the effort of pulling the charging mare to a halt.

Close. They'd come so close to the sheltering stone wall. Jillian blinked at it—it seemed to move toward her. And then she realized that a man had separated himself from the wall, a man so nondescript in size and dress that she hadn't even noticed him standing there against the stone.

"Is all secure, Mr.—" he began.

"Tell your lord all is secure, Robert." Cameron motioned for the man to approach, and when he stood alongside the wagon, Cameron leaned past Jillian.

"And ask Harrington to show leniency to a laborer's wife. She has need of the cottage even though her husband died tonight."

"The cottager's name?"

"Metcalf. Mary Metcalf."

"I'll speak to him."

"If he has any news, you can tell me when we meet tomorrow in the village," said Cameron.

The man nodded and melted back into the shadows.

Cameron turned back to her and studied her warily. "I will drive the wagon the rest of the way."

"Go," she said, scarcely able to speak past the anxiousness tightening her throat. "Go now."

They passed through the opening where an iron gate must once have hung. The drive curved through the trees, and it seemed to take forever to pass through the shadows cast by them. At last they cleared the woods and the moonlight gilded her house. It was but two stories, not half so grand as the townhome they'd left behind in London, but sturdy and secure. Shutters barred all the windows and stout oak doors presented imposing, impenetrable faces.

She caught a flash of movement near the stables, and yet another man moved from the darkness into the moonlight. She made a small sound of despair at understanding how thoroughly her stronghold had been breached.

"Martin," Cameron said. "The man I told you about. He'll see to the horse."

Freeing Jillian from unharnessing Queenie and brushing her down meant she could go inside at once and then stay in the house. Gratitude flooded through her, and she despised herself for it. That gratitude confirmed all of Cameron's predictions, but she could not help it. She shook with the need to be within the walls, to surround herself with her familiar things.

But she knew she had to pause at the door and let her father enter first. If she did not shepherd him inside ahead of her, he might linger outside for hours, or wander off and get lost. Her father seemed to drag his feet, and then at last it was her turn, but Cameron Smith sauntered through almost on her father's heels and delayed her for an impossibly long second more. He grinned down at her as he passed, amused no doubt by the irony of having her stand aside while he preceded her into her own home.

She stepped into her kitchen. She closed the door and then leaned back against it, waiting for her inner clamoring to subside the way it always did when she came home after being away for too long.

Cameron assessed her clean kitchen with a quick sweeping glance, and then bowed his head attentively once more toward her father, as if he were really interested in learning the difference between veins and arteries.

His presence altered the feel of the room. It felt smaller, and yet charged with energy. His low wordless sounds of interest bounced from the walls and struck her, somewhere deep inside, where the masculine rumbling stirred odd sensations into life. A not entirely unpleasant sensation . . . but certainly not the comfort she craved.

Stunned at her body's reaction, she clamped her eyes closed and clapped her hands over her ears to purge the sight and sound of him. To no avail. She inhaled his essence merely by breathing. Her skin prickled, as though awakened by the charged atmosphere.

She lowered her hands and opened her eyes. She had always prided herself on her ability to meld into the background, to accomplish her goals without calling attention to herself. Dubious accomplishments, but perhaps capable of saving her now, if she could call upon them to lull Cameron into underestimating her strength. She would have to stay alert for opportuni-

ties. She'd get nowhere by hiding her eyes and cowering like a frightened child.

And then she noticed that his physical presence
wasn't the room's only alteration. A bundle of clothing, and a hat with a cavalier's curled brim and plumed
feather, perched rakishly on top of the sideboard. She
could see into the narrow passage that led from the
kitchen into the bedchambers, and the door to her
room stood slightly ajar. She never left it open during
the day or when they had to leave the house, not even
a crack. Someone had been in her home while they
were out seeing to Jamie. Cameron had mentioned
sending a man to the house. Apparently he'd been
poking and prying where he had no business, leaving
his master's bundle out on Jillian's sideboard.

It was a potent reminder that Cameron had overtaken her life and commandeered her home—and
she'd just stood there now and quivered with pleasure
at the sound of his voice. She recalled with hollow
dismay his gloating certainty that she would come to
trust him, to depend on his strength. She might even,
he'd hinted, begin to develop a fondness for him.

Never. She vowed to stay alert for any show of
kindness, any hint of affection, for she knew they
would all be deliberately manipulative actions designed to shatter her will. She would never trust him.
She would plunge a knife into her own heart rather
than come to care for him.

She repeated the vows to herself again and again,
while she stood in the shadows and listened to her
father treat the interloper like the son she knew Wilton Bowen had always craved. The son he might have
had someday if Jillian hadn't run off, if she'd been
brave enough to save her mother on that long-ago
night.

They'd no sooner taken seats around the table when
Doctor Bowen launched into a discourse about blood,

about pulses, about the miracle of the human circulatory system. It was fascinating, compelling stuff that threatened to command all Cameron's attention when he ought to be paying mind to what Jillian was up to, standing deep in the shadows.

She might be on a surreptitious search for a knife. Or she might be fighting to regain her composure and maintain a bit of her pride. She would accept him, she would forgive him, so long as he did not strip her of her dignity.

But if she came running at him with a knife, dignity be damned.

He tensed when she began tending the fire. Overpowering a small female brandishing a dull kitchen knife was simple enough; an enraged virago swinging a long iron poker could break an arm or a knee before he got close enough to overwhelm her with his superior strength. She stirred the fire from its banked embers and added a few small sticks to strengthen the blaze. He watched while she hefted a knobby chunk of wood at least three inches thick and as long as his forearm. It, too, could make a formidable weapon if she tried to wallop him across the face with it. But she merely laid it atop the hungry tongues of flame.

When she began struggling with a large chunk of split oak, he found himself halfway out of his seat, intent upon helping her, before he realized what he was doing. He lowered himself back into the chair, grateful that Doctor Bowen didn't seem to have noticed, thankful that Jillian's back had been turned. Desperate highwaymen, dangerous kidnappers, had no business leaping to a captive's assistance.

And yet his hands gripped the arms of his chair, and the muscles in his forearm visibly tightened, ready for work, until she finished feeding the fire.

Doctor Bowen yawned in midsentence, and then sat there, mouth agape, staring at Cameron with dismay. "Where on earth will you sleep, my boy?" he asked.

"This house might appear spacious from the outside, but we're packed to the rafters as you can see. My Jillian is something of a hoarder, I fear."

"Women." Cameron pretended to commiserate while he swept a slow glance around the room. The tables, the sideboards, the paintings and assorted statuary that crowded the kitchen would suffice to furnish at least three rooms. Doctor Bowen seemed to be saying the entire house was similarly stuffed. Cameron's earlier investigation of the Bowens had told him that they'd fled a large, comfortable home in London for this secluded freehold. It seemed that Jillian had held on to as many things as possible to remind her of the life they'd left.

Benington had never been overfurnished—Cameron's father had maintained a soldier's abhorrence of clutter, and Cameron couldn't recall his mother well enough to know if she'd ever tried to soften the austere surroundings with feminine fripperies. Cameron had begun selling anything of value after Riordan joined the Royalist cause, sending the money through secret messengers in the hopes of keeping his brother's belly full, his feet shod, his tack in good repair. Benington had stood stripped bare as Cameron's soul on the day Commonwealth forces ousted him from his home.

"Mr. Smith can make do with a pallet in front of the fire," Jillian said, joining them.

"Nonsense," Dr. Bowen objected. "The furnishings from seven or eight bedrooms are crammed into this house. I'm sure you can rearrange a few things to make young Doctor Smith a private place upstairs, Jillian. Go on, you can dispose of a bit of your rubbish to clear a space for him."

She froze, looking as if she'd been shot through the heart.

Nothing would suit Cameron's purpose better than to force Jillian to shove furniture about, to discard

something she treasured, in altering her home to make
a place for him. It would reinforce the domination he
held over her. Yes, goad her with this complete evidence of her helplessness—when mere minutes ago
he'd scarcely been able to stand the thought of her
hefting a chunk of wood on her own.

" 'Tis late, Doctor Bowen," he said. "A pallet before the fire will suit me fine."

He fancied he read a hint of gratitude flicker across
her face, but it altered quickly. "You no doubt think
to keep watch so neither of us sneaks out the door.
Well, there is a back door, Mr. Smith, and windows
in each room."

"Aye," he said. "Your back door opens into the
rose garden. All the windows at the rear of the house
open there as well. I'd wager you and your father
enjoy the privacy provided by those high stone walls,
but I doubt either of you are capable of scaling them
without making so much noise that it would waken
the dead."

"There's a gate in the garden wall," she said.

"Rusty from years of disuse. My man tells me it
would screech louder than a kicked cat if anyone tried
to open it."

"I climbed trees for sport when I was a child, and
I'm very thin," she said, with a stubborn tilt to her
chin. "I could climb those walls or squeeze through
the bars in the gate."

"And your father would still be in the house, with
me."

"Of course I'll be in the house!" Doctor Bowen
cocked his head at Jillian and then Cameron in turn.
"Why would you want to go climbing walls and
squeezing yourself through iron bars, Jillian? If you've
so much pent-up energy, put it to good work making
a space for young Doctor Smith."

She admitted defeat with a slight, almost infinitesimal inclination of her head. No slumping shoulders,

no blubbering tears. Cameron did not know many men who could accept the inevitable so gracefully and with such unbowed pride.

He scarcely remembered his mother, but whenever he thought of her he remembered tear-tracked cheeks, nails bitten to the quick, red-rimmed eyes, and a body gone to fat. His father had taught him women had no substance, that they were useful for begetting a child or two and then worthless baggage thereafter. Cameron had never met a woman in the interim that had changed his mind.

Until now. He wondered at the quirk of fate that would saddle him with a woman he might respect at the very moment he required a weak-willed puddle of tears.

"I'll sleep by the fire tonight," he said. "Tomorrow, I'd like a place of my own—on this first level."

"You see, Father, Mr. Smith is quite content to sleep here tonight. He'll have the entire day tomorrow to choose a place and make it ready." She turned back to the fire and threw a final log into the growing blaze with enough force to tell Cameron that she understood full well that she'd lost a little, but gained a little, too. She'd admitted he might make a place for himself in her home—but she would not be the one to do it.

She lit a taper from the leaping flames and used it to light a half-dozen candles. The room glowed warm and golden, and he got his first good look at her.

He'd watched her from a distance, so he was familiar with the lines and shapes that made her. But he'd not been aware of the fine texture of her skin, or the thick abundance of the hair gathered into a sedate knot at the back of her neck. Her dress, a severe and utilitarian rusty red wool, no doubt served her well when working with her father in places where blood and various bodily fluids were always present. It did nothing to enhance her color, though, and seemed deliberately fashioned to bind down her breasts and disguise the delightful way her body curved from hips to waist. The unattractive gown, coupled with her severe hairstyle, seemed calculated to minimize her feminine attributes.

Odd. She had a lithe and lissome form that no amount of binding could disguise. She was not a true beauty, but attractive in the fine-boned, delicate way that some men found appealing. He'd known women possessing far less in the way of attractiveness who knew how to make the most of their good features. Jillian Bowen apparently scorned those female secrets—or she simply didn't care enough to learn them.

Not that it mattered. It suited him to have her mouselike and quaking. Except she wasn't quaking with fear, but with a barely suppressed rage.

That rage pleased him more than her fear would have. He did not want to analyze the reason.

"The problem," Doctor Bowen said suddenly, and with loud urgency, "is that the very moment blood escapes the body, it becomes bright red from the air, so there's no telling if it's from a vein or an artery unless you know . . ." His voice trailed away, and he looked as bewildered by his outburst as Cameron had been.

"You've tired yourself, Papa." Jillian shot a furious glare Cameron's way. "It's very late. You can continue this lecture tomorrow."

"Continue this lecture tomorrow," her father agreed. He tilted his head toward Cameron, and a question seemed to hover on his lips, as if he meant to ask him to identify himself. And then his expression cleared. "We must provide young Doctor Smith with some bedding, Jillian."

"He can roll himself into his cloak for tonight." She gently guided her father out of his chair. The old man swayed where he stood, looking as if he could drift off to sleep then and there. The only time Cameron had noticed such a quick descent into sleep was when babes or small children suddenly went from cranky grumbling into deep and restful slumber. Cameron had not enjoyed such restful slumber for years, but he could not envy Doctor Bowen's quick slide into oblivion. A good night's rest did not seem an adequate recompense for losing a lifetime's learning and experiences.

And yet Cameron knew he would crave a taste of that sweet nothingness for himself as he lay rolled in his cloak in front of the fire.

He shifted in the chair so he could stare into the flickering flames while the Bowens made their slow way from the kitchen and down the hall. He heard Doctor Bowen's occasional querulous questions and Jillian's calm, soothing answers.

The two of them—there. Himself—here. Just as it should be. And yet he felt uncommonly lonely. A strange, strange sensation for a man who prided himself on his solitary nature. And completely inexplicable, considering that he barely knew these people, and that he intended to leave them behind as soon as his mission was completed.

Providing they didn't all die in the meantime.

"It is not very cold tonight, Papa," he heard Jillian say. Her voice rose, became even louder. "Besides, if he feels a chill, he can always take a blanket from the trunk that lies to the left of the door."

She might not be willing to fetch a blanket for him, but she'd made it easy enough for him to learn where to find one. Cameron felt a quick stab of pleasure, which he quelled at once. She was merely behaving as expected. There was nothing personal implied in her lukewarm show of concern. She was just a puppet, bending according to the strings he pulled.

He sat in his chair for a long time, listening to the sounds of her making her father ready for bed, and later, to the soft thumps and scrapes from her own room. He then listened to the ensuing silence, and wondered if she slept, or if she lay there wide-eyed in the dark, plotting ways to escape him.

When the fire had burned low again, he found the trunk, and pulled out a soft woven bedcover. But he set it aside as he rolled himself into his cloak, and then folded it to use as a cushion for his head. The scents of lavender and soap drifted from the folded wool. Jillian must have washed that blanket before tucking it away. With her own hands she'd gathered that lavender, dried it, and layered the leaves between the folds.

He wished he'd left the blanket in the trunk. Even though the room had cooled a bit, he felt uncommonly warm.

5

The hours passed without sleep coming to grant some respite from Jillian's thoughts. So she bargained with herself: Each moment she stayed awake would erase one moment of the night before. If she stayed awake until dawn, then the entire previous night would be wiped clean.

She would walk into the kitchen and tend to their simple breakfast needs as usual. Jamie Metcalf would still cling to life. She would find no stranger sleeping in front of the fire, no glorious dark man who had sworn to bend her to his will, for whatever mysterious purpose.

As bargains went, it had one serious drawback: By not sleeping, she could not pass off the events of the past night as a bad dream.

Let him be a bad dream, the nightmare I first thought him to be, she prayed even as a full-blown image of Cameron Smith filled her mind. Dark, fathomless eyes, thick hair sweeping down and framing a face composed of strong angles and planes, full lips curved in a smile as they framed flashing white teeth. A strong hand extended to help her father. A light caress from callused fingertips brushed against her shoulder. Something inside her stirred, something soft, breathless, full of hope and yearning. She beat it down, angrily. She'd dreamed of handsome men before without succumbing to that sort of weakness. She had no business stirring at the thought of a man who had required only a quarter of an hour to upset the carefully balanced life she'd spent years creating.

The first hint of dawn, as insipid and insubstantial as her will, brightened her room. She eased from her bed, careful to avoid any motion that would lead the ropes to creak. She stole softly into the narrow passage leading to the kitchen. Relief, disbelief, swept through her, at seeing the front of the hearth lying bare. No sleeping scoundrel. No rumpled blanket.

She had to put her hand against the wall for balance. Touching her house, reminding herself of the safe solidity of her brick and plaster cocoon, always reassured her. Today, for some reason, that empty space in front of the hearth left an empty space inside her that her house could not seem to fill. She gritted her teeth against the urge to cry out.

It *had* been a dream, then. All of it. The solid warmth of Cameron's arm bumping against hers, the low rumble of his voice stirring those troublesome sensations in her innermost female reaches. A dream—those hot, interested glances that had made her think that one man, perhaps even one so magnificent, might see beyond her plain exterior to the woman within.

A dream. A nightmare. She should have known.

And now everything shall return to the way it was, she thought. Strange, that the realization brought no joy.

Her breath had been rasping in her ears, in counterpoint to the pounding of her pulse. She sucked in great lungfuls of air, her house's air, until her breathing steadied, and dropped her arm to her side when her knees regained their strength. A great tiredness gripped her.

The low murmur of male voices drifted through the passage, shattering her torpor. Two voices. Her father—and someone else. Nobody ever visited her fa-

ther. Ever. She had seen to that. So the other male
voice, husky and deep, could belong only to that
rogue, Cameron Smith.

The night before had not been a dream. Everything
that happened was real.

He was real.

Her heart lurched, but she told herself it was from
hearing her father speak with a verve and vibrancy
that had long been missing.

The voices drew her. She dragged herself down the
passage to her father's room and pushed open the
door. It swung wide to reveal her father gesturing em-
phatically at his prized anatomy chart. Cameron Smith
lounged back in her chair, *her* chair, his hands clasped
loosely over his middle, with one long leg straight out
in front of him and the other bent at the knee.

The pose invited her inspection, and without trying
very hard to fight the urge, she let her gaze drift from
the slope made by his bent knee to the firm flatness
of his belly, and up the incredibly broad expanse of
his chest. She realized with stunned surprise that the
top buttons of his shirt were undone and she could
see the wisps of sable-brown curls. He stared up at
her father, so that his firm jaw was revealed in its fine
symmetry, and his hair fell away from his face, revealing it in all its strength and splendor.

She shivered.

He was like a giant jungle cat, looking deceptively
at ease. But as one who knew intimately the shape
and ability of the human form, she knew those taut
and perfect muscles could, in the space of an eye-
blink, surge into swift and violent action.

Or, with one quick motion, he could catch a woman
in those bulging arms, pull her up against those taut,
perfect muscles, and let her feel all the things she
could not see.

She felt herself redden at the inappropriateness of
her thoughts and at that moment he sensed her pres-

ence, like the predatory creature she'd compared him to. He turned his head and fixed her with a slow, smoldering stare that skewered her in place.

She'd known he was magnificent. She had done her best to avoid looking at him the night before, instinctively knowing that her anger and fright weakened her and afraid to reveal those vulnerabilities to him, but she'd still been aware of his physical appeal. The images that had haunted her all night long had been but pale hints of the reality she saw now. Dawn brightened the windows behind him, and the lamp her father had lit sent flickering golden highlights over a face so fine and handsome that she had to catch her breath while something hungry stirred low in her belly.

He seemed completely unaware of the impact his handsomeness had upon her. If anything, he seemed embarrassed to find her staring at him, for she saw the telltale ruddiness rise from his neck to his cheeks.

"Jillian!" Her father spotted her and motioned her into the room. "Come, come. Young Doctor Smith's education is shockingly lacking. I want you to write a letter of reprimand at once to his professors at the University."

"Later, Papa. We must ride to see Lord Harrington right now. We promised to beg for his mercy regarding Mary Metcalf's cottage."

The rogue leaped to his feet. Every long, elegant inch of him drew tight as he brought his feet together and straightened his shoulders. Curse his hide, but it looked as though he meant to bow toward her! He made a stiff little jerk at the waist before a look of total dismay washed over him. He froze, and then twisted elaborately as if he'd risen only to stretch an aching muscle.

"There is no need to approach Lord Harrington," Cameron said. "I took care of it last night."

"Last night?" Puzzled, she ran over the events of the night before and remembered the almost-invisible fellow who'd disengaged himself from her wall and spoken to Cameron. She remembered Cameron saying something about Mary Metcalf. She'd been in too much of a panic then, too eager to get inside the house, to acknowledge that Cameron had made the promise to intercede with Lord Harrington and that he'd apparently done so through that odd little man.

"You sent him a message through a highly suspicious channel. Lord Harrington is not known to be charitable, even under the best of conditions."

"Harrington will do as I ask."

He seemed so confident, and looked at her with one brow cocked high, expecting her to heap him with gratitude. She wouldn't. *She* had made the promise to Mary, not Cameron. He'd usurped her there, as well, as if she weren't competent enough to handle it on her own—or simply to prove he could do it better than she.

Well, there was one area where she could best him. She approached the anatomy chart. "Young Doctor Smith doesn't know his musculature?" she asked with false sweetness, feeling a little thrill of triumph. She let her hand drift over the figure drawn on the chart. "Rectus abdominis," she said, pointing to the abdominal wall before realizing that was not a good place to begin flaunting her knowledge, considering her recent fascination with the way Cameron's hands had looped over the musculature in question. "Serratus anterior, Pectoralis major." She called out those muscles of the arms, and then found herself staring at Cameron's shirtsleeve and knowing it concealed warm, pulsing examples of the real thing, rather than the flat representation on the chart beneath her fingers.

Cameron's lips tightened; his eyes flashed in response to the challenge. He touched a spot on his chest very close to where a button gapped open. "Breast," he said. With a small smile tugging the edges of his lips, he ran his hand down his side. "Hip."

He paused there just long enough to lead Jillian to worry that he might take to identifying other body parts that caused her to blush merely to think about, and then his smile widened, and his fingers brushed a wrinkle midway between hip and knee. "Thigh." He sat back down, sprawling comfortably in her chair. *Her* chair.

"You see." Father slumped, his lips drooping in a glum line. "Doctor Smith knows little more than the most basic gross anatomy. We have many hours of intensive study before us, many hours."

"I'll fetch another chair," Jillian said, since the lout lounging upon the one that belonged to her seemed disinclined to abandon it.

"Oh, you have already mastered anatomy, Jillian. You need not attend these sessions. Why don't you fix us some breakfast? We shall need all our strength, all our stamina, if we are to correct young Doctor Smith's educational lapses." Her father shooed her away with a brushing motion of his hands.

His thoughtless betrayal all but paralyzed her. She told herself his faltering wits could prevent him from understanding the situation. But, a devil in her head taunted, those wits were strong enough to lead him to banish her from these studies. Even worse, her father expected her to serve Cameron Smith as if he were an esteemed guest instead of a bullying interloper.

"I won't," she said, with lips gone numb.

"And you should not." To her amazement, Cameron leaped once more to his feet. "Begging your pardon, sir, it is not your daughter's place to fetch and carry for an apprentice."

"Jillian always prepares our breakfast. One additional portion isn't much to ask." Father didn't seem the least bit astonished that his so-called apprentice chastised him on his manners. "Mrs. Podgett shall arrive at midday to tend to our other needs. Jillian would not be overtaxed to pour an extra measure of

water, or set one extra biscuit on a plate. Go along
with you now to the kitchen, Jillian."

Surely she imagined the regret that seemed to
briefly flit over Cameron's handsome features, the hint
of apology.

She blinked at Cameron, hating the emotions war-
ring within her. How was it possible that this rogue,
this kidnapper, understood her humiliation while her
father was completely oblivious to it? She hated the
gratitude she felt welling within her. She couldn't believe her traitorous self, responding so eagerly to silent
kindness from a man who had wronged her, who continued to wrong her by his very presence.

*You will come to trust me, whether you want to or
not. Captives develop trust for their captors. . . .* He'd
warned her, in that rich, beckoning voice—and already, without even a full day passing, she'd begun
to succumb.

Never. She would not, would not, provide breakfast
for that horrible Cameron Smith. She wouldn't. She
whirled without responding to her father, and made
her way blindly through the passage.

She heard a low growl of frustration and then heavy
male footfalls thudded behind her. She hurried her
pace, but wasn't quick enough to elude the hand that
caught her by the shoulder and spun her around. She
glared up at him, hating the fact that her eyes welled
with tears.

"Stop that!" she ordered, slapping his hand away
from her.

"Stop what?"

"Everything! You have forced your way into my life
until I have no choice but to go along with you. You
need not put your hands upon my person, or monopo-
lize my father's attention, or . . ." *Or bow and look
happy to see me, as if I were a pretty young miss who
roused your interest,* she finished silently.

"This is hard for you," he murmured, his voice low and husky.

"Of course it's hard for me! How would you like it if someone who had no respect for everything you hold dear suddenly appeared and snatched it all away from you?"

"I might understand that better than you think."

Pain flashed through him, toughening the grim line of his mouth, darkening his expression. She felt the ridiculous urge to trace a finger along the tic throbbing at the edge of his jaw. She wanted to ask him what he'd lost, and why it tortured him so.

"Who is Mrs. Podgett?" he asked, changing the subject.

She clamped her lips together and refused to answer.

"Jillian. You must know I admire your courage." The compliment sent a shiver coursing through her. "I will give you a word of advice. You must learn to expend that courage wisely. Answer my questions, and save your strength for more important battles."

"More words of wisdom from that chivalrous knight?" she taunted.

He did not answer. He went to the fireplace and crouched down at the hearth, balancing easily upon the balls of his feet. He reached over to the woodpile and shifted three large splits of oak with no more effort than it would have taken her to hoist feathers. She stared in helpless fascination at the way his shirt-sleeve stretched over the upper arm muscles she'd so recently identified, the way the stout cloth pulled tight across his back.

"Mrs. Podgett?" he prompted, stirring the fire with the poker.

The sight of him tending to one of her chores turned her mouth dry, and her attention riveted helplessly upon the strong clean lines of his thighs bulging against his breeches. He'd warned her to choose her battles carefully. She wondered if he suspected she already warred with herself.

"As my father said, she cooks and cleans for us."

Cameron rose with a fluid, graceful motion. He glanced around, taking in the good furniture, the elegant appointments, that she'd crowded into a space far too small. He didn't comment on the congestion, and she felt a twinge of gratitude, for she still smarted inside from her father's calling her a hoarder. She had tried telling her father that she held on to all of these things in the event his mind improved enough for them to return to London. She'd never admitted, not even to her own father, that the very thought of disposing of even one item that had been there during her early, happy years filled her with such overwhelming dread that she had to spend hours going through each room of the house, touching every object to reassure herself everything was still there.

"This is the home of a wealthy man," Cameron said. "Why no servants in residence?"

"You cannot possibly be interested in our domestic arrangements."

"Everything about you interests me, Jillian."

Her heart, over which she had no control, seemed to falter and then commence a joyous pounding that sent her blood singing through her veins. She curled her hands into tight fists, willing the silly giddiness to subside. His interest stemmed from nefarious intent. She must remind herself, every minute if need be, that he was a manipulator bent upon twisting her to his will.

"I suppose that the more you know about us, the easier it will be to gain our trust," she said.

She waited for him to deny the charge. Wanted him to deny the charge. Instead, he sent her a lopsided, apologetic grin that made him look as easily forgivable as a handsome, high-spirited youth caught stealing an apple from a prized tree.

She would not forgive him. She tucked the memory of his false interest in her away, just as she would record a debt owed by someone who borrowed money from her father. If she found herself tempted ever again to melt at Cameron Smith's words, to revel in his glances, she would call out that memory to remind herself of his true intent.

"What do you mean for us to do?" she asked. "Do you expect us to simply go on with our daily routine, act as if nothing has happened?"

He nodded. He folded his arms and leaned one shoulder against the wall, watching her.

She made a wordless sound of frustration and turned away from him.

He moved up behind her. She could feel the air warm between them, and she sensed but did not see his hand move to touch her and then pull away.

"If all goes as planned, the changes to your daily routine shall be minimal, Jillian. You need only take me with you when you ride about, to accustom people to the sight of me. On occasion I might ask you and your father to make a special trip at night. Other than that, you will scarcely notice I am here."

Her traitorous heart, her fickle blood, pounded and coursed, simply from his standing near. The very thought of riding in the close confines of the wagon with him, sitting at the table with him—oh, he was so wrong to think she would take no notice of him. He filled her every thought.

"Quid pro quo, Mr. Smith," she whispered, stepping out of range of his heat. She regained a little control with every inch she placed between them. "Something for something. I will answer your questions if you answer mine."

"Fair enough."

His acquiescence startled her. She shot a look over her shoulder and caught him watching her with a hint

of the hunger she felt clawing at her. Impossible. It
had to be her imagination.

"Why are you doing this?"

"I won't talk to your back," he said. "If you are
bold enough to ask the question, you must have the
courage to face the answer."

She turned. He'd come away from the wall and
closed the gap between them so she had to tilt her
head to look up at him. Beyond strange, and a little
frightening, to stand there and so openly accept an
answer when she'd spent years filtering questions
through her father, and listening with bowed head
while answers were directed toward him.

"What do you intend to make us do?" she asked.

"What do you think, Jillian? I'm sure you've developed a theory of your own."

She felt a flash of anger. "I expect an answer, not
another question. You're not holding to your bargain."

"I will. I suspect a sharp mind lies hidden within
you. I'd like to know whether I can count on its
strength."

She felt weakness pervade her at hearing him compliment her strength. She sensed no derision in his
expression, no scorn for a woman who thought to
match wits with a man—instead, he seemed almost as
breathless as she, as if eager to hear her confirm his
faith in her intelligence.

"You mean to use us to somehow help King Charles
escape to France," she whispered.

"Aye."

Such a simple acknowledgment, and yet it was filled
with a warm approval that started a glow within her.

"How?" she asked.

"Uh-uh." He admonished her with a waving finger.
"Quid pro quo. I answered your question. Now you
will answer mine. Why have you hidden yourselves
away here, miles from the village, with no servants?"

She supposed she ought to berate him for crowding two questions into one. But something within her welcomed the chance to explain it for once to somebody who seemed like he might understand. Even if that somebody was a loathsome kidnapper who had all but admitted to dragging her and her father into a treasonous activity.

"My father came from a wealthy family and so had the resources to attend the University of Padua, where he was graduated as a Doctor of Surgery. But you already know that." He nodded. "He was subsequently admitted to the Royal College of Physicians right here in England, and assisted his associate, Doctor Harvey, in serving King Charles."

"Before Parliament and Mr. Cromwell saw to it that King Charles was parted from his neck and thus placed beyond medical care," Cameron said.

She nodded. "But even before the king was assassinated, Father had left the royal service. Father has always possessed a rebellious streak. He alienated many of his peers by making no secret of his belief that physicians ought to work closely with barber-surgeons. He even studied their techniques himself and did not hesitate to employ them when he felt their methods might be beneficial to a patient."

"A true rebel," Cameron murmured.

"Aye. And now . . . now that his wits are deserting him, he fears more than anything that the strides he made in convincing his fellow doctors to consider alternative treatments will be passed off as the delusions of a broken mind. And so we are here."

"With no servants."

"We gave up long ago trying to find servants who could be trusted to hold their tongues about my father's condition."

"Mrs. Podgett being the lone exception."

"Oh, Mrs. Podgett devotes herself so wholeheartedly to her tasks that she wouldn't notice if an ele-

phant sat in our kitchen. . . ." Her voice trailed away
at the satisfaction that crossed Cameron's expression.

She'd told him, right out, that he need fear nothing
from Mrs. Podgett.

"No brothers, no sisters, who might show up
unexpectedly?"

Now she understood his obsession with their lack
of servants. "We are alone," she said.

"You are fortunate."

"Do you truly believe that? A brother or sister
might help carry some of the responsibilities."

"More likely, they'd ruin you altogether." He gave
her no time to ponder his statement. "Your turn."

"What will you make us do?" she asked.

"Nothing out of the ordinary." When she began to
protest that he'd already jolted her life out of the ordinary, he silenced her with a brush of his finger against
her lips. "For the next few weeks, you need only go
about your normal business, except I will be riding at
your side. You will tell everyone that I am your father's apprentice. I want everyone to become accustomed to seeing you driving with a tall, dark-haired
man accompanying you. I want the soldiers to wave
us through and the constable to ignore me altogether."

"I don't see how getting you entrenched in my com-
munity will help the king escape to France."

"You could be right—it is very likely we will play
no part at all in the king's escape. Charles should not
venture this way—he has excellent hopes yet of escaping through Charmouth or Bridport. He would have
to cross virtually half of England to reach the sea here
at Brighthelmstone. Nonetheless, we must stand ready
to serve him if he needs us. Our little group here is
only one of many that waits, hoping to be of service."

"Oh." Odd, but now that her interests were roused,
it seemed almost a disappointment to learn they might
not be called upon after all. She shivered. This sort of
disappointment had struck her once before, long ago,

when she'd been told she could not play a role, and disaster had resulted when she'd insisted. She tamped down the memory, the way she had for so many years. "So you might have terrified us and held us hostage for no reason at all, then. You might worm your way into the good graces of the townsfolk for no purpose."

"Perhaps," Cameron agreed with nary a flinch. "Or perhaps you might find yourself riding out toward the sea one night with Charles Stuart sitting alongside you in my place. A tall, dark-haired man whose presence should not be questioned, so long as I do my job well now."

"Who thought up such a witless plan?" she cried. "You look nothing like Charles Stuart."

"Are you so familiar with his looks?"

"I just told you that my father tended his father— of course, I saw Charles Stuart as a boy many times."

"He will have changed."

"He cannot change his face. 'Tis true you are both large, dark men. But Charles Stuart is coarse-featured, and you are . . . not."

Cameron's whole being seemed to vibrate with cocky delight. And why not—she'd all but admitted she found his features more pleasing than those of a king.

"Charles has been in exile for so long that few people are as familiar with his features as you are, Jillian. The soldiers know only to watch for a tall, dark-haired man. I expect that every soldier who sees me will at first suspect I am the king, and that is exactly what I want to happen. When you convince them I am merely an apprentice, they will lose interest in any tall, dark-haired man riding in your wagon. Charles could pass right beneath their noses and they'd think it was only me."

Now that he'd taken the trouble to explain in detail, she had to grudgingly admit that his plan made a bit of sense. But she didn't have to admit it out loud.

"Why didn't you just ask us straight out to help you? Why all this subterfuge?"

"You would not have helped, Jillian. You cling to the familiar with all your being. You do not take risks."

"Risks are dangerous. Taking risks can destroy the dreams of a lifetime." It felt odd to hear herself defending the principles that ruled her life. Perhaps his skepticism was what made her eager to prove his assessment of her wrong, so eager that she outright lied to him. "Driving you around in my wagon does not sound to be such a risky proposition."

He sobered at once, and this time he was the one to present her with his back. He must have folded his arms across his chest, because his back widened, tensing against his shirt. "Never make light of the danger, Jillian. You could be arrested at best, and executed at worst, if it is found you have helped the king in any way."

"So you have signed our death warrants," she whispered.

"Not if we succeed and manage to keep secret the roles we played."

"I see. My father and I risk our good names, our reputations, our very lives, and if you succeed in smuggling Charles Stuart back to France, you and the king go your merry ways. We are left to hide our role—if we can."

"If we succeed, Charles will see to it that you can return to London," Cameron said. "He will find a place for you and your father and servants who can hold their tongues."

"I won't go back to London. Ever."

"Jillian, it might be necessary."

"Then you have truly consigned me to death."

He turned back to her, clearly puzzled. "You lived in London for most of your life. You cannot possibly prefer this quiet, dull existence to the social life in London."

"A woman like me finds London a dull place."

"What do you mean, a woman like you?"

He had eyes; surely he could see that she lacked the charms men found appealing. But she'd be damned if she'd mention her lack of looks; he'd shown a surprising tendency to act the gentleman and he'd no doubt feel bound to offer some trite contradiction and tell her that he did indeed find her attractive.

She also did not want him prying beyond that surface reason and uncovering the shameful truth that she'd almost never gone outside the house in London. The mere thought of abandoning Arundel Forest, of losing the freedom she found here, scared her witless. "I can't . . . I can't leave here."

He stared at her with all the fascination her father might show if presented with an actual human body part to dissect. "Jillian, I once felt the same attachment to my home. I have come to learn that the heart can recover if provided with sufficient diversion."

"There is no man on God's earth who could draw me away from my home."

"Oh, love is not the only diversion of the heart, mistress. There is also revenge."

Cameron sought revenge. She wondered what wrong had been inflicted against him, to cut him off from his home and all he knew and send him on a mission seeking vengeance.

"I have no room in my heart for men or for revenge, Mr. Smith. I seek only to continue what I was doing before you blundered along. I pray to God you don't ruin everything for us. Without the occasional calls for his help, my father would be truly desolate, and might spin into an even steeper decline."

"Well, you could always take over for him."

"Impossible. The villagers would never accept medical care from a woman."

"You do not give yourself or these people enough credit, Jillian. Perhaps you hold yourself in the background needlessly. Perhaps injecting a bit of risk into your life will open possibilities."

His observation stung and seemed targeted straight at a part of herself that she had no wish to explore. She struck out against the probe. "No more questions. No more answers. We need not continue this discussion. You are forcing me to help the king, Mr. Smith. You are making me endure your presence. You are never going to convince me to like any of it."

He crossed his arms and scowled at her.

"And, Mr. Smith—fetch your own water and biscuits."

6

They spent the balance of the morning listening to Doctor Bowen discourse on anatomy. Jillian, despite her father's insistence that she need not attend the lesson, had claimed the chair Cameron had used earlier. She sat upon it with all the determination of a broody hen atop a clutch of eggs, her fingers gripping tight to the edges of the seat. Cameron could almost hear his father's ghost telling him that a ruthless man would dump her from the seat and take it for himself, remind her of who ruled her life now.

He fetched himself another chair.

He'd thought to go over his plans in his mind, but found himself absorbed in the dual pleasures of the lecture and watching Jillian. The subject, in Doctor Bowen's enthusiastic teaching style, held his fascination. As did Jillian—she grasped at every tidbit of information with such interest, such an obvious craving to learn, that it inspired the same within him. She reminded him of a sparrow, deceptively nondescript until one drew close enough to notice the iridescent sheen to the feathers, the quick bright intelligence, the determination to stake out an impossible nesting site and cling to it against all odds.

"Stop staring at me as if you mean to devour me," she said in a low voice.

He hadn't realized he'd been so obvious. He gave

a short laugh to hide his chagrin. "I'd go hungry, then, considering I've been thinking you look rather like a sparrow."

"A sparrow. I suppose you fancy yourself a hawk, then."

"A hawk. Hmm. It seems apt."

"Indeed?" Her brow rose. "I'd liken you more to a cuckoo. The sort of bird that confiscates another's nest and destroys everything the poor sparrow's worked for, and then flies off, leaving the sparrow to contend with the mess the cuckoo's made."

"I won't be flying for a while yet, Jillian." He wasn't sure whether he meant it as a warning, or whether he'd inadvertently betrayed how compelling he found this life led by the Bowens.

There was a seductive allure to learning the mysteries of his own body and knowing it was the same for everyone else. There was a sneaking and tantalizing glimpse of hope to think that a man such as he might one day learn enough to help people heal. All this after less than one day. He began, grudgingly, to understand how his younger brother might have so easily gotten drawn into the cause that had cost Cameron so dear.

He checked his thoughts. He had vowed to never look back upon matters he could not change. Somehow, talking with Jillian about diversions of the heart had opened old wounds, stirred old aches.

Jillian's head turned at a sound from outside. "That's Mrs. Podgett's pony trap." Jillian rose. "I'll go help her—"

"Martin will take care of her," Cameron said.

"Martin?"

"My man. The one who tended your mare last night, and who is sleeping in your stable."

"Oh yes, Martin." She flushed, embarrassed, and Cameron knew a moment's concern. He distinctly remembered telling her the man's name the night before, but in looking back, he recalled she'd been in something of a dithering muddle that started with her whipping her horse into a frenzy and ended only after she'd pulled the latch on the door behind her. He wondered if Jillian Bowen might be suffering from the same malady as her father. He found it surprisingly painful to dwell on that possibility.

She gripped the back of her chair, as if to assert she still ruled that small space, even if he'd overtaken her home and Martin her stable.

"Mrs. Podgett will be confused by all these sudden changes. I must greet her."

He mistrusted Jillian's insistence upon rushing out to meet the servant. He wondered if her hint that Mrs. Podgett might not even notice him had been deliberately misleading in the hopes she might be able to lull him into paying no mind while she schemed with the servant to have him arrested. He had to laugh at his own fancies. One moment he was doubting Jillian's intelligence; the next he was crediting her with manipulative skills his father would have approved.

"I'll go with you."

He'd forgotten to lower his voice, and thus disturbed Doctor Bowen's train of thought. "Where is everyone going?" Doctor Bowen asked.

"Just to the kitchen, Papa. Why don't you take a moment to go over your papers?" Jillian darted from the room.

Cameron followed, his long legs rapidly carrying him to where Jillian stood at the kitchen window. She stiffened, which brought the back of her head up against his shoulder. She whirled away, raking at her hair as if she'd backed into a swarm of wasps.

"I have told you, you need fear nothing from me physically," Cameron said, surprised at how it unsettled him to have her flinch away from his innocent movement.

"I don't fear you," she said.

I despise you. She did not say those words, but Cameron imagined them echoing within her.

Well, she would not be the first to hold such a low opinion of him. Nor was she likely to be the last, unless his plan failed and he found himself executed for treason.

She opened the door. Although she'd seemed determined to greet the housekeeper, she stood there in the frame, slim and supple and carefully blank of expression as the matronly Mrs. Podgett descended from her pony trap and launched into an argument with Martin, who'd appeared just as Cameron said he would. Somewhere in midscreech the housekeeper caught sight of Jillian standing there, and she shoved the reins in Martin's hands. She hurried up the flagstone walk, mumbling to herself.

"Strange goings-on everywhere I turn today, Mistress Bowen," she declared as she stamped her feet at the doorway. "Such a lovely cool day, with the flies all gone and nowt to pester the pony, but doesn't old Fraley scare me half to death and search my little buggy, claiming some half-starved ruffian's been seen lurking about. Searched *my* little buggy! As if I'd allow some hungry ruffian to crouch down underneath my skirts. And then to come here and find that man outside claiming to be your new stable lad."

She kicked the toes of her boots one by one against the doorjamb and then bustled into the kitchen. "And look here now—three cups, three plates, when all these years there've been but two. You've been breakfasting with the new stable lad, Mistress Bowen? Not proper at—"

She snapped her mouth closed in midsyllable when she caught sight of Cameron braced against the windowsill. She looked to Jillian for an explanation.

"And who might you be?" Mrs. Podgett queried when she regained her voice and the strained silence made it clear Jillian did not intend to make an introduction.

Mrs. Podgett was staring at him in a way Cameron had grown familiar with over the years. Women, no matter their age, found favor with his tall, lean frame, with the way his shoulders made a wide wedge of his torso. He sent her an easy grin and she dimpled back, a pleasant change from Jillian's scowls and arrow-shot flinches.

"Ah, Mistress Bowen must have forgotten to warn you of my impending arrival," he said, prompting one of those scowls from Jillian. "I am Cameron Smith, Doctor Bowen's new apprentice."

"Oh! Fancy Mistress Bowen forgetting to tell me you were coming. I'm so pleased to hear the doctor has got himself some help at last. He works much too hard for someone who sought a quiet retirement."

Jillian busied herself with scraping hardened wax from a candle holder, and Cameron felt a pang of sympathy for her. She had done such a good job of making it appear her father was still in full charge of his actions that nobody, not even the housekeeper, gave Jillian credit for all she knew and did.

"I brought the stable lad with me," Cameron said. "But I'm afraid the both of us will be more work than help for you, Mrs. Podgett. We men have prodigious appetites, and Doctor Bowen has whetted them with high praise for your cooking."

Mrs. Podgett, turning all aflutter, blushed and patted her bosom. "I do try my best to tempt the doctor's palate." She simpered with satisfaction, which shifted into mild alarm. "But, my goodness, for tonight, why, I'd thought boiled beef and cabbage, which is rather plain. Perhaps I might send that out to the stable lad and try something a bit special for your dinner instead."

"Boiled beef and cabbage will be fine for all of us," Jillian bit out.

"Nonsense! Not on this young man's first day. Most remiss of you not to warn me, Mistress Bowen." Mrs. Podgett frowned her disapproval at Jillian and then bustled toward the larder.

"I suppose you're very pleased with yourself," Jillian said. The energetic sounds from the larder—sacks being moved, crocks sliding along shelves—nearly drowned her out. "I did not suspect you would stoop so low as to flirt with an old lady to gain her approval."

"It worked with her. Would a bit of flirting help me win you, Jillian?"

He'd meant the question to be serious, to be an overture toward an uneasy peace rather than this discord that had sprung up once more between them. Somewhere between conceiving the words and saying them, they got twisted to mean something entirely different. *Win Jillian.* Win the right to loosen her hair from its tight clasp, to kiss her until her lips reddened and swelled like rosebuds and those glorious hazel eyes turned languorous with wanting rather than antagonism.

Her eyes widened into deep pools of agony. "You need not be cruel, Mr. Smith," she whispered. "Moving into my home, taking over my life, is mean and despicable enough. But pretending to . . . that would be cruel." She straightened her shoulders, and ran a quick hand over the tightly buttoned collar at her neck, and then back as if she needed to reassure herself that she was tightly bound and impervious to any loosening effects of a teasing word or an appreciative smile.

She confused him at every turn. She sometimes seemed to welcome his honest male appreciation, and then something would happen, some secret inner thought would occur to her, and she would lash out as if he'd struck her.

He had only himself to blame. He had, with his

own tongue, warned her that she could never trust his motives. How his father must be mocking him from Hell for allowing that misplaced bit of chivalry.

"Your father and I are riding into the village shortly," he said.

"Why?"

"I must make contact with Robert." Good God, how easily he fell into the lure of talking to her as an equal partner, someone who willingly pursued the same goal!

"I cannot allow it."

She was entirely too bold, and again, her misplaced bravery was his fault. He should never have taken her into his confidence about his plans. He'd allowed his fascination with her intelligence to overrule his common sense, leading him to hope she might lend her strength to his cause—to *him*—rather than fight with all her might. He'd treated her like a valued partner rather than a hostage. It was time for him to take back control, even if doing so meant driving an even greater wedge between them.

The size of the wedge did not matter. There was no possible future for John Cameron Delacorte, late of Benington Manor, and Jillian Bowen, daughter of the esteemed physician Doctor Wilton Bowen. Something rough clutched at his vitals at the realization, even as the part of his mind that he'd learned to always hold aloof approved.

"You have twisted things about, Jillian," he said with menacing softness. "My will is not subject to your approval." It made him feel like an alleyway thug when she flinched as if she'd taken a blow.

"It would frighten my father to venture out on his own."

"He will not be on his own, Jillian. He will be with me."

"You said you would not betray his affliction."

"I have no intention of betraying him."

"I do not trust you."

"You may come along with us."

"Why, thank you, King Cameron Smith," she said, her eyes flashing with sarcasm. "How nice of you to invite me to ride in my own wagon, alongside my own father."

He'd not cowed her as thoroughly as he'd hoped. Perhaps he should reassess his strategy and take advantage of her inner strength. A tough and feisty Jillian could be more of an asset than a weak, cringing female. Of a certainty, she'd be more pleasant company.

"King Cameron. I like the sound of that." He used the jest as an excuse to cover the smile he couldn't help. "We leave as soon as your father eats his noonpiece."

Jillian wondered if Cameron Smith had a secret list of embarrassments he meant for her to endure, a list that he consulted when her back was turned.

The ride into Bramber had been a torturous affair. Her last, cutting remarks to him in the house seemed to echo silently in her mind, as did the quick, angry way she'd torn the reins from his hands when he'd settled himself into the driver's position. She'd pushed him until with a wary frown he'd slid to the middle of the bench. Jillian didn't know why, but she could not sit there and let him drive her horse. She'd sounded and acted a proper shrew. One part of her mind said she had every right to lash out at him for his high-handedness—King Cameron indeed!—while another part deplored her loss of control.

She drove the wagon in an agony of silence, wondering what it was about herself that made her want to apologize and yet be bound and determined to make him suffer the same frustrations, the same sense of impotent fury, as she suffered herself.

But every time one of her barbs struck, whenever

she chanced to catch confusion creasing Cameron's proud brow, all she wanted to do was soothe it away.

Oh, how could she have lived all these years without realizing she was subject to such female urges?

Atop it all, her father's continued vitality mocked her, forcing her to acknowledge that Cameron Smith was responsible. She couldn't help resurrecting the old internal doubts that her father had always desired a son, that despite the untold hours he'd spent teaching her the mysteries of a physician's art, he would have rather spent the time tutoring a son of his loins. Witnessing his return to coherence in Cameron Smith's presence, she knew her doubts were based in truth, and she added that misery to the list of hurts he caused her.

She had always considered herself a practical, no-nonsense woman capable of maintaining a cool head in the worst of situations. But since that rogue's arrival, all she'd done was dither, lost in a swirl of confusion, beset even now by doubts and fears. He made her question her very existence, her justification for the life she'd so carefully crafted. He made her aware that all the walls she'd built, ostensibly to protect herself, merely enclosed a vast, echoing emptiness.

The village crier hailed them, jolting Jillian from her reverie. Her mind had wandered so far afield that she'd not noted the passage of miles. She'd not experienced the slightest twinge of anxiety at leaving her house, either. She supposed the larger worry of whether she would survive the invasion of Cameron Smith had crowded her old anxieties right out of her head.

"Who requires our help today?" Father asked as Jillian urged Queenie on to a favored shady spot.

"No one, sir," Cameron answered. "We came into Bramber so you might introduce me to your acquaintances."

"I might introduce you to my acquaintances. Excellent idea."

Cameron and Doctor Bowen climbed down from the wagon. Cameron paused. He slanted a look up at her and extended his hand, offering his assistance. "Come with us, Jillian."

She shook her head and then deliberately looked away.

She enjoyed rebuffing him. Especially since he could not know that she avoided moving among crowds of people whenever possible, not just because Cameron wanted her to accompany him.

He didn't insist. Didn't remind her that she had no choice in matters. He simply dropped his hand to his side and walked away as if she were no more significant than a fly buzzing round Queenie's muzzle.

Pride alone held her erect. She fixed her attention upon the peeling sign swinging above the door to the Vine and Sheaf. But nobody wandered in or out of the inn's door, and she could spend only so long studying the poorly rendered paintings of a grapevine, a swatch of grain.

So, with nothing to watch, she caught herself first peeking, and then blatantly staring, as Cameron and her father walked along the dusty village lane. She sat in the wagon seat, solitary and ignored, her cheeks burning with mortification, but unable to look away as the baker, the chandler, the tailor emerged from their shops. A few curious housewives, a number of servants, edged from the twisting side alleys to watch her father's progress. If she had gone with them, the panic would be setting in by now, fueled by the sensation of being surrounded and unable to fight her way back to her home.

But nobody barred Cameron or her father. They seemed able to move freely. They were laughing, having fun, and altogether unconcerned that someone could take hold of them and keep them from going back home.

Nobody seemed to notice that she wasn't at her father's side as he introduced Cameron Smith time and again, as proudly as if the rogue were his son instead of a scheming Royalist.

She told herself it was for the best that nobody noticed her absence. This brief spell of lucidity would do much to keep alive the fantasy that her father was in full charge. Perhaps . . . perhaps Cameron had arranged this little jaunt for just that purpose. . . .

You will come to trust me, whether you want to or not.

Would she never cease hoping that good intent lay behind his actions? Cameron Smith had engineered this false promenade for his own purposes. Any benefit to her father was secondary, if considered at all. She had no reason to feel grateful that Cameron's plans had the side benefit of keeping her deception alive.

She watched him walk with her father, one man so tall and lithe and graceful, the other a little slump-shouldered and stooped in the manner of a man who spent many long hours at study. Occasionally her father slapped the rogue companionably on the back. Once, Cameron's hand shot out and gripped her father's elbow just as her father stumbled over a rough spot in the road. She doubted she would have been able to prevent her father's taking a nasty fall. Cameron supported him easily until Papa regained his balance.

She watched their two heads—one a wild cloud of gray, one so dark brown as to be almost black and sleek as a seal—bend together until they almost touched. She could hear Cameron's quiet laughter, a gentle, infectious sound unlike the bitter and sarcastic mock humor he sent her way. The villagers bobbed curtsies their way, or tugged at their forelocks, or held out strong, willing hands to be shaken, something that had never once happened to her in all her years at her father's side.

Jealousy speared through her, cold and sharp as an icicle.

Jillian suddenly felt exposed and raw sitting there in the wagon. She should be plotting a way to extricate them from Cameron Smith's nefarious plan, not sitting there agonizing over doubts and weaknesses she'd thought long buried.

A bit of lace curtain moved at the window in Mrs. Hawking's house, a few doors away from the Vine and Sheaf. Though Jillian had by necessity held herself aloof from the other women in the town, there was something about the reticent recluse that struck a chord of kinship.

Mrs. Hawking had been acquainted with Jillian's mother and had been very helpful in recommending they consider this quiet, peaceful area when Jillian had sent a letter mentioning their desire to find a new home. Like Jillian and her father, she had come to this small village to escape London.

Nobody knew the whole story surrounding Mrs. Hawking; nobody had ever met the mysterious Mr. Hawking. Like Jillian, she lived a life apart.

The two women had become something more than acquaintances, but less than true friends. Jillian clambered down and raced for the uncertain sanctuary of Mrs. Hawking's home.

She fixed upon her face a bright, pleasant smile, and straightened her shoulders. The door swung open for her and Mrs. Hawking's maid gave her a cheerful little curtsey.

"Good day, Rose. Is Mrs. Hawking at home?"

"Mistress Bowen! Oh, Mrs. Hawking will be so pleased you've come to see her." She led Jillian to the parlor and announced her presence. Mrs. Hawking looked up with welcome lighting her face, and Jillian stepped into the room, intending to spend a few minutes, no more, in idle conversation.

But when she stepped through the doorway, when the maid closed the door behind her, it was as though she'd crossed an invisible boundary line that allowed her, for a moment, to show her weaknesses. It was a different sort of comfort than the one she found in her own home, but reassuring in a strangely liberating fashion. Jillian felt the tears pool in her eyes. Her lips twitched with a hundred suppressed screams, and, humiliatingly, all she could do was stand there and tremble.

"What has happened, Mistress Bowen?" asked the elderly woman, motioning her toward a chair. Jillian settled into it gratefully. The simple luxury of Mrs. Hawking's home surrounded her, furniture finer than her own, silks and satins and all manner of foreign artifacts that hinted at a life that had endured just as much upheaval as Jillian's own. She could do nothing but stare at her surroundings and wonder if Mrs. Hawking gained as much comfort as she did in clinging to things that reminded her of an Edenlike past.

Mrs. Hawking rang a small bell, and the maid popped her head through the door so quickly that Jillian knew she'd been lurking right outside. "Bring us water freshened with lemon, Rose," said Mrs. Hawking.

Jillian recognized in Mrs. Hawking's voice traces of the finely bred accent she heard in Cameron Smith's. Sitting there, waiting for the drink, gave her a moment to compose herself, but as soon as the maid left them with their refreshment, she found herself babbling.

"I've been . . . oh, Mrs. Hawking, I don't know what exactly has been done to me, but it's awful."

"Pray continue, child." Mrs. Hawking sat across from her, her posture as graceful and erect as a young girl's. "I assume your distress has something to do with the man who is outside with your father."

Jillian nodded. "He came upon us last night. He won't leave." Stated so bluntly, it did not seem sufficient to convey the depth of change Cameron Smith's arrival had brought to her life. She wished suddenly that she was close enough to Mrs. Hawking to call her by her first name, to feel comfortable enough to fling herself into the other woman's arms and sob out her frustration.

She'd never realized until Cameron's arrival how thoroughly alone she was, both by choice and by necessity.

Unable to remain in her seat for her agitation, Jillian went to the window and pulled aside the lace. Her father and Cameron Smith stood together in the middle of the road, surrounded by a group of laughing men. Dread curled through her at the sight, but then relaxed by subtle degrees as she realized no one meant her father harm. If anything, Wilton Bowen seemed to be enjoying himself. Immensely.

Mrs. Hawking joined her, and for a long moment they said nothing. Jillian wondered if the older woman was as captivated as she by the realization that Cameron Smith stood a head taller than anyone, his physical presence so compelling that the usually circumspect villagers gathered round him like hummingbirds circling a particularly brilliant blossom.

"Who is he?"

"I don't know. He has given me a name, but I know it is not his real one."

"What does he want from you?"

"I have guessed some things. He will confirm next to nothing."

Humiliating, to have to admit this. But Mrs. Hawking did not take her to task; indeed, she did not seem very surprised that a woman should find herself so overwhelmed by a man that she simply stepped back and allowed him to take control of her life.

"He is talking now with Robert Lindsay," Mrs.

Hawking observed. "He's Lord Harrington's man. I don't often see him around the village."

Jillian concentrated on the nondescript fellow who hovered near Cameron. With a start she realized he was the man who'd hidden by the stone wall the night before.

"So Cameron did not lie—Robert *is* Lord Harrington's man. You know this for certain?"

"Mm." Mrs. Hawking murmured a vague confirmation. "What do you think those two might have in common, Mistress Bowen?"

Jillian hesitated. She did not know Mrs. Hawking well enough to guess her political sympathies, and these days it was too dangerous to make assumptions. She'd made a mistake in coming here. If she confided that Cameron Smith meant to make the Bowens part of a Royalist plot, Mrs. Hawking could well betray her.

And then she felt Mrs. Hawking's hand grip hers with such warm concern that Jillian's tears threatened to fall all over again. "You can trust me, child."

"I do," Jillian whispered in return. "At least, I now realize that I must have all along, or I would not have come here when I am so troubled."

"And yet you could not admit it to yourself. How interesting that you should find yourself able to reach out to me now."

Jillian detected no sarcasm or hurt feelings in Mrs. Hawking's comment. It made her examine this new awareness that, strong as she was, she sometimes needed others, too. "I have caught myself looking at him and wanting to believe in him a dozen times already. He warned me that this would happen."

"Most men would take advantage. How honorable of him, to warn you."

Honorable? Jillian pressed a hand to her lips, wanting to deny it, but unable to do so. She remembered Cameron pretending to stretch his back as he fought his natural inclination to bow to her. She saw that firm, strong hand supporting her father and keeping him from falling.

"He says he learned everything he knows—good and bad—from a knight."

"Knights! When I was a girl, we would giggle together and dream of one riding to our rescue." Mrs. Hawking held the curtain away. "So he must be on a quest. I'd venture he's a Royalist, out to help Charles Stuart regain the English throne. Oh, don't look so stricken, child. I would have guessed merely by seeing him in such close conversation with Robert Lindsay."

And Robert Lindsay was Lord Harrington's man, and Cameron had mentioned having some influence with Lord Harrington. Good heavens, the whole village was ablaze with Royalist leanings, and Jillian, cowering in her careful shell of neutrality, had been aware of none of it.

"Besides," said Mrs. Hawking. "There's his hair."

"His hair?"

Mrs. Hawking's lips quirked in a youthfully feminine manner and Jillian found her gaze helplessly pinned on the way Cameron's hair, caught back in a queue, glinted with gold highlights beneath the sun. "He's not shorn like a Roundhead. Another knightly quality. I daresay he possesses others."

"He talks and moves in the manner of someone who has been raised in a gentle manner. He is polite, exceedingly so." Save for those rare flashes of humor he showed, which made her want to smile despite her fury, but she did not think she ought to bore Mrs. Hawking with such mundane details. "He is unfailingly considerate. He treats me like a lady. . . ." Jillian let her voice trail away.

Good God, she was citing a veritable litany of virtues that made Cameron Smith sound like a paragon of gentlemanly, knightlike virtues. She trembled even more when her newly sprouted bud of trust urged her to reveal everything to Mrs. Hawking. "I am aware every moment that I . . . he has overwhelmed me, Mrs. Hawking, and to my shame I have not fought hard enough against him."

"I have known men like him." Mrs. Hawking's eyes took on a distant cast, and Jillian wondered if she might be thinking of the long-absent Mr. Hawking, and also wondered, for the first time, if a doomed love affair might be responsible for someone of Mrs. Hawking's obvious refinement finding herself a lonely recluse in a small village. "You may have to be very brave, Mistress Bowen."

"He could bring Cromwell's men down upon as at any minute."

"Oh! I suppose that is so." Mrs. Hawking looked so startled at the notion that Jillian knew her caution to be brave had stemmed from another concern altogether. "More than that, child—he is a man unlike most others. The woman who finds herself joined with such a man must call upon all her inner resources to meet him on equal footing. Do you think you are capable of that much strength?"

"I don't want to be joined with him!" To Jillian's dismay, she felt all teary-eyed and shaky again. "I want only for him to be gone."

"Do you really?" Mrs. Hawking seemed even more shocked by hearing this admission. She turned back to the window, Jillian following suit, and she found herself staring once again at Cameron Smith and thinking that once he had gone, this village would be even quieter, her life more empty than it had been up until now. She hadn't realized, until now, that she'd thought her quiet, secluded life was dull.

Did she really want him gone? Mrs. Hawking stared, unperturbed, through the window, so obviously the question Jillian heard echoing sounded only in her head and not bouncing from the walls of the room. But still, the question hung in the air, and it should

be a simple matter to say, yes, I cannot wait to be rid
of him.

Her hands gripped the window ledge so hard that
she felt pain shaft into her fingers. Perhaps it was that
fleeting discomfort that made it impossible for her to
say that simple *yes*.

She watched a young maid blush and suck in her
belly when Cameron's gaze chanced to light upon her.
Another piercing stab of jealousy chilled her, different, somehow, than any she'd ever experienced.

What on earth was wrong with her?

7

Father sat dozing in his chair, one of his precious books propped haphazardly upon his lap. The fire flickered low. Jillian sat near the candle lamp tending to her mending, thinking the three of them would make the perfect picture of domestic contentment, except that Cameron continually paced between his chair and the window. Jillian could see the reflections of herself and her father, while Cameron cupped his hand against the glass and peered out at the night sky.

"I suppose you want us safely in our beds before you go to sleep yourself," she said, when his ceaseless pacing and peeking stretched her nerves close to breaking.

"I'm not tired."

"No? I would have thought that charming an entire village would be an exhausting exercise."

He gave her a little half-smile, and she stabbed her needle into the collar she was relining, knowing that she'd given herself away yet again. It was impossible to hope he had not detected the edge of resentment she'd suffered over his easy acceptance by the villagers.

"Come, Papa, off to bed with you before you drop your book into the fire."

"Is it so late? It cannot be." Her father frowned at her, obviously trying to puzzle something out, and then his expression cleared. "Why, you've not changed into your pretty gown, Jillian, and so we cannot go to bed. We must have been called out."

"No, Papa. It's simply bedtime."

"Nonsense. We must have been called out. You always wear your hair loose and dress yourself in pretty silks on the nights we stay at home." He sat back, pleased with himself for articulating the reason for his confusion.

"Not tonight." She bit her lip to keep from screaming at the amused expression on Cameron's face.

For fear of widening that smirk, she could not risk complimenting her father on remembering. Always, when he'd managed such a feat, she'd been profuse in her praise, trying her best to encourage him to cling to those wits that still remained. But she did not want to encourage this particular line of conversation.

She'd been ready to don her green silk earlier that evening. She'd held it up against herself and stared at her reflection in her glass, wondering whether it was the dress or the unfamiliar fluttering sensation inside her that had brought such a becoming flush to her cheeks. In her soul, she knew it was not the dress, but the thought of taking her meal at the same table as Cameron Smith.

Cameron Smith, who'd teased her, asking if it would be possible to win her through flirtation.

Cameron Smith, who'd warned her she could never trust his motives.

And so she'd hung the dress back in place and did nothing more to prepare for supper than brush off the front of her rusty red wool, and smooth her hands over her hair to make sure it remained in its usual tidy knot. A knowing smile would curve that lout's lips if he thought she'd taken special pains with her dress. She would simply perish if that smile curled with the derision of a handsome man who pitied a plain woman's attempts to primp for him.

She didn't want to think about how humiliated she would be if she fussed, and he took no notice at all.

"You remind me of your mother when you wear that green silk, Jillian. It makes the color rise up in your cheeks. You ought to put it on now."

"I gave it away, Papa," she said, lying. "You know how the Puritans frown on ostentatious dress these days."

"Aye, that is true. Sour-faced and drab-garbed lot. 'Tis almost enough to make me regret doctoring young Ollie Cromwell through his first bouts with the stone. Who would have thought England would come to this?" He shrugged and then yawned while alarm surged through Jillian. Her father seldom commented on the oppression imposed by Cromwell's rule. She did not know whether doing so now meant he'd been influenced by Cameron, who'd stated that observation practically word for word, or whether it was her father's increased awareness that brought it about. Either way, saying such things out loud could be dangerous.

"You tended Oliver Cromwell, sir?" Cameron asked.

"Aye. Time and again. He was a mere government underling, but never ceased pestering the royal physicians for treatment of one malady or another. Hypochondriac, no doubt, but the stone will get him in the end, you mark my words." Her father handed his book over to Cameron. "Study this well, young Cameron. I would suggest you concentrate particularly on those sections regarding musculature."

Cameron accepted the book wordlessly and pressed it against his chest as he paced once more from hearth to window. Jillian recognized something of her own awe for books in the way Cameron held that one against his heart, as if he wished he could absorb the knowledge it contained straight through his skin. He

paused there for a long moment before pacing back
again. He set the book carefully on the sideboard.

"Not just now. I must leave."

"You're going somewhere?" Jillian's heart fluttered.

"For a few hours."

"Must we . . . must we go with you?"

"Not this time. I'm eager to develop a certain familiarity with the geography that can only be gained on
foot."

"Where are you going?"

He did not answer.

"Now, Jillian, young men need their exercise. No
need to quiz Doctor Smith on where he means to go
walking. We need not be so harsh on our apprentice.
Run off with you now, young Cameron, but mind you
don't stay out too late."

"I daresay Mistress Bowen will barely get used to
my being gone before I show up on the doorstep
once again."

He went off to the medical supply room. Mrs. Podgett had cleared a bed for him upstairs, but when she'd
left for the day, Cameron and Martin had searched
the rooms on the first floor and settled on making
room for Cameron amidst all the medical supplies.
When he reappeared, he held a small, neat bundle of
his belongings in his arms.

Bringing his outer garments out there was another
example of the courtesy she'd mentioned to Mrs.
Hawking. A long-limbed man like Cameron would
have difficulty dressing without risking damage in the
small supply room, where shelves, crammed with bot-
tles of precious medicinals, lined the walls. Even so,
she wished he would have made himself ready in his
room—and then she chided herself for calling it *his*
room, as if he had a right to dress anywhere at all in
her home.

But he was terribly distracting. She couldn't help
watching the way his soft lawn shirt gapped away from

his breeches as he pulled a heavy wool jerkin over his head. He slid a sheathed dagger into his belt, and she realized with shock that she hadn't known he possessed such a deadly weapon. Another example of his courtesy, for he'd not employed it upon her to impress his will. He tested the fit of his boots and tucked his hair up into his hat, and then swirled his long black cape over his shoulders.

He was off to do something dangerous, she just knew it. Her heart hammered.

"Time for bed, Papa," she said to cover her agitation. She told herself her heart raced from the hope that Cameron might leave and never return, and not from the gut-deep certainty that he meant to go somewhere where he might be hurt.

"Martin will keep watch while I am gone," Cameron said.

He probably meant it as a warning to her that she must stay quietly in her bed and not make any attempt to escape. And yet a warmth blossomed within her, an utter certainty that he sought to reassure her and let her know that someone would be there to keep her safe throughout the long, dark night.

She bent her head over her mending so he could not see the foolish giddiness this awareness sent through her.

When a cool breath of air brushed her cheek, she looked up again. He'd gone, silently and without bidding her farewell.

The fleeting sensation of feeling cherished vanished as suddenly as he had. Her sewing hand wavered and she stifled a cry as she accidentally plunged her needle into the pad of her thumb. A spot of blood welled and then dripped down to melt invisibly into the rusty red wool of her gown.

She was glad, fiercely glad, she'd decided against wearing the green silk.

She got her father settled for the night and completed her own ministrations. She eased into her bed, tucked her covers all around her, and just lay there, waiting for the familiar sense of well-being to wrap invisible arms around her. Her breathing, her heartbeat, pounded out against the silence. The house must have always felt this quiet, this empty. Funny that she'd never noticed before.

She didn't know how long she'd lain awake—hours, she was sure—when she heard the shuffle and scrape of her father's slippers in the hallway. He came to her door. It was so dark that she could not see his face, only the pale blur of his gray hair fluffing out around his head like a nimbus.

"Young Doctor Smith has not come back yet, Jillian. I am very worried about him. 'Tis uncommonly dark out tonight."

She'd never caused her father the slightest bit of concern, housebound as she'd been, and now never venturing out without him. She'd certainly never even tried sneaking off into the night. It twisted her heart, to see how readily he'd adopted the habit of worrying about Cameron Smith. "Don't you remember how he checked the sky repeatedly before he left, Papa?" she asked, trying to soothe his agitation. "He waited on purpose until the clouds covered the moon. I'm sure he's fine."

"He's so new to us. What if he loses his way in the dark? We've left no candle burning for him."

She'd be damned if she'd leave a candle burning on the sill to guide that rogue home. "He'll find his way."

"He has yet to master musculature. Shocking, shocking. A university education doesn't mean what it did in my day. I've lain awake all night going over all the things I must teach him. I pray he does not stumble in the dark and jar his head."

Sympathy, and a clawing ache, assailed her. Her father's comment revealed that he'd improved, albeit temporarily, enough to mourn the loss of his mental capacity. Pray God it would last—but without the pain. If soothing his fears over Cameron kept him alert and functioning, then her pride could swallow the lighting of one small candle.

She threw off her covers and went to her father. She laid her hand against his arm. "I'll see to a light. Now, back to bed with you."

"Oh, Jilly, I hate sleeping the time away when my thoughts run so clear."

"I know, Papa." It had been a long, long time since he'd called her by her pet name. Her throat ached as he pulled her into his arms for a strong, comforting hug, the sort of embrace he never thought to give when he was at his worst and she needed it most. Standing there in her father's arms, she felt joy for being able to experience it once more, sorrow in knowing it would not last, regret to think that it had taken Cameron's arrival to bring it all about.

"We'll get through this, won't we, Jilly?"

"Aye, Papa." She could not be sure whether he meant Cameron's plan for them, or the dark netherworld of his own decline. It did not matter. They would muddle through, no matter the challenge. She felt strong, stronger than ever, and did not exactly know why. "But you'd best sleep now. It heals you."

"You'll remember that candle?"

"I'll remember."

She got him settled once more, and then fetched a stubby candle end from the larder. She fought with her conscience the whole time she struggled to light the nearly spent wick. She'd promised to light a candle for Cameron Smith, but she didn't have to use a fresh one that would burn the night long, nor did she have to set the candle in the window. She left the shutter braced open a few inches, and the candle stump burning on the mantel.

It wouldn't burn for much longer than an hour.

She should have gone easily to sleep then, secure

in knowing she'd upheld her word to her father while
at the same time doing next to nothing to ease the
return of Cameron Smith. But she lay awake. She did
not count the minutes, but her conscience had begun
to chide her for cheating on her word when at last
she heard Cameron come home.

The scuff of his boots against the floor paused, and
she fancied she heard a small sound of surprise, as if
finding the candle lit for him touched that cold, hard
heart in some manner. Nonsense. She heard the
whoosh as he blew out the candle. He made his way
into the hallway, heading for his bed, and then there
came a long pause. She knew it was silly to imagine
that he lingered for a moment, staring down the narrow passage to where her door stood slightly ajar, the
way it always did at night in case her father called for
her. He began moving again, and she heard the small
muffled sounds of him spreading his pallet in the dark.

Only then did she fall asleep, with the scent of
melted wax perfuming the air.

Mrs. Podgett had fussed the next afternoon upon
discovering only half a bread loaf remaining in the
larder. "I baked four loaves yesterday. Enough to last
the week," she'd grumbled.

"We're feeding two extra mouths these days," Doctor Bowen had reminded her.

"Men with prodigious appetites," Jillian had added
with a sharp look that told Cameron she suspected
he'd eaten the bread. He ignored her, for he did not
think it wise to discuss with her the unsatisfied appetites that raged within him.

Besides, he hadn't eaten the bread. He'd stolen it.

He'd hidden the bread in a small sack in his room
and had been plagued with guilt ever since. Imposing
his will upon the Bowens was one thing; pilfering their
food to fill the empty bellies of starving Royalist sympathizers was quite another.

A true warrior takes whatever he needs. He could hear his father's taunts echo in his mind. *You're too soft, boy. You'll never earn a knighthood. Why couldn't your younger brother have been born first? He had the guts, the makings of a knight! Go back to your farming. . . .*

The guilt over filching the bread had dampened his spirits, which perhaps accounted for his uncharacteristic lethargy, a laziness that had left him disinclined to pursue the activities that would make him a familiar figure in the village. He'd done nothing all day but stare at Jillian while she worked, while she studied, wondering what she looked like in the green silk gown her father said she sometimes wore, with her splendid hair unbound and curling about her shoulders.

He knew that if she had kneaded and baked that bread with her own hands, he would never have stolen it. It would be best to direct the conversation in another direction.

"Your smallfruit canes need pruning, and your vegetable garden shows signs of neglect," he said.

"The gardens were already derelict when we arrived," Jillian said. "Flowers are Papa's passion. We've managed to clear a small patch for his roses."

"I'll tend to the rest."

"Cameron—there's no need."

"There's a loose gutter on the left corner and a rotted windowsill on the second floor."

"You can rebuild my house from the ground to the roof and it won't make up for what you've done to us."

"I like fixing things, and I miss the feel of dirt between my fingers," he muttered.

And so he'd spent the full day outside, working up an honest sweat. He mended the gutter and windowsill. He cut spent raspberry canes and attacked the roots of overconfident weeds. So far as he could tell, Jillian hadn't glanced outside once to judge his progress. Not that he was doing any of this to impress her, he told himself as he heaved a heavy rock away from Doctor Bowen's straggling rosebushes. But he would have expected that sheer feminine curiosity would have brought her outside to see what he was doing to her house.

They had finished eating supper when he came in, and so he took his while standing in front of the fire. He bolted from the house the minute it darkened enough to provide a little cover. Before heading to the woods, he fetched the sack of bread he'd hidden in the stables.

The sackful of loaves thumped against his back now as he strode across the lower meadow, heading for the woods at such ground-swallowing speed that anyone would think Cromwell's men were hard on his heels.

He gained the safety of the woods. The wind buffeted the tops of the trees, so that the branches clacked like skeleton bones above his head. Leaves sighed their death throes beneath his feet as he crushed through them on his way to the meeting place.

The men had risked a fire; he could smell it while still a hundred yards away. But it had been well banked, for he could see no telltale glimmer.

Three men—Busko, Rothermel, Quint—awaited him.

"Where are the others?"

"With the plunder," said Rothermel. "Went deep into the woods with it."

Cameron nodded his approval as he unslung the sack of bread from his shoulder. He should have waited. Busko snatched the bread sack from his hands and Cameron knew there'd be nothing left for the men who'd gone off to guard the plunder wagon.

He tried not to notice their rough manners when they tore it into chunks and crammed it into their mouths; hungry men did not worry about the niceties. But forcing his thoughts away from the gulping and the chewing sent them drifting right back to Jillian, to wondering exactly how long her hair might be and exactly how much skin she bared above her breast when she wore silk.

He felt the urge to run again, as he'd run from the house earlier that night, but he knew there was no escaping a vision. No matter how fast or hard he ran, Jillian would haunt his mind.

"That's all you brung us?" asked Busko, swallowing the last of his bread.

"Those loaves were meant to feed the whole troop, not just the three of you," Cameron said.

"Bread." Busko made a rude gesture with his arm. "Soldiers need meat. You'll have to do better for us, or we'll be raiding the cottages."

"We can't raid the cottages, Buskie," said Rothermel, casting a nervous glance Cameron's way. "Lord Harrington said we might need help from them later."

"Lord Harrington never spouted such drivel when I ran this troop," Busko said. He sneered up at Cameron. "Then again, me not bein' a milord, I guess the old sot didn't deign to converse much with the likes of me."

"I'm no milord," Cameron said, inwardly groaning at the thought of once more engaging in the argument.

"We might need help from those cottagers later," Rothermel repeated. "You're too hotheaded by half to run this troop, Buskie. Lord Harrington told you so himself."

Cameron didn't find it particularly reassuring that only one of the men under his command seemed to cling to a bit of common sense. "Any man who goes near a cottage without my permission won't need to worry about the state of his stomach. No meals are served in Hell."

"Easy for you to say." Busko spat. "You got yourself set up nice and cozy. We ain't got servants cookin' meals for us and willing little wenches drivin' us all over the roads—"

Cameron's fist curled at his side. Quint leaped between Busko and Cameron. "We ain't hungry no more," Quint piped up. "Don't pay Buskie no mind. We just get a little bored sitting around, waiting for something to happen."

Busko, a local tenant farmer, had through sheer belligerence risen to moderate importance within the Western Association and had led this little band until Lord Harrington recruited Cameron. Busko made no secret of resenting being replaced as the leader and took every opportunity to goad Cameron. If he had a choice, Cameron would drum the man right out of the group, but it was so difficult to recruit men to the Royalist cause. Busko harbored a ruthless streak that could prove useful despite his unending resentment.

"I know it's frustrating for you," Cameron conceded, knowing Busko would ignore the apology implicit in his words. Quint gave him a quick nod and then crouched near the fire, placing himself between Busko and Cameron's fists. " 'Tis frustrating for me, as well. Tomorrow, I'll go into the village and see what I can buy in the way of foodstuffs without arousing too much curiosity."

"Only someone playacting at being an apprentice would say such a witless thing," said Busko. "Everyone knows masters underfeed their apprentices. Ain't nobody in the village would have trouble believing old Bowen starves you."

It rankled within Cameron to think of kindly old Doctor Bowen being thought of as miserly. The sooner he removed himself from Busko's presence, the better. "I'll go inspect the plunder."

"Didn't you filch anything from them Bowens to add to the heap?" Busko's chin shot out belligerently. His animosity seemed worse than usual, and there was nothing to account for it except that Cameron had installed himself within the Bowens' home. Cameron refused to rise to the bait.

"The Bowens are contributing enough to the cause. I won't force them to do more."

Busko muttered something.

"What did you say?"

"I said, your brother wouldn't have had such qualms."

"Well, my brother got himself killed, didn't he?" Cameron spoke easily while the pain of Riordan's death shafted through him anew.

"Aye. Got the last laugh on you, too, while he went about it." Busko sniggered while Cameron clenched his fist inside his cloak lest he smash it into Busko's snuffling countenance.

"I'll show you where Simon hid the plunder wagon." Quint leaped up and caught Cameron's arm.

"Aye, let's get out of here."

"Not without me," Busko said, spitting again into the fire. "I'll be stuck with selling that old rubbish. I can't wait to hear what impossible amount our leader claims it ought to fetch."

Cameron always assessed the value of the goods donated for the king's cause. He'd learned to do this when Busko had returned from selling several hundred pounds' worth of jewels and clothes for a mere handful of coins. To the tenant farmer, the sum he'd sold the goods for had no doubt seemed enormous. To a cause ever scraping for funds, the loss had sent them reeling. But it rankled with Busko to be given this proof that he did not know the value of quality goods, and Cameron tried to provide an estimate of what the goods should fetch without rubbing Busko's nose in his lack of knowledge.

It was a fine line he trod, a line he'd grown heartily sick of. He'd been doing it all his life, first with his father, and now, with Busko. Judging by his failure with the first, he had no reason to expect success with the latter.

The night was so dark, the moon so well shrouded, that he had to risk lighting a stick to view the plunder. He plunged a pitch-coated one into the fire and did his best to shield the flame within his cloak as he made his way to the wagon. Quint walked at his back, with Busko following behind, muttering beneath his breath the whole way.

Cameron greeted the men who huddled near the wagon and then waved the flickering light over the jumble of treasures piled in the wagon bed. He wanted to weep at the loss. His finger stroked a particularly beautiful silver crucifix and his heart ached. He wondered who had sacrificed a treasure that must have been passed down within their family for centuries, for the cross bore the marks of great age, and undeniably exquisite craftsmanship.

He knew all the steps that had been taken by whoever had given up this cherished heirloom—the surreptitious hiring of a Royalist-sympathizing chandler to cast a wax mold of the artifact, the handing over of the wax replica to a silversmith for a coating of the cheapest, thinnest silver plate, and then the substitution of the replica for the real treasure, just in case a Commonwealth loyalist happened by and questioned the whereabouts of a well-known artifact.

They were doing it all over England, the fathers and mothers of the young men who fought for the king, the wives and the daughters of the older men, stripping their walls and shelves, stripping the country of its heritage, destroying centuries of artifacts, decimating family fortunes. He'd done it himself with Benington's treasures, all for the sake of restoring Charles Stuart and putting England once more on a course of freedom and opportunity.

Silver, gold, all were heaped heedlessly. No need to take care, when it would all be melted down to provide coin for the king's underground army to subsist. Several trunks lay among the goods. He opened one to reveal armloads of furs, which would have to be smuggled clear to France for no one would dare buy them and wear them here in England beneath the Puritans' eyes. A second trunk revealed someone's wardrobe of silk. Good stuff, but it would fetch a mere fraction of its worth. Only the darker colors might not provoke too much frowning of a Puritan brow, providing the lace and embellishments were removed.

He dug through the well-packed trunk, hoping someone might have tucked boots in the bottom, but his fingers found only a canvas-wrapped packet of some sort. He yanked it loose and tugged open the string holding it closed. A slippery garment of silk spilled free, shining like molten gold beneath his light. A woman's gown, no doubt dear to the heart of whoever had donated it, considering the care that had been taken to wrap it.

Though it was difficult to tell in the flickering glow cast by his brand, he thought for sure that the gown would match the golden highlights in Jillian's eyes.

All his vague daydreams, his imaginings of what she might look like in silk with her hair undone came back to haunt him.

"I'll buy this one myself," he said, startled at the gravelly rasp of his voice. "I'll pay more than it would fetch through the usual channels."

Quint chuckled. "Now we know why yonder Cameron can't fill our bellies—he's too besotted with Mistress Bowen to be thinkin' of food."

"You be buying that dress for Mistress Bowen?" queried Rothermel. "Hey, Buskie, mebbe that's what you ought to've done that time you asked her to go out riding with you."

"You asked Mistress Bowen to go riding?" Cameron gaped at Busko.

"Nothing wrong with it. It weren't so long ago I

was well thought of in this village. Had me a nice farm, well set up. Wasn't overstepping my bounds to ask her to go for a drive—there's lots of gals would think it a fine honor. She set me down flat. Of course, I'm not the son of a *knight*." Busko spat the words. "I didn't have me no castle fallin' down around my ears."

Rage forked through Cameron, though he tamped it quickly. He'd made a mistake with the gown; it would be disaster to compound it by letting his temper show how much he disliked hearing them speak about Jillian as if she were an ordinary woman, a nose-in-the-air miss who'd declined a tenant farmer's invitation with snobbery. Knowing Jillian, she'd probably refused Busko's offer from a reluctance to leave her father on his own while she enjoyed herself.

"Now that I've been spyin' her out, I see she's too skinny, anyway," said Busko. "Too stiff of shoulder to suit me. No doubt stubborn, too. I like me a woman with nice pouty lips and dimples in her cheeks and nary a thought in her head save for pleasin' me."

The brand shook in Cameron's hand.

He had a better understanding now of why Busko hated him so. But he also knew that Jillian's stiffness stemmed from outrage at being caught in her predicament, and her lips were pressed thin to keep harsh words safely contained. He knew he wronged her by not defending her charms to these louts.

"That's enough about Mistress Bowen," he said.

"Will the lady be lettin' you put the gown on her— or will you be more interested in peelin' it back off?" Busko leered.

Cameron plunged the brand into the earth, squelching the flame, and at once two of his men launched themselves at him, pinning his arms to his sides.

The others weren't so gentle with Busko. Someone rapped him hard in the jaw, and he fell into a senseless heap at Cameron's feet.

"Don't you be minding Buskie," Quint rasped into Cameron's ear. "It set wrong in his craw when Lord Harrington turned this troop over to you. But I think it sits worse with him to see how easy you moved in on Mistress Bowen."

"She had no choice."

"Aye, and no doubt you ain't got no lustful intentions toward her. Just go easy on Buskie, Mr. Delacorte. We need every man."

Cameron was breathing as hard as if he'd run a full mile. He drew a great gulping lungful of air, and willed his body to relax. He gave a curt nod of acceptance. The men holding him sensed his control and let him loose.

"Tell that pig-eyed son-of-a-bitch he'd best fetch no less than four hundred for this lot," he said, amazing himself by the even tenor of his voice. But he could not be content with pretending Busko's insults had not occurred. "And you tell him that if Mistress Bowen's name ever crosses his lips again, he's a dead man."

"You know he likes to rile you."

"He succeeded. He'll regret it mightily if he irritates me again."

It took all his strength of will to keep from kicking Busko as he stepped over him.

"I'm going home now."

Cameron strode away into the welcoming quiet of the woods. Home. He hadn't said that phrase for two years now. Passing strange that he should think of his uncomfortable pallet on the floor of the medical storage room as home, but that was what it felt like, what drew him through that long, wearying trudge. He couldn't afford to indulge that thought. He had to take greater care. *Look at me,* he chided himself, *ready to kill a man for saying things any man might say.* The canvas-wrapped gown rubbed against his skin, where he'd shoved it into his shirt. Defending her honor, and bringing her gifts, and thinking of the place where Jillian waited as his home . . .

Home.

The very thought roused such an overwhelming yearning that he stumbled. He'd lost his home. And the course he'd chosen meant he would never have another.

8

![decorative flourish]

Cameron sipped at the peppermint tea Jillian had brewed but ignored his biscuit, as if he still smarted from her suspicion the day before that he'd stolen bread and meant to pay it back by starving himself today.

She waited for satisfaction to flood her. Instead, she noted the dark circles under his eyes, the unusual pallor beneath his darkened skin, and remembered how hard he worked digging at their garden all day. She wanted to urge him to eat his biscuit, and hers as well.

"My father and I are bid to Squire Horton and his gouty foot this morning," Jillian said.

He straightened at the news. "How were you bid?"

"One of Squire's servants came last night, while you were out."

"And he walked up to your door while I was away, bold as you please?"

"Martin heard him as he approached, and escorted him to the door. He stayed close the whole time while the servant stated his business."

Cameron nodded, but distantly, as if his only concern had been to hear that Martin had not failed in his assigned guard duties. She waited for him to ask if she'd held her tongue about his true purpose in being there, but he merely swallowed his tea at a gulp.

"I had begun to believe nobody ever called upon your father. I'll make myself ready at once."

"Oh, you are a poor excuse for a rogue!" Disgusted, she threw down her napkin. "I might have sent Squire Horton's man back home with a secret message telling him everything that's happened here. Commonwealth soldiers could be waiting there now to arrest you."

"Did you?" He leaned back and studied her through hooded eyes.

She opened her mouth to answer, and her anger dissolved beneath his piercing intensity. Being the subject of Cameron Smith's full attention, with those enigmatic eyes focused solely upon her, was extraordinarily unsettling. "Perhaps I did. Perhaps I did not. You would never know."

"I would know in my heart, Jillian, if you betrayed me. Just as you would know . . ."

Just as she would know if he meant her harm. Oh, God, she all but shook with the realization that she felt certain, bone-deep certain, that Cameron Smith would never willingly allow her to be hurt. She'd known that almost from the first, she realized, in some secret feminine place that had been thrilled rather than frightened by his touch. Cameron would no more hurt her than she would willingly take an action that would lead to his arrest, his conviction, the severing of that noble head from those broad, strong shoulders.

You will come to trust me, whether you want to or not, he had warned. *You will find yourself caring about me, and embracing my cause as your own.*

"You are so sure of me," she whispered. "That knight who taught you the ways of captor and captive—"

"This—" He interrupted her, and thumped his hand against his heart. "This has nothing to do with captor and captive. I do not wish to talk about it."

He pushed himself away from the table and rose to lean over her, with his hands braced upon the table-top. He said nothing. She stared up at him, her mind swirling with what he'd said.

From any other man, that touch to the heart could be tantamount to a declaration of love, an acknowledgement of tender feelings at the very least. From Cameron Smith, who'd taken her captive and vowed to watch her die if it suited his needs, it could be little more than a ploy to tug at her all-too-weak emotions.

"I will meet you outside when Martin brings the wagon around," he said, long moments later, when she still had not found the strength to say a single word.

Squire Horton's leg had swollen to such alarming proportions that it was impossible for him to don stockings. He'd propped the offending limb up on a small tower of cushions. So red and tight was the hair-speckled skin that it shone as if he'd been buffed from ankle to knee with a good coat of beeswax. Jillian felt a twinge of sympathy for the pain the old fellow must be feeling.

"You have been drinking port wine again," her father chided.

The squire's face blushed as red as his leg. "Barely a drop, Wilton."

"I have witnessed firsthand the size of your wine cups. You would have to pour much more than a drop merely to wet the inside, let alone leave something behind for you to drink." Dr. Bowen motioned to Cameron. "Have a look at this leg and then give us your recommendations, young doctor."

Cameron squatted down alongside the squire's up-raised leg. He scowled so fiercely at the swollen limb that Jillian wondered if he thought to force the gout away with sheer malice. He glanced covertly at her father.

The brick-red rising from Cameron's neck would soon rival the color of the squire's leg. Being put on the spot like this, forced to reveal his ignorance, was

proving to be humiliating for him. He peeked at the
leg and then at her father again, and Jillian fancied
she read a hint of apology at odds with his ferocious
glower, as if he wished he could apologize in advance
for how his lack of knowledge would reflect badly
upon his supposed master.

She ought to laugh. Instead, she felt a strange sensation to realize that Cameron cared, and cared desperately, about all this. He shouldn't. It made no sense
for a man of his nature, with no real interest in the
task at hand, to worry about embarrassing his supposed mentor.

Jillian couldn't shake the feeling that he'd suffered
a few too many such embarrassments in his life and
had grown heartily sick of failing to measure up.

In an ostentatious whisper, her father said, "Converse with him, young doctor, to divert his attention
from the pain while you examine him."

"Uh . . . Squire Horton, your orchard keeper has a
good hand with a pruning knife," Cameron said. "I've
seldom seen apple trees in better trim."

"Oh, you know a thing or two about fruit production?" Squire Horton leaned forward with interest, but
groaned when his movement sent the cushions shifting. He subsided back into the chair.

"Fruit production is . . . was . . . one of my abiding
interests." Cameron poked at the squire's leg as if it
were a peach he was testing for ripeness. The squire
gave a little yelp.

Fruit production! Jillian couldn't imagine a less
likely topic of interest to someone who claimed to
be a desperate highwayman. And yet it fit with his
determination to reclaim their kitchen garden from
the weeds and brush, and his getting his hands and
arms all scraped up while pruning their overgrown
stand of raspberry canes. She could so easily imagine
Cameron's hand cupping a crisp, juicy apple, or his

lean form climbing a tree to chop out the dead stuff and coax the fruiting branches into producing more.

"Your recommendations for Squire's leg, Doctor Smith," her father reminded him.

Cameron swallowed. He cleared his throat, and then swallowed again. "Leeches? Draw blood to relieve some of the pressure from within?"

The squire's startled gasp hissed through the room, and Jillian found herself wishing Cameron had honestly admitted his ignorance about treatments aloud rather than humiliate himself in such a fashion. Leeches and bloodletting were part of the reason people held such a mistrust of barber-surgeons that it sometimes carried over to physicians as well.

Squire Horton proved it. "Sucking parasites! Bleeding me dry!" he bellowed. "Since when have you taken up with blood-crazed barbers, Wilton? Sounds as though you should've left this lad out in the apple orchard."

"Now, now, Doctor Smith is but newly educated and they impart some radical knowledge at university these days." Her father strove to soothe the irate squire. "I'm proud to say I might have had some part in such a course of study. You know I'm of a mind myself that there's a time and place for the physician and the barber-surgeon to work together. This just doesn't happen to be one of those times. Doctor Smith will soon learn the distinctions."

"I bow to your superior knowledge, Doctor Bowen," Cameron said with just the right touch of chastened humility. He did indeed accompany the apology with a courtly inclination of his head, and something about that arrogant head bent but not bowed sent Jillian's heart skittering. "Mistress Bowen could no doubt offer an excellent recommendation."

"Hot compresses." Jillian spoke rashly, without waiting to filter the answer through her father as she usually did. "Begin wrapping at the toes and go up beyond the knee. Change every hour or so."

Squire Horton settled back with a pleased smile. "That sounds exceedingly comforting, Mistress Bowen." His hand twitched, as if he'd enjoy the remedy even more if he could wrap his fist around a cup of his favorite port wine.

Her father cleared his throat. "There's another method which I've read about, very old, no doubt cast aside in favor of modern methods. Tragic, I think, to lose touch with ancient wisdom."

"Well, don't keep it to yourself, Wilton."

And now her father cleared his throat again and looked rather sheepish. "It involves a dog."

The squire and Cameron cocked inquisitive heads while Jillian gaped at her father. She could not remember how long it had been since her father had called up a remedy without her prompting him to do so.

"What's this about a dog, Papa?" she whispered, half-afraid that his suggestion could be nothing more than the ranting of an addled mind.

Her father's brow furrowed with thought. "I seem to recall reading . . . ah, yes. It makes sense. Let an old dog, well past its lively days, curl at your feet and sleep. The sufferer strips his gouty foot bare and rests it upon the dog. The animal's warmth seeps upward through the leg and lends some relief."

"By God, that makes sense, Wilton." Squire Horton snatched up a bell and clanged it furiously. "Carson, fetch an old hound from the stables at once!" he ordered the servant who came running at the summons.

"Set a boy to keeping the fleas picked off as well. Nasty creatures, always crawling and sucking. You don't want to expose yourself to a new set of maladies," Doctor Bowen advised.

"The dog, plus the turn and turn about with those hot compresses suggested by Mistress Bowen, will set me right in no time." Squire Horton sounded his bell again and barked an order at the next servant to appear. "A glass of wine for all my guests, in celebration."

With the flurry of fetching the dog, and the goodwill cups of port wine poured over her father's protests, Jillian lapsed unnoticed into silence. Her head swirled. Telling a man who could not resist his wine to rest his aching foot upon a sleeping dog did not reflect very highly upon Wilton Bowen's reputation, but it was the first time in months, maybe in years, that her father had dredged even such a tiny tidbit from the mire and muck of his mind.

And Cameron Smith. The rogue had looked straight at her and dared her to prescribe a treatment. And she'd done so, without raising a gasp of outrage from the squire. He hadn't minded in the least that a woman would dare venture a suggestion affecting his health. The memory glowed, fueled by a tiny spark of accomplishment. She sipped at her wine, the first she'd ever been offered by the squire, and coming hard after her success, it tasted all the sweeter.

But the sweetness was tainted ever so slightly by the bitter knowledge that it had been Cameron Smith, Cameron Smith and his ridiculous suggestions, Cameron Smith and his outrageous daring, that had goaded her into stepping beyond the limits she had drawn for herself.

Still—Squire had liked her idea better than he'd liked Cameron's. He'd vowed to employ it, turn and turn about, with her father's suggestion. The warm glow intensified.

Mrs. Podgett was just leaving as they returned to the house. She fixed Jillian with a disapproving glare, and rested her hand upon the pile of bedding that Cameron had folded himself that morning and set atop the sideboard so that nobody would trip over it if they had to go into the medical storeroom.

The canvas-wrapped gown that he'd brought home the night before perched atop the bundle of bedding.

"Somebody cast Doctor Smith out of the room I made ready for him," Mrs. Podgett announced with a suspicious look at Jillian. "The bed's all covered up again, just as it was before. Not even a private place to store his goods."

"Blame me for undoing your hard work, Mrs. Podgett," Cameron said, sending her a secret wink to let her know he appreciated her concern. "I'm not accustomed to such fine lodgings. I found myself uneasy up there on the second floor and moved myself down here."

"Humph. I've never known such a bother about where a person can and can't venture." Mrs. Podgett dimpled at him forgivingly, and then fixed her disapproval once more upon Jillian. "Mistress doesn't like leaving the house. Young doctor can't sleep above the first floor. Next thing you know, old doctor will be saying he can't sit in the parlor." She sniffed and then took her leave.

Mistress doesn't like leaving the house. . . .

Jillian had said nothing during Mrs. Podgett's tirade. But now that the housekeeper had mentioned it, Cameron suddenly read new meaning into the way Jillian kept to the indoors. Most women were forever rushing to visit friends, or tend to marketing, or simply taking some air on a pleasant day. She had not even come outside to see the progress he'd made on her garden.

He resolved to ponder the matter further. For now, Doctor Bowen stared at the parcel with open curiosity. Jillian darted occasional sidelong glances toward it, but never quite looked at it outright.

"A package from home?" Doctor Bowen asked eventually.

"No, sir." Cameron was growing familiar with the fits and starts of the older man's mind, and he knew he had to veer him away from pursuing a line of questioning about Cameron's home. He never spoke of Benington. Cursing his impetuous acquisition of the gown, he decided to tell the truth. " 'Tis a gift. A gift for Mistress Bowen."

"For me?" Jillian tensed. Her eyes brightened with an excitement that told him her absentminded papa had not often indulged her with gifts.

Now that he'd admitted to bringing her a gift, Cameron couldn't wait to see her reaction. He fetched the parcel and placed it in her lap. Her fingers moved at once to the knotted string, and then she paused.

"Open it," he said, a little roughly, surprised to realize how it would hurt if she scorned his gift without even looking at it.

But she meant to refuse it. He could tell by the proud tilt of her chin that she suspected he sought to clear his conscience by bringing her a trinket or two.

"Go on, Jillian, open Cameron's gift," her father urged. "You've not received a special treat for a long time."

She looked at her father with the hungry hope that always greeted any sign of sensibility from him. Wilton Bowen peered at the parcel, and poked the canvas wrapping with a finger, eager as a child on Christmas morn. She gave her father a resigned smile and deftly undid the knots.

The stiff canvas fell open to reveal a puddle of honey-colored silk. The slippery cloth unwound and spilled down over her lap, garbing her from the waist in molten gold, a tantalizing hint of what would be when she wore his gift.

"You brought me a gown," she said tonelessly.

"And just the color to suit your eyes and hair," said her father. He clapped his hands, as pleased with the gown as if he'd bought it himself.

"I've noticed how well you sew, and I pray the fit comes close enough that you might alter it to suit, mistress," said Cameron. "The color—in the sunlight, that gold should just match the lights in your hair and eyes."

"It doesn't matter, for I shall never wear this gown." She'd gone pale, save for rose-colored splotches darkening her cheeks. Her repudiation of the gift rang out harsh and determined, even as her fingers caressed the shimmering cloth. She stilled, as if realizing she petted the silk as if she were stroking a cherished cat. She refolded the gown and wrapped it back into the canvas.

"Your mastery of me does not extend to dressing me like a doll, Mr. Smith," she said in a low, furious whisper.

"Come, come, Jillian," her father chided. "I am the master and young doctor the apprentice. You've gotten yourself all crossed about."

"Have I?" She set the packet away from her with such a grimace of distaste that she might have been handling a concoction of rat poison. "Why don't we ask Mr. Smith exactly what he had in mind by giving me this garment?"

"Nothing," he said, knowing it a lie even as he spoke. He'd imagined her, long-limbed and lush, shimmering gold from the tips of her toes to the highlights in her hair, and walking toward him with a smile on her face. "You have . . . lost much of late, mistress. When I heard you no longer had your gowns of silk, I thought—"

"I have all the finery I want or need. I make the effort to appear at my best when I choose, and of late, I have felt no inclination to do so."

She never backed down. He knew something of the strength of will it took to hold firm in the face of relentless good manners. Most women in her situation would have come around by now, would have begun flirting with him, would have latched on to the gift of the gown as evidence they'd been fortunate in having their lives commandeered.

Though he had not consciously seized upon the gown for this reason, in handing it over to her he'd been aware of an element of knowing that women were ruled by their hankering for fine clothes and jewels. Not she. Nothing about Jillian Bowen fit his knowledge of women. Nothing about her conformed to the lessons he'd been taught.

He wondered if he would ever learn to stop underestimating her.

He left the house again that night, after watching the sky until the sliver of moon disappeared behind a covering of clouds. He left without taking that wretched gown with him, and it sat in an untidy heap atop a side table, luring and mocking her at the same time.

Jillian couldn't believe that he'd brought it home for her. She couldn't imagine where he might have found such a luxurious thing at all, let alone happen across that exact color, the color she'd so often coveted but never dared buy. Such wondrous silks could be found only in London, but even while biding there she'd not been able to bring herself to order such extravagantly beautiful stuff.

They would have laughed, the few women who called upon her, to think of Doctor Bowen's plain, awkward daughter shimmering indoors in cloth of gold. They would have whispered behind her back at the impossibility of Jillian Bowen so bedazzling a man that he would forget her lack of graces, her inability to converse on topics of no consequence, her complete and utter failure to master the simplest feminine art.

Her head ached from the deliberately tight knot she'd gathered her hair into just before dinner, as if by so carefully binding it she would not risk remembering Cameron's glance falling upon a loose curl, and what he'd said. *The color—in the sun, that gold should just match the lights in your hair and eyes.*

Such words could almost make her think he'd given a thought to what she might look like with her hair loosened and falling about her shoulders. The rough wool of her serviceable dress scratched her skin with every move she made. The silk she'd refused, the silk she'd sworn she would never wear, would slide over her skin her like cool water.

Cool water. Rain had begun falling the moment Cameron had left, and now the wind howled, buffeting the house until she roused herself from furtively studying the gown. She drew closed the shutters.

"I do hope young Cameron does not take a chill out there tonight," her father fretted.

She had stood close enough to the rogue to know that he burned from within with a heat that could not be contained, a heat that enveloped whatever stood near. "He will fare fine, Father."

"Aye, he is a strong young chap. But you ought to have worn that gown for him, Jillian. He could have gone off to work tonight with the image of a pretty lady on his mind. I always felt heartened when your mama sent me on my way looking her best."

"He is not working tonight, and please do not compare Cameron Smith and me with you and Mama."

But her father was too caught up in reminiscing to pay any mind to her request. "Oh, how your mama looked forward to watching you grow up and fall in love, Jilly."

Papa pulled free the thong he always wore round his neck and opened the small locket to stare at the miniature within. "She told me she would teach you the knack of wearing bright colors, for you were complected the same as she. She planned to teach you a certain way of dressing your hair." She felt his glance skip over her dull gown and tightly drawn knot. "I wish I'd paid better attention when she talked of such things. You were too young when she died to remember."

"I remember she was beautiful."

Until those thugs had blackened her eyes and broken her nose, and Jillian had not seen any more because by then her mama was shrieking, Run, Jilly, run home. . . .

"I thought she was very beautiful," her papa whispered. "She never did. Told me I looked at her with my heart instead of my head. Here, Jilly—what do you think?" He pressed the opened locket into her hand.

Jillian had stared at the miniature a thousand times, wishing with all her heart that her mother would be more real than the occasional wisp of memory, the smiling likeness captured in oil paints. Jillian traced the tiny brush strokes with a featherlight touch. The same hair, the same eyes, the same nose as she saw when she looked in her glass, but with a subtle difference. Feature by feature, Elizabeth Bowen had not been a beautiful woman, but she'd possessed a flair that Jillian had never developed.

"Cameron looks at you with his heart," her father said.

The very idea of Cameron Smith ever looking at her with one-tenth the emotion her father had showered upon her mother sent Jillian's heart racketing.

"He has no heart."

"Nonsense. He'd be dead without a heart."

"I did not mean that literally, Papa. He just . . . he just pretends to care, to trick me into trusting him, to make me care in return."

"Oh, he has to trick you into fancying him? I thought him a rather handsome fellow. The ladies in the village seemed quite taken."

"Please, Papa, don't." Jillian desperately wanted to put an end to this line of conversation. It was bad enough to learn that her father harbored romantic illusions involving her and that scoundrel, but worse, something within her thrilled to the notion as well. It was all too easy to imagine twirling before Cameron in that gown of gold, watching his midnight-blue eyes

smolder with appreciation, those finely wrought lips
tilt with pleasure.

She ought to burn that damned gown. She would.
She would. She would give him one more day to get
rid of it and then she would hack the golden folds
into bits and feed them into the fire.

"You will have the devil of a time leaving a candle
burning for him tonight, with the wind howling so,"
her father said.

"He's explored every inch of the countryside over
the past days and nights. He doesn't need a candle to
find his way back home."

Her father looked at her sadly. "I did not realize
that you've never learned any of a woman's soft ways,
Jillian. I regret that I loved your mother too much to
ever take another wife. I have done you a great
disservice."

So now her father thought she lacked a woman's
heart, and after all she'd done to shield him over these
years. The pain that shafted through her buckled her
knees and she collapsed onto the settle while her father shuffled his slow way to his bedroom.

She did not know how she could endure this for
much longer.

She closed her eyes and drew a great, rasping
breath. She summoned her will, her strength, around
her like a cloak. Cameron Smith had said he would
take over her life for three weeks. Four days were
gone, only four. Seventeen were left. Endless in some
respects, but endurable. She could endure for another
seventeen days.

She rose to tend the fire for one last time that night,
but found that Cameron had taken care of it. He'd
carefully banked the ashes and piled a goodly portion
of logs onto the flames. She would wager her best
necklace that he hadn't struggled with the logs the
way she sometimes did. He hadn't asked her, either,

whether she minded his assuming a chore that was always left to her to do. *Her* chore.

She waited for the resentment to come crashing through her, waited for rage to shake her. Instead she found herself being warmed by the fire that Cameron had built for her and looking over at the gown of gold and wondering what drew him out on such a wretched night. A thirst for ale? A hunger . . . for a woman?

Maybe he'd find a way to slake those appetites on this storm-tossed night. Maybe he'd take the gown with him the next time he ventured out, and on her next trip to the village Jillian might spot one of the market stall women garbed in golden silk.

9

The loud bang of wood striking wood sent Jillian bolting upright. A shutter banging in the wind? No—a loose shutter would not have made such a solid thump, and loose shutters had to be refastened to keep from pounding incessantly. That one solid slam, forceful enough to rouse her from sleep, had to have been the kitchen door.

So. Cameron Smith had returned from whatever had drawn him out on this wild night.

And he'd returned drunk by the sounds of it. She heard the thwack of a booted toe striking a chair, sending it skittering across the wooden floor. He gave a muffled curse, followed by the woolly thump of a large male body plopping itself none-too-gently onto her mother's settle.

He probably sat there dripping rain and ale fumes and God knows what else all over the faded velvet upholstery.

She would not let that lout ruin her mother's settle.

Nor could she run the risk of allowing him to rise up and bumble about in a drunken stupor. Her father might awaken and take up where he'd left off haranguing her over Cameron's gift and Jillian's lack of womanly attributes.

Lightning flickered, and rain pelted her window. She could think of nothing that would draw her outside on such a night. Men, she knew, were different. No doubt Cameron had braved the elements simply to quaff a few pints of ale at the Vine and Sheaf. Perhaps he'd dallied with a serving wench while he was there. Perhaps he'd promised her a gown of gold silk. She'd been here, tossing in a fitful sleep, worrying, while he'd been out carousing and slaking various male lusts.

She snatched her wrap from its customary peg on the door and wrapped it well about her as she strode through the passage to the front room. She had plaited her hair into one long, loose braid for sleeping, and it got caught beneath the wrap. She reached behind her neck and pulled her hair free and when it flipped over her shoulder she noticed that the end of the plait had worked loose. She couldn't spare the time to fix it now, not if she wanted to save her mother's settle.

She had a hundred angry words, a thousand angry words, ready to fall and blister Cameron Smith's ears.

They all died unsaid at her first glimpse of him.

He slumped forward with his forearms braced against his thighs. His hair hung in wet strands, some sticking to his forehead, some shielding his face. His entire upper body wove from side to side. He would have presented the picture of exhaustion if she were not so convinced that he was drunk as a portside sailor.

But he'd been sensible enough, and taken the time, to spread a knitted coverlet before sitting down so that his wet and muddy self did not damage the settle's velvet upholstery.

Something inside of Jillian warmed and softened at the sight of that carefully placed knitted coverlet.

"Your boots have tracked mud clear across the floor," she said in a voice far less stern than she'd intended.

Cameron looked up at her then, lifting his head as if it weighed heavier than a sack of flour. She pressed a hand to her lips to keep inside the cry that wanted

to spring out at the sight of him. Fatigue etched his
features. His eyes had darkened into fathomless pools
of weariness. But even worse, a cut had opened above
his right eye and a trickle of blood oozed down his
cheek. A bruise darkened his jaw, bursting yellowish
and purple against his skin.

"You've been attacked," she whispered. "Oh, my
God, have you . . . are you badly hurt?"

He looked startled, as if it had been a very long
time since anyone had worried over his getting hurt.
Then a smile flickered briefly before pain altered it
into a wince. That well-pleased smile told her that if
any attacking had been done, he had been the one to
initiate the blows.

"You shouldn't have left your bed." He sounded
uncommonly hoarse; no doubt he'd taken a blow or
two to the throat.

"What happened to you?"

"Nothing."

"You're fairly painting my floor with your blood
and it looks as if a pound or more of flesh has been
scraped from your hide. Something happened."

"I kicked a thick-headed, braying jackass that
doesn't seem able to learn its lesson."

His flippant dismissal of her concern irritated her.
"Did you kill someone?"

He grew so still, the way a wounded creature does
when taking the final, fatal thrust of a knife. It seemed
impossible that she had caused that reaction merely
by articulating her suspicion. That would mean . . .
that would mean he cared about her opinion.

"I did not kill anyone," Cameron said at length. "I
merely reminded someone that I would not tolerate
unkind remarks about a person I admire and respect."

"He put up a good fight?" Jillian said while curiosity assailed her over who had provoked Cameron's
admiration and respect.

"Aye, he tossed me around a bit," Cameron conceded, making light of the size and strength of any man who could do such a thing.

"Well, it seems you must have landed on your head, for it appears there's no lasting harm done. I guess you won't require tending."

"Were *you* going to tend me, Jillian?"

The added huskiness in his voice must have been responsible for the rich timbre that made a caress of his calling of her name. And a lingering chill from the wind that had accompanied him through the door must have been responsible for the shiver that coursed through her.

"What, you would welcome a mere woman seeing to your wounds?" She didn't know why she lashed out at him with that snide edge to her words.

"I am guilty of many things," he said, "but never of minimizing your abilities as you regularly do to yourself. Good night, Mistress Bowen." He closed his eyes and slumped with weariness.

He had dismissed her from her own kitchen! She felt the stinging need to defend herself—but against what? Against someone who gave her more credit than she gave to herself?

He rubbed a hand over his face and she saw the raw scrapes creasing his knuckles. A half-circle of blood branded the tender skin between his thumb and forefinger.

"Someone bit you," she said, dread flooding through her at the sight. "You'd best let me look at that."

"I can bandage it myself. I've managed to learn that much, at least."

She decided she would wait until she was alone to try to figure out why he'd sounded so frustrated by his lack of medical knowledge. It seemed impossible that his playacting at doctor weighed hard on his soul, but his words, his tone, seemed to indicate that it did.

"Human bites often led to infections that no number of hot compresses or herbal poultices can relieve. We must act quickly to stem the possibility of infection."

He winced again as he flexed his fingers. "Jillian, I ache from head to toe. I cannot promise to hold my temper in check if you decide to fling more barbs my way just now."

She supposed he meant to frighten her, sitting there looking all fierce and bloody and warning her that he held but a tenuous grip on his temper. But she felt no fear, only a deep female certainty that Cameron Smith would never hurt her.

"If you think you ache now, wait until morning. That hand will be impossible to use unless you let me see to it properly tonight." There was no more time to indulge in her immature need to strike out at him, to verbally batter a man who held such a high opinion of her abilities. "Move down to the floor. I don't want you bleeding all over my mother's settle."

" 'Tis old," he said with a weary sigh, "and not as fine as your other furniture. I spread the cover. I won't hurt anything by sitting here."

"It's the most precious of all those things we brought here from London." He looked skeptical, and she felt compelled to explain. "I was only six years old when my mother . . . when my mother died, and it is difficult for me to remember the look of her. But sometimes, when I glance over at this settle, I can grasp a fleeting image of her sitting upon it, tending to her mending."

She didn't know why she had told the lout so much, except her conversation with her father had made it seem her mother was close in spirit to her that night. And perhaps she was feeling the smallest bit kindly toward Cameron for taking such care to spread the coverlet despite his not understanding how important the settle was to her.

Her heart lurched at the awkwardness of his movements as he lifted himself from the seat. She realized suddenly how much pure pleasure it gave her to watch him, to admire his lithe and well-shaped body effortlessly performing whatever he asked of it. There was little natural grace evident in the way he eased himself to the floor with a low groan.

She fetched healing ointment from the medical storeroom. She searched the shelves quickly, and tried not to glance at the bare spot on the floor where she knew Cameron would soon spread his pallet for what remained of the night. Such hard solid wood. Not even a layer of woolen blankets could make it a comfortable spot to rest battered muscles. Well—he had only himself to blame. He'd declined the comforts of a fine feather mattress upstairs in order to sleep here, on the floor, where he could keep her father and herself under constant scrutiny.

She ignored her foolish urge to run upstairs and drag a mattress down here for him.

The floor was dry, at least, she told herself, and a better place than he would likely find if he were sleeping outside in the rain where he belonged.

Back in the kitchen, she gathered a small bowl and rag. She always left a pail of water near the fire at night so that they would have warm washing water or the makings of a quick hot drink in the morning. She knelt at the hearth close to where Cameron sat sprawled, with one hand bracing him upright. He did not touch her, but something about the way his body angled seemed to pull her into his circle. She drew the bucket toward her and poured a little water into the bowl.

She dipped the rag into the warm liquid and then hesitated.

"You are afraid to touch me," he said.

"Nonsense." But she trembled as she made the denial. Of course she would have to touch him, whether it was a mere gingerly mopping conducted while she leaned forward and cleansed the gash over his eye, or whether she lifted his wounded hand into hers and bathed the soreness from it. She could not say why the thought troubled her so. "I must touch everyone who falls into our care."

"You are always so careful to hold yourself away from me that not even a thread from your gown brushes against my boots."

"That doesn't mean I'm *afraid* to touch you," she said. "I simply don't *want* to touch you."

It was a lie. Even as she said the words, her fingers tingled with the need to stroke Cameron's skin, to see for herself that no hidden damage had been done to him, and it was a need, a compulsion, that stemmed from her inner woman's core and not from the detached part of her that came into play when she acted as a physician.

She dipped the rag again and squeezed the water from it. The small, slight motions sent the material of her sleeping gown sliding against her skin, reminding her that she was bare beneath the thin wool. She knew that the moment she touched him, his heat would drift through the gap of her sleeve at the wrist, drift all the way up and warm her in places that had never been touched. Her breasts tightened in anticipation, and she was glad she'd pulled her wrap around her or else he might notice the way her nipples pushed against the fabric of her gown.

"Just hand over the ointment," he said when her hesitation dragged on so long as to become embarrassing. "I daresay I can rub it in myself."

"You must thoroughly wash the wounds first." Retreating into the safe and familiar role of healer helped ease the pounding of her heart.

"I'll wash tomorrow, Jillian. I'm not keen on the thought of swabbing at these hurts tonight."

"It's important to wash now. My father believes— or perhaps I should say, used to believe—that cleansing guards against infection and putrefaction." She did not want to skirt any closer to her worries about the nature of a human bite.

"Well, if he no longer believes such, why are you so eager for me to endure a scouring?"

"I never said he no longer believes in the theory. It's just that he doesn't often remember some of his most brilliant insights." She sent him a fierce glower to cover her sudden surge of melancholy. "You should understand. You're using his mental deterioration to your own advantage without regard to what a great loss it is to the world."

She could not tell if it was the flickering firelight that shifted over his skin, or whether regret darkened his features. He tugged the rag from her hand and then slapped it over his eye and began scrubbing away.

"Here, let me," she said, setting aside the bowl. "You're going at that like a scullery maid polishing badly tarnished silver. You'll have that cut bleeding worse if you gouge at it that way." She pressed the pads of her fingers against the cloth and in removing his hand Cameron's fingers lightly dragged against hers. She nearly dropped the blasted cloth from the tremor that shot through her at his touch. Reflexively, she pressed against him a little harder than she should have.

"Ouch. That hurts."

"You bleat like a little boy who's scraped his knees."

"You're tormenting me like a heartless governess."

"That's because I know what's good for you."

He grinned, and her heart lurched at the sight of that white, flashing smile curving so close beneath her hand. She could feel the light brush of his breath against the tender skin at her wrist. Her hand shook a little once more.

"Ow!"

"I swear you are less courageous than a mouse."

"Well, you're hurting me. Talk to me, to distract me from the pain."

"Talk to you? I have nothing to say to you."

A flicker of pain darkened his countenance for a moment, even though she'd done nothing to cause him to flinch. He waved his hand over toward the settle.

"Tell me about your mother, then," he said.

Her hand faltered. "No. We don't ever talk about my mother."

"Never? You must have, in order to overcome your grief."

"There is no overcoming it. All you can do is hold your pain close and hide it from the rest of the world. All you can do is guard yourself against ever caring so much about another person that losing them destroys you as well."

"But if that is what you do, you might never allow yourself to love someone again."

"What is the point in loving, if death can so easily snatch the loved one away and destroy you in the bargain?"

"The memories should enrich you and not destroy your hope. They should strengthen you, not make you slink away from life and cower in fear of ever loving again."

"What do you know of it?" she demanded fiercely.

"My brother died but six months ago," he said, his voice low and quiet with pain. "His death provoked me into doing things I'd had no interest in doing before."

"Such as racketing about the countryside, commandeering the lives of innocent people, getting yourself beaten to a pulp for no good reason." She sniffed. "A strange way of mourning, Cameron Smith."

"Some men might say taking up a noble cause is the only way to mourn, the only way to make sense of a senseless death."

"Who would say such a ridiculous thing? That ancient chivalrous knight who taught you the ways of a highwayman?"

"Aye. In this one instance, at least, I would not have disappointed him." His expression altered with remembered pain, and Jillian wondered exactly what had been the relationship between Cameron and the old knight who'd taught him such warped views of the world.

"Perhaps the old knight guided you in the wrong direction," she said. "Striking out against Fate accomplishes nothing."

"What if Fate has stolen everything from you?"

"Nothing will bring it back."

"Perhaps not. But hiding away and closing your heart to all feeling, running away from love, living in dread of losing someone you care about, strikes me as a poor alternative."

"You are impossible!" she hissed. "You tell me nothing substantive about yourself or why you do the things you do, and yet you criticize my choices. How dare you think that forcing yourself into my life gives you the right to cast aspersions on the way I've chosen to live it!"

He ceased talking then, and she missed the sound of his voice as she worked in silence, with only their breathing and the faint hiss of the smoldering fire making any noise. Until she reached the bruise at his jaw, and though she did not think she pressed any harder there, he flinched, and let loose with an involuntary grunt.

"The bastard broke my jaw."

The thought of Cameron's firm, strong jawline being permanently dented by a break sent an odd twisting through her stomach. "I'll check it for you," she said.

"You'll have to touch me with your bare hand, then," he said, and she realized that she'd been using the rag as a shield between herself and him.

"Stop talking. And clench your teeth together," she said, glad she had a logical reason to hush him.

She leaned closer, and her braid flopped down over her shoulder. A few more twists unwound from the loose end. Cameron lifted the heavy tail of hair, and the ropy loosened curls spilled over his fingers. "Soft," he murmured. "Softer than silk."

She thought of the silk gown he'd brought home to her. *The color—in the sun, that gold should just match the lights in your hair and eyes.* She'd scorned the compliment, thinking it a silver-tongued ploy to soften her heart. But his fascination with the hair he'd twined around his fingers drew her gaze down, and she saw the way the firelight sparked golden flecks amongst the ordinary brown strands.

Cameron hadn't spoken false; he'd noticed something . . . something beautiful about her. Truly noticed something about her that she'd never realized for herself. She tugged the braid from his fingers and tossed it back over her shoulder.

She traced the edge of his jawline, and then probed his beard-stubbled skin. Though he winced when she pressed at an obvious lump, there was no involuntary yelp such as would accompany the grating of a broken bone.

"You'll have a fine time explaining that bruise to our patients," she said to cover the breathlessness she felt at feeling him so warm and firm beneath her touch.

"No one will notice," he said. "My wretched beard grows as fast as weeds springing from a freshly turned furrow, and I'm a fast healer. By midmorning I'll be well on my way to sporting a beard that would hide far worse than this."

"So then you'll look exactly what you are," she said. "A proper scoundrel."

"Ah, no, because you see there is nothing remotely proper about me, Jillian."

He leaned back against the settle with his hands clasped lazily over his belly, his eyes half closed in the manner of a sleepy tiger. He was bloodied, muddied, and bruised, and yet she had no trouble imagining him dressed in silk hose and buckled velvet breeches with lace frothing at his neck and sleeves. A cavalier, with that elegant voice and those fine manners that not even a good beating could disguise.

"Now," he said, and that elegant voice held the edge of warning. "Get yourself off to bed and forget what happened tonight."

"What I remember won't matter if you walk about the village looking as though you'd been bested in a street brawl."

"Anyone so incautious as to remark on my appearance can be told that Doctor Bowen's new apprentice, being unfamiliar with his master's house, walked himself into the edge of a door."

"As you wish." She rose to her feet and made for her room. "I would be delighted if the entire village believes you are a clumsy oaf."

To her surprise, he grinned at her insult. She whirled away, feeling her nightgown swirl against her bare legs, feeling the weight of her plait brushing against her hips.

"Jillian."

She paused, held in place by his calling of her name.

"I was not bested."

She allowed herself a little sniff of disbelief.

"And Jillian—" She paused again. "I was not speaking lightly when I told you to forget about this. If anyone questions you about my whereabouts tonight, you must tell them that I fell asleep here at the hearth shortly after supper."

She didn't answer.

Nor did she sleep for the balance of that night. Her hair seemed to tug at her scalp until she raked loose the braid and let it tumble freely about her shoulders and beneath her as she tossed and turned. It would be a tangled mess in the morning but she couldn't face the thought of binding it up again just then. Her skin felt flushed. She undid the buttons of her gown from her neck to her waist and felt the brush of air against her breasts, but nothing seemed to cool the warmth that she'd absorbed from Cameron.

Her mind tormented her with questions, wondering where Cameron had been, how he'd gotten himself so battered.

She wondered what he had done that made it so imperative she lie about his whereabouts.

And she realized she *would* lie, if need be, for the sake of a smiling, teasing man who'd made her notice she had beautiful hair.

10

Jillian thought Cameron might sleep late. Or that he'd
sit near the fire, letting warmth and the passage of
time soothe his aches while he tried commanding her
to fetch and carry for him. She might be agreeable to
doing one or two small favors, under the circumstances, but only until the worst of his hurts faded.

Instead, he woke her by tiptoeing past her door
before dawn and easing himself through the kitchen
door at first light.

He couldn't be leaving again. Not in his condition.

She tore off her nightgown and shrugged into her
rusty red wool. She had it nearly buttoned when she
heard him at the back of the house, in the garden.
There was a thud, and then the scrape of a shovel
sliding through soil and rock. Again. And again. Soon,
he fell into the rhythm that came so naturally to men
who understood working with soil: the plunge of spade
into the earth, the involuntary grunts he made as he
turned over spadeful after spadeful of dirt, the metallic
tapping as he broke the clods into crumbles ready to
receive seed.

She knew a little—more than a little—about the
way a human body responded to the sort of beating
he'd endured the night before. Every bend of his knee,
every flex of his shoulder, had to send pain slicing

through his limbs. With every twist of his waist, his muscles would be screaming out in protest.

She threw open her shutters. He'd stationed himself about a hundred yards away from the house, with his back toward her. His dark hair, caught back in a loose queue, swung with each movement. He wore some sort of sleeveless undertunic, thin stuff that bared his arms and hung loosely around his neck. His impressive collection of muscles bunched and tightened with each plunge of the spade.

She could not look away.

She had stood well within crushing range of those arms. She had held those broad strong hands within hers, hands that bore the marks of fighting and violence, and felt nothing but strength and gentleness flow from him to her.

He worked with relentless effort, preparing her garden for the coming spring. Making it more fertile, more productive, capable of providing for her and her father once Cameron himself had gone.

He would be leaving. Two more weeks plus a few more days, and he would go. He had promised, and she believed him.

"Cameron." She called his name. "Cameron." She said it again, and it felt right on her tongue, the sort of name a woman could say while her thoughts swirled with trust and passion and the search for meaning in a dark, dismal world.

He had not heard her. She bit her lip, glad that he had not caught her out during this moment when she felt particularly vulnerable.

It was a frightening thing, to realize she was beginning to trust him. He had warned her that she might, but he must have been thinking about a casual sort of belief, not the faith she felt burgeoning within her now like tiny threads wrapping around her heart. Instead of feeling crushed and confined, she felt supported, nurtured. Trusting Cameron meant she could spend

all her days with those mighty, gentle arms holding her
close, and she wouldn't need the walls of her house to
make her feel safe.

The notion held joy as well as terror.

She prepared breakfast, but he did not come in from
the garden.

She woke her father and settled him at the table,
and Cameron still did not come in from the garden.

"Where is young Doctor Smith? Called out?" her
father asked as he bit into a biscuit.

"No, Papa, he's working outside."

"Ah. Mucking about in the dirt, I suppose." At Jillian's nod, he smiled. "Lad ought to have been in agri-
culture rather than medicine. Never saw a man so
keen on growing things."

"I think he might have been . . . before," Jillian
said.

"Before what?"

"Before . . ." Before descending upon them and
taking control, bent upon restoring the English monarchy, with revenge filling his heart. Driven by a loss so
profound he never spoke of it, carrying out instructions handed down by a knight of the realm, smiling
at her with the lazy grace of a cavalier, speaking to
her with the cultured elegance of an educated man.

She had been blind, thinking him a common
highwayman.

"Before he lost his lands, I think," she whispered.
"Papa, he spoke once of a younger brother who'd
been killed, and how his death pushed Cameron into
doing things he'd never thought he'd do—is it possible
that Cameron's brother got caught supporting King
Charles and Cameron's lands were confiscated by
Cromwell in retribution?"

"Cromwell in retribution?" Her father repeated in
complete bafflement.

"Cromwell's Commonwealth forces have confiscated property all over the country, ousted entire fam-

ilies, if they suspect even one son supports King
Charles. Oh, Papa, what if Cameron remained neutral
in this struggle, but his brother supported the king and
got caught? Cameron would have paid the price. If
this is what happened, it explains so much."

"Explains so much." Her father nodded, but tenta-
tively, looking not at all certain. "My fault, Jillian, for
saving young Ollie Cromwell from his first bouts with
the stone?"

"Oh, no, Papa, this is not your fault at all. I must
call Cameron in to breakfast." She pushed herself
away from the table. "He was hurt last night. He must
eat to rebuild his strength."

"Advise him to drink plenty of water." Her father
surprised her. "Sovereign remedy."

She ran into her room and leaned against the windowsill. Cameron worked, still. His arms glistened
with effort. His shirt clung to his back, and a broad
damp vee of honest sweat began at his shoulders and
arrowed down toward his belt. She summoned a deep
breath, ready to call out. And then she heard a quick
scurrying sound—someone running up the drive.

She ran into the parlor, which gave the best view
of the drive, the way she always did when she heard
someone approaching unexpectedly. This time it was
a boy. Red-faced and gasping for breath, his legs trembled so much that she knew he'd run all the way from
the village.

At once she set aside her half-formed theories about
Cameron and became her father's eyes and ears.
Someone needed them.

But Martin, silent and efficient Martin, intercepted
the boy. He caught him by the arm and bent low,
listening, while the boy blurted out words Jillian could
not hear. After a moment, Martin dragged the boy
beyond Jillian's line of vision. She ran back to her
room in time to see Martin haul the lad over to where
Cameron worked, oblivious to the boy's arrival.

He stopped digging when Martin pounded him on the back, and then shoved the spade into the earth and rested his arm atop the handle while he listened to whatever it was the boy had to say.

Martin dug into his pocket and handed a coin to the boy.

Cameron motioned for the boy to go on his way.

The boy, looking ready to burst into tears, protested.

Martin kicked some of Cameron's freshly dug dirt over the boy's boots and flung out his arm, indicating he'd been dismissed.

Cameron turned back to his work. He thrust the spade into the earth with a violence that hinted of desperation. Martin hunkered down next to him, obviously troubled.

Something was amiss. Jillian doubted very much that the boy was one of Cameron's clandestine spies. He had the look and demeanor of a swift-running village lad sent to fetch the doctor. Why had Martin so carefully shepherded him away from the house? Why had Cameron sent him away?

The boy, dragging his heels and casting miserable glances at the house over his shoulder, stumbled down the drive.

Jillian never left the house without first taking a few moments to quell the inner voice that begged her to stay inside. She always took at least a dozen great, mind-clearing breaths to fortify herself; always gave herself a brief, silent lecture on how foolish it was for a grown woman to fear venturing out of the house. She had no time for all that now.

She lifted her skirts to her knees and darted through the house, past her startled father, and out the door. She knew a shortcut through the trees that would bring her to a curve in the drive well ahead of the boy.

As she ran, her inner sentries shrieked their fright and pleaded with her to return to the house. Her pulse pounded stronger and stronger as those tentative threads of trust begin to unravel from her heart. She sobbed, both to regain her breath and to mourn the quick severing of that trust.

"Mistress Bowen!" The boy cried when she burst through the trees. His eyes lit with so much relief that she knew she'd been right in guessing he'd come to fetch her father, and it eased some of the panic fluttering inside. "Oh, please, mistress—you and the doctor must come. There's a dead man lying in a ditch near the Vine and Sheaf. Someone beat him to a right pulp."

Cameron raced around the bend in the drive and saw Jillian kneeling in the dirt, holding the boy tight against her chest.

They both turned their heads to look at him when his boot crunched a dried twig into shards. She'd been crying, or the closest thing to it, for her eyes were huge with agony and bright with the remnants of tears.

It bothered him more than he cared to admit that she'd run out of the house after the boy, but never came outside to see *him*.

"I told you to go home," Cameron growled at the boy.

The lad squirmed, but Jillian held him tight.

"You tell Martin to harness Queenie," she said. "My father and I must ride at once into the village."

"No." Cameron tightened his jaw while she froze with disbelief. "We stay here."

"This boy came to fetch us."

"The boy said the man is dead. There's no need to . . . to upset your father's routine for a dead man."

"What if he's *not* dead?"

"Oh, he's dead, mistress," the boy inserted eagerly. "Someone with great ham-handed fists smashed in his face and—"

"That's enough!" Cameron roared.

Squeaking with fright, the boy wriggled free of Jillian and bolted down the drive, making for the village.

She sat back on her heels. Her gaze flickered from the cut above his eye, to the bruise along his jaw, to his bruised and mangled fists. She had every reason to believe he had something to do with a dead man lying near the village inn, and yet it caused a pang of utter agony to see this proof of how little faith she had in him.

"I told you last night—I killed no one." The harshness of his declaration made him realize how it disappointed him to know she did not believe in him.

Nobody had ever believed in him. Not his father, who'd despised him for loving the land over battle. Not his brother, who'd scorned Cameron's careful neutrality, who'd derided Cameron's driving need to hold on to Benington Manor and secure the land for their family, for the ages.

And now, Jillian showed no faith in him. In some ways, this was the hardest blow of all to absorb.

"You have nothing to gain by forcing us to stay here, and everything to lose," she said, her voice even and devoid of any hint to tell him whether she'd accepted his assertion of innocence. "If my father and I do not go into Bramber after that boy ran all the way out here to fetch us, the villagers will question our absence. They will wonder why both Doctor Bowen and his new apprentice ignored their plea for help. You will undo all the progress you have made with them."

She made a calm, rational case backing up her desire to go into the village. He had no sensible argument to counter her stand.

"Do men often turn up dead in that village?"

"No."

"My instincts warn me something is wrong. It smells of a trap—someone who knows of the fight I had last night might be trying to implicate me in something I did not do."

She stood and stared down at her toes. He stood and stared down at the mess he'd made of himself while digging. He'd been wrong, thinking that punishing himself with work that strained his shaky reserves of strength would sap him so completely that he might forget the urges that had gripped him since the night before.

He wanted more from Jillian than a healer's probing touch. Grimy and sweat-soaked and curling his fists into aching lumps, even thus, he wished he could pull her into his arms and kiss away her doubts and fears. He wanted England back the way it had been. He wanted to walk her boldly up the wide steps of Benington Manor and sweep her inside and show her the view of his productive acres and his fruit trees and his pampered livestock. He ached to show her what he'd tried so hard to save, and share with her the dreams he'd had of children, and what had meant more to him than attaining the status of knight for the dubious privilege of being addressed as *sir*.

"You knew, when you descended upon us, that we would often be called away from this sanctuary." She was blessedly unaware of the turmoil within him. "You claimed to need our freedom of movement. Well, that freedom comes with a price."

"Perhaps too high a price."

She cocked her head askance.

"If I am somehow linked with this man's death, you and your father might be held to account."

"You told me from the first that you considered us expendable," she whispered.

"Aye. I knew full well the danger I placed you in. It did not seem to be so important . . . then."

Her eyes swam with tears. "And it's important to you now? How can I believe you—how can I *ever* believe you?"

He gripped her shoulders, heedless that the dirt clinging to his fingers might stain her gown. "My word, Jillian, is all I have left in this world. I give it to you now—I swear I had nothing to do with the dead man in the village. I swear I will do all in my power to see that you and your father do not suffer from helping me. Believe me. Tell me you believe me."

But he did not let her answer. He swooped low and captured her lips with his. She tasted of salt and tears and when she relaxed against him and made a sound low in her throat it took every ounce of his self-control to keep the kiss a thing of lips and tongues and not crush her against him or lay her down on the earth and bury himself inside the sweet haven of her.

She pulled away.

She took two steps back and stood staring at him with her hand pressed over her mouth.

"Jillian, I . . ." He closed his eyes while a wave of tiredness surged through him, reminding him of every aching bone in his body. "I'm sorry." He waved at everything, at nothing—at the partly shoveled garden, at the empty drive where the boy had bolted away, at her lips still swollen from his kiss.

"We must go to the village," she said.

He nodded.

"If anyone asks, I will tell them you spent the night playing chess with my father."

"You would do that for me?" he asked, his voice husky as hope hammered in his heart.

"Not for you." She glanced back at the house. "For my father."

She would protect him, Cameron, with the ferocity of a lioness, but not because she believed in him. Because he had sparked a glimmer of life in her father. It should not matter. He told himself a hundred times that it did not matter. But it did.

*   *   *

A knot of villagers stood near the ditch, marking
the place where the doctor was needed. Jillian
clutched her father's hand as they joined the oddly
excited group. The two boys who had found the corpse
while searching out kindling sticks stood with their
small skinny chests puffed proudly, their eyes alight
with excitement and their lips tightly pressed to keep
from smiling at such an inappropriate occasion.

Someone cried out, "Doctor's here!" The crowd
parted to let them near, but only a few tore their
attention away from the body in the ditch. Mrs.
Hawking, who smiled and reached out and gave Jillian's upper arm a quick, reassuring squeeze. A woman,
dimpling at Cameron. A tenant farmer who'd once
asked Jillian to go for a carriage ride—Husker,
Busker, some such name—looking as if he too, had
spent the night engaged in fisticuffs. Or perhaps in her
desperation to find a suspect other than Cameron, she
imagined the puffiness about the tenant farmer's eyes,
the swelling of his lips, for he seemed to be grinning
with a hysterical malevolence one would not expect
from a man who'd been recently beaten.

She felt something brush her elbow, and then the
solid, reassuring feel of Cameron's hand closed around
her, lending his strength as they approached the ditch.
His clasp made it easier, somehow, to move through
the close-pressing crowd.

She didn't want to trust the rogue. She'd wrestled
with her heart throughout the entire ride into the village. *Believe me,* he'd said, just before kissing her . . .
and once she started remembering that kiss, all her
sensible arguments against trusting him flew like swal-
lows fleeing winter's wrath.

"You don't have to look at him, Jillian," Cameron
said, his voice low and meant for her ears alone.

She ignored him. She tugged free of his grip, slipped
her arm through her father's, and stood as close to

him as she could while one of the villagers rolled the body over.

At first she saw only horror—blackened eyes, a hideously misshapen nose—that plunged her back twenty years while her mind echoed with the sound of her mother's final scream: *Run, Jilly, run home.* She trembled, and Cameron took hold of her again. He wrapped a strong arm about her waist and drew her close. Her ancient demons retreated from the influx of strength his touch gave her. She blinked, and her vision cleared. The face in the ditch was not her mother's. . . . She pressed her free hand against her lips to keep from crying out when she recognized the dead man.

Robert Lindsay. Cameron's cohort. His link to Lord Harrington and news of the king. Cameron could not possibly have had anything to do with the death of a man so essential to his plan.

He had begged her to believe in him; he had sworn he had nothing to do with this killing, and she had doubted.

"Took a right beating, he did," marveled one of the villagers.

Jillian studied the swollen features with a physician's detachment. Some of the puffiness, she knew, came from lying a full day in the open. But some had been caused by a heavy fist striking the flesh. Robert's hands bore marks showing he'd tried to defend himself.

Cameron's bloody face. Cameron's battered fists. Cameron's face bending over hers, Cameron's lips claiming hers . . .

A chill had descended this late in the day, but not enough to dampen the scent of crushed leaves as the villagers milled about, or the heavier, cloying odor that overlaid it all, to go along with the lazy flies buzzing around the dead man's head.

"Papa, is there nothing to be done for this man?" she forced herself to ask.

"Nothing to be done for this man." Doctor Bowen stepped away from the ditch with a regretful shake of his head.

His pronouncement came just as the thudding of hooves announced the arrival of mounted men. "Fraley." The name passed through the crowd in a hushed, rustling whisper.

A delegation of Commonwealth soldiers surrounded the constable. Fraley rode his horse to the edge of the ditch and sat looking down at Robert Lindsay's corpse for a few moments. With a jerk of his chin, he indicated for two of his men to climb into the ditch and deal with the body.

They heaved the body out onto the road and then leaped out themselves. One grabbed Robert Lindsay's legs and the other gripped him beneath the armpits. A few of the villagers began edging away from the crowd. Fraley barked out a command that stopped them in their tracks.

"None of you leave here until you tell me the name of that dead man."

Nobody answered. Mulish and sullen, the crowd glared its hatred at Fraley.

"Come, come," he said with false joviality. "There must be one man among you willing to earn the Lord Protector's goodwill this day. Imagine how grateful my lord Cromwell would be to hear that this man was a Royalist sympathizer, and that his treasonous plot had been foiled."

"Ain't no Royalists in this village, Constable Fraley," offered an old man in a voice that quavered more from fear than from age. "We seed that there fellow lurkin' about, but ain't none of us know him. He ain't never made himself sociable to no one."

Cameron caught a stall-keeper sneaking a look at him, a conspiratorial glance that said the stall-keeper

knew the old man hadn't exactly spoken the truth.
The dead man had been seen, just a couple of days
ago, talking to Cameron Smith. But nobody betrayed
him. His heart lurched, struck by an unfamiliar softness. They were protecting him—whether from loyalty
to Doctor Bowen, or a mutual hatred of Cromwell's
regime, it did not matter.

Fraley circled his horse slowly around the group,
and they herded together instinctively, much as a flock
of sheep would do. The exercise tasted bitter to Cameron, but he knew that failing to fall in with the crowd
would only call attention to himself.

He'd done what he could to disguise his own battered countenance. He had not shaved, and the beard
that was his daily curse darkened his skin from cheeks
to throat, doing a fair job of hiding the bruise along
his jaw. He wore a hat tugged low over his forehead
and the collar of his jacket folded high. He'd pulled
gloves over his swollen, protesting hands, the hands
Jillian had held and soothed the night before. He
blessed her skilled touch with the ointment, for the
gash over his eyebrow hadn't swollen very much and
a few moments of intent study in his glass before leaving had convinced him that he looked no worse than
any man who might've taken a fall on his way home
after quaffing a few too many pints of ale.

Fraley's sharp eyes spotted him. The constable stiffened, the way a good bird dog did when spotting
quarry. "You. I don't recall seeing you in this village
before. Get over here so I can have a good look at
you."

Cameron gave a curt nod and advanced. His heart
thudded the way it usually did after a hard hour's
digging. This would be the first real test of his plan.
He must at all cost appear calm and unaffected by
Fraley's scrutiny.

"He be doctor's new apprentice." The old man

who'd spoken before was obviously eager to earn some of Fraley's good will.

"I'll be the judge of who he is, and who he is not." Fraley leaned from his horse and swept Cameron's hat from his head. "State your name and your business in my town."

"Cameron Smith. Doctor's apprentice."

"Just as I told you," said the old man.

Fraley silenced the old man with a withering glance. And then his gaze swept over Cameron from head to toe. "Cameron Smith. The initials C and S. The same initials as that slinking jackal, Charles Stuart."

The crowd behind Cameron grew silent. He cursed inwardly. He'd never considered that aspect of his alias. Perhaps he could turn it to his advantage.

"Those initials, and my general build, have caused me much aggravation of late, Constable. Luckily for me, everyone knows that Charles Stuart is coarse-featured, while I am not—otherwise, I would have likely been arrested in his stead by now."

Fraley blinked, and Cameron wondered how close the man had been to ordering his arrest.

"Isn't it right, Papa, that Cameron looks nothing like Charles Stuart?" Jillian and her father had come to stand next to Cameron. It dazzled him, the feeling of togetherness that seemed to unite them against the constable.

"Cameron looks nothing like Charles Stuart." Wilton Bowen patted Cameron on the shoulder.

Fraley's chin jutted out. "Mistress Bowen! You made no mention of this man when we met on the road the other night."

"He had not yet arrived," Jillian answered smoothly.

Cameron stood there, mute with delight and apprehension.

Fraley glowered. "I specifically asked you, mistress, if you'd noticed any strangers—"

"Why, Cameron is no stranger!" Jillian's eyes widened with false amazement. "As my father can tell you, we knew Cameron in London."

"Knew Cameron in London," Doctor Bowen chimed in.

"Your servant," Cameron said, offering his gloved hand to Fraley. After a long, doubtful study of Cameron's features, the constable shoved Cameron's hat back at him and accepted the handshake.

"Cut that hair," Fraley advised, his grip tightening with angry intensity upon Cameron's wounded hand. "It adds to the likelihood of your being mistaken for Stuart."

Cameron made a noncommittal sound as he gritted his teeth against the pain.

"Oh, he can't cut his hair!" Jillian's hand reached out, as if she meant to defend Cameron's hair from Fraley's barber. "It is easier for him, and safer for the patient, if he ties his hair back in a queue while he's working."

Cameron racked his mind for something apprenticelike to say as he disengaged his hand from Fraley's. His heart hammered anew, but this time from the awareness that Jillian's defense seemed more spirited than one had a right to expect from a reluctant captive. "A lucky thing for us all that Lord Cromwell frowns upon drinking port wine, eh, Constable?"

"What?" Fraley appeared flummoxed, rather than impressed, but the confusion served Cameron just as well.

"Port wine. Gout. There's a medical connection, you see."

Fraley snapped his jaw shut and then issued a curt order. "Haul that corpse to the graveyard. Your servant, mistress," he said to Jillian, and then prodded his horse into motion.

The crowd heaved a collective sigh, as if they'd all been holding their breaths along with Cameron.

A variety of emotions assailed him. Relief, that he'd endured and apparently passed inspection by Cromwell's henchmen. Satisfaction, that his plan had succeeded and the villagers had accepted him into their midst. Amazement, that Jillian had held this opportunity in her hands to betray him, and she had not only kept his secret but deepened his cover.

But those feelings were nothing compared to the sorrow ripping deep through his soul. Jillian believed in him, enough to embroil herself deeper in plot. An hour ago, when he'd asked her to give him her faith, her promise to do so would have sent his spirits soaring. Now—now it was too late. The pain howled through him, taunting him with the knowledge that he'd at last been given what he'd always longed for— and he would have to trample that gift into the dirt and destroy the very thing he ached to possess.

One man who had known him and helped him had shown up dead in a ditch.

It was as though a bucket of ice-slivered river water had been flung into Cameron's face, waking him to the reality of how much he'd been deluding himself. He'd forgotten his own advice to Jillian, that she never underestimate the danger he'd placed her in. It hit him full-force now: He could not keep Jillian safe.

Enemies ringed him on all sides. He'd seen Busko lurking at the fringe of the crowd. The tenant farmer's hatred of Cameron could well have tainted his loyalty to the Royalist cause. Fraley had appeared supremely self-satisfied as he speculated about Royalist plots— he might know more than he'd revealed. Either man could have killed Robert Lindsay to flush Cameron from cover, to undermine the effort to smuggle Charles to France.

They would strike closer next time.

Jillian stood with her hands clasped in a prayerful attitude, her beautiful eyes shining with mingled exhilaration and trepidation. The night before, she'd told him a little about her mother's death. She'd confessed her belief that allowing herself to care about another person would destroy her as well. Jillian Bowen was a woman who'd closed her heart to love, a woman who believed there was no point in loving since death would only snatch it all away. She poised on the verge of abandoning those beliefs and needed desperately to see what he meant to offer in return.

He had nothing to offer. Not even his word, which Robert Lindsay's death proved he could not honor.

To save Jillian, he had to scorn her love and trust. He had to break her heart.

II

Something was wrong. Terribly, terribly wrong.

Jillian felt the change in him even before Cameron turned to her and chucked her beneath the chin the way a doting uncle might tease his favorite niece. He was pleased, and fond of her, but there was no indication that he felt any of the joy and anxiety that ebbed and flowed within her like waves crashing against rock. No hint of the man who had kissed her and asked her to believe in him. No sign of . . . passion.

"Extremely well-done, Mistress Bowen."

Jillian's smile wobbled, and she pressed her lips into a thin line for fear their trembling would be mistaken for anguish.

"Too bad your little act was all for naught." He gave a regretful shake of his head and followed it with a huge sigh. " 'Twas a good plan. It might've worked."

"What do you mean, *might* have worked?" She found her voice in her astonishment. A few of the departing villagers looked curiously over their shoulders at them. She switched to a low whisper. "Do you mean to tell me that you've abandoned your plan to save the king?"

"Of course. How could we go on, after this?" He looked at her with such wide-eyed innocence that she knew he was lying. Every drop of blood in Cameron

Smith's body was tinged with guile. He was up to something.

"Robert Lindsay wasn't that important to your plan," she said. "Everyone, you told me, is expendable. Robert's merely been . . . expended."

She didn't know if she made any sense, but she had struck close to whatever Cameron was trying to hide. His jaw tightened, and a tic betrayed his tension. "It's over."

"So you've given up," she said. "You will leave King Charles to fend for himself if he happens to be chased into this area."

He nodded.

"So you will go on your merry way, then. You expect me and my father to take up as we were, as if none of this had ever happened."

He nodded again. "As soon as I take my leave of your father."

Those tides of emotion surged through her once more. He meant to leave—the very notion made her want to cry out in denial. She wanted to wrap him close with every half-formed tendril of hope, every fragile thread of trust, that he'd brought to life within her.

And yet even as that frantic need gripped her, she felt a pervasive certainty that the Cameron Smith she had come to know would never abandon her, or her father—or his king—so lightly.

He confirmed her suspicions when his gaze flickered toward the ditch and back again. She understood everything then with a burst of utter clarity. She could not let her mind wander back to the sight of Robert Lindsay's beaten, battered, dead countenance without feeling revulsion twist through her, without a curl of dread snaking through her. Robert Lindsay had helped Cameron, and now Robert Lindsay was dead. She and her father had been coerced into helping Cameron to an even greater extent—they'd harbored him within their home, traveled with him about the countryside, afforded him a freedom of movement he could not hope to enjoy on his own.

Cameron was afraid for her. This glorious man who had lost his home, who yearned from the depths of his soul to succeed at something of importance, was willing to cast it all aside, willing to brand himself a failure, to keep her safe.

She could not let that happen. What use was a life spent cowering behind ivy-covered walls if every moment and every breath were tainted with the knowledge that she had let the man she loved abandon his dreams for her?

She blinked, startled by what she'd just realized.

She loved Cameron Smith. She loved a man whose real name she did not even know.

But she knew his smile, and the gentle touch of his big hands grown callused from hard work. She knew his heart and the careful way he'd involved her in his plan without breaking her spirit. It didn't matter what name he used. She loved him.

"Very well," she said. She summoned all her strength to take the biggest risk of her life. "You tell me the plan, and *I* will save the king, as you seem to have lost your nerve."

He gaped at her. She would have laughed if the stakes weren't so high.

"You can't save the king," he managed to say at last.

"Aha, I was right about you from the beginning." She stared down her nose at him, a difficult matter for a female who stood a head shorter than he. She had to angle her head quite far back, exposing her throat, and ignore the sudden longing she felt to have his lips tracing that sensitive skin. "You're as bad as everyone else, thinking me a brainless ninny simply because I'm a woman."

He narrowed his eyes at her. "You're up to something."

"So are you."

She took a breath, ready to launch into a litany of her suspicions regarding his motives. But before she could begin, she heard an urgent, "Please, mistress, over here." She glanced toward an oak and saw a young village woman standing there, holding an ominously limp-looking baby.

"Mistress." The woman kept her head bowed while she clutched her baby against her heart. "If your father, or the young doctor could just look at my little Tommy . . ."

She and Cameron reached the woman at the same moment.

"What is your name, mistress?" Cameron asked.

Startled by the question, the young mother gripped her baby all the tighter, raising an exhausted whine. "I'm . . . I'm Sairie, young doctor."

"Sairie." Cameron smiled at the frightened woman, a smile that served the dual purpose of bolstering Sairie while weakening Jillian's knees. He had quite obviously learned his lesson about distracting a patient with conversation. "Why don't you hand little Tommy over to Mistress Bowen so she can hold him while I, um, examine him."

Sairie complied, and then stood there twisting her apron in her hands while Cameron stared intently at the boy and Jillian ran a quick hand over his tiny body. His abdomen felt hot and distended, and he stirred sluggishly when she probed near his pelvic bones. She crooked a finger into his breech clout. Damp, nothing more. The signs pointed to a simple bowel impaction. She wondered why Sairie had not simply asked counsel of other women.

"What a quiet boy," she murmured.

"Only this past hour," said Sairie. "He's been screaming up a right storm for two days now."

"Squirming, and clutching at his belly?" Jillian prompted.

"Aye, mistress. Wriggling and clawing at himself something fierce."

"Eating well?"

"Until this morning. Now . . . all that crying, and now just lying there . . . I'm afeared, mistress. Help him, young doctor. Please help him."

"Oh, Doctor Smith won't need to help much." Jillian plopped the boy into Cameron's arms. "Hold him well away—I'd venture this little lad wants only to dirty his clout."

"Oh, mistress, it's been days. . . ." Sairie blushed, and stole a miserable glance at Cameron. " 'Tis my fault. I ill-wished him when he messed three clouts in the space of an hour. The devil bound Tommy's bowels, all because of me."

And she'd been too ashamed of heaping curses on her little boy to seek help from other mothers. Jillian could read the guilt plainly upon Sairie's face.

It was hard to summon the words of forgiveness Sairie needed to hear while Cameron cradled that little baby in his big, gentle hands. He held the child with a reverence for human life that Jillian had noticed only in her father. Tommy had Cameron's full attention; he seemed to have driven out all thoughts of death and secret plots and exiled kings, worried more about one tiny, insignificant peasant boy afflicted with constipation. Any lingering doubts still lurking in the recesses of her mind vanished.

"Babies do bind up sometimes." Jillian had to clear her throat. "Doctor Smith can tell you, there's a simple remedy."

"There's a simple remedy." Cameron accepted her coaching with an understanding grin, which shifted into a completely dazzling smile. He was enjoying this, taking sheer pleasure from helping an overwrought mother and her little boy.

"Truly?" Sairie stared at them with naked hope, which faded into alarm. "I have no money to pay you, Doctor, nor for any medicinals."

He pretended to consider that for a moment, his brow furrowing with thought. "Well, there'd be no need to pay *me* anything if Mistress Bowen tells you what to do."

Just that easily, he put the treatment of little Tommy openly into Jillian's hands. She waited for Sairie to object, but the young woman simply turned all her attention upon her, awaiting instruction. It was a dizzying moment for Jillian to realize that Cameron had been right—she had not given the villagers enough credit. She had allowed her own sense of inadequacy to convince her they would not accept her help. She'd been wrong from the first.

"An herbal clyster would work. Someone here in the village must have gathered and dried mallows over the summer." Jillian heard her confidence ring out loud and clear. Sairie nodded. "Make a weak tea of mallow flowers and leaves, and add just a pinch of red sugar. Strain it well before using it. Do you know how to administer a clyster?"

"Aye, mistress. I can borrow a tube and leather bag from the midwife." Sairie accepted her baby from Cameron. She pulled Tommy close to her breast and sent the both of them a look of melting gratitude, and then she hurried toward an alley.

"Will that fix him up?"

"I think so," Jillian said.

He stared at the place where Sairie had disappeared for a long moment. "You see, Jillian, that little boy and his mother are why you cannot be . . . expended. These people will need you and your father whether Charles Stuart is king, or whether Oliver Cromwell maintains his control."

He leaned toward the alley, almost as if he wished he could join Sairie and watch her little boy's return

to health. There was a yearning about him that told
her he wanted, more than anything, to know how it
felt to be so important to someone else.

"Cameron." She placed her hand against his upper
arm and felt the power and strength held in abeyance
there. He tensed beneath her, and she realized that
this was the first time she'd willingly touched him. The
first time, in fact, that she'd willingly touched anyone
other than her father or an ailing patient. She'd imagined touching Cameron a hundred times in her
dreams, but had never expected that doing so would
connect her so intimately to him that she would feel
the pounding of his heart, the heat sizzling through
his veins.

"That little boy and his mother," she managed to
say. "All of these people—they are the reason why I
cannot back out. I must help you finish what we've
started."

"Jillian—"

She hushed him with her fingers, shocked at her
own boldness and startled by the soft, dry firmness of
his lips. The connection to him was more profound
here, and she had to break it lest she begin trembling.
"We both know that my father won't be able to help
them much longer. If you let me retreat back into that
safe little world I prepared so carefully, nobody will
trust me to take his place. I will shrivel away, empty
and useless, without leaving my mark on the world."

She thought he might tease her. Women didn't leave
marks on the world—men reserved that right for
themselves. But Cameron did not mock her, only studied her with a blinding intensity that told her he had
unfulfilled dreams of his own.

"I don't have to accomplish anything grand." Articulating her modest dreams demanded a surprising
amount of courage. She had never dared admit them,
not even to her father, but somehow she craved Cameron's understanding. "I would be content to know

that I'd helped one child survive. Or that one woman who trusted me lived to nurture her family rather than succumbing to the heedless care of an ignorant barber-surgeon."

"Those are honest and admirable goals, and I can understand their appeal," he said. For a brief moment, no longer than a heartbeat, she thought she saw an echo in his eyes that said, *I'd like to do the same.* And then it was gone. "But I don't think you understand the risks, Jillian."

"I understand the futility of a life spent . . . waiting. You have been here for only a few days and already you've given me the courage to openly pursue my dream. I want to help you do the same."

Cameron went to the window again and again. Each time he pushed aside the drapery, he hoped he'd find clouds cloaking the moon. Instead, the sky remained relentlessly clear, so that even though the moon was a mere sliver, its glow and the light from the stars bathed the countryside in silver. Only the world's most foolish treasonist would consider venturing outside when his shadow would leap long, and his silhouette stand against the sky, visible for all to see.

"You cannot go out there," Jillian said, eerily echoing his thoughts. She stared at him, her eyes huge with apprehension. "The patrols can see for miles on a night like this. You could end up . . ."

"Dead in a ditch, like Robert," Cameron finished.

"Please, don't say that, even in jest."

"I tried telling you before, in the village, that carrying out my plan is a dangerous business. You insisted."

"But you don't have to go out tonight."

"I do. Something obviously went wrong. I have to find out what happened. My men will be expecting me tonight."

She had been mending, and she very deliberately

stuck her needle into a ball of thread. "Very well. My father and I will go with you. I will require only a few minutes to . . . to prepare myself."

He bit back a curse. She was forever turning the tables on him.

"This was your purpose in coming here, after all— to become a familiar figure riding with us at night. Nobody will think anything of it if they see us."

"No one has summoned us. Nobody is ailing tonight. Were we to burst in on someone unexpectedly, we could provoke, I don't know, a seizure of the heart."

Her lips quirked. "We seem to have switched roles, young Doctor Smith. You ought to be trying to convince me, rather than discourage me."

"I ought to tie you in your bed for your own good."

Her collar was unbuttoned, and the edge began fluttering as if the pulse beneath it had begun a new and furious beat at the mention of her bed.

"No, you ought to be telling me exactly why you are suddenly so reluctant to carry out your plan," she said. "Knowledge bestows power, Cameron. My chances are best if I know what to expect."

She was right. And if she was as determined as she seemed to carry her role through to its conclusion, she deserved to know what was in store.

"The best plans are simple plans." He closed his eyes, almost able to hear his father's voice drilling those words into his head. "But things could still go wrong, dreadfully wrong. Matters took a bad turn today, when you spoke up for me in town and claimed to have known me in London."

"I thought I was helping you."

Cameron ached to pull her into his arms, to erase the wounded dismay in her eyes.

"You did. But if the king does escape through here and I am somehow connected to the plot, someone will remember that you vouched for me. If Cromwell determines you played an active role in this subterfuge, you will be tried and punished as a treasonist. You could be put to death, Jillian. You and your father. So, pray Charles does not come this way. But if he does, pray that nobody ever learns from where he made his escape. I promise to provide you with an excuse to cover my disappearance, an excuse that will absolve you from guilt."

"Your . . . your disappearance?"

"I must leave here once my work is done."

"Leave?"

"We have all taken an oath to disperse once we pass the king through to the next station, save for those men who hail from this town, of course. If they disappeared, their families could be marked as monarchists. Cromwell has been known to employ . . . certain methods to extract information from those he suspects of helping the king. It is safer for you and your father, and essential for the lives of my men, that nobody who came from elsewhere stay here to be caught."

"You have always meant to leave, from the very first." She sounded almost numb with disbelief, and he could not understand her agitation.

"Aye. I told you, Jillian, three weeks, no more."

"So you did. You have always been . . . exceptionally honest with me, Cameron."

Odd, how a compliment such as *exceptionally honest* could make him feel like the worst sort of liar. And belatedly he knew why. He thought of that kiss he'd so rashly taken, of the golden silk he'd given her, and knew there was no woman in the world who would not read into his behavior the implications Jillian had read into them.

"I thought I'd made it clear from the beginning," he said. "I am sorry if I did not tell you enough."

"There is one very important thing you have not

told me." She swallowed. "You haven't told me your name. Your real name."

Oh, how he wanted to do it! His lips trembled with the urgency. *Cameron. I am truly Cameron, now, and will forever be,* he wanted to say, but he could not.

"It would be dangerous to tell you," he said quietly.

"Dangerous—for you?"

"Dangerous all the way around," he said.

Doctor Bowen refused to accompany them. Half asleep, his wits obviously flown for the night, he scowled and ordered them out of his room. "Tend to it yourself, Doctor Smith," he grumbled. "There's no point in having an apprentice if I must rouse these old bones every time someone thinks of a complaint."

"That's it, then," Cameron said when he and Jillian were once again in the kitchen. "You can't come with me. Once I leave the wagon, there would be no one to protect you. Robert Lindsay's murderer is on the loose."

"My father hardly provides protection, Cameron."

"The mere sight of a man sitting alongside you would suffice."

"Robert Lindsay was a man," she pointed out calmly. "Besides, if the murderer is out to destroy those connected with your plan, we could be attacked right here, in our beds, while you are gone."

He scowled at her. She was right. He would have to warn Martin to be extra vigilant. "Fraley knows you don't tend to patients on your own."

"Fraley knows I occasionally visit Mrs. Hawking."

"Not so late at night."

"Mrs. Hawking and I are both considered rather . . . unconventional. If Fraley happens upon us before you leave the wagon, I'll merely explain we're both going to visit her. If he stops me after you've already left the wagon, I won't mention you at all."

Cameron glowered at her. "You have a counter-point for my every argument."

"I am the sort of creature most men curse; an obstinate woman."

"Not obstinate," he said. "Strong."

"I'm not so very strong," she whispered. "I did exactly as you predicted."

His arms ached to pull her close and prove to her that bending did not mean capitulation. That she had managed to retain her honor and dignity while he had turned his back on his values to pursue a pointless revenge.

She was worth ten of his men, a hundred of him. Any man would be proud to call such a woman his, to walk with her at his side and announce to the world, *She is the one I love.*

He loved her.

He'd suspected it almost from the first, but he knew it for certain now, when it was impossible to change the tides of fate that would take him away from her.

And now he would be riding out alone with Jillian—not the romantic moonlight drive with his ladylove that his heart craved, but a stealthy rendezvous in the night, running the very real risk of discovery and death.

He harnessed the mare without rousting Martin, and Jillian was waiting near the door, her arms weighed down with a variety of objects, when he drove the wagon around to the kitchen. He jumped from his seat, and waited to help her into the wagon. She stopped a few paces away, just far enough so that he could not reach her.

"I've been climbing in and out of this wagon on my own for three years now, and I'll be doing so long after you're gone. There's no need to help me."

"I'm here tonight, and a gentleman helps a lady into a wagon." He held out his hand, surprised at how much he wanted to touch her, even in such a cursory fashion.

"I'll climb in myself, and *you* will lie on the floor."

She'd stymied him again. And she knew it. She smiled, a quick, secretly pleased thing that made him want to smile right along with her.

"I'd be in trouble if Fraley saw you sitting next to me, and then later saw me alone. But if you're lying on the floor, he won't even know you're there."

"Unless he stops you and searches."

"But if you're lying on the floor, reeking of ale, he'll believe me if I say you've gotten foxed, like apprentices are apt to do."

"Excellent plan," he conceded, "except I do not reek of ale."

"You will, once you splash this all over yourself." She shifted the goods in her arms, and then triumphantly held an aleskin aloft.

He shook his head, admiring her nerve as he accepted the aleskin. "Lord Harrington went to a good deal of trouble to recruit me for this area. I can't wait to tell him that he overlooked a truly devious plotter right in his own neighborhood."

It would never rank high among the numerous compliments he'd handed ladies, but Jillian's whole being lit with unabashed pleasure. He thought of all the endearments he could never say to her, all the sweet words he'd love to whisper in her ear. In later years, when he lay alone and dying, he'd get small comfort from remembering he'd most pleased the woman he loved by calling her a devious plotter.

He found himself oddly thick of throat as he poured a little ale into his cupped hand and made ready to rub it into his shirt.

"Oh!" Jillian pressed her hand to her mouth.

"What?"

"I didn't think—the ale might stain your shirt."

He cocked a brow. "If so, then half the men in

England would be walking about wearing ruined shirts."

"Maybe . . . maybe you ought to unbutton your shirt and just rub a little into your skin."

He held the aleskin in one hand, while ale dripped through the fingers of his other. She saw at once that any attempt at unbuttoning would accomplish the very staining she sought to avoid.

"I'll undo them for you," she said.

Her deft touch had his buttons undone in no time. But when she hooked her fingers beneath the edges to draw the shirt apart, her nails lightly raked his skin and parted the fine hair swirling across his chest. Desire shot through him, heating his blood and turning his lower body heavy with need.

She seemed to have forgotten to breathe. Her lips were level with the nipples on his chest, and her attention seemed riveted to the way they hardened from wanting her.

"I'll just climb into the wagon now," she whispered. The warmth of her breathing brushed his nipples with exquisite fire.

He welcomed the cold wet slap of the ale against his skin, but it wasn't enough to cool his body. The breeze quickly dried the ale, and he buttoned his shirt with shaking fingers, unable to forget the sight of Jillian's lips hovering mere inches from his flesh, the whisper of her soft breath warming his skin. He slid past the open half-door onto the carriage floor, and settled himself awkwardly with his legs wedged under the seat and his elbow braced under him for support.

"Should I make for Bramber?"

"Aye, but cross Scupper's field and follow the trail that goes back into the forest. There's a spot there where my men and I can rendezvous."

"How will I know when to stop?"

"I'll leave this door open so I can see." He unlatched the half-door.

She shook the reins and clucked her tongue, and they began.

They did not speak, and yet it seemed the very air surrounding them swirled with thoughts that remained unspoken. He couldn't help staring up at her, at the classic lines of her face limned in moonlight. She did not believe herself beautiful. At that moment, he ached with the need to convince her of her special beauty, and knew he would spend all his days envying the man who would one day enjoy that privilege.

In no time, they reached the small intake field that some long-ago, long-forgotten peasant had hacked from the forest. Finger-shaped thickets grew from the heart of Arundel Forest toward the field, as if the forest sought to claw back the land that had been taken from it. The only thing preventing the forest from reclaiming the land altogether were wide bands of boulder-strewn, rocky soil, which had been turned into traveling paths. Jillian chose the trail Cameron indicated.

"A quarter mile ahead," he said with a small movement of his hand.

She pulled slightly on the reins, slowing the mare by almost imperceptible degrees. Short minutes later they came to where a tangle of vines and dwarfed trees curled around and over boulders that stood as tall as a man. A small clearing lay beyond the boulders, another remnant of the long-dead peasant's industry.

"Don't stop," he warned. "Someone could be watching. I'll roll out onto the ground."

She flinched a little. "You could hurt yourself by falling from a moving wagon."

"It would take more than a fall from a wagon to stop me."

"When should I return for you?"

He hesitated.

"Cameron—you're not thinking of just running off, are you?"

"It would be best if we parted company here and now."

There, he'd said it. She deserved this option. Her bravery had brought him this far; she need not risk herself further. And yet a part of his soul screamed with the need to hear her say she would come back for him.

"You told me it was my decision, whether or not I wanted to carry on. I need to do this with you, to prove to myself—"

He caught a fold of her gown between his fingers and rubbed it. He fancied he could feel her life force vibrating through the scratchy cloth. He knew she could not feel his secret touch, could not see the hunger gripping him, could not know that he wished he could hold on to all of her and not just this edge of her hem.

"You do not need me." He sounded uncommonly gruff; or perhaps it was merely the echoing of his voice confined in the bottom of a high-walled wagon. "You have within yourself the strength and determination to bring your dreams to life. Go home and make them all come true."

She glanced down at him, her eyes bright, her lips lush and soft. He wondered what it would be like if he could slip away from this wagon with the feel of Jillian's kiss upon him. With the memory of her weight filling his arms and the imprint of her lush curves upon his flesh. He wished suddenly that she would ask for his promise to take care and return to her whole and safe—and wished even more that he had the right to want such a thing.

"If I go back into my house now . . ." Her voice trailed away and Cameron felt a tremor course through her. And then she tipped her chin stubbornly skyward. "You said I could choose."

He smiled, knowing she could not see his bitter-sweet appreciation of her determination. "You're right, I promised. But you must promise me to consider all aspects of your decision. I will return to this place in two hours. I hope I will not find you here."

His arms empty, his heart heavy with words left unsaid, he slithered through the open doorway and landed with a thud at the edge of the trail. Holding himself in a low crouch, he kept pace with the wagon for a dozen feet and then dove behind a thorn-crested boulder.

The wagon's slow crawl continued for another hundred paces, and then he heard her voice, clear and crisp and carrying in the night air. "Up with you now, Queenie. You can't go back to your stall just yet."

Love words of a sort—an explanation for the slowing of her wagon, spoken loudly, just in case someone lurked in the woods, spying. Just as telling her to stay away had been love words from him. There could never be anything more.

He stood behind the boulder, aching body and soul, watching until she disappeared around a curve in the trail.

He wondered if he would ever see her again.

12

I hope I will not find you here. I hope I will not find you here. The refrain echoed through Jillian's mind in time with the beat of Queenie's hooves, insistently, for every step of the miles it took to reach the village.

Cameron had scorned her help.

And in doing so, she feared he'd scorned her as a woman.

Her skin heated with embarrassment at remembering how she'd been unable to stop herself from touching him when she'd unbuttoned his shirt, how she'd let her fingers drift through the silky swirl of hair covering his chest. Her lips had paused mere inches from his skin and it had taken all her strength of will to hold herself rigid when she wanted to lean into him and press her lips against him and revel in his scent and his heat.

He was a man of experience. He had to know that when she cast her lot with him, the offer included more than her expert knowledge of the myriad byways cutting through Arundel Forest and the surrounding countryside.

Any woman possessing an ounce of spirit would demand revenge for being scorned. She ought to go straight to Fraley's house and tell the Lord Protector's henchman that he could capture a Royalist conspirator

near those large boulders not so far from Scupper
field, two hours hence.

It would serve him right if she did that.

But she could not betray him.

Run, Jilly, run home! The prickling sensation started
inside and threatened to grow overwhelming. She
could take the easy course and go straight home.
When the hour of rendezvous arrived without her
driving past the boulder, her absence would convey
her decision. Cameron would understand that she'd
put an end to their liaison.

She imagined him standing in the boulder's shadow,
watching the moon rise ever higher in the sky, until
eventually the velvet blackness lightened with the faint
hint of dawn. She wondered if he would worry that
something might have happened to her, or if he'd feel
saddened that she'd so obviously grasped at his offer
to end everything.

Run, Jilly, run home!

Her house, which had always glowed like a fire beacon in her mind, promising safe harbor . . . the beacon
seemed to flicker, warning that she would not feel so
secure if she hid herself away while Cameron remained outside at the mercy of Commonwealth soldiers. She had hidden herself away once before and
her mother had paid the price with her life. If she
went to her house now, she might never emerge.

Perhaps he'd sigh and congratulate himself for
guessing at the secret weakness that now threatened
to paralyze her. He'd simply move on to the next village and start all over again with another, more amenable captive, who didn't get all misty-eyed and weak
in the knees because he happened to smile at her once
in a while. Someone he could count on, a woman who
did not need to perform silly rituals before taking a
single step beyond her kitchen door. A woman who
wouldn't run and hide while vicious thugs hurt or
killed him . . .

She wondered if it bothered him at all to think of never seeing her again, the way it tore at her soul to think of the rest of her life spent without that flashing smile lighting her days and nights.

Oh, how she would miss the rogue. More than miss him—to have it end this way, with no final words of leavetaking, without one chance to brush his hair away from his forehead or thrill to the heat of his lips against her breast, would be akin to tearing out her heart just now.

She did not want to go home. For the first time in her memory, she wanted to lose herself in something warm and resilient, not the hushed, impervious stone of her home.

She was lost.

She was worse than a young girl. A young girl could be excused for believing that one day a mysterious stranger would burst into her life and teach her how to set aside her fears, how to open her heart to love.

Queenie halted, and Jillian blinked herself out of the trancelike state that had settled over her. They stood square in the middle of the village street, which lay deserted and eerily quiet. The sign on the Vine and Sheaf squeaked as it swung back and forth with the night breeze. A pig snuffled in a pile of muck near the farrier's stable. Otherwise, the daub-and-straw huts crowded up against the timbered houses with shutters drawn and doors barred, presenting a silent, impenetrable front.

Sensible people stayed in their houses after dark these days rather than risk detainment and questioning by Fraley and his men. With Robert Lindsay's murder, the villagers no doubt took extra safety precautions. She could sense the draperies being inched back, the curious faces peeping through gaps in the shutters and wondering what Mistress Bowen was doing sitting there all alone in her wagon while a murderer roamed somewhere out there. Queenie shook her head and stamped her impatience at not knowing where to go.

Where to go—Fraley's house, and do her patriotic duty while exacting a woman's revenge? Home, and spend all her days cowering away from the world? Or Mrs. Hawking's, and carry out the plan that would take her back to Cameron in two hours?

I hope I will not find you here.

Jillian slid from the wagon and led the horse to the rail nearest Mrs. Hawking's town house.

The short walk did nothing to clear her mind. Feeling like a puppet being controlled by forces she could not understand, she tethered the mare and drew a blanket over her back to guard against chill. She rubbed Queenie's nose and felt the warm whoosh of the mare's breath, the rumbling vibration of her affectionate nicker. Despite her senses swimming in things familiar, Jillian felt as though she were a stranger in her own skin.

Mrs. Hawking's serving girl boggled in surprise when she opened the door to Jillian's knock. She recovered at once and stood aside to beckon Jillian in out of the dark. "Come inside, Mistress Bowen. I'll take your cloak. Mrs. Hawking did not tell me you were expected, or I would have brewed a hot drink to take the chill from you."

"Good evening, Rose. I daresay Mrs. Hawking might have forgotten I would be here." Jillian lied smoothly, which heightened the sensation of being a stranger to herself. "We made only tentative plans to meet tonight."

The girl's eyes widened a little more, but she was obviously well trained and accustomed to her lady's idiosyncrasies. She did not press for more information as she escorted Jillian to her mistress.

Mrs. Hawking, impeccably gowned and coiffed despite the late hour, looked up from her sewing. Only the briefest flicker of surprise, immediately quelled, betrayed that she thought there was anything unusual in having Jillian Bowen call upon her at an hour when all decent women were at home.

"Ah, there you are, Mistress Bowen," she said.

Rose promised to warm some spiced wine and left them alone.

"Come here at once, my dear girl." Mrs. Hawking set her mending near the fire and held out her hands. Jillian, feeling ridiculously close to bursting into tears, rushed over and fell to her knees before her. Mrs. Hawking gripped her hands. "You're trembling, and pale as a moth's wing. What has happened?"

"He—" Jillian swallowed. There was no need to identify whom she meant; a liquid caress came to her voice, a softening, a breathlessness, at simply thinking of Cameron. "He wants to leave."

"Where is he now?"

"Off in the woods, meeting with his men."

"Because of Robert Lindsay's unfortunate death?"

"Yes. Cameron says something has gone horribly wrong."

"I should think so. I imagine it will be impossible for Lord Harrington to continue supporting the Royalists now—but enough of that. What is this about him leaving? I am confused—I thought you resented his intrusion into your life. Has he somehow threatened you?"

"Oh, Mrs. Hawking, that is the worst of it—he thinks that by leaving he will protect me. I cannot endure the thought of never seeing him again. He told me that I would come to accept him against my will, and he is right."

Mrs. Hawking's eyes softened with understanding. "He has captured your heart."

"Yes." Jillian closed her eyes, summoning all her strength. "I . . . I love him."

"Does he love you in return?"

Jillian swayed. "No. At least, I don't think so, even

though I am so besotted that I manage to read romantic intent into his most innocent actions."

"Such as?" Mrs. Hawking prompted.

"He kissed me, once. And brought a gown, a beautiful gown, for me to wear. But I pulled away from him, and I've never worn the gown. He hasn't kissed me again, or asked about the gown—and now he wants to leave."

She kept coming back to that. Cameron, gone. Something dark and empty opened within and threatened to grow until it swallowed her.

"My dear girl, men are exceptionally thick-headed when it comes to understanding females. You are a rather . . . restrained woman. He might be as unsure of you as you are of him."

I hope I will not find you here. . . .

"Could he be testing you?" Mrs. Hawking continued. "Men are notoriously demanding of themselves. Exceptional men require women capable of facing many challenges."

"He tests me all the time," Jillian whispered. "He makes me question everything I have always believed. He makes me look at my life in a new way, and I'm not at all sure I like what I see. It's as though I have lived with blinders, Mrs. Hawking, seeing only those things that will not frighten me and conveniently pretending the harsh realities do not exist."

"What a villain!" Mrs. Hawking remarked with a smile. "He makes you feel alive. Your mother would have loved to see this day."

Jillian was reminded that Mrs. Hawking and her mother had been acquainted in London, and it brought back all of Jillian's resolutions. Never love anyone. Never reveal your weaknesses. Never show anyone you care.

She could still remember those long-ago days following her mother's murder as if they'd just happened. Kneeling there in front of Mrs. Hawking's chair, she became for a fleeting moment that grief-sodden little girl, looking to a father too overwhelmed by his own loss to offer comfort and reassurance.

Everything had screeched to a halt: her schooling, the visits with friends, the gentle cuddles and storytelling before bed. There had been no one to hear her outpouring of guilt over begging her mother to take them both to the forbidden pleasure of a play being staged in an unsavory section of town. There'd been no one to absolve her for running home, hiding beneath the bed, while her mother's life's blood ran red in a London ditch.

Her father had immersed himself in his work. But a six-year-old girl had no work, and left alone to fend for herself she'd come to realize that if she never let herself love again, she would never find her world ripped out from under her. If she stayed quietly within her empty, echoing house, nothing awful would happen to her. The lessons she'd learned as a child had formed her as a woman.

Cameron was leaving. Whether she sent him away tonight, or whether she agreed to carry out his plan, he meant to go. Soon.

Loving Cameron, opening her heart even wider, would only expose her to a lifetime of emptiness and agony, the very things she'd sworn to avoid.

"I cannot risk it," Jillian whispered. "Even if I manage to convince him to stay a little longer, he has given his word that he will leave once the king is safe. No more than two weeks, Mrs. Hawking, and I will lose him."

"Ah, then that explains his failure to declare himself. Only a rogue would seduce you and leave you to bear the consequences once he's gone. As I said, men can be thick-headed. They take noble stands when soft touches and tender kisses are what's really needed."

Mrs. Hawking's expression shifted, and Jillian suspected she was thinking back to a time that had never been discussed between them. "Believe me, my dear girl, if you allow your fears and doubts to keep you apart from him, *that* is what you will regret for all your life. You will forever savor every moment spent with your beloved, but you will forever regret not summoning the courage to claim what might have been."

"He will hurt me when he leaves."

"Only the dead feel no pain. And pain is far, far sweeter than eternal numbness."

Rose arrived, balancing a tray. Mrs. Hawking moved to the sideboard and began to pour steaming wine into mugs with enviable composure while Jillian wrestled with cautions that had served her well for a lifetime.

"Does your young man enjoy mulled wine?" Mrs. Hawking asked as she handed Jillian a cup.

Jillian could feel Rose's eyes upon her, feel the young maid's curiosity. The old, familiar stab of insecurity led her to imagine Rose thinking, *Who on earth could be courting that old spinster?* She balanced that against the image of Cameron, glorious Cameron, his handsome face bent close to hers, his heart-stopping grin and the tickle of his breath against her skin.

She could picture every inch of him so clearly, but she didn't know so many things about him. She didn't know if he liked spiced wine. She had refused, that first day, to measure even a portion of water for him. "He most often drinks water," she whispered, feeling miserably guilty.

"Excellent for the digestion," Mrs. Hawking noted, concluding their innocuous conversation as Rose curtseyed her way out of the room. She closed the door, leaving Jillian and Mrs. Hawking alone and free to talk meaningfully once more.

"You must decide what to do," said Mrs. Hawking. "From all you have told me, he has left that decision entirely in your hands. It is a rare man who allows his woman such power."

His woman. Jillian Bowen, Cameron's woman. She shivered. "Do you think he would understand, Mrs. Hawking, that if I ask him to stay, I will be offering more to him than my skill at driving a wagon?"

"He may, if he has come to understand your nature. But keep in mind that he is a man, bent upon saving you for your own good. He might desperately want everything you offer but refuse to take it out of some misguided sense of honor and duty. It will be up to you to convince him you are willing to take the risks."

Willing to take risks after a lifetime spent avoiding them. Something very like terror raced through Jillian, and the only thing stronger than the terror was the absolute agony of thinking she might never see Cameron again.

The parlor clock chimed softly, and Jillian almost spilled her wine.

"The time!"

"Why, are you concerned about keeping an appointment, Mistress Bowen?" There was a definite conspiratorial smirk upon Mrs. Hawking's features. "I'd say you have a little while yet, before you have to leave."

On impulse, Jillian bent and brushed a kiss against the older woman's forehead. The gesture warmed something inside Jillian, and brought a pleased, startled expression to her friend's face. She should have made some overture to deepen their friendship years ago, she realized, the way she should have tried winning the villagers' trust instead of trying to fool them into thinking her father was still in charge. Such simple things. And yet she'd been paralyzed by fear, afraid to try anything.

Until Cameron had dared her to try.

Now it was up to her to dare even more.

"Let's enjoy our wine, but I'll watch the time," Jil-

lian said. "I don't want to be late for the most important appointment of my life."

Nobody had risked lighting a fire. The camp seethed
with tension, the only sounds the occasional awkward
shuffling and harsh breaths of men who knew things
had gone wrong. Cameron stepped carefully among
the trees, never certain whether a large dark lump in
his path would prove to be a rock or a man crouching
in the dirt.

"Is that you, Delacorte?" The low whisper could
have come from right in front of him, from behind a
tree, anywhere—but there was no mistaking the au-
thoritative owner of the voice.

"My lord," Cameron acknowledged Lord Harrington's query. Harrington's presence meant matters
were considerably worse than Cameron had feared.

"Over here."

Cameron turned his head at the direction, and
caught a glimpse of someone shifting, a black, velvet-
deep shadow briefly silhouetted against the dark sky.

Cameron marked the place. "Aye. In a moment."
He scanned the men scattered among the trees, unable
to make out any facial features. "Show yourself,
Busko," he said.

A brief, well-satisfied snigger greeted his order.

"Busko." Lord Harrington added his weight to the
command.

"Right here under the fancy milord's nose," Busko
said. "The way most things are that he don't notice."

"What were you doing in the village this morning?"
Cameron asked.

"Went to visit me mum. Feelin' a bit low, I was.
Whyn't you tell Lord Harrington why I had a hankerin'
for one of me mum's rare old poultices?"

Cameron wished he could thrash the man all over
again; he'd do a more thorough job of stifling his
mouth, given another chance, and he wouldn't need

the excuse of defending Jillian's honor to propel his
fists. "Did you have anything to do with Robert's
death?" he ground out.

"Be right stupid of me to kill the man who brings
us the information we need, now wouldn't it?"

"He's right, Delacorte." Lord Harrington absolved
Busko. "I have my own theory as to what happened.
I'd like to discuss it with you. Over here."

Cameron did not ignore the request a second time,
even though he would have preferred launching himself straight at Busko's head and grinding his leering
face into the dirt.

This animosity, this near-overwhelming urge to
throttle the man, puzzled and shamed him. A leader
dealt with the foibles of his underlings—his father had
taught him so in those long-ago days when he'd still
nurtured hope that Cameron would take his place in
a long line of Delacorte men who'd earned their spurs.
Old John Cameron Delacorte—*Sir* John Cameron
Delacorte—had never seemed to be able to grasp that
those days were gone, that knights no longer roamed
the lands, upholding the honor of their king.

No, Sir John Cameron Delacorte, who'd waited
until reaching his mid-fifties before siring his heir, had
gone to his grave railing against the fates for saddling
him with a son who'd chosen peace and prosperity,
who absolutely reveled in nurturing his lands and
seeing to the needs of his people rather than chase
the uncertain glories of service to the king.

Riordan should have been my heir, he'd complained
endlessly, especially during those last days when the
old knight was too frail to leave his bed, when he'd
had no ability to do anything save relive past glories
in his mind. *Riordan knows how to act like a man.*

Riordan—brash, hot-tempered Riordan—had died
doing exactly what his father admired most. And Cameron found himself here, sucked into the life he'd
never wanted by the actions of his younger brother,

risking his life and the lives of those he held dear, for the slim chance of saving the exiled English king. How his father must be chortling from his spot in Hell. Cameron clenched his hands at his sides as he picked his way through the dark lest he whirl about and pummel Busko into a useless lump of flesh.

Why Busko? Because of the man's constant antagonism, and more. When this business was finished and Cameron gone, Busko had the right to remain here, in Bramber, the village of his birth. Busko had pursued Jillian before, and now that he suspected Cameron's feelings for her, the tenant farmer would no doubt take a perverse delight in winning Jillian's love and affection for himself. Busko and Jillian. The very thought made Cameron's skin crawl with revulsion.

"What happened with Robert, my lord?" Cameron asked quietly when he reached Harrington's side.

"Let's go behind this tree."

"Right," Busko shot toward them in a loud whisper. "Wouldn't want those of us what has to carry out your schemes to overhear what you're plotting."

"Shut up, Buskie," muttered one of the other men.

"I'll deal with him," Cameron said and began to turn, but Lord Harrington stopped him.

"Later. For now, I have much to tell you. We've been compromised. Robert's murder proves it."

"Tell me."

"Shortly before you infiltrated your position with the Bowens, Robert had gone to meet with the king and his men in Broad Windsor. By then, Charles had been on the run for four weeks and eluded every trap set for him. I fear he enjoyed tweaking Cromwell's nose so much that it's turned him a bit overconfident. He and his men booked lodgings at the inn. Thank God they took the precaution of using a false name. They weren't there for ten minutes when at least forty parliamentary soldiers marched in, all intending to spend the night at the same inn."

"Someone recognized the king."

Lord Harrington gave a short, unamused laugh. "Not one of Cromwell's illustrious soldiers. The innkeeper himself. Robert said the innkeeper didn't declare his suspicions out loud, but kept sneaking glances the king's way. Robert feared that any moment the innkeeper would point straight at the king and ask, 'Be you Charles Stuart?' They spirited the king out of there."

"Where is he now?"

"Possibly still in Trent. That's where Robert went, at the king's request. He summoned representatives from every group like ours, all brought together for a master strategy session. They mapped out possible escape routes the king might try and explained the measures in place at each location. Regardless of where the king moves next, one of our groups will be in place to move him on to the next stage."

"But chances are slim he'd make his escape from here, if he's established headquarters in Trent." Cameron knew the geography well enough to understand that better and larger seaports than Brighthelmstone lay within easy riding distance of Trent.

"It will be difficult to know whether or not he'll need us," said Lord Harrington. He crossed his arms and turned in a circle, frustration and embarrassment emanating from him. "I must withdraw from the cause. I have been summoned to Cromwell's service, and I dare not refuse in light of Robert's death. I'm moving my family to my northern estate at first light, and then I will go on to London and serve the Lord Protector."

Cameron felt his gut clench. Without Harrington's financial backing, there would be no way to support another go-between. A man could be found—there were plenty of rabid Royalist sympathizers who would consider it a rousing adventure to take messages to and from the king. But few men these days could afford to keep a good horse capable of outrunning Cromwell's soldiers, or take out of pocket the bribe money required to pay for silence and information.

"Through sheer bad luck, as Robert was making his way back home, he came across the same troop of soldiers who'd been at the inn in Broad Windsor. He believed the innkeeper did indeed remark on his suspicions about the king, because it seemed to Robert that patrols had quadrupled, the way they do after the king's been sighted. And Robert also believed that one of the soldiers recognized him as being with the king's party. He feared someone had followed him back here."

"Robert would not have led them to you."

"No. We met secretly, as always. Nonetheless, I suspect that whoever followed Robert reported everything to Fraley. Robert's murder is Fraley's clumsy effort to flush his coconspirators out in the open."

"Aye. Fraley commented to all who had gathered that anyone providing information would earn the Lord Protector's favor." Cameron remembered how Fraley had studied every man in the crowd, including himself, waiting for someone to rise to the bait.

"Believe me, Delacorte, my withdrawal weighs heavily on my soul, but if anyone can understand why I must do so, it is you."

"Aye." Viscount William Harrington had much to lose if his role in the Western Association came to light.

"I have gone to great lengths to cover my venturing out tonight. These things had to be said to you face-to-face, man to man. But I stand here with my ears still echoing with my wife's pleas to bring an end to my participation."

Cameron thought of Jillian, and her brave insistence upon taking part in saving the king. He prayed she had considered his warning and that she would not return for him. The thought of a ring of angry soldiers surrounding Jillian's wagon, with their swords pointed at her delicate throat while someone searched and found Charles Stuart seated alongside her, left Cameron sick to his stomach. He could no longer recall why he'd thought pursuing revenge against Cromwell had seemed important enough to risk the lives of Jillian and Wilton Bowen.

"Well, my lord, since you have withdrawn, you will understand why I refuse to let Mistress Bowen continue to play the role we've chosen for her."

"You refuse . . ." Harrington sputtered. "Good God, Delacorte, we've gone over this a hundred times. It is essential that you continue to be widely seen with the Bowens. Don't you forget who's important in this matter—'tis the king. King of all England, not some aging physician and his spinster daughter."

Cameron had felt the same way, until a few days ago. Now, it stirred an almost overwhelming violence within him to hear Harrington make excuses for saving his own hide but insist upon putting Jillian and her father at risk.

"Long live the king," said Cameron, "but you had better find some way of getting word to him that our plans here have changed."

"Retract that threat," ordered the viscount.

"I made no threat. I merely told you the way things will be."

"Retract!" Harrington bellowed, before regaining his composure. He hissed a low threat of his own. "Say you will carry out our plan, or I'll remove command of this troop from you right this moment and hand it back to Busko."

A blackness having nothing to do with night settled over Cameron. He was back again at his father's bedside, listening to the old man curse him even in the depths of his delirium for Cameron's unwillingness to fight, to deliberately seek out the glory of battle no matter the risk to property or person. And now it was happening again.

He remembered that dark time as his father lay dying, completely oblivious to everyone and everything. Cameron had sat there day and night, the only time he'd spent more than a few minutes in his father's presence without the both of them losing their tempers. In the absence of anger, he'd found regret, and had bargained with the old devil. *I'll try it your way someday if it would make you care for me.*

His father had never acknowledged the bargain. He'd died without regaining consciousness. Cameron didn't know if the old man had ever heard the whispered offer. But God had heard. He did not know if the old man's dying relieved Cameron of his end of the wager in God's eyes.

Well, here was his chance to fulfill his part of the bargain. His father would have taken a sword to the belly before allowing someone to relieve him of command—and all because he'd promised a woman that she could decide whether or not to carry on.

"Busko's welcome to the command," Cameron said. "And you're responsible for any damage caused by the hot-headed fool."

Starlight glinted off Harrington's contemptuous sneer. "You've lost your nerve, or you've fallen for the wench. Either way, you're useless to us. Very well. I will send Quint to find the king and tell him you have jeopardized what has taken us weeks to arrange."

"You are conveniently forgetting your own abandonment," Cameron pointed out.

"Charles will understand. I have a title at stake, man! And besides, I might be able to do our side some good once I'm thick with Cromwell's cronies." He peered at Cameron in the dark, and for a moment he was the fair-minded man Cameron had always known him to be. "Tell me there's something more than lust for a skinny slip of a girl behind your decision, Delacorte."

"I'll return tomorrow night to hand over my maps." Cameron ignored the second chance Harrington had given him. "Your new troop leader will have need of them."

Harrington sighed.

"Quint, get over here," Cameron called. "Lord Harrington has a task for you."

He skirted the camp as he made his way back to the road. At the moment he didn't want to face Busko's sniggering triumph, or hear the disbelieving whispers move through the men. At the moment, he wanted only to sit next to Jillian and know that he'd done his best to keep her safe.

He wondered if she would return for him.

The largest boulder cast long shadows over the road, making it impossible to tell if anyone hid within its shelter. Jillian found herself aiming for the huge, unrevealing rockface with all the eagerness she usually felt upon approaching her home and knowing she was safe in the one place she belonged.

Ridiculous.

And yet her body seemed determined to come to life and wash away the numbness of fear. She felt a hint of perspiration dew her brow despite the cool night breeze. Her heart pounded too quickly, sending the blood surging through her veins. Her breath came in short, quick gasps. She betrayed all the symptoms of a fox trapped in a cage, except it wasn't fear that sent her pulses soaring. No, it was anticipation that rocked through her, making her all too aware of her woman's body and how rarely it had been stirred.

And all because Cameron Smith would soon vault himself into her wagon.

Or would he?

His offer to let her determine whether they would

continue this course plagued her now with a new meaning: He might have been hoping that she would take that opportunity and not make this rendezvous. He might be glad to be rid of her. And besides that, a hundred things could have happened to make him miss this rendezvous. He could have gotten drunk and lost his way. He could have embroiled himself in another fistfight. He could have been caught by Fraley and hauled off to jail.

Her lips moved in a silent prayer, but where just days before she had prayed that God would remove Cameron Smith from her life, she now prayed for his safe return. She knew that if she drove Queenie past that boulder and Cameron failed to slip into the wagon, then outwardly her life would resume its safe, predictable pattern. But she would have been rent apart inside, irrevocably damaged, nevermore content with the safe, quiet progress of the life she'd once sought.

She had fallen in love with the rogue, and it had changed her. Safety and predictability still had a powerful, almost overwhelming allure, but something else tugged at her as well, urging her to venture in search of it. The realization so astounded her that she eased her pull on the reins, and rather than slowing as they neared the boulder, Queenie eagerly picked up her pace. Jillian began to saw back at the reins, worrying *he will think I mean to escape him,* and then she heard the thuds of footfalls along the path and felt the vibration as something, some*one*, gripped hold of the frame outlining the open half-door. Her heartbeat, which had seemed to be pounding at twice its normal rate, speeded even more until all she could hear was its insistent thumping and her own internal plea, *let it please be him.*

"The road is clear behind," he huffed as he kept pace with the wagon. "How fares it ahead?"

"Clear," she managed to say.

With easy, elegant economy of movement, he found purchase on the step and then worked his way onto the bench seat beside her.

That first night when he'd come to her he'd all but overwhelmed her with his physical presence, so large, so warm, so vital that he seemed to absorb everything around him. It was the same now, and yet different, for rather than wanting to cringe away from him she yearned with all her heart to move close, to rest her hand against his breast and assure herself that his heart beat loud and strong, to run her hands over him from head to toe to make sure he was whole and unbroken, but with a lover's need to know rather than a physician's.

She was glad for the clouds scudding across the sky, for the shadows hid the need she felt sure was etched upon her face. And at the same time she wished for a brighter moon, for she would sell her soul to decipher the expression in his eyes as he slanted a sideways look at her.

It seemed . . . it seemed . . . that he looked at her the way a man looks at a woman. It seemed that glorious Cameron Smith found favor with her, Jillian Bowen, a woman who'd spent so many years in seclusion that she'd never learned a woman's arts or developed the social skills to keep him fascinated. She'd maintained such a rigid isolation that not even her father's considerable prestige had drawn suitors. But she could not tell if Cameron's smoldering gaze was a mere trick of the moon, or if her own wanting for him to look upon her with desire made it seem that he did.

"You came back to me." There was a low, exultant possession in his voice that touched something secret and hidden within her.

The sensation frightened her, unlike any fear she'd ever known. This was not the sort of inner clamoring that could be stilled by enclosing herself in her house.

This was an invasion of the soul, awakening feelings that had never been stirred.

She poised on the brink, torn between wanting to plunge across the artificial border she'd erected in her heart and the long-ingrained need to protect herself against such vulnerability. She wished she had more experience with men, with the verbal sparring other women engaged in so easily, for she did not know the right things to say to let him know she was willing to risk everything for him.

"Cameron," she whispered, wishing he might give her some hint of how he would react to the declaration she had to find the strength to make.

He reached toward her, touched her lower lip where it trembled. She felt the heat and power of him surge through her at his touch. "I am sorry you are so frightened. I want you to know . . . tonight I disengaged you and your father from this scheme. I know your presence here means you were willing to continue. But certain developments have made it too dangerous to continue with the plan I'd developed. I've given up command of my troop. After tomorrow, I'll be gone."

The half-fledged hope that had fluttered within her died, crushed by the finality of what he'd done. "Tomorrow," she said, knowing she sounded stupid, but her throat had gone numb from practicing the words that would now never be said between them. "Tomorrow. So soon."

The next three weeks of your life belong to me, he had said. Those first few days had seemed an eternity. Now, she was conscious of every minute slipping by. She'd spent less than a week in his company. She was entitled to two more, but it was not to be.

"You will suffer no lasting consequences."

The promise chilled her. He would soon be gone. He had no intention of staying. That promise that there would be no lasting consequences was a blatant reminder that her silly, womanish stirrings of love, of hoping that he might desire her for herself, were but foolish fancies. She had been briefly useful to Cameron Smith, nothing more, and she'd pleased him this night by returning to him, eagerly proving that she'd grown as amenable as a falcon tamed to its master's hand.

She was filled with self-loathing. How could she have forgotten, even for a minute, that she had been forced to go along with him? How could she have forgotten his warnings that something within her would come to care for him and actually embrace his cause?

She felt a surge of anger at Mrs. Hawking for encouraging her to think along the lines of love. She felt even angrier at herself for falling like some silly simpering miss for the occasional hot glance, a single kiss, the gift of a gown she would never wear, bestowed by a man who had every reason to want her cooperation.

She'd been all atremble at his touch, poised at the brink of revealing some of the feelings raging inside her, but he had been off somewhere in the dark, planning how to cut all ties with her.

She did not even know his real name.

"So, then, after tomorrow night I shall be rid of you and all this intrigue." She clipped her words with the same efficiency she used to slap the reins against Queenie's sides.

"Aye. 'Twill be as if none of this ever happened."

"Good."

She clucked to the mare, even though Queenie needed no encouragement to pick up her pace. Despite her brave facade, Jillian knew she'd just spoken a lie. Nothing would be the same for her, ever again.

13

~~~~~~

Jillian sat at the kitchen table, staring at the plate of uneaten breakfast biscuits. Anxiousness thumped through her with the dull insistence of a headache. She never felt this sense of dread *inside* her house, never, except for this morning, when she'd woken to find Cameron already gone, her father missing from his room.

Much as she yearned to go outside and hunt them down, the anxiety held her in place. She sat trapped into immobility, wanting to go but too weak to stir; despising the need to reassure herself that Cameron was still there, and equally despising the gut-wrenching fear that she'd find out he had indeed left for good.

And so she sat, staring at biscuits, until she heard the light clip-clop and squeal of a small-framed horse pulling a pony trap. Mrs. Podgett must have arrived for her day's chores. It didn't seem possible to Jillian that she'd sat there for half the morning. She couldn't let Mrs. Podgett see her like this, hair uncombed and sloppily dressed. Jillian gained her feet and was half-way to the hall when a sharp rapping at the door stopped her. Mrs. Podgett would not knock.

She peeked through the kitchen window before going to the door, and then almost could not reach the door quickly enough. Mrs. Hawking, come to visit!

She had never done so before. Jillian threw open the door and wished that the indrawn whoosh of air would somehow push Mrs. Hawking straight into Jillian's arms, for she felt in dire need of a comforting embrace and did not know how to get one.

"Mrs. Hawking."

"Mistress Bowen."

"Won't you come in?"

"I will."

Jillian closed the door and then turned to watch as Mrs. Hawking swept her gaze over the room. Just as Cameron had, she seemed a bit taken aback at the amount of goods Jillian had crammed into the room's confines. "I see you have kept many of your mother's things."

"All of them."

"Does doing so give you the sense that she is somehow still with you?"

"No," Jillian whispered. "I know she is gone. . . . I did not take care of her, and I have vowed to care for her things, always."

"Oh, my dear girl, your mother would never hold you to such a bargain." Mrs. Hawking curved an arm around Jillian's shoulder and gave her a quick hug. "I worried about you so much all night, wondering how it went with you and your young man. I had to drive myself out here this morning for reassurance."

Last night. Jillian shivered, remembering how Cameron had announced he'd planned Jillian right out of his life and how she'd pretended to be pleased. "I've been revealed as a coward," she said. "I tucked my tail between my legs at the first sign of an obstacle."

Mrs. Hawking led her to the table and they sat. "So you retreated behind your reserve again."

"The way a frightened little squirrel darts into a hollow tree. And I . . . I spent some time this morning feeling angry at *you* for encouraging me to think he might love me. He is gone, Mrs. Hawking. I'll never see him again."

"Of course you will."

"No, he is gone."

"I passed him not three hundred yards away from here. He's with your father at the far corner of your garden."

"He's still here?" At once Jillian's hand flew to the tumbling mass of her hair that she had not bothered taming this morning. "I must comb my hair, and—"

Mrs. Hawking reached for a small decorative glass adorning a sidetable. She pressed the glass into Jillian's hand. "You look just fine, Mistress Bowen. See for yourself."

Look at herself in a mirror, in front of another person? Jillian gave the glass a perfunctory glance, and then her hand tightened around the glass, and she looked again.

She touched her cheek. Her skin bloomed with a freshness and color she'd never noticed. Her eyes snapped and sparkled with the surging excitement that had greeted Mrs. Hawking's announcement that Cameron was still here. Her hair, that wild cloud of curls, shone with softness, as if it intended to tempt Cameron to run his fingers through and hold her captive while he claimed a deep, drugging kiss.

"You look very pretty," Mrs. Hawking said. "Nothing suits a woman more than the anticipation of romance."

Jillian couldn't help it—she giggled. It was a low, unusual sound that she felt obliged to apologize for making. "I'm sorry, Mrs. Hawking. I'm not laughing at what you said. I don't know what's come over me. I never giggle."

"Well, maybe it's past time you've begun. I enjoy a good giggle myself every now and again."

"You do?"

"Oh, yes. And I must insist you do so in the future.

There's no need for a woman to act like a simpering simpleton, but it is quite nice if you can giggle and flirt and provoke your beloved into mindless passion every once in a while."

Jillian stared into the glass again. She never looked at herself in a glass for longer than it took to check that every hair was in place and that an appropriately serious aspect was plastered over her features.

The aspect that looked back at her now—eyes soft and dreaming, and lips already quirking with the need to giggle—just might be capable of sparking a little mindless passion.

"I'll leave now," said Mrs. Hawking. "Unless you would like me to help you dress."

"I need only brush this off and shake out the wrinkles." Jillian ran her hand down her familiar rusty red wool. It felt rough and scratchy against her fingers.

"Seems to me I remember hearing something about a gown of golden silk that the young man you're trying to capture brought home for you to wear."

Jillian—out to capture Cameron. After he'd already taken her captive, and in doing so had led her to unbind her hair, let her spirit soar, lift her heart in the search for love. By taking her captive, Cameron had set her free. The notion made her smile. "Thank you," she whispered.

Mrs. Hawking cupped her hand against Jillian's cheek. "Someday we'll have to have a good long talk about men," she said. "You've more important things to do today."

She left. And Jillian went to the medical storage room and hunted for the canvas-wrapped packet that held the dress. It would be a ruined mass of wrinkles. But she couldn't find it. She searched every shelf, peeked behind every bit of furniture in case it had fallen behind. Conceding defeat after lying on the floor and feeling blindly beneath a cabinet but finding nothing but dust, she sat back on her heels while tears pricked at her eyes. He must have taken it away and given it to someone else.

But then her gaze fell upon a muslin shroud hanging from a hook. The muslin had been wrapped with great care around something. Her heart pounding, she looked. Dear, dear Mrs. Podgett must have found the folded dress and pressed it, for it hung there well protected by the muslin with each glorious golden fold shimmering as she revealed it to the light.

Back in her own room, she pulled on the dress, which was a bit overlarge everywhere, a little too long, nothing that her expert needle could not fix. She would tend to it later, after she'd found Cameron and said all the things she should have said the night before.

If she had, would Cameron have spent the night in her bed?

She bunched the extra inches of silk in her hands to keep the skirts from dragging along the floor as she hurried to the kitchen, so light of heart that she scarcely noticed her feet touching the ground. But just before the threshold, she had a pang of doubt. What if she offered him all she had to give—and he declined?

Her heart hammered so violently at the thought that it took longer than usual to prepare herself to leave the house. When she finally emerged, she listened for the muted thunk of shovel striking earth. Mrs. Hawking said she'd seen him in the garden. He meant to leave her today—and he'd chosen to spend his last hours tending to a backbreaking chore, giving heart to the soil so it would nourish Jillian and her father for years to come.

Nurture Cameron, too, if she managed to convince him to stay.

She followed the sound and saw him working near the back wall of the flower patch, where her father had been trying but failing to coax his roses to thrive. Her father was there with Cameron, just as Mrs.

Hawking had said. He hovered close, his head moving back and forth following every swing of Cameron's shovel. She would have to bare her heart before her father. The thought made her hesitate, but only briefly. Cameron would have to believe her if she declared her love for him out loud, in front of a witness.

Cameron. Cameron was . . . magnificent. Despite the early morning chill, he'd removed his shirt and a light sheen of honest sweat gleamed from finely rippled muscles as he dug into the ground and heaved the heavy mud aside. He'd tied his hair back out of the way, and she could see the beginnings of the beard shadowing his cheeks, a dark hint of the finely swirling hairs that crested over his chest. She couldn't help staring at the way the hairs joined together in a thin line and plunged with an arrow's straightness down beyond the waistband of his breeches. She nearly forgot to breathe for a long moment while her body soaked in the sight of him the way drought-parched earth swallowed the rain.

She had to keep him with her. She would shrivel and crumble into dust if she didn't.

"Jillian!" Her father caught sight of her and beckoned for her to join them.

She bunched the silk even more, knowing she'd have to hold it high to avoid ruining it while she crossed the garden. Her hands clenched. Cameron had turned rigid as the handle of his shovel when her father called out to her. He stood looking down into the ditch he'd dug as if he'd rather stare into its muddy depths than meet her in the eye.

Her newfound resolution wilted. Beneath the all-revealing sun, she had to accept the blatant evidence of his disinterest.

Her father, his face wreathed in smiles, motioned to her again. "Come see how young Doctor Smith means to dry out this mucky spot. He can divert the dampness with a trench, Jillian—he says water can be channeled through the earth the way Doctor Harvey says blood flows through the body."

Cameron turned his face toward her. Dark smudges below his eyes told her he had not slept any better than she. But he'd obviously spent the night confirming his resolution to leave rather than dreaming of what could never be. His glance flicked over her, but instead of the appreciative grin she'd hoped he'd flash upon finding her wearing his gift, his lips thinned as if she'd angered him in some way.

"Cameron?" she whispered.

"I have no time for chatter, Jillian. I want to finish this before I go." He turned away and bent to his digging once more, dismissing her even as he confirmed his intention of leaving.

The wind sent a lock of her unbound hair tickling over her neck and into the gap where the too-large bodice bagged away from her. She felt acutely conscious of how she must look just then, brazen and bold, appearing in full light with her hair blowing wild, garbed in shimmering gold silk that had been given to her as a bribe.

She clapped her hands over her mouth to stifle the cry welling in her throat, even though doing so meant dropping the hem against the earth. But then she couldn't run, because the long skirts threatened to trip her, and so she held one side high and bit her teeth into the flesh between the thumb and forefinger of her other hand, hoping that the pain would outweigh the agony spearing through her soul.

"Now why would she run away like that?" she heard her father complain as she stumbled for the sanctuary of her home. "Jillian's been bemoaning this damp corner ever since we moved to this place. I would think she'd be as delighted as I am with what you've accomplished, young doctor."

"Another bucket?" Martin asked doubtfully.

"Another." Cameron gritted his teeth and closed

his eyes as Martin drenched him with water still icy from the well.

"I'm not at all certain that this is good for you," said Doctor Bowen as Cameron motioned to Martin to prepare another bucket. "Your flesh has gone as pale and pebbled as the skin on a freshly plucked chicken."

Aye, and his teeth were chattering so hard that he'd be lucky to survive this without cracking one or two of them. "I work up such a sweat while digging I don't notice the cold at all," Cameron lied. "Another bucket, Martin."

"Last time I saw lips so blue, 'twas on a corpse," Martin muttered as he doused Cameron once more.

If only, Cameron thought. If only his whole body, his heart and soul, were as unfeeling as a dead husk.

He should have left the Bowens hours ago. He should have packed his maps last night and struck straight back to the camp under cover of darkness. He could have spent this entire day helping Busko develop new tactics, a new plan for moving the king through to Brighthelmstone. Instead, he'd dabbled in the mud and listened with gritted-teeth fascination to Doctor Bowen's theories about the workings of the male reproductive system, a subject the old man felt should be discussed only in Jillian's absence.

Cameron wondered what Jillian's father would have done if he'd known that the whole time they worked, Cameron's all-too-demanding reproductive urges were tormenting him with thoughts of ravishing the physician's daughter. All the while Cameron wrestled with the knowledge he should be leaving while his heart clamored, his soul demanded, one more glimpse of her. Schoolboys did such things, lurking about and waiting for a glimpse of their little loves. Not desperate highwayman spies who ought to be off developing alternate escape plans for fugitive kings.

A man could grow to love this quiet English coun-

tryside, with its gentle breezes still carrying a hint of
the sea's freshness but far enough away that it need
not suffer the harshest chills. A man who but recently
thought his life loomed endless and empty could lose
track of the time when his mind was occupied with
the surprisingly fascinating study of medicine. A man
who'd lost his home could feel he'd found a new and
better one in a place where every villager's eyes sparkled with welcome, where his hours were occupied
with an art that merited respect, where a woman like
Jillian Bowen rode at his side day or night.

His heart had lurched at seeing her wear his gift.
Her hair, whipping free in the wind, had set his skin
to tingling with a craving to feel those silken tresses
stroking against him like the flutter of an angel's wing.

It had been the hardest thing he'd ever done to turn
away and stare into the muddy trench he'd dug and
wish he could crawl inside rather than hurt her as he
knew his pretended indifference did.

She had stood there with love trembling from her
lips and shimmering from every inch of her, so inexpe-
rienced and innocent that she had not realized how
she betrayed her vulnerability. She could not know
that in appearing to scorn her, he'd given her the
greatest gift he had to offer.

She would hate him for all the rest of her days. She
would not pine when he left; she would relish the sight
of his back as he walked away. She would not know,
she must not know, that when he left her, he would
be leaving his heart behind.

"One more bucket," he said, and braced himself for
the chill that did not cool the fever in his blood.

Mrs. Podgett called them to dinner.

"I'm not hungry," Cameron said immediately. "You
go on, Doctor Bowen."

"Nonsense. You dry yourself off and come to the
table with me. All that digging. Bound to leave a great
gaping hole in your belly."

If only, Cameron thought again. If only that were the reason for the emptiness inside. "I know you eat informally in the kitchen, but these clothes are ruined and my others are too rank to wear to dinner."

"I'll lend you some breeches and a shirt," said Martin.

"I couldn't."

"Oh, 'tis no trouble." Martin shot him a wicked grin, showing a mischievous side Cameron had never suspected.

Martin's shirt would not button over his chest, and the breeches skimmed the lower edges of his calves, making him look as ridiculous as he felt, but he had no excuse for failing to eat his meal with the Bowens.

Jillian sat at the table. Cameron felt a surge of pride in her strength—it would have been so easy for her to remain in her room until he'd gone. She had changed garments. No more golden, shimmering silk, but her staid old rusty red wool. She'd tamed her hair into its usual knot at the back of her neck. Save for the fact that her skin had turned pale as porcelain, she betrayed none of the hurt he knew he had caused her.

She held herself, always, with a straight-spined dignity and a confidence in purpose that increasingly held him in thrall. She maintained, always, a serene expression that revealed nothing of what she thought. Perhaps her very serenity had something to do with the failure of so many to recognize the true beauty that she possessed. No fashionable pouting lips, no eyes quick to glitter with manipulative tears—Jillian's was a calm beauty born of strength and intelligence. Beauty a man could savor, and revel in knowing that it was the outward manifestation of a proud spirit and not a mere pretty dressing for an empty mind and soul.

"We have had the most interesting day, Jillian," said Doctor Bowen. "Young Doctor Smith and I had quite the rousing discourse on the . . . oh, dear. Never mind." He lowered his head and devoted his full attention to shoveling beans from his plate into his mouth.

"Studying, young doctor?" Mrs. Podgett cast a questioning glance at Cameron's still-wet hair, and at the poor fit of the clothes he'd borrowed from Martin.

"Matters of . . . of the human heart," Doctor Bowen shouted, then made an elaborate wink in Cameron's direction.

Jillian gave a very unladylike snort.

The sound lifted Cameron's spirits a little—he'd not crushed her completely.

"I suppose you and Doctor Smith will have to devote hours and hours to that subject before he masters it," Jillian said.

"Oh, I hope not." Doctor Bowen frowned at her. "I have plans for this afternoon. I am most anxious to watch the water drain into that ditch Cameron dug."

"Sounds right boring to me," Mrs. Podgett said, plopping a custard down on the table. "What will you be doing today, Mistress Bowen—going along with your father to watch muck seep into a trough?"

"I believe I'll rest in my room for the rest of the day." Jillian wiped her lips. "I may ride into the village tonight to visit with Mrs. Hawking."

"It's good to see you going out and about on pleasure for a change, mistress. But do take your father or young doctor," Mrs. Podgett urged. "No woman's safe, not since that poor fellow showed up dead the other day. Too dangerous by far to go out alone."

"I'll go with you, mistress," Cameron said, his heart commencing a heavy thump at the idea of riding out alone once more with Jillian.

"I seem to remember you telling me you had other, very firm plans for this night."

"Aye. Riding along with you will get me to my destination all the quicker."

Jillian glowered at him. "Then you must come, too,

Papa. You would be interested in a visit with Mrs. Hawking, wouldn't you?"

She didn't want to take that final ride with him alone. Cameron could not blame her. But as disappointment rocked through him, he realized he'd seized on the thought of spending one last hour alone in the wagon with her. For what, he could not say. He did not dare tell her the truth about his feelings for her, which left only the impossible: Jillian, in his arms, yielding and loving and healing the wounds no one but she knew existed.

Her eyes met his for the space of a heartbeat. Not enough to read into her soul, but enough to sense her vulnerability. She radiated an incredible, aching sadness that plucked an echoing chord at his core. He looked down at the beans congealing on his plate, forcing himself to concentrate there so he could not act on his impulse to shout aloud that he'd meant none of this cold indifference.

"We will ride into town together," Jillian prompted her father.

"We will ride—" Doctor Bowen began.

"The ditch, sir," Cameron interrupted. "You've been telling me all day how you're looking forward to reclaiming that ground for your roses."

"My roses!" Doctor Bowen straightened and cast a hopeful look at Jillian. "You would not mind if I stayed here, Jilly, would you? Just this once?"

She softened at her father's barely contained exuberance. "No, Papa," she whispered. "You stay here and plan your new rose garden."

Cameron exulted. He would have his hour. Even if he did nothing more than sit next to her, absorbing her scent and committing every line of her face to his memory, he had his hour.

"Well, then, eat hearty, the both of you," said Doctor Bowen, showing a good example by loading his fork with a towering portion of beans. "You don't want to be hungry when you and young doctor ride into town."

"That's very wise advice, Papa." She pried a sliver of meat free from its gravy and brought it to her lips, but set it back down without tasting. "Appetites can be so troublesome, and indulging them can lead to nothing but distress."

14

The light coming through the window altered, shifting from yellow-gold to gray, until Cameron could barely see the faint traces on his maps that indicated roads and byways. His eyes burned with fatigue. He hunched lower, squinting at the maps, but had to admit that after hours of futile studying, he still could find no miraculous route that would lead Charles Stuart to safety.

He leaned back against the wall with a defeated sigh. Well, it was Busko's worry now. Perhaps the tenant farmer had a better eye for terrain than Cameron. Perhaps another nobleman had come forward to fill the place vacated by Viscount Harrington.

Perhaps cows would sprout wings, and Jillian Bowen would burst into this room, demanding Cameron make love to her before he left her forever.

He swallowed a bitter laugh, and then almost choked when the door to his room did indeed swing open to frame Jillian.

He would always remember her standing in a frame, he realized. She was always on the inside, looking out through a window, a door. He'd never noticed her stepping out onto a stoop to judge the day's weather, or darting out to the garden to pluck a few flowers for the vials and vases crowding her tabletops.

"What am I to tell my father when you don't come

back home with me?" Jillian demanded. "And the
people in the village when they ask after you? You
and all your planning, have you given a single thought
to what we . . ."

Her voice trailed away at the sight of his maps
spread all about. Notes bearing his distinctive, slashing
writing. Arrows indicating possible escape routes.
More arrows and dotted lines mapping out impossible
escape routes.

"Those maps have been here all this time."

He nodded. "If Fraley had decided to search your
house and happened to find these, you and your father
would have been branded as monarchist traitors."

She paled, but said nothing as he rolled the maps
and stuffed them into his pouch. She had to understand now that he had not exaggerated the danger his
presence placed her in. He couldn't help nurturing a
tiny spark of hope that this understanding would lead
her to forgive him someday. Not that he would ever
know.

"How am I to explain your sudden absence?" she
asked after a while.

He'd thought long and hard about the best excuse
she could use. He prayed she might accept the one
he'd selected. "Tell them I've run off."

"Run off?"

"Apprentices sometimes do."

"Everyone speaks badly of apprentices who desert
their masters. I can tell everyone that you were called
back home to tend to an emergency."

"I don't have a home." He felt a queer thickening
in his throat to think that she would rather use an
excuse that reflected well on him, instead of badly.
"Tell everyone I've run off," he repeated. "In great
haste, saying nothing to your father. I've prepared a
note for you to show anyone who asks. I selected the
words with great care." He pulled from his pocket a

rectangle of paper that he'd torn from the edge of a map.

It would be easier to hand it over to her and let her read it for herself, but he knew he could not take that cowardly way out. He had to read it aloud, had to sit there and not flinch or attempt to deflect the outrage she would have every right to heap upon him.

He cleared his throat but the ache gripping it tight did not ease. " 'I cannot face Doctor Bowen after last night. Nor am I free to make things right. I am sorry, Jillian. Sincerely, Cameron Smith.' "

"An apology to me?" She accepted the note from him and bent over it. It was harder than he'd expected to watch her wrestling with the puzzle, attempting to figure out why he was so adamant about the words he'd chosen. Horror dawned as she comprehended. "Anyone reading this will think . . ."

"Will think I took advantage of a naive female and ran away before your father held me to account for ruining you, before you made demands I was unwilling or unable to meet. There is no man alive who will question you further after reading this."

She pressed her hand against the door frame for balance, and it took all Cameron's strength to remain seated rather than leap up and grab her into his arms and tell her he would never willingly humiliate her in this way.

"I won't do it," she said.

"Think it over. You will come to the same conclusion I've reached. My support of the king could come to light one day, and by association, you will be put under suspicion. Nobody will hold you to blame if it seems you were an unwitting dupe, someone who fell for the charms of a practiced seducer."

"Is that all it ever was?" she whispered, almost to herself. She set her hand atop the pouch where he'd folded away his maps. "Plans and more plans and yet more plans, topped with contingency plans. Was seducing me until I cooperated high on all of those lists?"

He could not deny her accusation without admitting his cold rejection was a mere diversionary ploy. Nor could he manage to lie and say: Yes, that kiss I claimed, the pain tearing through me now, are false. He had compromised many things in his life, but he refused to make a mockery of the love that gripped his soul.

"You are an intelligent woman, Jillian. What do you think?"

Intelligent, yes, but heartbreakingly uncertain of the strength and beauty that called to him even now. He watched as tears welled in her eyes, and admired the strength of will that allowed her to conquer them without shedding a single one.

"I will never forgive you for that," she said.

"Nor should you. Your reputation will be—"

She silenced him with an impatient wave of her hand, as if the destruction of her good name was a matter too inconsequential to consider. "You made me believe that someone might value my intelligence. And yet you never thought me better than feeble-minded, and worse, I behaved as though that were true. You had only to appeal to my intelligence to gain my cooperation, Cameron. You did not have to create false illusions and then destroy them for me."

She stunned him into speechlessness. He had never considered that his evasions would cause her to lose even more faith in herself. He had truly harmed her, in so many ways. She left him standing there with his mouth agape, feeling himself to be the one lacking sense.

His hand curved around the neck of his pouch. The maps, the notes, rustled in protest, the only remaining evidence of an obsession that in that very moment vanished like vampires were said to do at dawn. Revulsion churned through him, for what he had let his life become, for how he had let his obsession taint the lives of others.

He had done many things in his life that he was not proud to claim, but he had never before been ashamed of himself.

She could do this, Jillian told herself. She could manage this one final ride with Cameron Smith, and she could watch him slip off her wagon, and be glad to be rid of him.

She could do it. She could.

She thought to ask her father to accompany them after all, to provide some sort of buffer between herself and Cameron Smith, but Papa was still entranced by the garden pattern Cameron had fashioned for him using threads and a notched board. Cameron had also raided her herb bins and provided her father with dried rose petals in varying hues. The petals just fit in the squares formed by the threads, with each petal representing a different sort of rosebush. Wilton Bowen, esteemed Doctor of Surgery, noted colleague of the Royal College of Physicians, sat before the fire, shifting dried rose petals from square to square as he planned the rose garden he might not have the memory to plant come spring.

That spring would surely come, no matter how dark and frozen this winter without Cameron turned out to be.

"Ready?" Cameron asked. "The mare's been harnessed."

She nodded, and watched while he stuffed his pouch into his belt and folded his cloak securely around the small bundle he'd made of his extra garments, his shaving tools. Once the black packet was tucked under his arm, there was no evidence to prove Cameron Smith had ever lived in her home. It caused a pang to see how little impact he'd made on this space. The wood, the plastered walls, the furniture—nothing bore his imprint. She supposed that outwardly she might appear unmarked as well. Inside was a different matter.

He opened the door and held it for her. She knew a moment's panic. She'd been in such a muddle, trying to come to grips with Cameron's leaving, that she'd forgotten to prepare herself for walking out of the house. She required a moment to summon her courage.

"Aren't you going to say anything to my father?"

His jaw tightened. She felt, with a sickening lurch, that it would be harder for him to take his leave of her father than it was for him to say good-bye to her.

"I could not make him understand."

"Nor will I be able to," she countered.

"But he will have you, Jillian, as he always has, to smooth things over. And you will have him." He shot a glance toward Wilton Bowen, a glance laced with longing and affection. "I daresay he will forget all about me in no time."

The hurt vibrated from him, and she felt an inexplicable pang of sadness. Cameron envied her relationship with her father. Even though Wilton Bowen was but a wreck of the physician and scholar he'd once been, Cameron had come to know the man within, perhaps even to love him, just a little.

He stood back while she climbed into the wagon, the way he had every time since she'd lashed into him for trying to make her grow accustomed to a courtesy she could not expect to enjoy for long. She had only herself to blame for the regret that niggled her. Just this once, she would have liked to feel his strong hands wrap around her waist and the lean power of him as he lifted her onto her seat.

"What about Martin?" she asked. "Won't he be going with you?"

"He'll stay for a time."

"To make sure I don't have a change of heart and report you to the authorities?"

"No, Jillian. To keep watch over you, in case of trouble."

He swung easily into his own seat, and settled down precisely far enough away to avoid touching her.

The reins felt slippery in her hands. She realized her palms were sweating the way they sometimes did when she'd been away from the house too long.

"Up with you, Queenie," she cried, and slapped the reins against the mare's back. Queenie bore into her traces, and Jillian surreptitiously wiped her hands against her skirts.

The twilight gloom deepened. The soft lamplight emanating from the house's windows faded behind them. The air settled around them, damp and promising fog. The heaviness in the air held in the sound of Queenie's movements so that hooves striking stone and hard-packed earth seemed to ring out, impossibly loud. It felt . . . it felt like that first night, Jillian realized, when Cameron had swooped in out of the dark and changed her life forever. The air, too heavy. The trees, too still. The silence, too deep so that the sound of her heart threatened to overpower the magnified pounding of Queenie's hooves.

"Something is wrong," she said. "I think . . . we are being watched."

Cameron looked askance at her, but did not mock her fears. She felt a little thrill of pride in knowing he valued her instincts. And then she grew angry with herself once more. She was doing it again, taking joy in the tiny crumbs he threw her way, even as she was carrying him out of her life.

"Leavetaking," he said eventually. "It can sharpen the edge of tension."

She understood *that* well enough. Her whole being still quivered with the need to deny that these uncomfortable moments would be the last she ever had with him. She wanted to cry out and protest that the memories she'd amassed were too few to enrich the rest of her life. But those tensions had nothing to do with the danger she felt swirling about them, as clearly as the first fingers of fog bleeding from the ground in curling wisps.

"Oh, for a slinking rebel, you have uncommonly poor instincts! On the night you . . . when you arrived, I knew, I sensed, that someone was out there in the dark, waiting for me. I feel that sensation again now."

"Well, I am right here beside you, Jillian."

"Not for very long."

"No. Not for very long."

Her breath grated harsh against her ears, and she hated it, she wanted the noise gone from her ears so she could concentrate instead on the rich timbre of Cameron's voice saying these final words to her. She wondered if she tried apurpose to memorize the sound, whether she could. She could not remember her mother's voice, save for snatches of lullabies that came to her in good dreams, the anguished screams that echoed through the bad. *Run, Jilly, run home!* Soon, too, Cameron's voice would be lost in the void of her past.

"You will find happiness, Jillian," he said.

"I will," she vowed rashly. "I will sing and dance and make so merry that people will wonder how I've managed to keep myself quiet for so long."

He laughed, low and soft, not at all offensive. "That would be something to see."

You could see it, Cameron, she wanted to say. *I would come to life for you.*

"I, too, hope you will find whatever it is you seek," she said at length.

"Oh, I found it, Jillian. Held the promise of happiness within my hands, but had to cast it aside before I destroyed it."

Her traitorous heart leaped with delight. He was

talking about her—about *them*. She knew it. She could feel it in her core.

But Cameron stared straight ahead, as if the view framed between Queenie's ears was the most compelling sight he'd ever seen.

She took herself sternly in hand. She could get through this. Less than an hour and he would be gone from the wagon, gone from her life, forever. All these premonitions of disaster, this pathetic yearning to read meaning into his most innocuous comments, had to stem from the tension of the situation.

She lost herself in the clopping thud of Queenie's hooves, trying not to mark the distance as the road rolled beneath the wagon. She tried not to notice the brightening of the stars, for each infinitesimal increase in their light meant the unstoppable passing of this final hour with Cameron.

It did not matter that she ignored the time, the distance. All too soon the forest thinned, heralding their imminent approach to the collection of boulders. Within minutes, Cameron would leave. Queenie, already becoming accustomed to a routine that would now be discontinued, slowed her pace as they approached the grouping of huge rocks.

She felt Cameron stir as he recognized the same. She had one more moment, one breath's worth of words, to end things with him.

"Will you tell me your name?" she whispered.

She thought for a moment that he might. He fixed a long, brooding look at her, and she would swear that his hand reached out in the dark and came very close to brushing her face.

"I cannot," he said. "Good-bye, Jillian. Martin will keep watch over you for as long as you wish him to stay."

And then he was gone. Just a soft click as the half-door swung shut behind him, and the dull thump of his boots hitting the road.

She didn't want to look. She told herself she
wouldn't look even as she twisted in her seat and
craned her neck around the high wall, searching
through the dark for a last glimpse of his form. She
found him. So tall, so elegant in motion, she could not
look away until he disappeared behind the boulders.
She tried to force herself to believe that, for the moment at least, he was safe.

She closed her eyes, burning the imprint of him into
her memory. She would never see him in the flesh
again.

The agony welled, strong and hot. Such blinding
pain should obliterate the nagging sense of dread that
seemed determined to pluck at her nerves.

But it didn't.

Cameron would never again discount Jillian's
premonitions.

He'd stood in the shadow of the boulder for longer
than he should have, watching her wagon disappear
down the road. And then he pushed away from the
stone. She was gone.

He'd barely entered the clearing behind the boulders when he heard the chuffing of a horse, the jin-
gling of tack. Someone was riding among the trees,
and not worrying about being heard. Not one of his
men—they all knew better.

He froze, knowing he'd lost the protection of the
boulders' shadows. He cursed the moon, which each
night had spread its width a little more and was now
near half, a shining beacon on this dark night. Light
bathed the area, pinpointing him in the clearing with
as much clarity as if he'd stepped out onto a gallows
in front of a crowd of thousands.

The unseen rider caught sight of him. "You there!
Halt!"

Cameron tensed. He could run. But a man on horse-
back would run him down in no time. He could stand

and try to brazen it out, but if the challenger recognized him, Jillian would be implicated. Damn the fates!

He dodged back behind the boulder. He felt a pang of longing for the small Italian *scoppietti* he'd once owned, but he'd given it to Riordan when his brother went off to join the king. None of Riordan's effects had been returned, nor had Cameron expected to see his firearm again. The Royalists suffered a chronic shortage of armaments—someone had no doubt confiscated Cameron's firearm the moment Riordan fell to the ground.

And it was too late to regret abandoning his sword. He'd been reluctant to use it when making the initial contact with the Bowens, and had never felt right about wearing it in front of them afterward. He carried only a knife, not his weapon of choice, for employing it was a bloody, messy business that posed as much risk to himself as to his attacker.

The challenger burst from the woods. Muttering dire insults against his assailant's parentage, Cameron clambered to the top of the boulder. Perhaps he could leap down onto the man's back and knock him from the saddle, make an escape before the man caught a glimpse of his face. It could work. He crouched, poised to leap, when the man reined his horse to a plunging, snorting stop and gaped up at Cameron as if he were a dead man come to life.

"Good God, 'tis Charles Stuart!" The attacking lout stared upward, stupefied, at Cameron's face and form looming over him.

The likelihood of convincing this lout that Cameron was nothing more than an innocent doctor's apprentice seemed rather dim. Besides, there seemed little point in doing so when he wanted nothing more than to disassociate himself from the Bowens. So much for soldiers coming to believe Charles Stuart was only

Cameron Smith—this time Cameron Smith would be
Charles Stuart.

"Then bow down before me!" he roared, and
launched himself straight at the man's shoulders. They
both tumbled to the ground, but the idiot under attack
had not had enough foresight to drop the reins, and
so his frightened mount whinnied and stomped in a
panicked effort to escape the men rolling and grunting
beneath its hooves. It proved unsuccessful. The soldier
sent a solid, punishing blow to Cameron's midsection.
The horse's hoof glanced off his forearm and thudded
solidly against his ribs. Jillian would have a mass of
bruises to tend, Cameron thought distantly . . .

But Jillian was gone. He'd sent her away. If he got
killed this night, she would never know how much he
regretted what circumstances had forced him to do.

The soldier bucked beneath him and Cameron
smashed a telling blow into the man's face. The soldier
went limp, and the horse bolted free.

Cameron lay there for a moment, breathing hard,
and then winced as the pain seeped into his bones.
He heaved himself away from the unconscious soldier
and sprawled in the leaf-strewn dirt with his arm flung
over his eyes.

He had a choice. He could slip the blade of his
knife between the man's ribs and put an end to the
threat he posed. Or he could let the soldier live, knowing the man had seen his face and might be able to
identify him.

With a sinking heart, Cameron knew he couldn't
kill the man. The soldier had only been performing
his duty. Cameron's own carelessness and pure bad
luck had dropped him at the boulder at the same time
the soldier reconnoitered that stretch of woods. A few
minutes earlier, a few minutes later, and they might
never have met.

He could not summon enough hate to murder a
man he did not know. His father had been right about

him—he lacked the cold-hearted dispassion of a true warrior. But instead of the self-loathing that usually gripped him when confronted with the evidence of his lack of manliness, all he could think was, Doctor Bowen and Jillian would understand.

For these past two years he'd burned for vengeance against anyone associated with the Commonwealth forces that had stolen his birthright. It should have felt particularly sweet to plunge his knife into a man who bore Cromwell's insignia emblazoned on his tunic. Cameron's innards churned with revulsion at the very notion. How could he slip the blade of a knife into the miracle of a human heart? How could he spill blood that coursed through arteries and veins so divinely designed?

He lacked the cold-heartedness for both kidnapping and killing. As Jillian had commented, he was pretty much a washout as a rogue. With all his fumbling about, seeking revenge, he'd finally come to understand what he had been born to do.

Now that it was too late, he'd found his heart's desire as well as his life's work. With Jillian Bowen at his side, he would have made a truly fine doctor.

15

~~~~

Jillian's anxiousness grew, and apparently communicated itself to the mare, for Queenie tossed her head, fighting the bit. *Home*, Jillian promised herself. She could not ride blithely into Bramber while her hands shook with worry, while her heart pounded in dread. She could not sit in Mrs. Hawking's parlor sipping hot spiced wine as if nothing was amiss.

What she wanted to do made no sense. She wanted to patrol in and out of the woods all night long, to be close if Cameron needed her.

Cameron didn't need her. By now he would be deep in the woods, nearing his secret camp. If he knew she harbored this near-overwhelming desire to protect him, he'd be angry—or extremely amused. Perhaps he'd feel pity, thinking she could not let go of him now that matters were ended between them.

She would just go home. Home. The promise of home always eased her dread, but not now. It could be because two excruciatingly long miles passed before Jillian spotted a likely place to turn. The maneuver was a bit tricky, and took so long that her heart pounded out a rhythm that resonated with the warning *hurry, hurry*.

The panic would ease now, she thought, once Queenie and the wagon were turned and they set off, retracing the path that had led them here. The anxiety always eased, notch by notch, when she knew she was heading home. But the expected relief did not come, and she began suspecting she was not suffering her usual panic that struck from being away from home for too long. Her instincts were urging her to go back to Cameron, whispering that Cameron needed her.

She knew a sudden spurt of envy for all women who knew they were essential to their men. She had locked herself away from such a possibility. She had willingly chosen dull, passionless safety. She had convinced herself that it was too dangerous to become accustomed to the simple pleasure of watching a man she loved walk toward her with a welcoming smile on his face, with his arms outstretched. She had denied herself love that could last a lifetime, fearing it would end too soon. As a result, she'd never known love at all.

Until now.

How foolish she'd been! Oh, if she had only two or three such memories of Cameron, they could sustain her for a lifetime. Mrs. Hawking had been so right about that. She knew now that it hadn't mattered that she'd never tasted love before, for no man other than Cameron Smith could ignite the fire in her soul.

She heard the drumming of hoofbeats, and she hurriedly composed herself, practicing the lie she'd chosen to explain her presence in the woods at this time of night. Within moments, she realized it was a riderless, terrified military horse that galloped straight toward her, with reins trailing dangerously close to its flailing hooves, stirrups flapping against its sides. The horse screamed out in frenzy as it charged past her, as if it meant to warn her that terrible danger lay ahead.

The sight of the frightened beast terrified her more than if it had been Fraley and a veritable army of Commonwealth soldiers. Oh, God, her premonition of danger had been right! She slapped Queenie into a faster pace. She did not think she breathed at all until she reached the boulder where she'd left Cameron.

A man's boot stuck out beyond the edge.

"Dear God, no," she murmured while tears sprang to her eyes. She stopped the wagon and clambered down. Heedless of the vines and thorns ripping at her gown, she was nearly around the back of the boulder when strong arms grabbed her from behind.

"Don't go back there. The sight is not fit for your eyes."

It was Cameron. She'd known from the instant his hands gripped her. His voice washed over her like a balm, soothing her trembling, calming the panic. He was alive, and safe . . . and no doubt responsible for the deathly stillness of the foot lying behind the boulder.

"So, the war has begun for you," she whispered.

He spun her gently without losing hold of her, pulling her so close that she had to lean back a little as she looked up at him.

"I did not kill him, Jillian. I wanted to—but I couldn't."

"Oh, Cameron, I'm glad you didn't, but . . ." She reached up to lightly trace the proud curve of his jaw. "If killing him meant your staying alive, I would plunge the knife into his heart myself."

His arms tightened around her. His head tipped low, and she thought he meant to kiss her, but then he bit off a curse and held her away from him. "Wait here."

He fetched a length of rope from the back of the wagon and then disappeared behind the boulder. She could not just stand there waiting; she got into the wagon and urged Queenie off the trail until the mare and wagon were hidden from any chance passersby. Still no sign of Cameron, but she could hear him dragging something across the leaf-strewn ground, and then long minutes passed when she could hear nothing save the pounding of her heart. Cameron might be killing that man even now, with the sound of her endorsement of such an action ringing in his ears, with a length of her own rope strangling the life from him. Or he might merely have bound the unconscious man and was now dragging him well out of sight.

She didn't care, she realized with surprise. She didn't care what Cameron did, so long as he came back to her.

And he did. He emerged from the shadows, silent as a panther, with a jungle predator's command of its surroundings. He nodded his approval of her moving the wagon. "He saw me, and thought I was Charles Stuart," Cameron said. "I let him believe so. You must know this, for it changes everything."

He had not killed the man, then, or he would not feel it necessary to warn her. Relief flooded her, along with something else. Cameron's holding his rage in restraint seemed like a sweet gift given to her at great cost. She did not know how to acknowledge it.

Her heart sank. And then surged with hope. "But that is the very best thing. When he regains consciousness, he will raise a hue and cry, claiming that he's been attacked by the king. The townsfolk and Fraley know you are not the king. Nobody will blame you for this attack."

But he did not seem to share her sense of relief, for such bleakness washed over him that she had to press her fingers to her lips to keep from crying out. "I allowed my personal feelings to take precedence over my mission," he said. "I have jeopardized everything. It is far worse if the soldiers believe Charles is in the area. They will increase the patrols. It will be impossible for the king to pass this way."

She saw his fist clench at his side, saw him reach for the knife at his belt, and she knew he'd decided the soldier must die after all.

"Cameron . . ." She didn't know why she felt so certain that a cold-blooded killing would weigh hard

on his soul. She just knew, in her woman's heart, that
it would change the essence of him. "Blows to the
head often erase a person's memory of events that
immediately preceded the blow. There's a chance, a
small one admittedly, but a chance that the soldier
will awaken with no memory of how he's gotten himself into such a fix."

He believed her. She could read it in the slight softening of his stance, in the way his hand swung away
from the knife. He trusted her and believed her
enough to put all his faith in her, to risk the destruction of all he had worked for. The realization seemed
to light a flame inside her.

"It will be a long time before he regains his senses.
And even longer before he can free himself from the
restraints I placed upon him. We need not worry
about him working himself loose until dawn at the
earliest."

"Dawn is many hours away, Cameron." For some
reason, confirming that the soldier was securely imprisoned and that she and Cameron were alone, truly
alone, sent her pulse racing.

He sheathed the knife. He flexed his hand and
winced. "I've made a mash of my fists again."

"Let me see," she said. "You might have aggra-
vated the bite and worsened your bruises."

He moved closer to her. She wished he might take
her in his arms as he'd done when first she came there,
but he merely offered her his hand, palm outstretched.
She balanced it within both of hers, feeling its size
and weight and shocked at the wanton urge she felt
to have that hand stroking her skin, pressing her
where she curved, teasing shivers from her most sensitive places.

"You have a gentle touch, Jillian," he murmured.

She trembled, and her fingers closed around his,
with the pad of her thumb rubbing against the calluses.
He shivered at the light caress. His huge body

seemed at once less threatening and more powerful, and she knew the awesome power she possessed as a woman to both bring him to his knees and be so overwhelmed by him that she would never be the same again.

"You have always shied away from touching me," he said, with an added gruffness that told her how her flinching had hurt him.

"You have avoided touching me as well," she whispered. She knew the fluttering in her voice betrayed all the pent-up longing she'd tried so hard to hide. She didn't care. Standing there, holding him bruised and battered, brought home to her so forcefully that the fight with the soldier could have easily gone the other way. She might have returned to this place and found that the still body lying beyond the boulder was Cameron's, and that the soldier had not had an attack of conscience. Cameron could well be dead, and she would never see him again, never even know the truth of who he was, never know the ecstasy of his lips claiming hers.

"Jillian." Her name was a husky groan. And then he pulled her hard against him, wrapped her in his arms, and held her so tight that it ought to have choked the breath from her, but she found herself breathing wonderfully well, with each indrawn rush of air smelling of Cameron and cold clear night.

He pressed her head against his chest and she felt the thundering of his heart beneath her ear while his hand moved with featherlight grace through her hair, loosening it, setting it free to mingle with his own wind-blown tresses. This should have been enough to reassure her that he was fine. His body, resilient, felt hard and strong and solid as the boulder they stood beside. But she wanted more, she wanted to burrow into his flesh while he did the same to her.

She must have made some small sound to betray her hunger, for he made a low moan and managed

somehow to both draw her closer and tip her head
back, baring her neck in a vulnerable arch. If he had
tried doing this that first day, she would have kicked
and clawed and fought her way free. Now, she moved
closer against him and trembled in an agony of ecstasy
when she felt the brush of his bearded cheek against
her jaw, and then the incredible, impossible softness
of his lips against her throat, her neck, tasting her,
branding her.

She was his.

She had always been his, from the very first
moment.

Somehow, despite the awful nature of his coming
to her, her woman's instinct had recognized him as
the one man for her, had been convinced despite the
evidence that he would never hurt her or her father,
never wantonly destroy. Her whole body glowed now
with the joy of finding those deeply held beliefs to be
true. She felt the last vestiges of doubt melt away like
frost beneath the morning sun.

His hands ran down her sides, molding the swelling
of her hips, tracing the shape of her ribs. Without
thinking, she let her hands flutter over the front of
him, unfastening the buttons of his shirt until it gaped
open and gave her access to the broad planes of his
chest. She pressed her forehead against him, inhaling
his scent, relishing the tickle of fine, curling hair
against her eyelids, against her lips.

He lifted her into the wagon, a quick, effortless motion that made nothing of her height and weight. She
wrapped her arms around his neck to help while he
fumbled beneath the seat for the blanket she always
kept there and soon he lowered her upon that thin
woolen cushion. She was open to him, vulnerable, and
he took advantage, loosening her buttons and pushing
her gown away, tugging free the ribbons of her un-
dershift, divesting her of everything until she was
naked for him, her skin bared to the cool autumn

night. She shivered from the sensation; she'd never before bared herself to the wind. He mistook her reaction as being cold, which he soon remedied by shucking his own garments and pressing his heated length against hers.

His lips claimed hers, his hand cupped her breast, and lower, against her hip, she could feel him hard and insistent, waiting to breach her most secret place and claim her as his, forever. She shivered again, thrilled at the notion of being so thoroughly possessed by him, of having him inside her and all over her at the same time. She arched against him with her wordless demands, and returned his kisses, answered his caresses with tentative, demanding touches of her own. His mouth closed over her breast and she cried out at the sensation that surged through her.

The sound inflamed him more and soon his lips were everywhere, his tongue tracing the valley between her breasts, his lips pressing with damp sweetness against the softness of her belly. He murmured her name against her flesh and the vibrations seemed to pass straight through her skin into her inner core, which spun and released a thousand splinters of delight.

She cried out again, in protest, when he lifted himself away from her, and lay there trembling with emptiness and wanting while he loomed over her, her dark and beautiful highwayman. He stared down at her, hunger burning in his eyes while the moon silvered his hair, and she knew he was offering her a choice, to follow where he wanted to take her, or to push him away.

"Cameron," she whispered her surrender. With a low growl of triumph he moved over her, his weight a burden that her body craved. She reveled in the sensation of being crushed beneath him, wanting more, not knowing what she wanted until she felt him throbbing and insistent at her center, and knew she

wanted him inside. With a low moaning cry she arched
to meet him.

"Yes, Jillian, come to me. Come to me so I can
show you how much I love you."

"You . . . you love me?"

"Let me show you."

She expected pain, but never realized it would be
tempered by the sensuous slide of him within her,
never realized that her body would respond with such
liquid delight. She had always felt giving herself to a
man in this way would be the ultimate invasion, the
final abandonment of her individuality to the will of
another. Making love with Cameron was nothing like
that. He was inside her, surrounding her, and yet she,
Jillian Bowen, had never felt more alive, never felt
so strong.

She felt a change in his rhythm, and his glorious
body tensed within her arms. He lifted her hips and
brought her stomach hard against the firm, rippling
muscles of his, and she shattered inside, an explosion
that engulfed him and carried him into the swirling,
joyous void along with her.

She didn't know how long they stayed, wrapped in
each other's embrace, breathing hard, heartbeats gradually subsiding toward normal. Eventually the roaring
inside her dimmed until she could hear the rustle of
dry leaves skittering over the ground, the resigned huff
of Queenie's breathing, the soft sound of the wind
singing through crevices in the boulder. And she lay
there naked and wanton in a highwayman's embrace,
content as she had never before been in all her life.

Cameron held her while his blood cooled. His body,
not yet replete, demanded he take her again while his
mind, gradually regaining its sense, taunted him with
the cold hard truth of what he'd done.

She'd been a virgin. She was gently born, and had
fashioned a life for herself that demanded she behave

with utmost propriety. He had taken her on a wagon bench, fornicating alongside the roadway like a pair of adolescents. He had nothing to offer her to compensate her for what he'd taken. Nothing. No title, no lands, not even the promise of his love ever after, for it would be impossible for him to remain here with her.

And he would do it all again, starting that very moment, if she proved willing.

A low chuckle rumbled through the night, and it took him a moment to recognize it came from him.

"Cam . . . Cameron?"

His laughter died, stifled by his recognizing the chains of uncertainty that still imprisoned her. His Jillian could not yet believe she had the beauty to drive a man senseless. He shifted them so that he lay with his back against the bench, then pulled her on top of him so she could feel for herself what she did to him.

"Ah, Jillian, holding you in my arms like this makes me realize my old father was right."

"Right about what?"

"A man proves his worth by taking action. By claiming what he wants, and to hell with the prickles of his conscience."

"Is that what you truly believe?" She struggled up onto an elbow. Her hair tented over them both, creating an intimate, rose-scented cocoon.

"After the action I've just taken, I feel like a king," he said. She moved slightly and he grinned like a fool at the exquisite sensation of her skin moving over his. "I tell you, Charles Stuart would envy me now, for what we have done."

"But Cameron, if you did not heed those prickles of conscience, you would not be the man I . . . we would never have done what we just did."

His hands gripped her waist, and moved up the delicate curve of her ribs. He pressed her closer to his heart, which hammered with a need to hear what she was saying.

"Your actions toward me and my father were often quite despicable." She hushed his half-hearted attempt at a protest with a quick kiss. "But every moment I could sense the honor and integrity of the man beneath the cold-hearted facade."

"You do not know who I am."

"True, I don't know your real name. I no longer care, because that name belongs to the man who believes he should act without conscience. 'Tis Cameron, the man inside *your* skin, I've fallen in love with."

He crushed her close. With movements that required no thought at all, he rolled her beneath him once more and drove into her hot depths with a thrust born of equal measures of need and triumph. "Say it again," he demanded, when she was his. "Tell me again."

"Cameron." She gave a small breathless moan when he shifted his hips and proved his possession of her. "I love you."

He plunged deeper, and again, and again, until she blossomed from within and filled the emptiness that had left him hungry for all his life.

He would have lain with her all night. Every fiber of his being ached to do so. But he permitted them only another quarter hour before he caught her close for one last, desperate embrace.

"You are in turmoil," she murmured against his shoulder.

"Aye. It grieves me to abandon the king's cause."

"Then don't. Let your actions match the worth of the man inside. Help save the king, Cameron. We can do it together."

"No."

"I don't want to lose you."

"I have to leave, Jillian. I explained why I cannot risk being captured until all my men have made it safely away from here. I swear to you, I will return once the king is safe and when I am sure no suspicion can be attached to you and your father."

"Oh, Cameron." Her laugh ended in a tiny sob; he fancied he felt the wet heat of tears trickle against his chest. "The thought of losing you frightens me more than the thought of being arrested."

Confused, he could only repeat his vow. "I will return to you."

"Don't you see? If you can turn your back on what your heart tells you is the right thing to do, then I will have lost you—the real you. The Cameron I love could not leave me or abandon his king."

Her unerring understanding of his essence humbled him. "Jillian, the risk is great, and it could be for naught. Charles Stuart might never come this way."

"But he might. Do you have faith that those men out in the woods will guide him safely through to the sea?"

"Some faith." After a long pause, he admitted, "Not much."

"You could do it. *We* could do it—together."

He curved his arm around her and drew her as close as he could without squeezing the breath from her, while shudders coursed through him. Jillian believed in him.

"I'll take you home," he said. "And then I'll go back to the camp and see what the men have come up with. If they've managed to develop a good plan, I'll stay out of it."

"What if their plan includes me?" she asked.

"I will help them find another way."

"Could you live with yourself knowing the king came here, needing you, and you'd abandoned a plan that would have saved him, just to keep me safe?"

"The guilt would be mine, and not yours," he admitted. "But I would rather live with guilt than lose you now."

"Then," she said, "we'd better not fail."

16

Cameron took her home. He saw her safe to her room, and though it was the last thing he wanted to do, he left her in her bed, alone, while he went outside to tend to the horse and explain to the confused Martin that he'd changed his mind about leaving the Bowens.

And then he struck out through the back fields. The fog rolled and thickened as he went deep into the woods, taking a careful roundabout course to the camp. He figured he would join the men at the outermost fringe of the group, and as he'd bargained with Jillian, he would keep to himself the information that she wanted to continue helping the cause. With luck, Busko would have developed a new scheme, and she would be completely out of danger.

He met none of Cromwell's soldiers. But he couldn't quell his disquiet when he also failed to encounter any sentries standing guard for the Royalists. He stole to the edge of the camp, completely undetected, and though he searched the entire perimeter, he did not find a single sentry.

Cameron gave up all pretense of stealth and strode into the camp, angry that discipline had eroded so far after only one day under Busko's command. A fire blazed bright in direct violation of all the orders he'd ever given. A handful of men crouched around its flickering flames, more intent upon warming their fog-dampened selves than worrying about Commonwealth soldiers patrolling the area.

Nobody even noticed him until Cameron kicked dirt onto the fire. He would've doused the flames altogether, but shock stopped him when he recognized the first man who looked up at him in protest. Quint. The man Harrington had sent to warn the king there would be a change in plans.

"You can't have found the king and returned already. What happened, Quint?"

Before Quint could answer, a sneering challenge came from behind Cameron's back. "Well, if it ain't the milord what used to be in charge of this troop."

It didn't improve Cameron's spirits to realize that Busko had at least moved with stealthiness. He stiffened, wondering if he'd just exposed himself to a knife blade slipped between his ribs. A moment passed, heavy with Busko's hatred, and then Quint scrambled to his feet.

"I went looking for the king, just as Lord Harrington bid me," Quint said. "But I'd gone no farther than the Western Association camp at Hambledon, when a runner come staggering in. The runner told us he'd been sent by the king to tell us the king had to move from Trent. He's headed *this* way. He's moving sneaky-like, staying away from the better roads, and there ain't no certain way of getting a message to him."

"So the king knows nothing about Harrington's withdrawal of support. And you weren't able to get word to him about the new plan Mr. Busko developed?" A plan, Cameron fervently hoped, that excluded Jillian and her father.

Uncomfortable silence greeted Cameron's question.

Dread curled through Cameron's gut. "You did develop a new plan?"

"We're aiming to make one tonight," Busko said. "You're holding us back."

There was an edge of uncertainty in Busko's voice. The men hunkered around the campfire looked up at Cameron with the mute pleading of sheep who'd been handed into the care of a thick-headed, dull-witted shepherd.

Cameron swore. He'd been stripped of command, and Busko wouldn't relinquish it to him without a fight Cameron had no time or energy to waste upon.

And he didn't care, Cameron realized somewhat distantly. Saving the king was the important thing; it didn't matter who led the charge. Yet another of his father's ingrained truisms that crumbled beneath the harsh light of reality.

"Take these maps, *sir,*" he grated, shoving the pouch into Busko's gut. The lout clutched the pouch against his heart as if it were a shield. Cameron glared around the camp, and one by one the men bent to inspect their boots, or fiddled with their shirt collars, or simply shifted their eyes to avoid meeting his. "I am sure your hawk-eyed sentries have already reported this. I came across a Commonwealth soldier in these woods not three hours ago. He came to a bit of mishap. I daresay that when he's discovered, these woods might be searched more thoroughly."

One of the men made a small whimpering sound. He dashed the dregs from his cup into the fire, then he rose, stretched elaborately, and bolted for the woods like a kicked dog. His thrashing, crashing fight against the underbrush could be heard for many long minutes.

"Aren't you going after that deserter?" Cameron asked mildly.

Busko snapped at him. "Don't have a place for a man like him in *my* troop."

"We got a place for *you,* Mr. Delacorte," Quint offered. "I mean no disrespect to Mr. Busko, but you always was a fair hand with maps and planning and such."

Busko said nothing, tacitly echoing Quint's sentiment.

"I liked that other plan of ourn," Rothermel said with a wistful sigh as he edged closer to Cameron. " 'Twouldn't be nothing simpler than for us to sit here, waiting for the king, and then heaving him into Mistress Bowen's wagon so she could ride him into Brighthelmstone. I liked that plan."

Several of the other men muttered ayes, and Cameron felt his heart sink.

Busko provided no real leadership. The men's spirit had been sapped by Harrington's withdrawal, Cameron's demotion, the recent desertion. Cromwell's soldiers combed the woods, and the king was nowhere to be found. Without some dramatic gesture to pull the small band together, they'd disappear one by one into the shadows of the forest, and if Charles Stuart did indeed find his way here, he'd find naught but the cold empty ashes of a campfire that should have never been lit.

"Our original plan." Cameron fought to force the words through a throat that locked against saying them. "That plan could still work."

Busko's head snapped up, and his features altered for a brief moment into a resentful gratitude. Someone—it sounded like Rothermel—muttered "Thanks be to ye, God."

"There would have to be some changes made," Busko said, no doubt needing to assert his authority.

"Aye." Cameron welcomed the man's insecurity, for it allowed him to offer alternatives which might offer some small protection for Jillian. "You are the leader of this troop, Mr. Busko, so it's up to you to decide whether or not to use my suggestions."

"Aye." The stubborn tilt of Busko's chin wavered a notch.

"For example," Cameron said, "we can't just sit

here waiting for the soldiers to come upon us. Also, since we don't know where the king could be, we'll need to keep a sharper watch than ever for him. Every man should fan out, posting themselves a half mile apart. We have enough men to provide a line of coverage from here to Arundel Hill. Whoever finds the king can spirit him to the Bowens' house, or to those boulders near Scupper's field."

The men began nodding, seeing the wisdom of the idea. A tide of excitement washed out the despair that had gripped them all. They were once more united, loyal Englishmen out to save their king.

"And you'll just be sitting on your milord butt whilst Mistress Bowen rides you back and forth through the woods," Busko said, but though the cutting words were there, the usual razor edge had been blunted.

"Shut up, Buskie," said Quint.

They all looked to Cameron for the quick, curt nod he always used to seal a plan with his approval. He gave it. He'd won them back, every man of them, and it hadn't been because he'd used his strength and sword to cut down his opposition. Busko, for all that he possessed the qualities Cameron's father claimed were the marks of a true leader, had not been able to hold on to his men for more than ten minutes after Cameron reappeared.

Jillian. She had urged him to come back here, to act as his honor demanded and do all he could to save his king. If not for her urging, he would not be savoring this quiet sense of accomplishment right now.

He'd had to put her back at risk to do it, though. His gut roiled. He vowed he would do anything, anything, to minimize the role she would have to play.

The men crouching near his feet shifted by subtle degrees until they surrounded him like a flock of dirt-encrusted, hairy ducklings. His men. His command. His king, given a glimmer of hope because one small woman believed with all her heart in a man she knew only as Cameron Smith. It mattered nothing to her that he had been the first Delacorte heir in three hundred years to fail to earn a knighthood. It mattered nothing to her that Benington Manor had been ripped from him, parceled out to a dozen Commonwealth loyalists, and would most likely never come back to him.

He would tell her his name, Cameron decided, right before he asked her to marry him.

Providing, of course, that they both survived.

Jillian stretched as morning's first shafts of sunlight flooded her bed. She winced at a new tenderness and sense of heavy satisfaction in her body, and then smiled, recalling every moment of how those new feelings had come about. She had been loved by Cameron. Her hand brushed the bare space next to her, and she dared to hope that someday he might lie in that space alongside her, every night.

She would *never* leave the house then—so long as Cameron was inside.

A bird welcomed the dawn with a glorious burst of song that exactly matched the music in Jillian's heart.

She hugged herself, remembering their lingering touches in the wagon as they'd given Queenie her head, trusting the mare to see them home. The kisses, stolen at first by her and then claimed by him. She'd been shameless and demanding and he'd tried so hard to act the gentleman, to no avail, until her skirts had been bunched into a cushion beneath her hips and he'd taken her again right there on the wagon seat. She'd gone wild, with Cameron surging within her, the wagon vibrating them from without.

She smiled to herself, a secret thing, even though nobody could possibly see. It seemed . . . risky . . . to gloat openly and revel in erotic memories, aching for a repeat, plotting ways to make it come about. She

scolded herself. The old Jillian Bowen feared taking
risks, even one so small as daring to hope she had
found love. The new Jillian Bowen, the woman she
had become in Cameron's arms, would risk anything.

An intuitive warning curled through her, urging caution. She was strong because being with Cameron
made her strong, the inner voice warned. Without him,
she was a meek, unobtrusive spinster who spent her
days living a lie and hiding from the world.

She wanted to fight against the voice. She did, but
it hammered inside her with the full force of truth.
She closed her eyes against the agony of knowing she
was not as strong as Cameron thought her to be. Not
as strong as she wanted to be.

But, God willing, she would have a lifetime to learn.

The birdsong ended on a shrill note and the flutter
of departing wings. From the way it sounded, someone
had frightened the bird away. Footsteps pounded up
the drive, with the speed of the truly desperate.

But the footsteps halted, and she heard Martin's
voice, low and menacing, as he challenged the newcomer. She slid from her bed and raced for the
kitchen. Throwing open the door, she saw Martin
grappling with a youth, no more than thirteen or four-
teen years old.

"Martin, no," she called. "He's probably come for
me and my father—"

With a bellow of outrage, Cameron launched himself from between the trees lining the drive and
bowled Martin and the youth down into the dirt.

He'd come home safe to her. She whispered a silent
prayer of thanks even as she lifted the edge of her
nightgown and hurried to the thrashing tangle of male
limbs. "Cameron! Martin! Stop what you're doing at
once and let this boy tell us why he's here."

Martin rolled away, groaning as he clutched his
head. The boy curled into a ball and lay there quiv-
ering like a mistreated puppy expecting another kick.

Cameron raised himself on one elbow and cast an apologetic grimace down toward the frightened stripling he'd been pummeling.

And then he looked up at her. His hair had worked loose from its thong and waved down over his brow. Dark blotches smeared his shirt from where he'd plowed chest-first into the dirt. He looked utterly devilish sprawled there on the ground, utterly appealing. A slow smile broke out as he swept his glance over her from head to toe. She realized from the shadow stretching out in front of her that the rising sun lit her from behind. Sheer male appreciation beamed from Cameron; she had no doubt that her gown had gone transparent.

"I've come home, Jillian," he said.

"Yes." Her throat had gone tight all of a sudden. "Yes, Cameron, you're home."

And she had raced out to meet him without sparing the slightest thought upon preparing herself to leave the house. She caught her breath, waiting for the panic that was sure to ensue. But her pulse remained steady—until she looked again at Cameron. And then it fluttered in a way that sent heat spreading through her lower reaches.

"Let's see what this boy wants," Cameron said. "And get yourself out of that light, Jillian, or Martin's head will be swimming from more than that lad's blow to his head."

A squeaking came from where the boy had his head planted against his knees. Cameron bent his head to listen, and all his lazy sensuality tightened into apprehension.

"His mother's ill—Jillian, fetch your father."

"Of course." She knelt, though, and touched the boy on his shoulder first. "What ails her?"

The youth, wiping angry tears from a face that had made the subtle shift from childhood but not yet firmed into the face of a man, took a huge rasping breath. "Agony of the gut, mistress."

"Here?" Jillian asked, pressing her hand against her lower abdomen, praying it would be anything else.

"Aye, exactly there. Leastwise, it started there. She be writhing right good now, though, and crying that she hurts everywhere."

"How many days has she had the pain?"

"Three, mistress. Tonight . . . last night, late, it went different. She be screaming with it now."

All Jillian's lightheartedness faded beneath the certainty that nothing could be done for the boy's mother, nothing but to dose her with soothing potions. It grieved Jillian to think of the woman enduring one more moment than necessary of an agony so excruciating that some gouged open their bellies, desperate to eradicate the pain.

"We must hurry," she said.

"Aye, please hurry." The boy gave a little sob. "But them soldiers be clogging the road all the way. Stopped me a dozen times, they did, making me state my purpose over and again. My mum—she expected me back by now. She'll be thinking I dawdled."

"We'll get through to her," Cameron promised. "Mistress Bowen knows shortcuts through the woods."

They hurried. Jillian scarcely remembered dressing herself, but she roused her father and had him ready, too, just as Martin led Queenie around to the kitchen. They made a tight fit, all four of them crammed onto the bench seat together. She settled the weeping boy beside her father and Cameron took the place next to her. He'd changed, too, into the spare garments he'd bundled into his cloak when he meant to leave her for good . . . a mere half-day, and her life had changed completely.

This was not how she had dreamed of marking his homecoming. She was bursting with questions about his meeting in the woods, and she knew those matters consumed his mind. And yet, his jaw clenched with determination as he focused on the road ahead.

"Pray we meet no patrols to slow us down," he said.

His brow furrowed with worry and concern for a woman he'd never known. As the wagon lurched into motion, Jillian felt complete in a way totally different from the thrilling ecstasy Cameron had brought to her earlier, so different, and yet just as satisfying.

"I, too, hope we meet no troops. But if we do— Cameron, I'm accustomed to dealing with road patrols. No matter how they goad, please let me handle them."

Cameron shook his head, but not in denial. Rather, in the way of one who finds himself admiring something unexpected.

"You trust me to do this, don't you?" she asked, uncertain whether she sought a confirmation, or the simple pleasure of him articulating his faith in her out loud.

"My father must be screeching through the halls of Hell to hear me say this, but aye, I trust you to get us past the soldiers, Jillian."

"Your father had a low opinion of women?" she guessed.

"No, he had *no* opinion of women. Claimed they were useful for begetting heirs and naught else."

"Surely your mother convinced him otherwise."

"My mother." Cameron tensed, and then relaxed. "She was no more than a child when he took her to wife, and he a near-doddering old man of fifty and five. She died the year after my brother was born. Nobody ever spoke of her again—'twas as though she'd never existed. I've often wondered about her dying. My father had a low tolerance for things that did not fit his idea of usefulness."

She gathered the reins into one fist and slid her free hand along his forearm, where it rested along his thigh, then moved it down further until her fingers twined with his. His hand closed over hers, holding it tight.

Until the first soldiers stopped them.

"Halt!"

"State your purpose."

"Travelers must show a permit issued by Constable Fraley."

Save for one half-swallowed, angry growl of frustration, Cameron honored his word to let Jillian deal with the soldiers.

The soldiers ringed the wagon. One swung a lantern, though by now the sun rode high and thoroughly flooded the wagon. "Good God—look at him. Do you suppose we've found . . . "

"You have stopped Doctor Wilton Bowen," Jillian interrupted the soldier. "We require no permit to travel, as my father and his apprentice are often called out unexpectedly to tend to the sick. We are on our way to an ailing woman right now."

"Bowen. That's all right, then. I heard about that apprentice that looks like the king."

"And look who else they're carrying—it's that little whelp what ran up the lane a bit ago crying he had to fetch the doctor for his mum." One of the soldiers peered intently into the back of the wagon. "There's no problem here. Let them pass."

They'd gone another mile, no more, before they were stopped again. Once more the soldiers circled the wagon. Queenie, unaccustomed to being surrounded by other horses, stamped and whinnied her confusion. One of the soldiers grasped the reins as if he feared the mare would bolt, while his officer demanded that Jillian reveal the contents of her father's medical bag.

Cameron sat rigidly beside her, saying nothing, staring down the trail.

"Why are you delaying us?" Jillian railed at the officer. "A woman is very ill and needs our help."

"One of my men was beaten near senseless last night, mistress. He says 'twas Charles Stuart himself who bludgeoned him with bricks and a great, thick branch of oak."

Cameron's jaw tightened. He had told her what had happened with the soldier, and Jillian knew that the account had been greatly exaggerated. No doubt the soldier had sought to avoid personal humiliation with his tale.

She'd suspected that the increased patrols had stemmed from the soldier being found, but hearing the fight recounted in this enhanced version convinced her as nothing else could that Cameron had been right in warning her of the danger to come. The soldiers simmered with fury, hungry for a chance to retaliate on behalf of their fallen comrade-at-arms.

"Well, my father is certainly not hiding Charles Stuart in his bag of medicinals," she retorted.

"Maybe that's him sittin' right next to you."

"That is Cameron Smith, my father's apprentice. Surely Mr. Fraley has told you about him."

A soldier made an affirmative grunt. "Aye, you're right—up close he doesn't look anything like the poster of Charles Stuart."

"Lift your skirts, mistress," the officer said calmly.

Cameron's icy control threatened to crack then, but Jillian laid a restraining hand against his arm. "I'm assuming you mean to make it possible for you to check beneath the wagon seat, sir."

"Exactly so, mistress."

She angled her legs first to the right, and then to the left, while the soldier plunged his sword into the darkness beneath the seat. He grunted and stabbed with enthusiasm, but when he withdrew his weapon, he'd only succeeded in shredding Jillian's blanket.

"Let them pass," he called.

Two hours had flown, the time it usually took to ride all the way into Bramber. They should have risked taking the main road, Jillian realized. They approached the collection of boulders where Cameron had struggled with the soldier the night before and spotted yet another patrol blocking the trail there.

Not content with a visual inspection, they ordered everyone from the wagon. Two soldiers climbed inside, two others climbed onto the roof, and yet another rolled underneath to inspect the undercarriage.

"Nothing," he spat disgustedly as he brushed the dust from his uniform. His gaze settled on Cameron's boots, and then swept up Cameron's full length, taking in his height, his hair, his mustache. The soldier's eyes widened with shock, and then narrowed with suspicion.

Jillian's blood ran cold.

"We've been looking for Charles Stuart," said the soldier. "Could be we've been looking for the wrong man. This man ain't the king, but on first glance could well pass for him."

His fellow soldiers converged around them like wolves scenting a bleeding, wounded deer.

"Who did you say you were again?"

"Cameron Smith."

"Doctor Cameron Smith," Jillian amended. "My father's apprentice."

"My apprentice," Doctor Bowen agreed.

"Doctoring's become a rough business these days?" the soldier asked. "You look a bit battered about the face."

"Anyone can see those bruises are days old," Jillian said. "And yes, doctoring can be a rough business. Doctor Smith was struck earlier this week by a patient flailing out in pain."

The soldier made a noncommittal sound of acknowledgment. "Can anyone vouch for your whereabouts last night, *Doctor Smith*?"

"No," said Cameron. "Only my bed."

One of the soldiers closed his fist around his sword hilt. A low murmur swept through them.

"That's not true," said Jillian quickly to forestall them from attacking Cameron. "I can vouch for Doctor Smith. He was with me last night."

"I'm talking about someone who can mark his presence for the whole night, mistress, not just a few evening hours."

"So am I, sir." Jillian tilted her chin, meeting the soldier's appalled gaze unflinchingly.

"You are saying that the two of you were together the whole night?" the soldier clarified.

"All night," Jillian whispered. "From dinner until dawn's first light."

"Watching that ditch fill with water, no doubt," Doctor Bowen muttered as he climbed back into the wagon without waiting for permission.

"*Plowing* a ditch, more likely," sniggered one of the soldiers at the rear of the group. It was an insult beyond bearing, but it served to ease the tension. Jillian could endure any amount of speculation, so long as Cameron was safe.

Their leader studied Cameron a moment longer. "She's right. That's an old bruise on his jaw." He gave his permission for them to return to the wagon with a jerk of his head. "Let them pass. Sorry to have . . . interrupted your journey, mistress."

Jillian felt his eyes upon her, hot and speculative, as she levered her foot onto the step. And then Cameron came up behind her, blocking her from the soldier's leering regard.

"You deliberately led them to think the worst of you," he said quietly when they were moving again.

"You gave me the idea," she said. "The note you said I was to show everyone, hinting that you'd debauched me and run away rather than face the consequences."

He closed his eyes and quivered as if he'd been

arrow-shot. "My own arrogance astounds me at times."

"I lived through it, Cameron."

"More than that." He stared down at her, his eyes hooded. "Jillian—you seem uncommonly exhilarated by all this."

"I . . . I am." She swallowed, and felt a tremor of excitement course through her. Perhaps this was the way her mother had felt, all those years ago, tweaking propriety and taking the risk of getting caught doing something she shouldn't be doing. "I have a fearsome taint in my blood. My mother passed it to me."

"What sort of taint in your blood?"

Jillian cast a nervous glance toward her father, but he seemed absorbed in something the boy was confiding to him in soft whispers. "My mother had a compulsion to act in stage plays. It would have been a terrible scandal if she'd been found out. My papa disapproved, but he was away from home most of the time, in service to old King Charles. Mama would steal away at night and sing and dance in tiny theaters that were hidden away all over London."

"From what I have seen, you don't possess a drop of this so-called taint in your blood."

"Oh, but I did! She taught me lines, and I would help her practice. I begged and begged to see her perform, and when I was five years old she took me as a birthday treat. That's when we both discovered I had the taint, for nothing would do except that I, too, perform on the stage. I pleaded with her until she let me take a small role in one of her productions. I was Esmeralda, the youngest daughter of an earl, in my first play."

"Your first. So there were more."

Jillian nodded, but a little stiffly, because memories held too long at bay stirred and snarled, warning her away. But somehow, with it being Cameron asking the questions, she felt an almost overwhelming desire to talk about it. "There was another play, a very special one, the playwright said, with a part for a pretty young girl of no more than six. My mother did not want me to do it. She would never say why, and I accused her of being jealous because the play had no part for her. I can scarcely believe what a wild virago I became. I was shameless, threatening to tell on her to my father, threatening to tell all her proper friends what she did, if she would not let me take the role."

She couldn't say any more. Her throat seized on her, until Cameron's hand closed over hers and his warmth pervaded her suddenly clammy skin and sent warm tendrils clear to her heart. "And?" he prompted.

"That's when . . . when it happened. We had stolen out to rehearsal and it hadn't gone very well. I didn't like the story and the playwright looked at me in a way that made me feel very frightened. I couldn't wait to get home and tell my mother that I'd changed my mind, but he would not let us go for hours. It was so very late when we left rehearsal. She was worried and wanted to hail a cab, but none were to be found."

It had been foggy that night, too, and their footfalls had scraped against stone, sending harsh sounds bouncing off the silent, dark houses. When she'd first heard the heavier shufflings and thuds, Jillian had thought them to be echoes, weirdly distorted. But they weren't.

"And then . . . then the footpads came upon us. They had been following us, they said, and knew my mother was no common actress but a woman of quality. They were enraged when she had no jewels and only very little money on her person. They beat her, Cameron, and at first she made no sound but she began to scream and they beat her harder to quiet her and she screamed even more, telling me to run."

Run, Jilly, run home. . . .

"And I ran. Or, I tried—and one of the men caught

me and I thought he would choke me to death, and I
could not get away, could not even scream, and everything was growing dark. But my mama somehow
kicked him and he crumpled into a ball and let loose
of me."

Run, Jilly, run home. . . .

"I could scarcely breathe, from my neck swelling
and from being so afraid, but I ran. I ran and ran.
They killed her. And it was my fault, all my fault, for
forcing her to allow me to perform in that play. And
she died because I ran away, when I should have
stayed and kicked them as hard as she had kicked to
save me."

"Jillian." Cameron bent over her and enfolded her,
reins and all, into his arms. His forehead pressed
against hers. The rasp of his skin, the hot brush of his
lips, the security of his embrace, drew her away from
the awful time and brought her back to him. "You
were a child. Six years old. You could not have saved
her. Your mother ran a great risk every time she stole
through London's streets at night, alone. She must
have known she would run out of luck one day. She
probably counted herself lucky that you escaped."

"We should have stayed home and not left the
house. We should have practiced using other, secret
routes from the theater so that those men who waited
to attack us would have been lurking all night for
nothing."

"And you have lived your life trying to correct what
you perceive as your mistakes. Jillian, no six-year-old
child could have prevented those men from doing
what they did."

"Aye." How strange, that with one small syllable
she could acknowledge a truth she'd spent years deny-
ing. That long-ago attack, and the way that thug had
entrapped her and nearly choked her to death while
she struggled, marked the beginning of her retreat
from the world. She realized now that she had consid-

ered her confinement a justifiable penance. She had always simply accepted her irrational need to be safe inside her home, her compulsive drive to learn myriad routes through the twisting byways so no one would ever know exactly where she and her father would be and block them from going back home.

She was a woman grown, but in many ways still that frightened girl of six who held herself accountable for destruction wreaked by criminals. Cameron had given her the strength to make the first tentative steps toward forgiving herself.

"Jillian?"

She leaned into him, too dazed to speak.

"Could you do it again? Could you take a risk in the night, and act the role of your life?"

"I don't understand."

"If there was ever a time I wanted to stay, and hold you close, it is now. But I must go."

She blinked. "Go? You can't leave! We discussed this—we are in this together!"

He shook his head, with a slow sweet smile that spoke of finality, and an agony in his eyes that told her he bled for her. "All these soldiers snarling the roads and byways, this poor boy's mother suffering because we are delayed in reaching her—it is all my fault."

"And my fault, too. I begged you not to kill the soldier."

His gaze remained steady without the slightest flicker of blame sent her way.

"If you had killed him, Cameron, these men would not be combing the area now, looking for Charles Stuart."

"But they are here. Because I allowed my heart to rule my head, the real Charles stands no chance whatsoever of using these byways to make his escape. Not a flea could pass through here undetected, unless . . ."

"Unless what!" Jillian felt a sense of doom settling over her. Her question brought a wistful tilt to his lips.

"Unless I rectify my mistake. Look at me, Jillian." She did; she wanted always to look at him, his dark hair waved in the wind, thick and dark as the king's. He touched his mustache—dark and full as the king's. And she had an intimate knowledge of Cameron's body, knew it to be extraordinarily tall and fit, lean and athletic as the king was said to be. "Tell me what you see."

"I see a man about to do something foolish for the sake of a lost cause." Her voice choked on her observation.

"That's my brave girl." He chucked her lightly beneath her chin. "I will simply turn my plan about. Tonight, when this current crop of soldiers is relieved by fresh troops, I will let them catch me, and I will not protest that I am Cameron Smith, humble apprentice. I will allow them to believe I am Charles Stuart."

"What would that accomplish?"

"It would clear the roads, Jillian. It would lend the soldiers a false sense of accomplishment. They'd no longer be on the lookout for a tall, dark-haired man. Charles could pass through here with impunity."

"Cameron, no. They'll haul you off to London, or wherever Cromwell crouches like a spider, waiting for Charles Stuart to become entangled in his web. Cromwell might . . . Cromwell might kill you when he realizes you've deceived his men."

"I know," Cameron said, accepting a death sentence with a soft smile.

And she knew there was nothing she could say to dissuade him. He had told her, from the very first, that his life was expendable to his cause.

"When?" she whispered.

"Now." He touched her beneath the chin, lifting her face, and rubbed the callused pad of his thumb over her lips, just once. "Charles could already be here, waiting for something to happen. We must clear the way for him."

"We will lose each other. Cromwell will imprison you, or he will kill you."

"Now you know why I fought so hard against falling in love with you. Why I tried to make you hate me. I should . . . I should regret claiming you as my beloved, but I cannot."

"Nor can I." And she did not regret it, not one single pang of regret.

"You will endure, Jillian. You have survived far worse."

Oh, God, he thought she was strong on her own. Right then she felt impossibly weak, too shaken by the effect of those old memories and too uncertain of her newfound strength to know how to proceed. She was not sure she could find the answers without him there to hold her. She was not even sure she wanted to live at all if Cameron was not part of her life. But how could she tell him so without seeing that proud light fade from his eyes, without watching his confidence in her shift into contempt?

"Promise me something," she said.

He inclined his head, a cavalier acknowledging a demand from his lady.

"Promise me that you will not openly boast of being Charles Stuart. Promise me that you will allow the soldiers to reach their own conclusions."

His eyes glimmered with understanding. "Aye. Perhaps I could plead the case before Cromwell that my arrest was merely a case of mistaken identity. It gives me some hope, Jillian."

It was a thread of hope, nothing more. It did nothing to lighten her heart.

"How long will it take you?" he asked. "The lad's mother—how long to take care of her?"

Jillian shook her head. "Impossible to say. Hours, perhaps."

"If you just see her, and leave with her the things she can use to ease the pain, how long?"

"Why, Cameron?" She could not imagine why he seemed so concerned. The minute he left this wagon, he would be gone from her life forever.

"Because you must return to your home as soon as possible. Pack the wagon with those things that are of vital importance to you. Leave the rest behind and strike out at once for London."

"Leave . . . leave our home?"

"Aye. When word spreads that Charles Stuart has been captured, Constable Fraley, or one of those soldiers who have stopped us today, might remember seeing you with a man who fit the same description and wonder why I am no longer here. He might even believe he allowed Charles Stuart to slip through his fingers thanks to your lies, and his rage would be boundless. You must leave this place before the questions begin."

Leave her home? Leave the haven she'd crafted with her own cunning and guile? Although nothing could match the terror of losing Cameron, the thought of losing her home as well seemed too much to bear. All her dreams of the future had included Cameron coming to live with her and her father, an idyllic scene where they'd continue treating the sick and retiring to their snug little home in the woods.

Her heart began thumping erratically. The old memories she'd stirred tonight had helped her understand that she might one day conquer fear, but that day had not yet arrived. She would need time and the steadying strength of Cameron to help her. "I cannot leave my home, Cameron. I cannot do it."

"I will wait until tonight before allowing myself to be captured. You will have ample time to tend to the woman and return home and pack your things." Cameron issued instructions as if she hadn't raised any objections. "By nightfall, this current lot of soldiers will have been relieved by the next shift. I will try to get captured by a group of soldiers that has not seen us together."

The trial curved, and through the trees they could see the humps and lumps that would prove to be men and horses as they drew closer. They were running out of time.

"Tell Martin what I've done. He'll report everything to my men. Tell him the roads will be clear and it will be safe to smuggle Charles through without your assistance. I have calculated how much time we can safely expect to go undetected. It should take a day and a half of hard riding to get me to London and hand me over to Cromwell. A day, perhaps less, for Cromwell to recognize that I am not the king and to do with me what he will. Two more days for the soldiers to return here in disgrace. Perhaps—if we are lucky—five days in all. Plenty of time for the king to get through, and for you to be gone and safe from Cromwell's wrath."

"Leave my home?" Her protest sounded embarrassingly like a whimper. "Cameron—I cannot go into London. I cannot."

"You'll spend no time at all in London save to ask someone to point you toward the road to Chelmsford. Ask for Chelmsford, so that if anyone chances to remember you, they'll remember only Chelmsford in their mind. But follow that road beyond Chelmsford and on into Linchester. Ask for Howard Firthington. Linchester. Howard Firthington. Say the names."

"Linchester," she repeated hollowly, knowing she could not, would not seek it out. "Howard Firthington."

"Tell him John Cameron Delacorte sent you, and that you are precious to me. He will take care of you for me. I will come to claim you there if I am able to escape Cromwell's wrath."

"John Cameron Delacorte."

He gave her a crooked, bittersweet smile. "This is not the way I planned telling you my name, Jillian."

Oh, God, he'd told her his name and she'd been so wooden with despair that she hadn't even realized it. It struck her as a terrible omen, as if he'd taken on a whole new identity to mark his transition from this life to a new one, a new one that did not, could not, include her.

"You . . . are *Cameron*."

"Aye. I am Cameron, my love. I've always been Cameron." He brushed the lightest of kisses over her lips, his breath mingling with hers.

And then he vaulted himself over the half-door, and he was gone.

17

Cameron leaned back against a tree trunk, gasping for breath and fighting annoyance at the same time. He was beginning to understand how Charles Stuart had managed to elude the Commonwealth forces for more than a month.

For the best part of three hours, Cameron had dodged through the trees at the roadside edge of the forest, running heavily and clumsily so as to make as much noise as possible. He'd frightened away every bird and wild thing in the woods, but raised not the slightest bit of interest from the troops relentlessly patrolling the road.

An hour or so back, he'd sworn he'd heard soldiers moving deeper in the forest. By the time he'd fought through the underbrush, they'd moved on. He'd returned to the road, thinking that a man skulking among the trees there ought to draw some interest. They never noticed him.

Good God, Cromwell's men were so incompetent, so oblivious, that for the first time he believed the tale he'd heard, that Charles had merely climbed into an oak tree at Boscobel Wood and took himself a good long nap while Cromwell's soldiers supposedly combed the area looking for him. At the rate his sacrificial arrest was proceeding, Cameron would have to march straight down the middle of the road, perhaps walk

right into the soldiers' midst, before they took any
notice of him.

He wished their captain would whip them into
shape. All this dashing back and forth was wearing
him down both physically and mentally. Having himself mistaken for the king was growing less desirable,
while thoughts of bracing himself in the hard, uncomfortable crook of an oak tree for a night's sleep
loomed nigh unto irresistible.

But there would be no sleep for him, he knew. The
moment he closed his eyes his mind would taunt him
with the memory of all Jillian had told him. When she
most needed his strong arms around her, he'd pushed
her away and told her to be strong for herself.

Guilt roiled through him, poisonous and stinging,
and yet he could not shake the feeling that pushing
Jillian away had been the right thing to do.

She had courage in full measure. She had to recognize her own strength and know it stemmed from
something wonderful within herself. Not a taint in the
blood, but a glorious spirit that had been locked away
for far too long. She would never know the fullness
of it if she believed someone else was responsible for
setting it free.

He pushed off from the tree and sprinted across the
road. He caught the trunk of a sturdy sapling in the
curve of his arm and let his momentum swing him
around until he stared down the road.

No luck. The soldiers couldn't be more than fifty
yards away, and not one of them had caught sight
of him.

Well, he would just have to get closer and try it
again.

He stomped through the underbrush, snapping
fallen twigs, stirring piles of leaves. It was a horse that
caught him, swiveling its head and blowing a warning
through flaring nostrils while its ears twitched with
curiosity.

"Who goes there?" challenged the rider.

Summoning a great bellow from the depths of his chest, Cameron burst out of the woods and made for the center of the road. He crouched there, brandished his arms aloft and howled like an African ape to make certain the louts caught sight of him, and then spun and pounded down the road, away from the soldiers.

The man who'd challenged him raised a shout and soon a contingent rode hard on his heels. Cameron dared looking over his shoulder, and his mock flight took on a new intensity. Battle-lust raged from his pursuers, and for the first time he realized that they were so spoiling for a fight that they might kill him before recognizing he'd make an excellent hostage.

Not now, he prayed. He had to buy more time for Jillian before he died. Besides, it would do him little good to meet his death now. It was imperative that the soldiers believe him to be Charles Stuart and take him to Cromwell. Then, he could die.

Despite his rationalization, his instincts demanded he run. His tired legs pumped harder, faster, in a mindless effort to outrun his pursuers. But only for a few yards. His sense of honor and responsibility overruled his yearning to escape. Stumbling to a halt, he lifted his hands in defeat.

"I yield," he cried. "Do not kill me."

The soldiers pulled up, skidding to a stop as they encircled him. To a man they pointed swords at his heart. One held a small firearm trained upon his head. "Why shouldn't we kill you?" challenged one of them. "Running away from the Lord Protector's patrols is a crime punishable by death."

Jillian had asked him to allow the soldiers to make their own assumptions.

"Don't you know who I am?" Cameron asked softly. And then he held his breath, wondering if his daring impersonation would pay off.

It didn't seem so. A few stared at him with bewilderment, one man yawned, another glowered and said, "It matters not who he is. Kill him."

Cameron waited, not daring to breathe, praying one of them would countermand the order. Instead, some frowned at him and others fingered their weapons. He smothered another sigh and shook his head to free his hair from its queue. Then he ostentatiously lowered one hand to stroke his mustache. He stretched his hands even higher, adding inches to his height. Finally, one of the gape-jawed dullards bolted upright in his saddle. " 'Tis the king!" he cried. "We've captured Charles Stuart!"

"Charles Stuart is no longer the king," grumbled one of the men, but he was ignored by the others who whooped with triumph. They soon had Cameron trussed with ropes binding his arms to his sides, his feet hobbled with a short length of leather thong.

"Are you the king? Charles Stuart, I mean," demanded the captain.

Cameron did not answer.

"He is!" shouted another. "Admit it, you!"

"I would have to be a fool to admit such a thing," Cameron said.

A rousing masculine cheer greeted his half-truth.

"We must report our success at once and then go straight with this man to the Lord Protector," announced the fellow who'd first identified him as the king. "Cromwell is sure to reward us handsomely."

"Aye, but how will we get him there?" asked another. "He can't ride with his ankles tied together, and you can't throw the king of England over the back of a horse like a sack of flour."

"Charles Stuart is no longer the king of England," asserted the same man who'd said so before.

Cameron swallowed his annoyance and had to avoid rolling his eyes in exasperation while the argument on how best to transport him raged around him. And then he heard the clopping of hooves, the squeaking of wagon wheels, as distinctive as a familiar voice.

'Twas Jillian and her father.

Cameron's heart sank. The hour was hard on midnight. Her errand of mercy should have concluded long ago. She should have been on her way to London. But he supposed he had known, somewhere deep in his soul, that she would not leave the bedside of a suffering woman merely to buy herself a little extra time to make an escape. He had only himself to blame for telling her he calculated they had five days to work within. Five days. He took reassurance from the thought. Even after tarrying so long, she would be safe in Linchester well before the hue and cry was raised.

Providing she would leave her home. He swallowed his doubts. She would do it. She had to do it, if they had any chance of ever being together.

"Commandeer that wagon," snapped the soldier in charge.

The troop waited, simmering with excitement, as Jillian approached. Then one of the soldiers rode up and hailed her. Cameron could not hear the discussion, only the low murmur of the soldier's voice and Jillian's sharp dissent.

One of his captors pressed the point of his sword between Cameron's shoulder blades. He stumbled forward, hampered by the hobble and not particularly interested in walking toward the wagon. He did not want Jillian to see him. Even though he'd sought this arrest, he found it humiliating to be seen standing there, subdued and tied. The sword pricked again, and he could feel a warm, thick track of blood inch down his back.

"Get a move on or this blade will slide in a little deeper next time," growled his tormentor, the soldier who'd grumbled that Charles Stuart was no longer the king. "Pierce straight through to your heart, I will."

There was a certain allure to the notion of letting

the soldier do as he threatened and end everything for Cameron here and now. And then he thought, *this is Jillian. She will understand. She will not think me a failure as a man for letting another's warlike ways seem to prevail.* A faint smile hovered over his lips, and, feeling remarkably strengthened, he inched toward Jillian with as much dignity as his hobble would allow.

The argument between Jillian and the commander became clearer as he approached. He heard the end of a phrase, ". . . to carry Charles Stuart."

She had to understand what had happened. But she betrayed nothing, not by so much as a tiny hitch in her voice.

"I don't care if Good Queen Bess has risen from the dead for the sole pleasure of taking a ride in my wagon," he heard Jillian's voice raised in argument. "The Lord Protector himself says royal blood does not entitle anyone to special privileges. You may not take my horse and wagon just because Charles Stuart fancies a ride in it."

"You have no choice, mistress. We will trade two mounts so you may return to your home. Your mare and wagon will be returned to you unharmed. You have my word as an officer."

"And what are we to do if someone calls us out?" she challenged. "How are my father and I to . . ." her voice drifted away as she caught sight of Cameron.

Her lips parted. Her eyes widened. She paled. A fine trembling moved through her, and with a pang of desire Cameron remembered how she'd felt vibrating against him.

Another pang, too—one of dread. If she did not recover her composure quickly, she could give everything away. *You've got it within you, my girl,* he said to her silently.

With horror, he watched her hand rise. For one blinding second, a devil's voice shrilled inside him. She'll point you out. She'll betray you. But she merely pressed her hand against her heart, keeping her beautiful eyes upon him.

Her father sat beside her, hunched and terrified. Rage raced through Cameron, to think that these soldiers frightened that gentle man. As if his regard drew the doctor's attention, Wilton Bowen turned and saw him.

The old man's posture straightened. Such pure joy at finding Cameron standing there flooded his features that Cameron's throat tightened. His own father had never looked at him with such fond regard.

"Why, it's . . ." Doctor Bowen began.

"Father, look—the soldiers say they have captured the king, Charles Stuart," Jillian said.

"The king, Charles Stuart?"

Cameron could not tell if the soldiers caught the uncertainty in Doctor Bowen's voice, or the look of confusion he exchanged with his daughter. But at Jillian's firm nod, a fleeting, temporary awareness sharpened the old man's features. "The king, Charles Stuart," he repeated. "Why, I suppose it might be." He leaned back and studied Cameron. "You've grown a bit since last I tended you and your father, eh, young Charlie? I would not have recognized you."

"My father was once a Royal Physician," Jillian said, her eyes bright and her voice ringing with pride in her father.

"And you can rest assured the king will never forget his valued service," Cameron said softly. He was so proud of her. It surprised him that the rope binding his arms did not shred from the swelling of his chest. "It is a relief to me that you and your father are tending to the health of the English people, mistress."

She understood that he was asking how she'd fared with the sick woman suffering agony of the gut. "We do our best," she said. "Those we cannot help are put at ease."

"You can do no better than your best. And mistress, I suspect your best is very good indeed."

The captain cut off the conversation with a short chop of his fist. "Enough yammering, *your majesty*. I'd heard you were a rum hand with the ladies, but I never thought you'd go so far as to flirt whilst wrapped in rope from head to toe."

Cameron gave a wry smile and a shrug of his shoulder as if to say he could not help himself. "You must admit the lady would provoke any man's admiration," he said.

"Enough of this chatter. Out of your wagon, mistress. I'll give you my own horse and . . ." his gaze drifted over his mounted men, and he indicated one with a jerk of his chin. "That one over there. We'll take good care of the wagon and mare. We'll return them to you later tonight, after we report the capture of yon Charles to the constable. My guess is he'll be so pleased with the news that he'll give us the loan of his official wagon."

The constable. Fraley. Cameron's blood ran cold. The man would know at once that he was not Charles Stuart. Curse it! Every time he thought he'd wormed his way out of one mess, he found himself caught fast in another.

"Oh, how kind of you," Jillian warbled. "I did not realize that Commonwealth forces had to report to the local constabulary."

"We do it as a courtesy, madam."

"Well, no matter. I am sure Mr. Fraley will be thrilled when you hand over the king to him," said Jillian. "He will be so delighted to take credit for capturing this elusive rogue."

"He wouldn't take credit!" objected a soldier.

"Of course he will. You are within his jurisdiction, I believe."

The captain and his second-in-command exchanged appalled glances. "On second thought, we have no time to waste upon courtesies. I think it best if we press straight on to London with the prisoner," said the captain. "You, Edmonds, will ride into the village and report our capture of the king to the constable. *After* you see the lady and her father home."

His second-in-command waved to another soldier. "You ride the road ahead and hail all troops you see. Advise them that Captain Walker and his men have captured Charles Stuart and mean to turn him over to Lord Cromwell at once. Tell them we have sent a special emissary back to Bramber to advise Mr. Fraley of our success. No one need bother to make a special trip." Captain Walker gave a slight nod of his head to indicate approval of the plan, which would ensure credit stayed right where he wanted it to be.

Jillian accepted a soldier's help and climbed out of the wagon. She patted her horse and said conversationally, "Queenie is tired, and accustomed to short journeys only. She will make no speed whatsoever to London. But I'm sure that suits you, because you are no doubt eager for Constable Fraley to catch up to you."

The captain's lips thinned.

Cameron had to bend his head because he was not sure he could stifle his smile. His Jillian was quite the glib-tongued sorceress, divining just the right things to say at just the right time. Taint in the blood—he prayed all their children would be born with it.

"I don't particularly fancy being bounced about in the back of that old wagon," Cameron said, trying to sound as pompous as he imagined the real Charles Stuart would sound at such a time. "I give you my word that if you let me ride a horse, I'll make no attempt to escape."

He was afraid he might have sounded too eager, but it didn't seem so. Thanks to Jillian's skillful goading, it was plain to see that Captain Walker's mind had

seized on the thought that he could very easily lose
the glory of this capture to Fraley.

"Very well, the doctor may keep his wagon,"
Walker said. "Edmonds, you will give up your mount
for our prisoner."

"Why not Scully?" Edmonds countered. "I out-
rank him."

"By virtue of your father's title, not by rank in this
common man's army," Walker said. "Off your horse."

"Are you going to make me walk all the way to
London while that treasonist rides?" Edmonds
asked, aghast.

"No—you ride to the village with the mistress and
her father and inform the constable of what's
happened."

"We have just come from Bramber. Our home lies
some miles ahead," Jillian said. "My father is tired. It
would be unkind to force him straight back to
Bramber right now."

Walker brightened. "Never let it be said that we
soldiers are unkind. You are absolutely right, mistress,
you and your father should be taken straight home.
Edmonds will see you home safely, and then he can
walk into the village."

"Miles," grumbled Edmonds.

"I have never walked it myself," said Jillian. "But
lads will oftentimes run out from Bramber to fetch
my father. I hear tell it takes no more than three hours
or so. I'll see to it that you have a good meal and
perhaps a brief nap before you set out."

Edmonds did not look much happier, but the captain beamed.

They cut the thong hobbling Cameron's ankles, and
though Jillian's heart flinched when the knife neared
his flesh, she realized that the men were treating him
with a muted, but deferential respect. They truly believed him to be the king, and even though as Com-

monwealth soldiers they owed loyalty to Cromwell, they were Englishmen first, with the inborn reverence for their king. She wondered if they rued their part in grinding the spirit of England into the dust.

She studied Cameron from the beneath the cover of her lashes. Her whole being surged toward him. He stood proud and unbowed despite being bound and at the soldiers' mercy. His hair whipped in the wind like a bold banner declaring his untamed spirit.

She wanted more than anything to run to him, to press against him and drink in his scent and the feel of his flesh against hers. But such behavior could not be explained away, even if she declared herself to be an ardent Royalist.

If he was to survive this daring impersonation, she had to play the role of her life. Only if the soldiers continued to believe he was Charles Stuart would they refrain from hurting him.

When they presented him to Lord Cromwell, who surely knew the true face of Charles Stuart . . . she did not know what would happen to him then.

And she might never know if he lived or died. If they executed Cameron in London, word might never filter back to Arundel Forest. And if God smiled down and Cameron was set free, he would go straight to Linchester, expecting her to be there, waiting for him. Her absence would declare she had chosen her home over him. A man as proud as Cameron would not come back here to demand an explanation. He would forget all about her.

It was an awkward business getting Cameron mounted with his arms tied to his sides, and so with another promise from him that he would not try to escape, the soldiers cut free those bonds and settled for binding his wrists in front of him, so he could hold the saddle horn for balance while another soldier held his horse's reins.

They took off at such a pace that Fraley would have

the devil of a time catching up to them, even if this
soldier Edmonds left this very moment and ran all the
way to the village.

Cameron never looked back.

Nor had she expected that he would. She had no
need of one final glance. She would go to her grave
savoring the smile he'd given her, his look so filled
with love and trust. And now he'd made the supreme
sacrifice for his king, risking everything to provide
Charles Stuart with a slim chance, a very slim chance,
of survival. No true knight could do more.

His father would have been proud. Very, very
proud.

Edmonds stood with his arms crossed, watching the
departing troop. A bad-tempered frown grooved his
face. He would not make a pleasant companion on
the wagon ride home.

Constable Fraley would be livid at hearing the king
had been captured in his area. He'd head straight to
London, and if his horse was fast enough he might inter-
cept Captain Walker's men and tell them all that they
had the wrong man, they held an imposter, not Charles
Stuart. Cameron would no doubt die on the spot.

She had to stop Edmonds from telling Fraley the
news.

It would not be impossible. She'd promised the soldier a good meal and a rest before walking to the
village, and he did not appear all that eager to make
the journey. He had the disgruntled, spoilt look of a
privileged man accustomed to better treatment. Her
medical storeroom was filled with herbs and potions
known to plunge its takers into deep, long-lasting
sleep. She could dose the soldier and keep him senseless long enough for Cameron to be carried all the
way to London; for the Lord Protector to be summoned from wherever he might be; for the entire English army to be made to look like fools.

And then what? What would all of this scheming,

the sacrifice of Cameron's life and their newborn love, mean if Charles Stuart got himself captured anyway?

Jillian did not know Cameron's men. She knew only that his faith in their abilities was less than rock-solid. Even so, he had instructed her to tell Martin that plans had changed, that the men should smuggle Charles to Brighthelmstone without her. She knew he had ordered this change in plans to protect her.

But what if . . . what if she carried on?

If she could convince Martin that Cameron wanted her to carry out his original plan, then Cameron's men would still be on the lookout for the king, would still deliver him into her hands if he chanced to appear. Cameron had believed in her strength, her ability to see this through. She could do this for him, so his death and the loss of their love would not be in vain.

That taint in her blood, that troublesome and seemingly useless ability, could well save the king and lend some meaning to the empty life awaiting her.

She began trembling at the sheer audacity of her thoughts.

"Jilly—what's wrong?"

"Papa." She found his hand and gripped it in her own. She glanced toward Edmonds and judged he stood far enough away to be unable to hear them. "Do you understand what's happened to Cameron, Papa?"

"Why, yes, I—" But in the midst of his confident beginning, her father blinked, and the uncertainty clouded his eyes. Jillian wanted to cry as she watched her father struggle, and fail, to reassemble his thoughts. "I—I think I understand. Young Doctor Smith has . . . why, he's been crowned king!" Her father straightened with amazement. "Quite astonishing. I daresay he won't have much time now for his medical studies. A pity. He has a natural aptitude, just like you."

Wilton Bowen's wounded mind had fabricated a

mishmash of truth and fantasy. Her father could not help her through this. The decision would be hers alone to make, though her father would by necessity pay an equal price. All the strength required would have to come from within her.

"Would you like it if Cameron came back to us someday?"

"I would quite like it. A most pleasant and polite young man. Excellent digger, for a king. I do wish I had my new rose garden pattern with me."

"We'll be home soon, Papa, and you can work on your pattern."

Edmonds swiveled on his heel. "Let's get going," he said. He crowded onto the seat next to her father.

Jillian got them moving. She cast all yearning, all sadness from her mind. She had very little time to think. She could not count on her father. She would have to trust Martin with the truth and hope he would agree to let her carry out the original plan.

Her life would be forfeit regardless. She had already misled the parliamentary forces with half-truths, and now she meant to drug one of Cromwell's soldiers for the purpose of keeping vital information from the local constable. She would be tried and hanged for treason. Just like Cameron.

She was startled to realize they'd almost arrived at her house. She'd been so busy weighing her decisions in her mind that she hadn't noticed the time and the distance flowing by.

She had to decide. Retreat like a quiet little mouse and pray luck would help her beloved's dreams come true, or take the biggest, boldest risk of her life, knowing that succeeding would not necessarily return her beloved to her, but knowing that even in failing she would prove herself worthy of the man she loved.

"I am sure you are hungry, Mr. Edmonds," she said. "Our housekeeper will have left a meal for us. And I myself will brew you a special tea before sending you on your way."

18

Jillian knew Martin would be watching for their return. She silently cursed the construction of the wagon. The high walls boxed them in against the elements, but also protected them against prying eyes. Because of the way it was built, she had always felt so safe in the wagon that it almost felt like an extension of her home.

And now, Martin might not be able to see inside well enough to realize that the third person in the wagon was not Cameron, but a Commonwealth soldier. She hoped that her appointed guardian wouldn't walk out of the stable to fetch the horse and wagon, suspecting nothing amiss. But nor did she want him to confront the soldier the way he'd accosted the poor lad who'd come to them the night before.

Stay hidden, she prayed. *Trust me to deal with this.*

And it seemed her prayers were answered. She caught the merest glimpse of Martin's flitting form as he melded into the deeper black shadows cast by the stable.

"Well, here we are at last, Mr. Edmonds," she said. Her voice quivered with the effort it took to keep herself planted firmly on the bench seat. Her whole being shook with the need to run into the house. She had been away from those sheltering walls for too many hours. But balanced against the panic was the

awareness that the longer she kept Edmonds away
from Bramber, the longer she delayed Fraley hearing
the news, the better for Cameron.

She'd driven as slowly as she could. Queenie had
been impatient for home and Jillian's arms ached from
the effort of holding her back. She'd had to fight herself, for she and the mare wanted the same thing, and
she had yearned to whip the mare into a gallop. And
now they'd arrived and her home beckoned, promising
to soothe her jittering nerves—but she could not go
inside. Not until she'd informed Martin of what had
happened and won his promise to help.

"I'll just see to my horse and be right back to warm
our dinner and prepare that tea I promised you."

She held her breath, praying the soldier wouldn't
remember his breeding and turn chivalrous on her and
offer to unharness and brush down Queenie.

He did not disappoint her. Edmonds held fast to
the bad-tempered sulk he'd maintained throughout
the ride, and he followed her father into the house
without casting a single glance toward the sweating
horse.

Martin, however, closed his hands around Queenie's
reins the minute Jillian gained the inside of the stable.
"Can you tend to her in the dark?" Jillian whispered.
"It would be best."

"Aye, I'm sure you'd like that," Martin snarled.
"No light to shine on your face and show you for
a traitor."

The insult stung. Martin had kept to himself since
being installed in her stable, and Jillian had not gone
out of her way to befriend him, but she felt sure that
Cameron would have told him she could be trusted.

Cameron. Simply thinking his name made her quake
with worry. She forced herself to regain a measure
of calm.

"I did not willingly invite that Commonwealth lout
home with me."

"Where's Mister . . . where's Cameron?"

"Mr. Delacorte—" She gasped at the sharp twinge of pleasure that came from saying the name he'd entrusted to her. John Cameron Delacorte. It suited him so well, noble and proud and vibrating through her like a drumbeat. "Mr. Delacorte has been captured by Cromwell's troops."

Martin hissed his disbelief.

"He let it happen apurpose, Martin." She rested a hand against the man's arm, sensing how the news had rocked him. "They believe him to be Charles Stuart. They are taking him right now to London. The byways have already cleared of soldiers—we weren't stopped at all this past hour."

"Then why did you bring yonder arsehole home with you?"

She explained, as quickly as she could. "We cannot let that man go into Bramber," she said. "If he tells Fraley what happened, Cameron will be exposed as an imposter."

"So what do you expect to do with him, then?"

She told him that, too.

"You expect a Commonwealth soldier to fall senseless from sipping leaves and roots?" Martin gaped at her in disbelief. "And Mr. Delacorte agreed to this plan?"

"Not . . . not exactly."

Enough light filtered from the moon to illuminate Martin as he crossed his arms and narrowed his eyes at her. "What *exactly* does Mr. Delacorte want you to do?"

Jillian decided that a judicious mixture of fiction and truth would serve her best.

"He wants me carry on. And then once we've saved the king, I am supposed to pack my things and go with my father to a place called Linchester."

At the mention of the town, she sensed a subtle

softening in Martin's antagonism. "Well, that's all right then, mistress. He's sending you to his home."

"His home?" The news staggered her. "I thought, from things he'd said, that his home had been confiscated when his brother went off to Scotland to fight for the king."

"Aye, they stripped Benington out of his hands, 'tis true. But there's plenty of folk in Linchester who would sell their souls to help Mr. Delacorte."

"That's what he's doing for the king, Martin. We cannot let him fail."

"I don't see how keeping yonder arsehole dosed with herbs will help Mr. Delacorte off there in London."

"Mr. Edmonds has been charged with the task of reporting to Constable Fraley. Fraley will make all haste to catch up with the soldiers so he might share in the glory. We cannot allow that to happen."

"What difference would it make to have one more Commonwealth lackey following in Mr. Delacorte's wake?"

"Fraley has seen Cameron. Examined him up close. He knows Cameron is not the king and would say so at once. The soldiers would be infuriated to learn they'd been duped, and Cameron is their prisoner, bound and helpless." She shivered.

"Ah." Martin nodded his understanding.

"Fraley does not command the road patrols outside of Bramber. He will not know that the patrols have been canceled. The longer we can keep this information from him, the easier it will be for King Charles to get through."

"I'll make straight for the camp," Martin said. "The lads have to know of these changes—"

She remembered Cameron telling her about the hot-tempered yeoman left in charge of the troop. She could not risk him learning that Cameron had been captured and that she, a mere woman, proposed saving the king on her own.

"No, Martin. There's no time, and the fewer people who know the truth, the better."

She had sounded too anxious, and Martin had caught it. He frowned at her and jutted his jaw stubbornly. "I don't like it. I'm not so sure Mr. Delacorte would ever stand for you hauling the king without himself there to watch over you. My guess is he wants you to go to Linchester."

"Well, I'm not going." She performed a little jaw-jutting herself, though she doubted her chin had the impact of Martin's.

"You'll go if I say—"

"Martin. Please," she begged. "For every moment since Cameron decided to do this, I've lived with the knowledge that he could die. That would be hard, harder than anything I've ever known. But those of us who love Cameron could cling to some comfort if we know his death was not in vain. The king must be transported safely back to France. He's on his way here, and he won't be expecting a change in plans. He will be expecting to travel into Brighthelmstone with me. Can't you see that the only thing we can do is save the king—to honor Cameron?"

Martin sighed. She wasn't sure, because of the light, but she thought a suspicious-looking trickle wended down his cheek and he dashed it away. "All right. You shove tea down Edmonds's gullet, and I'll truss him up and introduce him to a right cozy straw heap next to Queenie. I daresay if he complains about the accommodations I can give some personal attention with a chunk of wood against the back of his head."

"Thank you," she whispered.

"But I have a condition," he said. "Two nights, no more. If Charles Stuart hasn't turned up by then, you'll pack and be on your way to Linchester."

"Four nights," she bargained.

"Three."

She nodded, pretending acceptance even as her body shook with the need to get into the house. She would never be able to go to Linchester. "Now we are treasonists," she said. "What do we do?"

"We do what treasonists mostly do. We wait."

"He ate all my dinner," Jillian's father complained the moment she walked into the kitchen.

Mr. Edmonds leaned back in his chair. Jillian clenched her fists in the folds of her skirts. Her relief at closing herself inside the house was overwhelmed by her fury at seeing Edmonds's arrogant assumption of Cameron's chair. *Cameron's* chair. Edmonds lounged casually, tipping the chair back on its rearmost legs. She wanted to dump the soldier right onto the floor.

"Mrs. Podgett should have left enough . . ." *for three*, Jillian finished silently.

"There was enough for a woman," Edmonds said. He slanted a sneer toward her father. "And a half-wit."

Jillian dug her fingernails into the pads of her hands. She'd known it was a risk to leave her father alone with Edmonds while she consulted with Martin, but she'd had no choice.

"Doctor Smith never once ate my portion," her father grumbled. "A true gentleman, young Doctor Smith."

"Who's Doctor Smith?" asked Edmonds.

"My father's apprentice. He's not here just now."

"When's he coming back?"

"I'm . . . I'm not sure," Jillian said.

"So it's just you here with the crazy old gent." Edmonds shifted in his chair. "And me."

There was something about the way Edmonds looked at her that stopped her from admitting Cameron would never come back. "Doctor Smith could return at any moment."

Edmonds studied her for a moment, speculatively, and then his lip curved in a knowing smile. "I'll take that tea now," Edmonds said. "Or maybe you could lock this old fool away and bar the door for the night—and fetch the two of us some ale."

There was no mistaking the lascivious intent behind his suggestion. Nor his confident belief that no mysterious Doctor Smith would be coming into this kitchen at any time soon.

"We don't keep ale in our home. I'll go the storeroom and fetch the tea."

Jillian hurried to the medical storeroom. She grabbed at the bundles of herbs that would strike Edmonds temporarily senseless. It took all her strength of will to keep from bursting into tears, knowing she stood upon the place where Cameron had slept. Cameron had never once, from the first moment of his arrival, given her cause to want to dose him into unconsciousness. She paused for a moment, taking deep, gulping breaths to stop the shaking, and then she returned to the kitchen.

Her father had been right to call Cameron a true gentleman, Jillian thought. Cameron had never battered her father with insults, or used his position of strength to confiscate more than a fair share of what was available, or looked at her the way the self-styled gentleman Edmonds was doing now, with anticipation lighting his eyes, eyes that seemed to be fixed firmly upon Jillian's bosom.

Well, she thought, working while loathing shuddered through her, at least with his mind fixed upon her female charms, Edmonds wasn't in a hurry to leave for Bramber.

When the brew had steeped, she let it cool as long as she was able to endure Edmonds's staring. The stuff had a vile aftertaste, and she was afraid Edmonds might refuse more than a sip or two if it was so hot that he couldn't drink it straight down. She placed it in front of him. He sniffed at it.

"What's this?"

"Tea."

"No tea like I've seen."

"We live simply here, Mr. Edmonds. We drink herb teas, not the new China tea. Here, Papa—you have a cup as well, and I'll fix you something to eat."

It would be easier to have her father asleep than to worry about him saying something that would destroy Cameron's chances. Her father took a sip, and then looked at her with cheeks bulging from not swallowing the brew, shock widening his eyes.

"Go on, Papa, drink your tea," she urged.

He swallowed obediently. "But Jillian, this is—"

"I know, it is our very best. We must offer the best of our poor hospitality to Mr. Edmonds."

Edmonds, smiling, tipped his head back and quaffed his tea down without pausing for breath.

Jillian had never noticed before how empty were her days. For two days now she'd done little but trace the printing on the medical text she held in her lap. She hadn't spent a minute concentrating on the words.

Doctor Harvey's theories on the human circulatory system were so much easier to understand, now that her father had spent so many hours explaining the text for Cameron's sake. And yet she could rouse no interest in mastering the nuances of the movement of blood, the role of the pulse. She'd developed a sudden aversion to studying anything related to human functions ruled by the heart.

The theories seemed to be without validity, consigning the heart to the role of mindless muscle. How could that be? Hers ached so much, yearning for Cameron, that she would not be surprised if it simply stilled and stopped its endless pumping.

This house in the woods had always seemed perfect. Now, it echoed, empty despite the *things* crammed into every inch, crying out for Cameron's presence. Their isolation, once so treasured, seemed to press in on her. She'd never been so aware of the lack of human sound, even small sounds like the scrape of a man's boot against the floor, the rasp of a file notching wood, the thud of shovel turning earth for a garden that would now never be planted.

She was lonely. She had always been lonely, but it was worse now that Cameron had been there and showed her what it felt like to burn with love. She suddenly envied her father's drifting wits. If only she could lose entire chunks of her memory and sit there, waiting, without this ache permeating her every fiber. . . .

No. She wanted to forget nothing.

All across England, wives and mothers kept their silent, secret vigils for the men who'd stolen away to support the king. Many families, like Cameron's, had been uprooted from ancestral homes. None of those women lost heart.

She had to have faith that she would see Cameron again. She had to believe. Cameron had made her feel intelligent, strong, worthy of a magnificent man's love. She intended to prove him right.

But what were her tools? She was a woman, trying hard but still uncertain of her strength. She had a wagon. A familiarity with the roads and byways leading to Brighthelmstone. A furious soldier bound and gagged in a corner of her stable. As weapons in the fight of her life, they seemed pitifully inadequate— and yet Cameron had been convinced that they were capable of changing the course of world history.

She shook her head, wishing she could as easily dislodge her doubts. And then she prepared herself to go outside and ask Martin to hitch the mare. It was time to ride the roads, waiting for the king.

*   *   *

"You are idiots, the lot of you!"

Oliver Cromwell's neck and face beaded with fearsome sweats as he swept a shaking arm to include Sergeant Walker's entire contingent of soldiers.

Tertian ague, Cameron thought, marking the sweats and the shaking. The Lord Protector could fall into a fit then and there. Doctor Bowen would recommend dosing with tincture of *quina-quina*. . . .

"This man is *not* Charles Stuart!" Cromwell roared. He surged against the table as if he meant to attack, reminding Cameron that he was standing there with his hands tied at the wrists, his ankles hobbled, and no means of defending himself. He ought to be thinking about his own neck rather than the state of the Lord Protector's. "Who in God's name *are* you?"

Cameron remained mute, as he had done ever since leaving Jillian.

"He said he was the king!" Captain Walker defended himself.

"I never did." Cameron ended his silence with agreeable mildness. "You all assumed the worst of me merely because I am cursed with dark hair and long legs."

Walker paled. One of his minions, obviously desperate to please, leaned close. "Thass right, sir, he didn't call himself the king," he said in a harsh whisper that echoed through the room. "Jacks over there, he said sorter like, 'Admit ye're Charles Stuart,' and this fellow said something sorter like, 'I admit nothin'—"

"Oh, shut up!" Walker pushed the man so hard he stumbled over his own feet and fell to the floor, arms flailing.

"Not well-done of you, Walker. Not well-done at all."

The rebuke came from the back of the room. The click of bootheels against marble marked the speaker's movement toward the front of the hall. Cameron recognized the cultured voice—Harrington.

A tiny frisson of hope wriggled its way up through the muck of despair. Harrington was the king's man, here because he'd been summoned and wanted to divert suspicion. But with Harrington's next remarks, Cameron's hope died aborning.

"Because of your stupidity," Harrington said, pausing before Captain Walker, "the roads between here and Bramber are unpatrolled. A full regiment of the Lord Protector's finest forces abandoned their orders to escort this . . . this . . . *imposter* to my Lord Cromwell's presence."

Walker and his men hung their heads. Harrington took two more steps and stood before Cameron. He tilted his head back and looked at Cameron down the length of his nose. Cameron could read no silent complicity in Harrington's icy regard, no hint that Harrington meant to keep silent about what he knew.

Cameron felt as if his neck would snap from the anger surging through him. Harrington was a traitor! Everything made sense now—the disastrous murder of Robert Lindsay, Harrington's withdrawal of support at the most crucial time. He'd been out to compromise the Royalist cause from the beginning, and Cameron had been fool enough to trust him.

And Harrington knew all about Jillian.

"I've seen this man before," Harrington mused. He clasped his hands behind his back and circled Cameron, one heel clicking against the toe of the other boot, and then again. "Can't quite remember . . . I daresay it will come to me."

Cameron's rage ebbed, but swelled in a new direction. Harrington knew him as well as he'd know his own brother. His failure to identify Cameron seemed to hint he did not mean to betray him—but why the coyness? Perhaps the man was enjoying this metaphorical grinding of Cameron's face into the dirt in repayment for that argument in the woods. Perhaps he merely prolonged the suspense before divulging all he knew of the Royalist camp headquartered near Bramber.

Cameron couldn't risk that happening. He had to do something to divert attention away from there, and his scrambling mind could only think of one way to shield Jillian. He would fling his true identity in Cromwell's face. The Lord Protector would realize that Cameron had every reason to despise the parliamentary government, and there'd be no further reason to delve into what Cameron had been doing near Bramber, or whom he'd been doing it with.

"I am Delacorte," he said.

Cromwell stared hatred at him, but betrayed no indication that he recognized the name.

Cameron straightened his shoulders and ignored the pain that shafted through his back from his bindings being too tight. "John Cameron Delacorte."

The blank incomprehension marking Cromwell's expression never shifted.

Fury surged through Cameron anew. How could Cromwell not remember the name of the man who'd been stripped of his lands, every inch of which Cameron had worked with his own hands? Benington. Lush and verdant Benington—and Cromwell remembered naught?

And even worse, bold and spirited Riordan had been killed when the self-styled military genius now sitting before Cameron ordered a repugnant rear attack on outnumbered Royalist troops. Cromwell did not even remember the name of a man whose death weighed upon his black soul.

"Delacorte," Cameron said again, through gritted teeth.

A hushed silence followed Cameron's violent spewing of his name. And then laughter, rich and mocking, echoed through the hall. "Oh, listen to him, my lord,"

Harrington said. "He's so swell-headed over being mistaken for the king that he thinks his worthless name ought to mean something to you."

Harrington had deliberately silenced him before Cameron could say anything more. And still he did not betray him. Cameron dared to hope—just a little.

Cromwell leaned back with an exaggerated sigh. "You said you know him, Harrington. What does his name mean to you?"

"Nothing yet, my lord. But it will come to me. Let's lock him away until my memory is jogged. Since this fellow's so filled with kingly pretensions, he might appreciate the comforts of the Tower. 'Twas built by a king, Mr. Delacorte, and has housed a most illustrious list of guests."

With a brief flicking motion of his hand, Cromwell ordered it done.

So, too, must it have been with the confiscation of Benington, Cameron realized as they pushed him none-too-gently toward the door. Someone had made the suggestion, the Lord Protector had ordered it done. A barely considered request; a meaningless gesture. And Cameron's life had changed.

It had changed for the better, he realized. Instead of spinning out his lonely years on Benington, convinced he'd failed by never earning the designation of *sir*, he'd found Jillian. He'd had the heady thrill of knowing he was important because of what was inside of him, not because of an honorable title or accolades. He'd been chasing the wrong dream, nurturing the wrong doubts, for all his life.

He couldn't help laughing. He knew exactly what would make him happy, now that he had no chance on this earth of achieving it. Simple pleasures—studying with Doctor Bowen, becoming important to people because of the skill he learned at the old man's knee, loving Jillian, raising children to be proud of themselves and their dreams, no matter how modest.

The soldiers dragging him to the Tower exchanged glances with brows raised as his laughter bounced from the walls. Perhaps he annoyed them; for whatever reason, they poked and prodded him with their pikes to the highest reaches of the Tower, where his comfortless cell had a sweeping view of the city and the roads snaking out from its center.

They cut his bonds before they left, and so he was able to grip on to the bars of his window as he stared out, aligning himself. He blessed God for incarcerating him a cell providing a view of the road to Chelmsford, the road he'd told Jillian to follow.

Would she, though? He could not shake the memory of the pale, stark terror that had come over her, the numb resignation in her voice when she'd told him she could never leave her home. Had he pushed her too hard, too fast, expected too much?

She had to come to him. She had to.

He would keep a vigil over the road, watching every minute. He vowed not to sleep, not to eat, until her wagon passed and he knew she and her father were safe.

19

Twice each day, Jillian drove into Bramber, always taking a different, twisting course, but managing to pass the boulders near Scupper's field, coming and going. Martin had told her that if Charles Stuart came to Cameron's men, they would bring him either to the boulders, or straight to Jillian's house.

Twice each day she passed the boulders on her right; twice each day she passed them on her left. She drove with the half-doors on each side of the wagon braced open. Each time her heart racketed against her ribs and her breathing labored as she waited for the muffled thumps, the scraping sounds that would mean her royal cargo had arrived.

They had arrested Cameron on Saturday, and it was now Tuesday. Although Martin had not said anything to her so far, she was all too aware that this was the last day she'd bargained to be allowed to carry on. If Charles did not arrive, then Martin would expect her to close up the house and go to Linchester. Martin would also go into the woods and concoct a new plan with Cameron's men.

She wondered if she'd have any luck dosing Martin with herb tea and trussing him up alongside Edmonds.

She went to the stable to tend to Edmonds before leaving for the day's first foray into the woods. She knelt there in a horse stall, spooning soup into the soldier's mouth while he glared his hatred at her. A long shadow loomed on the barn wall. Tall and broad, the newcomer moved with an easy, elegant grace.

"Cameron!" she cried, spilling the hot soup straight into Edmonds's lap. He yelped in pain while she whirled, her arms wide, a smile threatening to split her face in two.

But the man who stood there was not her beloved.

"You're not Cameron," she said her arms dropping. She knew she sounded stupid, but her disappointment was so severe that she could do nothing but stare at his too-short hair, his too-narrow shoulders, his equal height, and find him lacking.

"Many years have passed," said the stranger. "I daresay I have the advantage over you, for I was just a boy when we met last. You have not changed so much, Mistress Bowen, as I have."

His easy way of moving marked him as a young man scarcely past his teens, certainly no older than his early twenties. Exhaustion lined his features and darkened the skin beneath his eyes. His face was streaked with dirt, and his garments bore the marks of hard riding and rough wear.

A glimmer of recognition pierced her despondency. "Oh! You must be the king."

"Charles Stuart, your servant, mistress." With a weary smile, the tall stranger bent at the waist and sent her a cavalier's bow.

He's not half as elegant as Cameron, she thought.

Edmonds's groaning ended in a little yap, like a beagle that had scented a rabbit.

"How fares your father?"

"My father is in good health," Jillian said. "Your hair—it's shorn like a Roundhead's."

"Aye." Charles rubbed a hand over the sweat-matted locks that had been roughly cut to fall just below his ears. " 'Twas meant to be a disguise."

"Cameron did not know, or he would have cut his as well," Jillian said.

Men—perhaps a dozen in all—moved from the outside to surround the king. "Who be yon howler?" asked one scruffy fellow, angling his jaw toward Edmonds.

"One of Cromwell's by the looks of his uniform," said another. "How do ye come to have a Commonwealth soldier trussed up in yer stable, mistress?"

Stammering, she explained what had happened during Cameron's arrest.

"Ye mean they got our Mr. Delacorte, and we got naught but *him*? You never told us, Martin." The scruffy fellow glared accusingly at Martin, who flushed and stared at his feet.

"Kill him," said the king.

"But—" Jillian began to protest.

"Not Martin. The soldier—ain't that right, sire?"

"You can't kill either of them."

"Kill him, but after the lady and I have left the premises," the king added. He caught her around the fleshy part of her arm and gently drew her away from Edmonds.

"You can't just kill him! He's bound. He can't defend himself."

"He chose the wrong side, mistress. He knew the risks. Come. Walk with me."

She walked through her horse pasture arm in arm with the king of England. But all she could think of was that in the place where Cameron had been taken, *he* would be considered to be on the wrong side. He might already be dead.

No. She shook the thought away. She would know, in the deepest part of her soul, if Cameron was gone from this earth. She would know.

"Can you feed us?" asked Charles. "Wilmot and I must be on our way quickly. Bread and cheese will

do, and then you can tuck yourself into bed knowing
you served your king well.''

"Tuck myself into bed?" She blinked in confusion.
"Not for many hours yet . . ." Oh, how *should* she
address the man whose life was in her hands? "Your
majesty. Don't you know the plan? I will be the one
transporting you to Brighthelmstone.''

"But you told us that Mr. Delacorte had been
arrested.''

"So he has. I mean to carry out his plan.''

Charles looked poleaxed. "Mistress, I do not think
you comprehend the danger. My men and I rode into
Bramber earlier today, expecting a quiet village, and
found soldiers swarming everywhere.''

"The constable. Fraley. He must have heard by now
that the man they've arrested is not you. He will have
summoned soldiers to help him search the district.''

And Cameron had not returned, which meant
Cromwell had kept him . . . or perhaps he'd gone to
Linchester, expecting to find her already there, and
knew by now that she did not mean to come.

"Would they have released Mr. Delacorte, sire,
when they realized he is not you?"

The king shook his head. "Knowing Cromwell, he'll
lock Mr. Delacorte away for a good long time.''

So then Cameron would not yet know that she
hadn't gone to Linchester. The thought gave her no
comfort, not while thinking of her proud, daring highwayman locked in some hellhole of a prison.

"I wanted to turn and run when we approached
Bramber," said the king. "But my man Gunter said
we'd look suspicious. We rode in bold as you please.
From what we overheard, the Commonwealth soldiers
have been set with the task of guarding Bramber
Bridge.''

"That makes sense," said Jillian, amazing herself by
speaking so calmly while her heart had just shattered

anew. "The easiest road into Brighthelmstone crosses that bridge."

"Wilmot and I left Gunter to his own devices while we took to our heels back to Arundel Forest, praying to find Mr. Delacorte's camp. His men knew nothing of Mr. Delacorte's arrest or they would not have brought me here." The king paused, and a wistful longing overtook him. "I don't know what's become of my other men, and I don't know how we can travel through to Brighthelmstone now."

"There are small trails and lanes that make for rough travel, but if we use them it is possible to bypass Bramber altogether. Queenie and I will see you delivered safely to Brighthelmstone." They'd come to where Queenie stood grazing. Jillian stopped and stroked the mare's silken side. "I know I'm only a woman, sire, but I assure you that nobody knows these byways better than I do."

"I have no doubt of your competency, mistress. I was merely taken aback for a moment—and I had no reason to be. If not for the brave women who have helped me along the way, my head would be mounted upon a pike and my body moldering in a grave somewhere."

"Brave women?"

"Aye." He told her how he'd ridden boldly through the countryside pretending to be the servant of Jane Lane, who rode pillion to him the whole while. And Juliana Coningsby, who'd pretended to be his runaway bride to give everyone a good reason for why he remained secreted in a room at an inn, and later, the same Mistress Coningsby traveled as his wife, helping Charles sneak through an area where the patrols were looking for fugitive men without women. "And there was a widow near Stonehenge, who went above and beyond in providing solace to her king." A devilish twinkle lit his eyes.

"Your majesty!"

He sent her a cocky grin that reminded Jillian that
the king of England was but twenty and one years
old, despite amassing experiences that would do credit
to a man twice his age. His delight in his memories
made her smile, too.

"I doubt that what I'm prepared to do will linger
so fondly in your mind," Jillian said. "Your bones will
be rattled and your teeth will likely be cracked by the
time we reach the water's edge."

"So long as I live to see the sun rise in France, you
will certainly be added to my list of memorable
women. For you see, mistress, you have just given me
new heart. Gunter swore he had the connections to
secure certain passage to France, and now we cannot
get through. I have survived so many disappointments
these past weeks, but to be so close, and watch my
every hope disintegrate once more . . ." The king's
voice trailed away, and a shudder coursed through
him.

"I understand, your majesty," Jillian whispered.
"You have gained your homeland and now you must
leave. I would not—I *do* not—have the courage to
leave my home behind."

The king cocked his head, clearly puzzled. "My dear
Mistress Bowen, what does it matter where I live, so
long as I *do* live? Wipe any such sympathies straight
from your mind. The goal of the heart is what matters,
not where a person lives. I mean to take my rightful
place as King of England. It matters naught where
I live betimes—France, or even off in the wilds of
Virginia Colony."

*The goal of the heart is what matters, not where a
person lives.* Loving Cameron, being loved by him,
were the goals of *her* heart. Cameron had tried convincing her of that very thing. But that same heart
pounded a refusal to leave the house in the woods
behind.

"If you can indeed transport me to Brighthelmstone, by this time tomorrow, or next day at the latest, I shall be in France—and I shall thank you for it, every day of my life."

"Not I," she said. "John Cameron Delacorte."

"He chose his cohorts well, mistress. Since you mean to carry out his plan, remind me of its details."

"Aye. You and he are very much alike. Physically. It was his plan that people around here become accustomed to seeing him riding my wagon with me, so that you, dressed in his clothing, would not be remarked."

"Simplicity is always ingenious." The king nodded.

"It always seemed too simple to me."

The king laughed. "So many men have heard my description. Fewer have ever seen my face in portraits. Far fewer, in person. Your Mr. Delacorte played excellent odds with his gamble."

"On the day Cameron was arrested, soldiers stopped us repeatedly. If Fraley has set them swarming again, we might well be searched and you could be discovered."

"Today, mistress, whilst leaving Bramber, we thought ourselves pursued. Thirty, perhaps forty, of the Commonwealth's finest troops came straight at us at top speed. I thought certain I'd met my end. 'Nay, sire, slow down and let them pass us,' my man Gunter suggested. We did so, and were deluged with soldiers the way a quiet beach is stormed by the sea. And just as a wave recedes, so too did that swell of soldiers ride straight on past, without giving me a single glance. They had me within their sights twice, and failed both times to sniff me out. I am feeling exceptionally lucky today."

She heard a sound from the stable, a prolonged, wheezing gasp, that brought Queenie's head up and sent the mare backing away in fright. Edmonds had met his death with more dignity than Jillian had expected.

Charles curled his hand around hers and pressed it

against his heart. "It does not weigh easily on my mind, mistress, to kill a man who would have been my loyal subject if not for the overweening ambitions of Oliver Cromwell. I apologize for causing you distress. I know it will not ease your mind to think so, but killing that traitor will make matters easier for you, and easier for us all. There is no way we could have released him without jeopardizing my escape, or without implicating you and Mr. Delacorte even more."

"I understand," she whispered.

"And now—that bread and cheese?"

She had a bad moment while watching Charles swirl Cameron's cloak about his shoulders and tilting Cameron's hat at a jaunty angle upon his head. If she closed her eyes, opened them, and closed them again very quickly, she could almost imagine the cavalier standing before the fire was Cameron. Cameron who fingered the brim of his hat, who leaned over her father's shoulder and with no hint of mockery whatsoever shifted a dried Tudor rose petal from one threaded square of the rose garden pattern to another.

"Inspired placement, young doctor," her father said, nodding his approval, but obviously confusing the king for Cameron.

"We'd best be on our way, sire," Jillian said. "Come, Papa, we must go."

"I'll have to pack up my pattern and petals."

"There's no time."

"Of course there's time. It always takes you a while to get yourself through the kitchen door, Jilly."

Funny how thinking of dawdling even one more moment while the king had such need of her seemed like a foolish waste of time. "Not tonight, Papa."

They tucked a disgruntled Mr. Wilmot beneath the seat, which amused Charles greatly. "Wilmot bears great disdain for disguises and subterfuge," he said. "I shall never let him live this down."

The twisting trails had never seemed so narrow, the ruts so huge, the shadows so impenetrable, the woods so silent. The wagon's familiar rocking soon put Jillian's father to sleep in his corner of the seat. Jillian focused upon one landmark after another to mark their progress, because without doing so it seemed that they were mired in mud, that Queenie plodded along some endless ribbon of earth that kept curling back upon itself, keeping them in place.

"Tell me about Mr. Delacorte," said the king, and Jillian wished it would be proper to reach over and squeeze his hand in appreciation, knowing he spoke to help relieve the tension. "How did he come to my cause?"

She told him about Cameron's brother, and how Cameron's lands had been confiscated from him as punishment when Cromwell had learned that Riordan Delacorte fought for the king.

"Ah," said Charles. "I knew the surname sounded familiar. I remember Riordan Delacorte. He fell with the men at Preston, when Cromwell attacked from the rear, revealing himself for the blood-soaked backstabber he is. There were times then that my men had naught to keep them alive save for the money and food smuggled to Riordan from his brother. I'd wager your Mr. John Cameron Delacorte plundered his own house to keep my men's bellies full, and to keep my hopes alive."

Jillian felt ashamed suddenly of the way she'd clung to every piece of jewelry, every painting, every tiny treasure. She'd thought she was honoring a vow, keeping her mother's memory alive. Mrs. Hawking had told her that her mother would not have expected it. Now that she'd allowed herself to think about her mother, just a little, Jillian learned that she carried

290   *Donna Valentino*

more vibrant memories of her mother inside than ever could be found in inert, lifeless *things*.

"I've never seen Cameron's home," Jillian said.

"You will. Linchester. Benington Manor. You tell your Mr. Delacorte that I will fix all that, straight away, when I am back in my rightful place."

"Cameron says it can't be restored," she said. "He says the land was divided and parceled out and—"

"My dear Mistress Bowen." Good humor laced Charles's voice. "I am the king of England. Once I am placed on the throne that is rightfully mine, I can do whatever I want. Now, tell me the goal of *your* heart."

It seemed a harmless way to take their minds away from the near-paralyzing foreboding that whispered they could be apprehended at any moment. Far better to spin wild, never-to-be-realized dreams with a man who was fleeing for his very life in a medical wagon and yet proclaimed his divine right to rule all he fled.

"You can get him back for me," she whispered.

"Your Mr. Delacorte?"

She nodded.

"Ah, you have me there." Charles gave her a look of utter regret. He did squeeze her hand then, and she felt commiseration radiating from him. "That's one thing I cannot do for you. If you want your beloved back, you'll simply have to go get him yourself."

A small troop, no more than four or five men, thundered straight toward them.

"Shall we brazen this out, Mistress Bowen?"

"We have little choice, sire. There's no room to turn on this trail, and even if there was, they would overtake us before we'd finished."

She urged Queenie onto the side of the road and pulled up. Her heart thudded against her ribs.

The mounted men slowed when they caught sight of them. Jillian recognized the lead soldier who'd stopped them the day they'd traveled into Bramber to tend the woman with agony of the gut. And he recognized her. She felt his gaze flicker over her, over her father . . . over the king. Puzzlement furrowed his brow for a moment, and then cleared. He said something to the men riding with him, and they spurred their mounts back up to speed and shot past them down the trail.

Cameron's plan had worked.

Pride shot through Jillian. She couldn't wait to tell him . . . but she would never be able to tell him.

Go get him yourself. The king's suggestion echoed through Jillian's mind.

A few miles later, a lone horseman standing sentry atop a small hillock shielded his eyes to study them. After a moment's regard, he seemed to recognize the wagon, and sent them a wave, passing them through.

Go get him yourself.

The refrain pounded through her throughout the balance of their journey to Brighthelmstone. And even beyond, for they found upon arriving there that the king's trusted Colonel Gunter had indeed secured the promised passage—a ship bearing the name *Surprise*. Gunter had also bespoken a room at the George Inn, for the ship would not leave until the early hours of morning.

"And we'll be sailing from Shoreham, your majesty," Gunter said. " 'Tis but a few miles from here, and the roads lay quiet and free of soldiers."

The king gave Jillian his leave to depart, but she refused. She wanted, for Cameron's sake, to see for herself that Charles Stuart had climbed the ladder to the ship *Surprise* and sailed for France.

The king offered her the bed secured by Gunter, but once again she refused, and asked him to allow her father to sleep there instead. She knew she'd not close her eyes at all that night. She kept watch with Gunter and a rumpled-looking Wilmot while Charles

Stuart, accustomed by now to snatching sleep wherever he could, slumbered peacefully alongside her father in the next room until the deep dark hours
following midnight.

The short drive from Brighthelmstone to Shoreham,
not more than nine miles, passed without incident.
The *Surprise* rocked gently in its mooring, fitted and
ready to sail. Charles clambered up the ladder. He
exchanged quiet greetings with several men on deck,
and she thought he would vanish then into the bowels
of the ship.

Instead, Charles Stuart turned to look to her. He
waved, and with a grand gesture swept Cameron's hat
from his head. He treated her to a bow that nearly
had his head scraping against the ship's decking. And
then he did a most unkingly little jig, and leaped in
the air, kicking his heels together.

She should have savored that bow for hours, should
have spent the return trip in a daze of wonderment,
knowing that she, Jillian Bowen, had helped save the
king of England. Instead, her mind kept circling
around Charles Stuart's suggestion: *Go get him
yourself.*

To leave Arundel Forest and all the familiar roads,
all the safe corners of her home and never shelter
herself in their familiar comfort again . . . at the mere
thought, her pulse began racing, her heart fluttering
within her breast like a wild thing.

She fought to tame her fear, at least enough to think
things through. If, *if* she found the courage to ride
into London, what would she do? Demand . . . what?
Please return the man who captured my heart? From
what she'd heard of Cromwell, the Lord Protector
cared nothing about matters of the heart.

"Jillian?" Her father woke, and leaned forward,
studying the countryside. "Why, we are approaching
Brighthelmstone from the west. Have we been to
Shoreham?"

"Yes, Papa."

"Well, we shan't do that again. We shall send Doctor Smith the next time. No point in having an apprentice if I must drag my old bones from bed before dawn."

"Cameron isn't here anymore, Papa."

"Then you must tell him to come home. 'Tis against the law for an apprentice to run away."

Go get him yourself. . . .

Against the law for an apprentice to run away . . .

Against the law for an apprentice to be taken away from his master, as well.

Doctor Wilton Bowen would have every right to appear before Lord Cromwell and demand the return of his apprentice, whom the soldiers had arrested through mistaken identity and hauled off to London. Cameron had been careful to avoid identifying himself as the king. Jillian had taken equal care with her words. But that would not prevent one of the officers from saying she had not identified Cameron as her father's apprentice. She quelled the surge of fear that ran through her. By now, the soldiers they'd tricked would have been banished from London in disgrace.

She could do this. She and her father could storm Westminster Hall and seize Cameron from Cromwell's clutches.

Her father. Her burgeoning hope deflated. Jillian dared not attempt a rescue that depended upon her beloved, mind-wounded papa confronting—and confounding—Oliver Cromwell.

"Oh, Papa, I do love you!" Her father smiled happily as Jillian leaned over and planted a loud, smacking kiss on his forehead. She hoped he could not hear the tremble in her voice. "But we cannot fetch Cameron. He's off in London."

"London! Why, I would quite enjoy visiting London. Have friends there, you know. And there's your mama's grave."

Remorse, sorrow, faint hope—all of it swirled through Jillian. In sheltering her father and creating a new haven for themselves, she'd gone too far. Isolation suited her, but Wilton Bowen had spent most of his years surrounded by colleagues and learned men, and he must have keenly felt their absence, though he'd never complained.

And her mother's grave. Jillian's chest ached, as she thought of how long it had been since fresh flowers had adorned that lonely slab of marble. Her mother had loved flowers, always, and Jillian had never visited the grave, even once.

Go get him yourself. "Papa . . . Papa, would you like to try to go to London?"

"Try to go to London." He parroted her easily.

"Never mind," she whispered, certain that he did not comprehend the full import of what she was saying.

"London. I would quite enjoy visiting London, but . . ." Her father frowned, and she could almost feel him struggle to hold on to his thought. "Could you do such a thing, Jilly?"

Her father had rarely commented on the weakness that affected her for so long. He gripped her hand, and she sensed in him a yearning to make things right for *her*.

"I don't know, Papa," she said, and almost at once dread certainty settled over her. "No, no I couldn't. You're right. I could not go so far from home."

"London." Her father squeezed her hand a little tighter. "I would quite enjoy a bit of a visit."

A visit.

Jillian seized on the concept. A visit. She could hold the terrors at bay if she knew there was an end, if she knew she could come back home the minute she saved Cameron. "Will you help me try, Papa?"

"Help you try." He smiled, a sad smile that acknowledged his awareness of his limitations and shafted straight into Jillian's heart.

"I will have to coach you," she warned.

"Have to coach me." He nodded. "Always do, Jilly."

Could it come about? Could a woman fearful of ranging too far from her house, and an old man whose wits were half-flown, brave the Lord Protector's stronghold? Could that taint in her blood give her the ability to act the outraged lady of quality and demand the return of her father's apprentice, who had for some reason been arrested by Commonwealth soldiers? Expecting such a plan to work would be as crazy as . . . as imagining that she would one day help the fugitive King of England escape to France.

She felt the laughter bubble to her lips. "Papa, we're going to London."

It was a simple plan. Simple plans were best, Cameron had said. Simplicity is always ingenious, the king had said. But was this plan ingenious? Fraught with pitfalls, of a certainty. For instance, if those soldiers who'd arrested Cameron were still on hand and remembered that she had denied knowing him . . . or if Cameron himself had weakened under torture and admitted the truth about his plan . . . no. Cameron had told her the soldiers would be sent home in disgrace. Cameron had vowed he would never betray his men or his king.

Go get him yourself.

Jillian wished she had one more moment with Charles Stuart, to tell him that kings could indeed do anything they wanted to do: He had reminded her that she had the strength to make her wildest dream come true.

Queenie would never be able to make the long journey to London; returning home through the same convoluted byways might alone have been enough to

break the mare's stamina. Jillian had to risk taking
the easy route, straight from Brighthelmstone through
Bramber. By the time they gained the village, the
mare shook with fatigue, and Jillian knew the horse
could go no farther. She dismounted and gripped the
bridle, and guided the mare to the post in front of
Mrs. Hawking's town house.

"Just a bit more, Queenie, just a bit," she soothed,
while guilt assailed her for driving the poor mare so
hard over these past few days.

Mrs. Hawking herself threw open the door. She
quickly assessed the sweat-soaked mare, Jillian coated
with dust. "What do you need?"

"Your horse, Mrs. Hawking. I'll leave Queenie in
your care. I'll be back for her . . . a week, perhaps
less."

"I'll have my stable boy tend to it. You and your
father come inside."

"There's no time—we must go."

"You'll go nowhere until the horses have been
switched. In the meantime, you will restore yourselves
with food and drink. Wouldn't you like a bite to eat,
Doctor Bowen?"

"Like a bite to eat. What with soldiers stealing my
supper and kings eating all my cheese, I've been uncommonly hungry of late."

"Hush, Papa," Jillian warned as he helped her father climb from the wagon. The village was astir with
early morning business, and though no one stood near,
she did not want to risk anyone overhearing anything
that would pique curiosity.

"Tell me everything," Mrs. Hawking said after she'd
brought them inside and sent the maid off to fetch
food and drink.

Jillian related the events of the night, feeling detached from the telling, as if it had all happened to
someone else. Someone bold and brave, who would
risk breaking her horse's legs on dark woodland trails;

someone courageous enough to spend a sleepless night in an inn with two men she barely knew, keeping watch over a sleeping king, heedless of her good name, caring only about carrying out the goal of a man she might never see again.

"You are your mother's daughter," Mrs. Hawking said, when Jillian came to the end of her story. "She would be so proud."

"She would not be proud if she knew I still quake with fear at the mere thought of leaving these familiar places."

"You need my horse to go save your young man," Mrs. Hawking guessed. "So you aren't just thinking about leaving. You are going to do it."

"Aye. I'm going to go to London and save Cameron." She shook from head to toe and thought it a very insipid sort of declaration. "I will return the horse in no more than a week."

"Oh, my dear girl, that horse is the least worry on my mind. Rest assured that if you can't come back, I will cherish your mare as if she were my own, and you do the best you can by my gelding."

"I will come back," Jillian said. "With Cameron, if God wills it."

"Mistress Bowen," Mrs. Hawking said gently, "I don't see how that can be possible. Your Cameron can never come back here after what he's done."

Jillian's tentative determination wavered. Her old inner demons swirled, reminding her she would only be safe if she abandoned this dangerous scheme and simply fell back into the old, familiar, safe ways of doing things.

Her mind, on its own, ran over all the possible pitfalls of going home and doing nothing. Her part in the king's escape need never be known. But if suspicion somehow fell on her, she need only show the letter from Cameron to prove she'd been duped by a master manipulator. She would tell anyone who inquired that

Mr. Edmonds had delivered her safe to her home and gone on his way. With this newfound rediscovery of her playacting ability, she'd have no trouble pretending ignorance and shock that Edmonds had never gone into Bramber as he said he would to report his news to Constable Fraley. The troop passing her in the woods the night before never stopped to realize she had been driving the king, and her presence here in Bramber was common enough that nobody would question it.

"If I return home, lock myself behind the stout oak doors, everything will go on the way I always wanted it to be," she whispered.

"Would it be the same?" asked Mrs. Hawking. "Would it resolve anything?"

No, it wouldn't. Cameron would rot in jail, or end up executed. Hiding behind the walls of her home would no more help Cameron than locking herself away all these years had brought Jillian's mother back to life.

Run, Jilly, run home. . . . But what if home was not that mass of brick and plaster, but the loving circle of Cameron's arms? What if her mother had not been urging her to hide, but to run forward and live life to its fullest?

The maid appeared with a heavily laden tray. "Mark says to tell you the horses have been exchanged, madam," she said to Mrs. Hawking.

Jillian's father attacked the tray with zest. Jillian's whole being churned with terror, with such an overwhelming need to see Cameron, that she knew she could not swallow so much as a sip of water.

"What are you going to do, my dear?" asked Mrs. Hawking.

"Could you ask Rose to pack some food for me? I don't think I can eat just now." She took a deep breath, swallowed, and said the words out loud, "I will get hungry, later, on the road."

20

The swill they pushed through a slot in Cameron's door each day was so foul that the flies didn't even bother with it. The funny thing about not eating, he mused, was that it left him feeling giddy and elated and not at all inclined to sleep. Which made it easy to honor his vow to keep watch over the road to Linchester. Hour after hour he watched, marking the shape of each wagon, studying the form of every female on the off-chance that Jillian had traded her precious mare and wagon for a pair of riding horses.

He counted the scratches he'd made in the wall with the edge of a battered pewter candleholder that had not held a candle for years, so far as he could tell. He studiously ignored the endless procession of marks gouged by one of the previous occupants of this room. Six days he'd been here. And Jillian had not passed along the road. *I can't leave here, Cameron,* she'd said, and he had refused to accept the finality of those words.

She had not passed through London. He would have felt it in his heart.

No, he refused to believe she'd buried herself back in her house. Perhaps he *had* fallen asleep. The light-headedness that gripped him sometimes left his head swirling, and sometimes he caught himself blinking at the sky and wondering how the sun had traveled from the eastern edge of his window to the west.

He refused to believe that Jillian had chosen to cloister herself behind the walls of her house, moving only along the paths and lanes she trusted. Not his Jillian. She had come too far to embrace the path of emptiness, when love awaited her with arms opened wide.

Providing he ever got out of here.

The door to his cell crashed open. He crouched there, near the scratches in the wall, and blinked up at the soldier who motioned with his sword for him to rise. He must have been more light-headed than he realized, for he would swear the soldier looked exactly like General Monck, Cromwell's most trusted advisor.

"You've been summoned."

Cameron braced his hand against the wall and used its support to inch up slowly, for he knew that rising too quickly would bring on a surge of dizziness. He cursed his over-sensitive stomach. He ought to have forced himself to eat, even if only a little, because now when he most needed his wits and his strength, he was dull of mind and so exhausted that he stood weaving and ready to fall over.

His clothes hung loosely, he'd lost so much flesh these past six days. His hair hung from his head in matted strings, and the inability to shave had left him with a beard. Still, he felt no shame when the soldier's scornful gaze reminded him of his filthy state. 'Twas none of his own doing.

"Hard to imagine you ever being mistaken for that rogue, Charles Stuart," said the soldier. "I told the Lord Protector so myself, but he seemed disinclined to take my advice on that particular matter."

"And he takes your advice on other matters."

"Consistently."

"You *are* General Monck."

"At your service."

"Provide me with a bath and the means to shave, and I might one day be mistaken again for Charles Stuart."

"Not likely—unless you hie yourself to France and get yourself mistaken over there."

France. In his slow-witted state, it took Cameron a moment to understand the significance of the comment. "He did it. The king made it back to France."

A mistake, there. He'd betrayed his Royalist leanings. Stupid. But Monck either had not noticed—or the faint smile hovering at the edges of his lips hinted he might be a secret Royalist sympathizer himself. Impossible.

"So say the rumors."

"How? By way of which seaport?"

"The details—if there are any—will be known soon enough. If you fancy keeping your head fastened to your filthy neck, you'll wipe that smile off your face and keep this to yourself. The Lord Protector's been in a foul mood even without hearing this latest . . . rumor."

"Cromwell doesn't know yet?"

"Don't make me repeat myself, Delacorte."

The king was safe. Jubilation surged through Cameron, though anguish followed hard on its heels. What did it matter if Charles Stuart regained the throne some day if Jillian Bowen was not at Cameron's side to savor the triumph of Cromwell's downfall?

Cameron might not be there, himself. Although Monck did not seem overly concerned, this summons raised a sour note of warning from Cameron's instincts.

"You're taking me to Cromwell?"

"Aye, if you ever shut your mouth long enough to move through this door."

Cameron held out his hands to be bound. Monck laughed as he wrapped a leather thong loosely around his wrists. "Seems a waste of good leather. You look as if you couldn't squash a louse."

Cameron's head had cleared a little by the time they reached the vast, echoing hall that Cromwell favored for conducting business. Awareness sharpened enough to sense the grim, chill atmosphere settle around him like a shroud.

The Lord Protector sat behind a table stacked high with books and rolled maps. The sweats and redness had gone, to be replaced by a white-lipped rage that seemed to waft across the hall and envelop Cameron in its wake. General Monck left Cameron in the charge of another soldier and then the general went to stand just behind Cromwell's shoulder.

"Step closer, Mr. Delacorte," Cromwell said without bothering to look up.

A sense of inevitability swept through Cameron as he walked, carefully to avoid stumbling, to stand before the Lord Protector.

"You've been remarkably tight-lipped about yourself," Cromwell said, astounding Cameron with the affable tone of his voice. Well, so too did cats play with mice before making the final, lethal pounce. "A pity. It might've gone easier for you if you'd been more forthcoming."

Cameron remained silent. He'd been found out. The best thing—the only thing—he could do was go to his grave keeping his secrets.

"As I told you, my lord, Mr. Delacorte has a secretive bent." The comment came from amidst a group of advisors standing in a shadowed corner. Cameron gritted his teeth. Harrington. Betraying him. And all else, no doubt. Cameron could go silent as a monk to his grave, and Harrington's tongue would rattle on, condemning every man who'd risked everything for the Western Association. Harrington's tongue would condemn Jillian.

But perhaps he hadn't done so yet.

I'll kill him, Cameron thought. Right then. He possessed all the strength of a scarecrow, scarcely capable of keeping his head from wobbling. But a fine and pure rage lent him vigor. His hands had been bound in front of him, and loosely bound at that. He could clench his fists together into a sort of battering ram. He turned, by slow, imperceptible degrees toward Harrington.

But before he could strike, a door opened. And Cameron knew he was too late. Jillian and her father, with a phalanx of soldiers following close behind, walked into the hall.

She stood staring at him for a long, timeless moment. Her eyes were wide and liquid with longing. Her face was streaked with dust—they'd driven hard to get here. His rage surged anew.

"There she is," said Harrington. "The young lady who jogged my memory."

"Is this the man you told us about, Mistress Bowen?" Cromwell asked.

Cameron reeled. He wished then that starvation had killed him. Death was preferable to hearing betrayal from Jillian's own tongue.

Her lips trembled. She blinked. She reached for her father's hand. "Yes. He is the one."

"You are certain?" Cromwell asked. "This is extremely serious business, Mistress Bowen, and we must be certain there is no possibility of error. I've seen the rogue but once before, and his appearance now is remarkably different."

"He is the one. I would know him anywhere." She took a deep breath.

Cameron felt his spirit desert him, and he wished his bones and flesh would follow, for he did not know how he would endure hearing her pronounce his death sentence. He watched, even now fascinated with the lush curve of her lips, the slight tilt to her chin that hinted at her inner fire.

"Lord Cromwell." She stepped forward a few steps. "Lord Cromwell, please cut that cord away from my father's apprentice and give him back to us."

"It might not be a good idea—" Cromwell began before Cameron sorted out the full force of what Jillian had just done.

"Is that you, young Ollie Cromwell?" Doctor Bowen shuffled to the front of the hall to stand in front of Cameron. He bent and peered ostentatiously at the Lord Protector. "By God, it is you."

"Doctor Bowen?" Cromwell gaped at the old man in surprise. "Doctor *Wilton* Bowen?"

"Of course, Doctor Wilton Bowen. How many Doctor Bowens do you think there are, out hunting down their apprentices? Don't tell me you're the one who's been making such a muddle of things."

"Muddle?" Cromwell's voice sharpened.

"He means mistaking his apprentice for the king," Harrington inserted smoothly. "Is that not correct, Mistress Bowen?"

"Exactly so," she said.

"Humpf." Doctor Bowen glared at the Lord Protector. "You were contentious as a youth, and now your entire nature's turned bilious. Choler in your skin, as well. Still suffer from the stone, no doubt."

"Why yes, sir, I do." Cromwell blushed.

Cromwell *blushed*?

Cameron blinked, certain he was dreaming.

General Monck nodded to the soldier standing guard over Cameron. The soldier drew his knife and sliced the leather binding Cameron's wrists.

Doctor Bowen motioned for Cameron to join him in front of Cromwell. And then the old man gripped him by the neck of his shirt, though it was a good long reach for him, and shook Cameron as if he were a boy caught plucking the petals from one of his precious roses. "You've malingered long enough. Time to go back to work, young doctor."

Jillian had moved away to stand near the wall, her head down, pale and with the old meekness shielding her so thoroughly that Cameron doubted anyone but he was aware of her presence any longer.

"Come along now, Cameron." Doctor Bowen gave him a gentle push. And they made it nearly as far as the door before the Lord Protector called them to a halt.

"Doctor Bowen?"

"Yes, young Ollie?"

"We no longer have Royal Physicians."

"I should say not, or I would still be here in London, wouldn't I?"

Cromwell blushed again. "But you've continued your practice. Have you perchance learned of a cure for the stone?"

Doctor Bowen blinked. "The . . . the stone?" With horror, Cameron realized that the brief spurt of sensibility that had gotten them this far had come to an end.

"There is no cure for the stone. You will probably die from it," Cameron said, not knowing if it were true or not, but taking a rather sharp pleasure from the stricken expression with which Cromwell greeted his diagnosis. And then he gripped Doctor Bowen with one hand, and Jillian with the other, and took them out into the sunshine.

He let her lead him as far as the wagon, her familiar wagon despite the strange horse between the shafts, and then he caught her into his arms.

"You came," Cameron said, holding Jillian about the shoulders, his whole being shaking with the delight of touching her, breathing her scent.

She nodded.

"You took a terrible, dangerous risk, in coming

here." He would be infuriated later, thinking of the risks she'd taken, but for now his ecstasy was too great.

She nodded at that, too.

"And now we shall go to Linchester."

She stiffened, and then she shook her head. "No."

"Jillian, I cannot go back to Arundel Forest."

"Neither can I. I have come to realize I must never go back to that house."

"But you refuse to go to Linchester."

"Aye."

He was baffled. "Well, where then?" And then he remembered that the Bowens still owned a home in London. "Here, in London?"

Jillian turned her head. He followed her gaze and saw her father squatting near the ditch that ran along the edge of the road, peering down at a leaf caught in a tangle of dying weeds. People walking along the road took great pains to keep a wide berth as they passed him, the way one might skirt a raving lunatic.

"We cannot stay here," she said.

"Cannot stay here," her father said. He looked over at them and sent his daughter a huge smile. "Remembered all my sentences."

"Yes, Papa, you remembered every one of them— and added a few outstanding sentences of your own."

Her father beamed, pleased by the compliment.

"A fine ditch here, young Cameron. You ought to come inspect it with me."

"Aye. In a moment, sir." Cameron closed his fingers over Jillian's shoulders and drew her closer, pressing her against him. "We could just stand here in the street for the rest of our days, if that's what you choose, but I warn you now—I will not let you go."

"Oh, Cameron, I . . ." She sniffled. "I don't want you to let me go. Cromwell refused to see us when we first arrived, and while we were waiting for your friend Mr. Harrington to gain admittance for us—"

"Harrington?" Cameron interrupted her. "Harrington helped you?"

"Yes. He said he'd had you locked away to keep you out of Bramber until the king made it through. Lord Harrington had this notion that you might do something . . . reckless . . . to keep me out of trouble."

"He was right." Cameron had to admit his weakness where Jillian was concerned, and knew Harrington had remarked it when Cameron cast aside his command. Harrington had always, always been the king's man.

"I . . . I made arrangements, and I'm not at all sure that you'll like them." Jillian's agitation drew all Cameron's regard.

"Arrangements for what?"

She rummaged in the pocket at her waist, and then withdrew a paper. "I've booked passage for the three of us. The ship leaves in four days."

"Ship? To where?"

"Italy."

"Italy?"

"The University of Padua is in Italy, Cameron. It could take years to graduate as a Doctor of Surgery, but Mr. Harrington said it might be best for us to leave England completely, for a while, anyway, and I could study along with you at night and learn with you, and I had thought that at times you seemed to enjoy helping my father, and—"

He stopped her nervous babbling with a kiss.

And his head spun, but from sheer exhilaration.

"Four days! We have time to return to your house and pack the things you need—"

"Cameron, we stopped there before coming here. I don't want to go back. We don't have to go back. I brought everything we need."

He lifted the lid on the box bolted to the back of the wagon. A crate of medical books. The rose garden pattern he'd made for Doctor Bowen. And a canvas-wrapped parcel. He tugged at the string holding it together and the canvas fell open to reveal a puddle of shimmering honey-gold silk.

"I brought my wedding dress," she said. "I'm sorry, but the king kept your fine cloak and hat. You'll have to—"

"The *king* kept my cloak and hat?"

She nodded. "You did intend them to be part of his disguise, you know."

"Jillian, how exactly did Charles Stuart get to France?"

"Must you know right now? It's a long trip to Italy, and I'm rather anxious to find an inn where I might . . . rest and prepare myself for the journey."

She rose to her toes and planted a light, warm kiss upon his lips, proving she didn't care that he had the stink of prison upon him, or that uncounted people swarming the London streets could see him. Cameron pulled her into his arms and kissed her the way he'd dreamed of doing for all those endless days and nights since he'd been apart from her.

He felt the tug on his sleeve distantly at first, but then could not ignore it as it grew more insistent.

"Young doctor, I'd quite like to go home now."

"Aye." Cameron wrapped an arm affectionately about the old man's shoulders, and kept a more intimate touch upon Jillian as he drew her hard against himself. "Let's go home."

May 25, 1660

The crowd gathered on the Dover shore had cheered the raising of every flag, the herald of every trumpet. But when the boat carrying Charles Stuart began rowing toward the beach, twenty thousand voices roared their approval so mightily that they drowned out even the sounds of the sea.

General Monck was the first man to welcome the

king back to English soil. It was only right that Monck should be the one to do so, after working so diligently for these past five years to bring about the restoration of the English monarchy.

The Restoration. The power and glory of England had been handed back into Charles Stuart's care without shedding a single drop of blood, without firing a single gun, without unsheathing a single sword. Any physician would be pleased that human suffering had been avoided, but there was a special sweetness in the triumph for Doctor John Cameron Delacorte.

"You ought to be standing there alongside the general," Cameron said to his wife. "No one played a more important role in keeping Charles alive to see this day."

"Charles remembered—he saw to it that we have this excellent spot to watch—" Jillian squeezed Cameron's hand in conclusion, for a fresh burst of cheering drowned out the balance of her words. The booming of cannon commenced as soon as the vocal din ebbed. Smaller guns lent punctuation, in a sweeping tide of joyous thunder that no doubt spread clear to London. On a nearby hill, a huge bonfire leaped to life, followed a few minutes later by another fire on another hill, and then another, until eventually a trail of flame seemed to beckon the king straight into the country's heart.

Jillian pressed close, and Cameron wrapped his arm around her shoulder. "He'll never recognize us," Jillian said, running a hand over the bulge of her belly. She'd almost talked herself out of coming to watch the king's landing, claiming polite women did not show themselves in public in such an advanced state of pregnancy. Cameron had silenced her protests with the kisses and touches that reminded her he always thought her at her most beautiful this way, swollen with his child.

"He might not recognize *you*," Cameron agreed,

teasing her. "But not recognize me—his mirror image?"

By now the king had come close enough that Cameron was able to make out some of his features. Charles Stuart was no longer the brash, boyish youth of twenty and one, but a mature and sober man of thirty who looked every one of his years and more.

"Nobody would ever confuse the two of you now," Jillian said, stroking a finger along Cameron's jaw in a shockingly intimate public gesture. Cameron grinned. He would never grow tired of his wife proving she found him pleasing to look upon.

The king's guard formed a protective phalanx around him, keeping the crowd at bay, but Charles did not seem to mind the hoarse cries battering at his ears, or the desperate hands flung his way—he acknowledged personally many of the shrieks, and brought the palm of his hand up against innumerable others. His progress would take him right past the spot where a uniformed guard had installed Cameron and Jillian, but the seething crowd threatened to block Jillian's view.

"Under ordinary circumstances I'd offer to lift you," Cameron said. "But considering your astonishing girth I'm not so sure I can." She smacked him playfully on the shoulder and he smiled to think how such a jest, in the old days, would have had her withdrawing behind her protective façade, afraid he'd meant to insult her.

But there was no need to lift her. To his astonishment, Charles Stuart caught sight of them, and with a side comment to his guard, he made a path straight for them.

"Doctor and Mrs. Delacorte," he said. And the king of England bowed to *them*.

Cameron struck a bow of his own, and Jillian tried to curtsey, but Charles stopped her with a hand on her shoulder. "None of that is necessary between us, madam," he said.

"Your majesty."

Charles's gaze flickered around them. "Your father is no longer with you?" Jillian shook her head, and her eyes took on an instant glisten. "Did he ever get to enjoy that rose garden of his, madam?"

"Oh, yes, sire." Jillian's voice shook, while a smile lit her face. "Cameron dug him a beautiful garden in Italy, and my father spent happy years there, sitting in the sun, amid his roses, with his first two grandchildren at his knee."

The king, who could not possibly have a pleasant memory of his own father's last days, seemed pleased. One of his guards leaned toward him. Charles listened, and then nodded.

"Well, they tell me I must be on my way. But I want you to know I haven't forgotten. Linchester. Benington."

Jillian gasped, while Cameron felt surprisingly little pain at hearing the place names that used to mean so much to him.

"I . . . I never told my husband what you promised, sire," she whispered.

Charles cocked a disapproving brow at her. "Tut, tut, Mrs. Delacorte—I gave you my word. I daresay I shall be deluged with petitions from this moment on, and my advisors tell me I can grant but a few. Yours shall be one of them."

"I . . . I don't understand," said Cameron.

" 'Tis simple, man. Your wife won your estate back for you some nine years ago on a most circuitous route to Brighthelmstone. Though I cannot promise it will happen overnight, Benington will be placed back into your hands. Certainly by the time of the ceremony, for you will require a proper residence after that."

"The ceremony?"

"It has been nigh unto twenty years since the King

of England has installed Knights of the Garter. I mean
to do so in conjunction with my coronation. And you,
Mr. Delacorte, will be the first to feel my sword tap
your shoulders as I dub you Sir Knight."

"Jaclyn Reding is a rising romance star!"
—Catherine Coulter

JACLYN REDING

□**WHITE MAGIC**　　　　0-451-40855-1/$5.99

In Regency London, a young lord sets out to discover the circumstances surrounding his friend's suicide by locating the lady who spurned him. What he finds is an enchanting, beautiful woman with some peculiar hobbies: nocturnal activities the lord believes to be sorcery—and an affectionate relationship with a wealthy gentleman. But nothing prepares him for the most startling revelation of all—a passion that suddenly consumes them both....

Also available:

□	**STEALING HEAVEN**	0-451-40649-4/$5.99
□	**TEMPTING FATE**	0-451-40558-7/$4.99
□	**WHITE HEATHER**	0-451-40650-8/$5.99

Prices slightly higher in Canada

Payable in U.S. funds only. No cash/COD accepted. Postage & handling: U.S./CAN. $2.75 for one book, $1.00 for each additional, not to exceed $6.75; Int'l $5.00 for one book, $1.00 each additional. We accept Visa, Amex, MC ($10.00 min.), checks ($15.00 fee for returned checks) and money orders. Call 800-788-6262 or 201-933-9292, fax 201-896-8569; refer to ad # TOPHR2 (4/99)

Penguin Putnam Inc.　　　Bill my: □Visa □MasterCard □Amex_____(expires)
P.O. Box 12289, Dept. B　　Card#_____
Newark, NJ 07101-5289　　Signature_____
Please allow 4-6 weeks for delivery.
Foreign and Canadian delivery 6-8 weeks.

Bill to:
Name_____
Address_____City_____
State/ZIP_____
Daytime Phone #_____

Ship to:
Name_____ Book Total　　　$_____
Address_____ Applicable Sales Tax $_____
City_____ Postage & Handling $_____
State/ZIP_____ Total Amount Due　$_____

This offer subject to change without notice.